Praise

"A shocking story about two young women accused of the unthinkable. Chafin's bold debut will keep you *Shaken*."
VALERIE TAYLOR, AUTHOR OF *A WHALE OF A MURDER:A VENUS BIXBY MYSTERY*

"Gripping debut... a complex story about the nuances of love, grief, loneliness, and the moments of fear or rage that can change lives."
BARBARA CLAYPOLE WHITE, BESTSELLING AUTHOR OF *THE PERFECT SON* AND *THE PROMISE BETWEEN US*

"A fantastic debut! Chafin understands the complexity and nuances of the human condition, of the psychological impacts of guilt and grief, and she weaves them into memorable characters with an unforgettable story."
LISA TOWLES, AWARD WINNING AUTHOR OF *CODEX, TERROR BAY,* AND *SALT ISLAND*

"Both heartbreaking and riveting, *Shaken* sticks with you long after the last line and announces Chafin as a tour de force novelist with a keen eye for the emotional gut punch."
MICHAEL KEENAN GUTIERREZ, AUTHOR OF *THE TRENCH ANGEL* AND *THE SWILL*

"A raw, unflinching look at the highs and lows of motherhood, exposing the unspoken taboos with piercing honesty. It's a story that lingers long after the final page."
CAITLIN WEAVER, BESTSELLING AUTHOR OF *SUCH A GOOD FAMILY* AND *THINGS WE NEVER SAY*

"I am shaken."
Randell Jones, editor/publisher, Personal Story Publishing Project and 6-minute Stories podcast

"*Shaken* examines dark psychological aspects of motherhood that are not discussed nearly enough in popular culture ... The more we address child abuse, medical neglect, and shaken baby syndrome, resources can be made more readily available to struggling parents."
Jennifer Donovan, Reedsy Discovery

"A smartly plotted, character driven drama written by an author who's not frightened of exploring a difficult subject."
The Wishing Shelf

About the Author

Jill Amber Chafin earned an advanced diploma in creative writing from Te Pūkenga (New Zealand Institute of Skills and Technology) and a Bachelor of Arts degree from University of North Carolina at Chapel Hill. Her short-form prose has appeared in *The Personal Story Publishing Project* and *Motherfigure* and has also been honored as a Finalist for the Penelope Niven Creative Nonfiction Award, Honorable Mention in the New Millennium Writing Awards, and Third Place winner in the anthology *America's Next Author*. She lives with her husband and two children in Chapel Hill, North Carolina where she works as a freelance writer, editor, and circus arts teacher. *Shaken* is her debut novel.

jillamberchafin.com

Shaken

JILL AMBER CHAFIN

Happy Reading! ♡ jill a chafin

VL

www.vineleavespress.com

Shaken

Print Edition
ISBN: 978-3-98832-137-4
Published by Vine Leaves Press 2025

Cover design by Jessica Bell
Interior design by Amie McCracken

To my grandparents: Robert and Barbara Shaw
May your bright spirits and unconditional love live on forever

Chapter 1

Sally

Day one: Friday, September 7

Sally knew she wasn't supposed to shake a baby. She saw the message everywhere—on pamphlets, brochures, in baby books, on posters prominently displayed at the doctor's office. Who could miss it? This was a problem for social services. They'd come and take Morgan away. They'd tell her she was a bad mother.

But you'd see doting fathers playfully tossing their babies around, flipping them over their shoulders, swinging them in circles—around and around, the babies dizzy with glee. That was no crime. Even Charles played rough with Morgan. He'd saunter down the hall, holding Morgan upside down by his ankles, letting him swing like a pendulum—"Where'd Morgie go? Have you seen him?"—while Morgan exploded into a fit of giggles.

Had she crossed the line?

Morgan lay in his crib now, curled on his side, snug in his Winnie-the-Pooh sleep sack, his thumb resting between lax lips. Fast asleep, although his breathing sounded labored. Didn't it? Was that a sign? Or could he just be congested?

She wanted to shake him awake, to make sure he was all right, to make him laugh.

But maybe it was too late. Maybe she caused damage—brain damage. Like she'd read in the newspaper the other day, that dad who attacked his toddler with a baseball bat. She couldn't understand how any parent could do that, how anyone could hurt their baby. And yet, here lay little Morgan, her sweet boy, in pain. She knew he was hurting.

It had started with another screaming fit, Morgan wailing nonstop for no apparent reason. She tried everything. She gave him his favorite ball. His Elmo. She turned on "Wheels on the Bus" and sang along. She squatted and quacked like a duck, jumped like a wild chimpanzee, crawled on all fours, and barked like a dog. He stared at her and continued to howl for hours. *Hours!*

Then she snapped.

"Shut up!"

He paused, taking in a sharp inhale, his face red and splotchy and dripping with tears. Then he tilted his head back, opened his mouth wide, and let loose another ear-splitting shriek.

"Stop! Stop! Stop!" Sally repeated, her voice rising higher and higher.

She needed him to be quiet for just one second. She'd only gotten around three hours of sleep last night. Head buzzing, she furiously rubbed her eyes, trying to think straight.

The cat meowed and pawed and licked at the dirty stack of dishes. The washing machine whirled and clanked from down the hall. A cockroach scuttled across the carpet. The TV blasted "If You're Happy and You Know it." Her phone rang and vibrated like it was having a seizure on the counter.

In one quick swoop, Morgan was in her arms. "Shhh, please stop crying. I need you to stop." It was just a little shake, a warning: Please stop. Please let mommy have a break. Please let mommy think. *Please please please pleasepleasepleaseplease.*

But Morgan didn't stop. He screamed even louder, snot sputtering into his open, wailing mouth. Her heart pounded, sweat pooled under her arms, her legs weakened.

She thought of carrying him downstairs, exiling him to the basement again. Last time she'd left him down there for several hours, alone in his playpen with only a bottle of milk and his Elmo. She hadn't known what to do during that time. She'd sat on the couch, stared at the wall, then studied the checkered blue and white squares on her socks. It had been quiet. Unusual, eerie. But quiet. Really quiet.

And when she'd finally gone to retrieve him, he was quiet. Morgan was quiet. Red-faced, teary-eyed, exhausted quiet. Had he screamed and cried and protested in the dank, musty basement? Sally had no idea. She didn't set up a baby monitor, she didn't even leave the door cracked open.

Charles recently asked about the playpen in the basement. Simple answer: She was storing it there. He shrugged his acceptance. He didn't investigate. He didn't ask why it remained set up, with a sheet inside.

Something about the playpen made her feel guilty. Later, after he'd mentioned it, she wrestled it into the basement's storage closet, shoving it against the caked bottles of cleaning supplies and moldy mops, leaning her body into the door until it latched shut. Out of sight, out of mind.

She even contemplated getting rid of it, hauling it over to Goodwill. But in the end, she couldn't. Because every time Morgan had one of his animalistic episodes, she needed a way out. A moment of peace.

But today, with Morgan's face inches from her own, she hadn't made it to the basement. Instead, she grasped her baby firmly under his armpits, his legs kicking and arms waving in fury. Just a little over one year on this planet and he already had that much vigor and defiance in his lungs, in his limbs, in his soul.

"I said stop. Stop. Stop! STOP!" Sally screamed so loud her throat hurt and her ears rang. She squeezed her eyes shut and when she opened them, Morgan was completely silent, his head hanging limply to one side, his eyelids fluttering to stillness. She hadn't even realized she'd been shaking him. And now he was quiet.

But not the good kind of quiet.

"Oh God," she gasped. "*Oh my God.* My baby." She needed to call 911. Should she do mouth-to-mouth?

She pressed her ear to his chest and held her breath. She heard a ragged, gasping sound—he was breathing! She exhaled, then quickly carried him down the hall to his room, changed his soggy diaper, stroked his forehead, zipped him into his soft sleep sack. She clutched him to her chest, his head nestled in the crook of her neck. She paced, waiting, wondering what to do next. She longed for him to howl again. Her stomach twisted.

She'd hurt Morgan. What would she tell Charles? What would they do with her?

He just needs sleep, she told herself. Sleep will make everything better. She placed him in his crib, tucking his tattered Elmo under his arm. His breathing was raspy, but steady. She watched him for several minutes, her knuckles gripping the edge of the crib, before forcing herself away.

She stumbled down the basement stairs, tripping over an old tennis racket and Charles's bowling bag. She yanked open the door to the storage closet. Morgan's playpen filled almost every inch of the space. She should've brought him down here, let him scream his heart out, and then he'd be exhausted, angrily exhausted—but still conscious.

After crawling into the creaky playpen, she tugged the door shut. It was tight, but she fit, curled into a ball. It was dark and still and quiet.

So very quiet.

Her own sobs finally broke the silence as she cried herself to sleep.

Chapter 2

Charles

Day one

"Charles? It's Charles, right?"

Charles looked up from his screen. The woman from the next cubicle, the new temp, stood next to his desk. What was her name? She smiled broadly, a piece of spinach stuck between her front teeth.

"Yes?" he asked.

"Your phone." She nodded toward his desk. "It's ringing."

"Oh," Charles said, briefly glancing at the flashing light, then back at the temp. Should he tell her about the spinach? He never knew what to do in these situations.

"You should answer it," she said before disappearing behind the partition.

He slowly lifted the receiver. "Print Solutions. This is Charles Hay—"

"Charles. Your report. The formatting is all wrong," his boss hissed. "And why are you still using the old version of Excel?"

"Wait, there's a new version of Excel?" He clicked his pen a few times. He always ignored those annoying boxes that popped up, stuff about system updates and whatnot.

"Just redo it, okay?" she said. "By the end of today."

"I need to redo the *entire* report?" He glanced at his watch. "But it's already four—"

"Then you've got exactly one hour to get it done." *Click.*

Charles listened to the dull tone before sighing and hanging up. He unlocked his cellphone—still no word from Sally. She always sent a picture after lunch, Morgan's face covered in peanut butter and jelly, blue yogurt smeared in his blond hair. But not today. He'd called around two, as usual, knowing how much she cherished the afternoon check-in, but she hadn't answered.

You OK? he texted her.

He knew Sally had her rough days. He'd often arrive home to dishes and laundry piled high, crumbs scattered across the counter, a soiled diaper abandoned on the living room floor. How long did it take to load the dishwasher or toss some clothes into the washing machine? What did she do with all those hours, especially when Morgan napped? She complained of being tired, but damn, she was lucky to get to stay home all day, going for walks, soaking up cuddles. Meanwhile, he slaved away in this stuffy, soul-crushing office, the too-bright fluorescent lights buzzing above, the constant *click click click* of keyboards making his head crackle and ache.

"I can redo your report."

Charles spun around. The temp was back in his cubicle, holding a clipboard to her chest. She ran her fingers through her wavy auburn hair, tucking a strand behind her ear. Smiling. That piece of spinach was still there.

"What?" he asked.

"Sorry, I overheard." She blushed. "I've mastered the new version of Excel."

"Why?"

"Why did I spend hours working on Excel or why am I willing to help?"

"Um, both."

"I don't have anything better to do," she said with a shrug. "I finished my work for the week."

He eyed her, trying to size up her motivation. Either she wanted to steal his job out from under him or this was an office crush.

He rarely received attention from women. He was still amazed that Sally, a woman entirely out of his league, fell for him. Their paths had collided on a Friday afternoon, at Target of all places. He had run in to grab an ice cream bar when he heard a loud commotion, turned, and took in the sight: a flustered blonde in a watermelon-patterned sundress, all wide-eyed as a dozen pints of Ben & Jerry's thundered to the floor.

"Oh gosh. I'm so sorry. It's just ... well, I like grabbing the ones farther back," Sally explained, scrambling to pick them up. "They're more fresh."

His clueless response: "Can ice cream actually be fresh?"

"Of course," she said, brushing her radiant blond hair out of her eyes, batting those long lashes up at him.

He helped put the pints back and had every intention of returning to his work conference—he was, after all, already married—but then he admitted he'd never tried Chunky Monkey, to which Sally protested: "What? This is the best flavor ever. C'mon, you gotta try it."

They sat balanced side by side on one of those iconic red balls outside and by the time their spoons scraped the bottom of the pint, he knew her entire life story: the recent loss of her mom (damn you, cancer), dropping out of college, having nobody stable in her life. She endeared herself to him, like a wounded bird fallen from the nest, plaintively calling for help. He wanted to get her back on her feet—that was all.

Or that was what he told himself as he left that day, her number scrawled on the Target receipt.

But this temp? Yeah, she seemed closer to his age and kind of nerdy, with sleek, green-framed glasses balanced on her button nose, mismatched clothes, a gawky smile. But c'mon, he thought, surely she has better prospects than *me*. Instinctively, he touched his head, pushing thin strands of hair forward to obscure his receding hairline. No, she just wanted to land a permanent job here, nothing more. It seemed silly, though, trying to impress the boss by doing *his* work.

"I work fast," she said. "Really."

He glanced at his watch again. He could pawn this job off, grab a pack of muffins from the bakery downstairs, and catch the express bus home. Get some extra time to horse around with Morgan before his evening Uber shift.

"Sure, knock yourself out," he said. "I'll email you the document."

The temp clasped her hands together. "Excellent! You won't be disappointed." She rattled off her email address. Mandy. That was her name.

"The boss lady said five—today."

"On it," she said as she bustled back to her cubicle.

Who cared if she did his work? She'd probably ask him to put in a good word for her. Sure, he could do that. He clicked *send* and stood. "See you Monday," he told her. She happily typed away, sitting up perfectly straight, as if she'd read an article about how good posture improved productivity. Good for her.

"Yes, have a good weekend." She smiled up at him. The spinach was gone. "And I'll show you the ins and outs of the new Excel next week."

"Yeah. Sure. Whatever," he said, his shoulders tensing. Maybe he should just quit? Switch to working full time for Uber. Imagine that, never having to look at another damn spreadsheet again. They'd give his job to Mandy. Clearly she was better at it. He could gather his stuff, email his resignation letter over the weekend—screw having to give two weeks' notice.

He picked up the framed picture of Morgan at six months old, remembering the magical photoshoot. They'd gone armed with his favorite toys—Elmo, bubbles, toy trumpets, the works. But then the photographer handed Morgie a green plastic duck and he pawed at that squeaky toy like it was made of gold, sitting motionless for several minutes, and glancing up to flash the most adorable smile whenever they called his name. It was incredible. Until they had to go home and leave the precious duck behind—then all hell broke loose. That kid might be small and cute, but he sure could wail.

Charles exhaled as he set the frame back on his desk. What was he thinking? He couldn't quit, not with them struggling to pay the mortgage. He picked up his phone again. Not a peep from Sally. She never ignored him all day.

What the hell?

✦

Charles stepped out of the cool building into a blast of heat. He wished he could work in T-shirts and shorts. North Carolina didn't start cooling down until late September, sometimes mid-October. What was the point of wearing stiff shirts and strangling ties when only co-workers saw each other? Who were they trying to impress?

He carried the cardboard box of muffins—blueberry, Morgan's favorite—huffing his way to the bus stop just in time for the express, a forty-minute ride compared to the hour-long regular service. Beth, his ex, had insisted they live all the way out in quaint Oak Wood ("Oooh, I love their parks and schools!"). Back then, the commute to Durham by car seemed manageable. But now he left their one car, a Volvo station wagon, with Sally during the day so she could take Morgan on outings. And for emergencies, of course. This left him at the mercy of public transport.

The five-minute walk from the bus stop to home resulted in a sweat-soaked shirt. Charles took a few deep breaths to clear his head, to mentally prepare for whatever state Sally was in. It had to be bad if she hadn't managed to answer her phone or even shoot him a text. He imagined absolute chaos—Morgan sprawled on the floor in complete meltdown mode, Sally attempting to throw together something that resembled dinner, the cat clawing at the couch, the TV blaring cartoons. Charles never imagined having a family would be quite so messy and chaotic.

With Beth, everything had been orderly, predictable. He received a proper scolding if she found a towel on the floor. Now, with Sally, abandoned towels piled up in every room and he struggled to keep up with it.

"This was your choice," his mother had lectured him. "Now you have to move forward, embrace what you've done."

What you've done. Leave it to his mother to be so damn judgmental. But she'd loved Beth, everyone had loved Beth.

Charles shoved the key into the lock and paused, tracing his hand along the green trim. He'd bought this house with Beth six years ago, brimming with excitement as the real estate agent ushered them from room to room, sharp heels clicking on the kitchen's linoleum floor. "Plenty of space for whatever you need, you know, babies and such," she'd said with a sweeping gesture and a wink. He and Beth interlocked hands at that, blissfully unaware of the countless fertility treatments that awaited them.

They'd picked out the interior color—Dusty Indigo—after mulling over dozens of sample cards strewn across the kitchen counter. Really, it was Beth's choice, Charles just nodded along. Beth made the curtains, using thick, cream-colored fabric, the sewing machine whirring late into the evening.

And then bam—the freshest pint of Chunky Monkey ice cream changed everything.

Charles slowly opened the door. The lights were off. The house dead silent. What was going on?

"Sally?" he called out.

The cat, Mr. Moops, tentatively crawled out from behind the couch, as if he'd been hiding from something.

Chapter 3

Sally

Day one

Sally's eyes fluttered open. She squinted in the darkness and sat up, feeling something creak and shift under her. Her head throbbed, her mouth felt grimy, her tongue heavy. Reaching out, she groped the mesh netting of the playpen.

Everything came flooding back: Morgan's screams, followed by her own screams as she grabbed him, the anger and desperation racing through her blood. She trembled, remembering the way his head flopped to the side. Did that really happen? Did she really shake him?

It had started out as a typical day, despite the fact that between Morgan waking up several times and the cat accidentally getting locked outside, she'd only gotten a few hours of sleep. Charles squeezed in quality time with Morgan while Sally made breakfast. She could handle breakfast. Somehow life felt easier in the morning: everyone in a chipper mood, no headaches from a day tainted with tantrums.

She usually liked to brew her favorite herbal tea, Country Peach Passion, while scrolling Pinterest for a nutritious yet delectable meal. But today she needed the caffeinated boost of full-strength coffee. In her sleep-deprived state, she couldn't even bother with cream and sugar. Blinking, her eyes landed on the perfect recipe: Frittata. It required a dozen eggs, along with spinach, bell peppers, mushrooms, and crumbled goat cheese. Then she discovered they only had five eggs. No fresh spinach, but she found a crystallized box in the freezer. Bell peppers Charles had grown, slightly shriveled from being in the fridge too long. No mushrooms but a tomato would do—again from Charles's garden. And goat cheese? When did they ever buy goat cheese? Cheddar slices would work.

"Why must you use every dish in the house when you cook?" Charles often complained.

She couldn't help it, always underestimating how food changed and expanded. Like today's eggs, frothing and foaming over the bowl's edge, needing to be transferred to something bigger. Then a bowl to mix veggies, a skillet, measuring spoons, cutting boards. In the end, the sink overflowed with slimy dishes.

They sat at the round, white-tiled table, like a normal family—Charles sipping his coffee while skimming the paper, Morgan shoving egg chunks into his mouth and spitting out the peppers, Sally downing her third cup of coffee and feeling optimistic: *Today's going to be a good day.*

"Time to get going," Charles announced. He stood and planted a kiss on Morgan's head.

"Stay a little longer," Sally begged, grabbing his untucked shirt. She hated when he left, when the peaceful morning ended.

"You know I can't be late," Charles said, fiddling with his tie, tucking in his shirt. "And I've got work tonight. I've got those—"

"Those airport trips," Sally finished. "I know."

"But I'll be home for dinner." He gave her a quick peck on the cheek. "I promise."

Morgan played with his sippy cup while Sally cleared the table. Then they headed outside. Morgan squealed as she pushed him in the baby swing, his chubby fists banging together in baby sign language: *more, more, more.* The oppressive heat didn't seem to bother him, even though Sally's shirt was already damp.

"Maybe we should go to that playgroup," Sally said during his morning snack. "What do you think, little pumpkin?"

Morgan peered up from the highchair, grinning widely, exposing his four puny teeth.

Playgroup happened every Friday, at eleven. She glanced at her phone: They had half an hour. Charles kept insisting they should go—*Morgan needs baby friends*—but something always came up. Truth be told, she was terrified to meet those other moms, feared they'd judge her as a phony, a fake. They'd whisper behind her back about how she stole someone else's husband, someone old enough to be her father. *What a scandal!* She scanned the pictures they posted on Facebook afterward, older moms—all smiles, hair nicely done, the kids playing calmly with fancy wooden puzzles (which, she knew, Morgan would try to eat). Who were these moms, having time to get all dolled up with toddlers running amuck? Deep in her gut, she knew they'd kick her and Morgan out at the first sign of her boy's wild side.

"We should go anyway," she said, suppressing a yawn while pulling Morgan out of his highchair. "A change of pace will do us good, don't you think?"

She stuffed diapers and wipes into the yellow corduroy diaper bag, packed a snack, filled his water bottle. But Morgan had another idea. He scurried across the living room floor on hands and knees, like a wind-up toy, and grabbed the TV remote off the coffee table.

"Morgan, no," Sally said.

He threw the remote across the room and it crashed into the wall, batteries flying. Sally quickly scooped up the parts and set them on a high shelf, taking deep, steady breaths.

She crouched down and Morgan smacked her right across the face, repeatedly, before hurling himself dramatically to the floor, spread eagle style. Then came his screams. Those terrible, powerful screams.

Over the next few hours, she tried everything. She even offered lunch, thinking—*hoping*—it was hunger. She frantically slathered peanut butter, the bread slices tearing apart, her hands shaking from too much caffeine. Morgan choked down a few bites. Sally sighed with relief. But then he flung everything off his tray and Moops slunk in to devour the rejects.

It spiraled out of control from there.

✦

Sally pushed the closet door open, then heaved herself over the edge of the playpen, knocking over a mop in the process. It whacked her in the face.

"Shit!" She wrestled the mop back into place. Her eyes adjusted to the darkness as she shuffled forward, making sure not to trip over the bowling bag again.

At the top of the stairs, she paused and blinked into the late afternoon light streaming through the windows.

"Morgan," she whispered.

She opened his door. His body was a motionless lump. She walked closer, holding her breath, then lightly touched his chest, his cheek, and ran her fingers under his nose. Still breathing. Should she let him keep sleeping?

Google. She needed to google the effects of shaking your baby. Maybe he had a concussion. Could you get a concussion from shaking? Should she take him to Urgent Care, say he fell down the stairs? But he didn't have any bruises.

Perhaps it wasn't as bad as she thought. The details were fuzzy, how much or for how long she'd been shaking him. He could've just dozed off in her hands. Or perhaps, maybe, he was tired from all that screaming.

She found her phone next to the open jar of peanut butter and swatted away the flies. There were five missed calls: two from Charles, the rest from work. Shit, they wanted her to come in. Today, of all days.

Her phone's screen radiated the time: 5:21. Charles would be home in an hour. And then he had those airport trips—what time was that? The effort at rational thought made her brain ache, her hands tremble.

She rummaged through the pantry and found the extra-strength Tylenol and a bottle of merlot. She struggled with the cork, tossed two pills in her mouth, then tipped the bottle to her lips. Just a few sips, she told herself. She needed to stay in control.

Food. Morgan must be starving. Snatching a baby food pouch—Peaches n' Plums—she bounded down the hall.

He'd been asleep for, what, two or three hours? A sickness rose in her throat. Why had she left him that long? She pulled him into her lap and sat on the glider.

"Come on, pumpkin. Mama's here." She rubbed his back, hummed "You Are My Sunshine," and tickled his chest until his eyes fluttered open.

"Oh God. *Thank God.* You're awake. You're okay. Are you okay? Are you hungry?" Her voice broke. She held the pouch to his mouth. He took a few slurps. "There you go, there you go," she cooed.

He pulled away and buried his face in her chest, leaving a purple streak across her white shirt.

Her phone rang, back on the kitchen counter. She carried Morgan down the hall. Krista's name flashed across the screen, her manager at Denny's.

"You want me to come in," Sally said, balancing Morgan on her hip. He clutched her shirt.

"Hey Sal! Yeah, Greg's sick, some stomach thing. And of course it's game night," Krista said. Sally imagined her rolling her eyes. "Any chance you can get here by 7:30? And do four or five hours?"

"My son … he's …" Sally hesitated, looking down at Morgan. His soft blue eyes looked wary, sad, as if he knew, too, that something was wrong. "I—I need to find a babysitter."

"Gotcha. Call me back asap."

Sally set down her phone. Her breath came out in gasps. "Everything's fine. You're alive. You're going to be okay." Morgan peered at her. "Isn't that right, little pea? You're okay."

She quickly typed out a message to Alyssa: **Can you babysit tonight? 7? Work emergency.**

Dinner. She had to make dinner; life had to appear normal. She placed Morgan on the floor, pulled out a frozen pizza and started heating the oven, then hoisted an ice bucket up to the fridge's dispenser. She furiously banged the button, and ice spewed out, a few pieces scattering across the floor. Taking one last swig, she shoved the merlot into the bucket and set it on the table. She reached to the high shelf, pulling down their only two wine glasses. Might as well make the open bottle look intentional—an attempt at romance. She yanked out the bottle, took one more sip, then one more.

Morgan stared at her, his face blank. She expected him to at least lunge toward the fallen ice but he didn't move a muscle.

A shower. She needed a shower. She tugged at her clammy shirt. But what about Morgan's possible concussion? Shit, she forgot to google it.

Her phone beeped. Alyssa said yes, she'd be there at seven. Sally typed a confirmation text to her boss, who responded with: **You're the best! You always do the work of three servers!**

Morgan squirmed, a nasty, pungent odor floating up. A code-brown situation.

"Okay," Sally said, scooping him up and grabbing a juice box and cheese stick from the fridge. Back in his room, she changed his diaper, then balanced him on her lap in the chair. He took a few tentative nibbles of cheese, chewing slowly, before pushing it away. He guzzled down the juice box, then leaned his head against her chest.

The front door slammed. "Sally?"

Her stomach did a full flip. What? Charles was home already?

"Okay, sweets. Okay, okay, okay," Sally said, standing, still holding Morgan. She spun in a circle. What to do? She couldn't let Charles see him like *this.* He'd know, he'd know something was up.

She quickly maneuvered Morgan into pajamas as he whimpered softly. "Shhh, it's okay," she whispered as she slipped him into his sleep sack, then gently lowered him into his crib. He curled up, tugged Elmo close, and shoved his thumb into his mouth. Once his eyes drowsily closed, Sally flicked on his starfish nightlight, whispered *I love you,* and carefully closed his door before making her way to the living room.

"Hey honey," she said, squeezing the empty juice box between her hands. "You're home early."

Charles loosened his tie, kicked off his shoes, and placed a box from Angie's Little Bakery on the counter. "How's Morgie?" he asked.

"He didn't nap this afternoon, so I put him to bed early." She tossed the empty juice box in the trash, then grabbed a napkin and swiped at the blob of baby food smeared across her shirt.

"Really?" Charles glanced at his watch. "It's not even six."

"He was rubbing his eyes and everything. Yawning up a storm." She yawned too, stretching her arms overhead.

He flicked on the kitchen light. "You look rough. You okay?" He put his hand to her forehead. "You're not getting sick, are you?"

Sally took a step back. "Me? I'm fine. I didn't sleep much last night and well, it's been one of those days."

He studied the tower of dishes, the scattered food items, the toys strewn across the living room floor. The cat circled his ankles, meowing incessantly. "I can see."

She leaned in, kissed him on his stubbly neck. Breathed in his musky cologne, a touch of sweat. "I'm glad you're home," she said, trying to keep her voice steady.

"I'm just going to take a little peek," he said, starting down the hallway. "I'll be as quiet as a mouse."

"No!" Sally grabbed Charles's hand. Then, more softly, "He's fought sleep all day and I *finally* got him down. Let him rest." She led him to the table.

"Oh wow, the merlot. I forgot we had that," he said, then stopped. He pulled it out of the ice bucket. "Sweetie, you're not actually supposed to chill merlot."

"Oops, silly me." She forced a smile.

He exhaled slowly, turning the bottle in his hands. "Okay, let's let Morgan sleep. But this weekend, I want to do something fun, as a family. I could whip up my pasta alfredo dish, the one you love, and maybe go to Flowers Park again? Let Morgie ride the train. Last time he rode it for at least an hour straight. Remember that?"

Sally stroked Charles's back as she stared out the window. The low sun's glare bounced off the dusty vases, illuminating Morgan's collection of rocks and dried leaves and beloved twigs on the windowsill. "Yes, of course," she murmured. "That'd be great."

"Frozen pizza again?" he said, looking at the counter.

"Like I said," Sally said, "it's been one of those days."

"Well, let's unwind for a minute before I'm off again."

"Oh, I forgot to tell you." She walked over to put the pizza in the oven. "I got called in tonight. Alyssa's coming to babysit."

"What? You've got to tell them no." He shook his head. "You can't drop everything whenever they need you. It's not worth it."

"It's an *emergency.*"

"But look at you," Charles said. "You look exhausted. You should stay home, rest up."

"It's Friday night, plus it's a game night. The tips will be worth it." Her heart hammered harder. She chewed on her nail. "And I don't want to get fired."

"Babe, c'mon. You barely break even after paying Alyssa." He sat down, pouring himself a glass of wine. "They're not going to fire you for turning down one emergency shift."

"They might."

"We'll be okay without this job." He swirled the glass around.

"Will we?" Sally knew about the unpaid fertility treatments his ex had left behind. Except, well, Beth wasn't officially an "ex"; she'd up and disappeared before Charles could file for divorce, taking a chunk of his money with her. The wedding—Charles and Sally's ceremony—had merely been an excuse to dress up, a facade to placate Charles's nosy relatives as Sally neared the end of her first trimester. The ring acted as a placeholder until they tracked down Beth. How hard could it be to find someone?

"Sally ..." Charles took off his glasses and dug his fingers into his temples. "I've had a long day, too. I don't want to argue."

She lowered herself next to him and buried her face in her hands. She knew using their finances was a lame excuse. She *should* stay home in case Morgan got worse. Oh God, what if he did get worse? But she needed to get out, to get away from what she'd done.

"I know you like your job," he said. "You should go, if that's what will make you happy—"

She tried to hold it back, to stay strong, but the ugly sobs broke loose. She longed to tell him, to blurt out everything that had happened that afternoon, but the words wouldn't budge. Charles wrapped his arms around her, holding her trembling body, probably thinking she was just being an emotional mother pushed to complete exhaustion after a long day with a rebellious toddler on nap strike.

She knew he'd never believe it: *I lost control and hurt our baby.* The words, this unbearable truth, remained trapped, stuck at the back of her throat. For if she actually said the words, released them for the world to hear, it would make it all true.

Chapter 4

Alyssa

Day one

Alyssa walked up the sidewalk, her backpack slung over one shoulder. From the outside, the Haywoods' house looked normal. Nice, actually. They lived in the affluent part of Oak Wood, on Whispering Wind Drive, with bursts of pastel-colored flowers, manicured lawns dotted with oak trees, old-fashioned streetlamps that flicked on at dusk, and a decked-out playground a five-minute walk away. Their house reminded her of a blooming sunflower, painted bright yellow with green shutters. It stood out from the boring gray and beige and pearly-white neighboring homes.

But inside? Yikes! What a dump. The carpet was wrecked, the walls had weird stains, and the dishes—ugh, what a mess. Not to mention the cat's litter box, forever expelling a smell of ammonia and urine.

Charles worked at some office over in Durham. He never said the name. The dads never talked much. Usually, the moms did all the talking—the interviews, references, bookings. She did know, however, that Charles also worked as an Uber driver. His profile popped up one night when she and Jess were searching for a ride to the movie theater.

"Oh my God. That's Morgan's dad," Alyssa said when she saw his wire-rimmed glasses, the slightly receding hairline, those tired brown eyes. "Why on earth is he working for Uber?"

"Maybe he's a drug dealer," Jess said.

"Are Uber drivers known to be drug dealers?" Alyssa asked.

"Seems like an easy way to spread the goods, if you ask me," Jess said. She swiped to the next driver.

Alyssa knew Sally worked as a server at Denny's because she'd comped the theater club—the entire cast of *Annie*—a massive tray of loaded nachos back in May. It seemed odd, though, Charles and Sally working three jobs between them. Could they really be druggies?

She pressed the doorbell and a moment later heard fumbling inside. The door flung open.

"Come in, come in," Sally said, glancing nervously over Alyssa's shoulder. She had red splotches across her cheeks, as if she'd been crying.

"Are you okay?" Alyssa asked as she tentatively stepped inside.

"Oh, I'm fine." Sally scurried over to the couch, chewing on her lower lip as she struggled to slip on a pair of black Toms. "Thanks for coming on such short notice. Work. They couldn't find anyone else. I'd rather not go, but you know how it is."

Alyssa hovered by the door, watching as Sally heaved toys and books off the coffee table, presumably looking for something. Keys?

"Morgan's already asleep. He went to bed early. Probably a little bug." Sally smoothed down her black button-up shirt. "Just watch TV, help yourself to some snacks, you know the drill. There's even leftover wine. Merlot."

"Um, I'm still only fifteen," Alyssa said in a dry tone.

"Oh, snap! That's right. I've only been able to legally drink since February. I get it."

"Are you sure you're okay?" Alyssa moved toward her, close enough to smell the sour scent of booze on her breath.

Sally tugged her knotted hair into a sloppy ponytail. "Oh me? Sure! I just lost track of time, that's all." She smeared pink lipstick over her quivering lips. "I hate when work does this. As if they don't have other people to call. But it's fine. It's totally fine. I'm just grateful you were able to come."

"Of course. No prob."

"How's that chemistry class going, by the way?" Sally asked, squinting in the oval mirror by the front door. She hurriedly redid her ponytail, then licked her fingers to smooth back stray wisps of hair.

"The AP class? Ugh, the teacher—Ms. Beasley, otherwise known as *Beastly*—is terrible. She keeps putting random stuff on the quizzes, stuff we've never covered in class." Alyssa sighed, hauling her backpack to the couch.

"God, I hate it when they do that."

"We've got our first exam this Wednesday. I'm legit worried." Alyssa fiddled with her necklace—a purple My Little Pony on a gold chain—one of the few mementos left from her dad. She could still remember the unicorn wrapping paper, the crinkly pink tissue paper, her dad's satisfied chuckle: *I knew you'd love it.*

"I'm actually taking chemistry for the third time this semester, at the community college. Maybe we could study together sometime?" Sally's eyes darted around the room. "And you're in another musical, right?"

"Yes, *The Wizard of Oz,*" Alyssa said. "That's in December, after Thanksgiving break." She watched as Sally whirled around like a tornado, grabbing her oversized leather purse, phone, and finally discovering her keys strategically hidden under Mr. Potato Head.

"Ah, well, let me know when we can buy tickets. Morgie ... he'll love it." She heaved the door open and scanned the road. "My Uber's here. I'll be gone for at least four, maybe five hours. Charles should be home by eleven, at the latest. Call or text if there's any problem." She turned back, a pained look on her face. "But please, just let him sleep. He's had a rough day."

And with that, she slipped out the door and gently closed it behind her.

Alyssa let out her breath and scanned the suddenly tranquil living room. She'd never seen Sally quite that worked up or spastic before. Perhaps she'd gotten into a fight with Charles? They were always super nice, the nicest of all her babysitting families, but still, they were an odd couple—Sally barely old enough to drink, Charles probably twice her age.

Alyssa had Jess to thank for this job. She designed a stunning flier and helped Alyssa plaster them across town—at the library, cafes, that boisterous indoor trampoline place with a zillion wild kids. Alyssa even instructed her mom to take them to her various temp jobs: "Pin them up on every bulletin board you see." And now, almost six months later, this had become one of her most steady babysitting gigs.

She secured the deadbolt on the front door, then picked up flung magazines, scooped toys into bins, folded blankets, and fluffed couch pillows. She wandered into the kitchen to examine the snack situation. Pouches of baby food. A jar of mixed nuts—only shriveled peanuts remaining. Celestial Seasonings herbal tea boxes. A few bars of Hershey's chocolate, one already open. Oh, and a white cake box from Angie's Little Bakery. Inside were four pristine blueberry muffins with a crumbled sugar topping, untouched. She closed it. Like all savvy babysitters, she knew the unspoken rules:

1. Don't touch anything that isn't already open
2. Never finish something completely
3. Don't even consider the expensive items

The cat mewled in the corner, pawing at his bowl. Alyssa found a bag of cat food and sprinkled in the remaining kibbles, then noticed a puddle of pee on the floor.

"Oh gross. This was you, right?"

The cat gave a fierce hiss before hunching over and devouring his food. Alyssa sighed, pulling a handful of paper towels off the roll. "I bet your litter box is overfull again. But guess what?" She tossed the soggy towels into the trash and washed her hands. "That's one thing I'm never gonna touch."

She grabbed the opened Hershey's bar and the unfinished bottle of merlot, as well as a plastic Big Bird cup since all the regular glasses were dirty. She stared at the pile of dishes—she often did little chores when she could since it was the golden ticket to a generous tip—but decided it'd take at least a couple of hours. With a quick flick of the light, the kitchen was forgotten.

Back in the living room, she paused to study the framed pictures. Their wedding day, with Sally's simple but elegant white cocktail dress, sun-tinted blond hair cascading over tanned shoulders, glittery pink lips, brown eyes sparkling with a hint of lavender eyeshadow. And skinny—gosh, she was insanely skinny back then, like anorexic-thin. Not that she was grossly obese now, just plumper, more curves. But still pretty. *What does she see in Charles?* Alyssa wondered. He kind of reminded her of that short, stocky guy on Mom's *Seinfeld* reruns, but a little taller. And not totally bald, at least not yet.

Next stood a gold frame with engraved words: OUR HONEYMOON. Sally and Charles lip-locked on some pristine beach, turquoise water spanning for miles, a scattering of luscious palm trees behind them with coconuts piled at their feet. It looked like Hawaii. How could they afford a honeymoon in Hawaii but not new carpet?

Alyssa heard a cough through the baby monitor. *Morgan.*

She should check on him. Their baby monitor was basic: only sound, no video. She hated it; you could never tell if he was properly breathing. The news was full of gut-wrenching stories, things like *sudden infant death syndrome.* Talk about a babysitter's worst nightmare.

She set the chocolate and wine on the coffee table, headed down the hall, and sneakily opened the door. She tiptoed to Morgan's crib, paused, and listened to his soft, raspy breathing, his chest moving up and down, the room slightly aglow from the starfish nightlight.

All good.

Back in the living room she couldn't find the remote, so she switched on the TV from the back. A documentary about the migratory patterns of whales flashed on. She couldn't change it, so she settled into the couch, broke off a square of chocolate, and carefully poured a tiny amount of wine into the Big Bird cup.

She was still stumped by Sally's erratic behavior from earlier.

Many things didn't make sense about this family, this house. Like the playpen set up in the basement. She'd discovered it during her third or fourth time watching Morgan, back in March.

It didn't seem *that* unusual, not at first. Parents usually stored baby gear in their basements, attics, or garages—folded strollers, chipped highchairs, those brightly colored musical toys that belt out annoying ballads at the slightest touch. She had ventured down there in search of Morgan's favorite chicken nuggets and hurried because the lone flickering lightbulb hanging from the cobwebby ceiling made it a perfect setting for a horror movie. She bounced Morgan on her hip, pushing aside hunks of plastic-wrapped meat in the large freezer. Then Morgan squirmed, wanting down, so she gently lowered him to the floor. "Stay right there," she told him, digging deeper into the freezer. When she looked up, he was gone. "Morgan!" she shouted.

She heard giggling from behind a tower of boxes. Rushing over, she found him pointing to Elmo, who was draped over the edge of the playpen. Elmo looked guilty, as if caught in the act of trying to escape. Morgan yanked him down and cooed happily, babbling in his secret baby language.

"Morgan, watch out!" Alyssa was concerned about the precarious stack of boxes. But then she noticed a sheet inside the playpen, and a bottle jammed in the corner. A bottle? Confused, she picked it up, shook it, and stared at the floating chunks of milk. What, Morgan played, or slept down here? *In this gross basement?*

Morgan tugged at her pants, reaching for the bottle.

"No," Alyssa said. "It's yucky." She tossed the bottle back into the playpen, scooped him up with Elmo, and bounded up the stairs. Morgan howled in protest. She totally forgot about the chicken nuggets.

Later, she brushed it off, figuring there must be a logical explanation for the playpen in the basement. She had noticed a toolbox next to the freezer. Maybe Charles plopped him in the playpen while he was downstairs repairing things. Or while stocking the freezer from his hunting trips, although that seemed a thing of the past—she had seen a hunting rifle gathering dust on a high, cluttered shelf in the basement. He did seem to like hunting back in the day, judging by that creepy stuffed rabbit in the living room, next to a framed picture of himself holding the rifle and said rabbit by its bloodied feet.

But why would they have the playpen in the far corner? And behind a dangerous tower of boxes? She shook her head. That happened months ago. The playpen was probably packed away by now.

When Alyssa told Jess about it all—playpen, dead rabbit, gun—she suggested looking under their bed.

"Under their *bed?*" Alyssa repeated.

"You might find a big pile of meth under there. Then you'll be an accessory to the crime and they'll haul you off to juvie." Jess looked up from her bedroom floor where she was painting her big toenail neon orange. "And say *buh-bye* to your babysitting job."

"Okay, when did you ever hear of people stashing drugs under their bed? That's like, so obvious."

"That's the point," Jess said. "Everyone thinks nobody would be that stupid, that's why they don't look there. Like that movie, that guy who murdered his girlfriend. He stashed the dead chick's phone in his gym bag, *under his bed.* Cops never found it." Jess smirked. "I'm telling ya, this fam? They sound totally sketch."

Alyssa had shrugged it off, as she did with most of Jess's harebrained theories. But now, maybe, she should take her advice and go sniffing around. But the couch was so comfy, the few sips of wine seeping into her core, and the North Pacific humpback whales had just embarked on their six- to eight-week journey south to mate, give birth, and hang out for the winter months. She pulled out her phone and thought about texting Jess, updating her on Sally's frenzied state. But she already knew her response: *Check under their bed!*

Instead, she swiped through her photos, looking for her hunky new neighbor. She'd named him Luke. He looked like a Luke—like a bad boy Luke. She'd snapped the first pic last week, at dusk, as Luke stepped out of his shiny blue Prius, a duffel bag in one hand (gym bag, maybe?), his phone in the other.

She pulled a pen and her leather-bound journal out of her backpack, feeling a wave of guilt when she saw the dreaded chemistry book (soon, she told herself). A brochure for The Congress of Future Medical Leaders stuck out from the top. Her chem teacher had given it to her, explaining that it was a convention held in Boston next summer for students serious about the medical field. "It'll look really good on your college applications," her teacher had added.

Alyssa dreamed of becoming a doctor, that part was true. But dang, that AP chem class was slowly destroying her life. She flipped to a blank page in her journal and wrote:

Friday, September 7:

Today we officially met Luke. Almost *being the key word. But as usual, Mom blew it. Here's what happened:* We *arrived home at the same time, mom dressed from what appeared to be another failed interview, me dragging my backpack up the steps (I swear, that thing's full of bricks). She asked why I wasn't at rehearsal. I told her the director canceled it, had the stomach flu or Ebola. Anyway, I saw Luke pull into his spot and pointed him out to Mom.*

She was like, "What new guy?"

WTF? How could she not notice the tall, sandy-haired, blue-eyed man living directly below us? Broad shoulders. Tan complexion. HOT. A tad too old for me but perfect for Mom (or give me a few years).

But no, Mom thought I was nuts. "He could be a serial killer for all we know."

The truth: Mom's hopeless when it comes to dating.

Alyssa sighed, hoisting her feet onto the coffee table, tapping the pen against her journal. Still not ready to tackle the chemistry book, she picked up her phone and continued scrolling to the pic taken just last night, again from her bedroom window. It was becoming a series: *Hunky Man Next to Prius with Mysterious Bag.* The time stamp was midnight, right on the dot. And he was staring up at her—he noticed her.

Morgan's piercing cry rattled over the monitor, along with a scratchy cough and a gagging sound. Alyssa swatted chocolate crumbs off her chest. It wasn't like him to wake up after going to bed.

She raced down the hall and turned on his light. "Hey little guy, it's me, Lissy," she said in the soothing, nursery-rhyme voice reserved for little kids. "What's going on?"

Morgan stared back, blinking. She noticed purple streaks and gross chunks covering the sheet, on his jammies. Poor Elmo was drenched.

"Oh gosh, you really *are* sick," Alyssa said. "Let's get you cleaned up." She couldn't find fresh jammies but found a plain white onesie in his bottom drawer. He let loose a sharp yelp when she changed him. "Sorry, little guy," she said. She tossed the soiled stuff, along with Elmo, into the washing machine to deal with later.

What to do after throwing up? Hydrate.

"Let's get some milk," she announced.

She settled him on the kitchen floor, then opened the fridge. She found a half-filled bottle and gave it a sniff. Fresh enough. She closed the door, ignoring the clutter of finger-paintings, pictures, white-board grocery list, and a clipped-out obituary. She warmed the bottle and vigorously shook it, then squatted to Morgan's level, waiting for his clap of excitement or his giddy nod of approval. He stared right through her, as if she weren't even there.

"Morgan, it's me," she said, sticking out her tongue. "Blaaaaaahhhhh."

His face remained blank.

"Oh, you poor baby." She scooped him up and paced the kitchen floor, humming his favorite tunes. After a minute, she headed to the couch and laid him in a cradle position across her lap.

Morgan always guzzled his milk, fast and furious. It was his go-to comfort, except for the times he had those uncontrollable screaming fits. Those were the worst. Alyssa usually resorted to nestling him in the stroller and pushing him around the block several times. Somehow the fast, jiggly pace, along with fresh air and a change of scenery, calmed him every time.

After a few labored sips, Morgan pushed the bottle away. He stared at the TV, watching as the whales dove head-first into a feeding frenzy, downing mouthfuls of krill.

She knew she needed to text Sally and Charles. She hated doing that, it always made her feel like a failure, having to reach out for help. But barfing was inarguably on the list of *When to Contact the Parents.* She quickly sent a message to both of them: **Morgan threw up. Just wanted to let you guys know.**

"What do you need?" she asked Morgan. He seemed calm but unsettled, scanning the living room as if he'd never seen the room before. How odd.

But, what else could she do? She had dutifully checked off the most common actions—feed, burp, change, comfort. Now sleep? He shrieked as she maneuvered him into a new sleep sack. She lowered him into the crib and switched on the sound machine hanging on the rail, set to "industrial vacuum"—his favorite.

"Just let me know if you need anything, 'k?" She planted a firm kiss on the top of his messy hair. She stood there a moment longer, eyes locked with his, before turning off the light. Outside his door, she braced herself for the bellows of protest.

Silence.

It was like a totally different Morgan.

Her curiosity finally taking over, she tiptoed into Charles and Sally's room to see if she could dig up some dirt on who they really were. She opened closet doors, pulled out nightstand drawers, gingerly fished around in each dresser—nothing but a few tampon boxes in Sally's underwear drawer. And yes, she even crouched to shine her phone's light under their bed, only to discover abandoned cat toys and a rainbow-striped ball. Feeling guilty, she shuffled down the hall. But then, she stopped. The third bedroom. What was in there? She fiddled with the handle but it didn't budge.

Jess would go ballistic: A locked bedroom! *Just think of all the secrets.* Alyssa made a mental note to ask her how to pick a lock. If anyone knew, it'd be Jess.

Alyssa returned to the living room just in time to see the whales returning home from their epic migration, white-spotted gray calves twirling and diving and snorting behind their proud mamas. She picked up her phone—Charles had written back.

Chapter 5

Charles

Day two

A sharp wail broke the early morning stillness. Charles jolted awake and fumbled for his glasses, kicking off the sheets.

"I'll get him, honey," Sally mumbled, grabbing his arm.

But it was *his* job to get Morgan. He always got him in the morning, Sally always did breakfast. That was their routine.

"It's okay," Charles said. "I haven't seen him since yesterday morning. I miss the little guy."

"He's sick. I don't want you to catch it," she said, her voice coarse with sleep.

Alyssa texted them both last night when Morgan had thrown up. Charles had immediately wanted to cancel his last ride, but Alyssa reassured him it was under control, that Morgan had drunk some milk and fell right asleep. When he arrived home, she seemed a bit flustered, apologizing for not starting the washing machine—"I couldn't find any detergent." She had hand-washed Elmo in the sink with soap and left him to air dry over the vent.

"I'm amazed he managed to fall asleep without him," Charles said.

Alyssa nodded in agreement, her brow furrowed. "I'm so sorry."

"It's not your fault," Charles told her. "You did everything right."

Morgan's whines now crackled over the monitor. Charles gently patted Sally's arm. "Trust me. I can handle a sick kiddo."

Sally jumped to her feet, looking as if she had enough energy to run a marathon. "No. You stay here."

"Seriously, I've got this," he said, standing. "You got home past midnight. You deserve some extra sleep."

"I didn't even see Alyssa's text until I finished."

"I know." He opened the blinds, trying to gauge the day's heat as fresh rays burst through the clouds. "Don't worry. I'll go and—" He turned. She'd already left the room. "Sally! What the hell?" He hurried around the bed and bumped into the corner that jutted out, then cursed as he hobbled out of the room.

Sally cradled Morgan on the glider chair. He weakly sucked his thumb.

"Does he have a fever?" Charles asked, kneeling in front of them.

"I don't think so."

Charles rested his hand on Morgan's forehead. His boy's eyes fluttered open, looking tired and pained. "Oh, my poor little munchkin," he said.

Sally rocked him rhythmically, humming softly under her breath.

"We should take his temp, just to be sure," Charles said, standing up.

Sally murmured her agreement, clutching their boy a bit too firmly, as if he was about to jump from her lap.

"Where do we keep the baby thermometer?" he asked.

"Bathroom, bottom drawer. On the left, I think."

Charles headed toward the door and paused. Sally gently rubbed Morgan's cheek. "It's going to be okay, it's going to be okay," she whispered, a few tears seeping out of the corners of her eyes.

I should say something, he thought, anything to reassure her. It was probably a harmless bug or maybe something he ate. Morgan had practically inhaled that frittata yesterday. It'd made Charles queasy. That was often the case with Sally's cooking, his stomach protesting while he made the obligatory *mmm, this is good* sounds, sneaking a microwaved Hot Pocket after she left the room.

In the bathroom, Charles dug through the bottom drawer, pulling out three different baby thermometers.

“We’ve got a rectal, ear, and forehead option,” he said as he returned to Morgan’s room.

“Shhh,” Sally whispered, “he’s fallen back asleep.”

“Oh wow, really? He must be feeling so lousy.”

“What should we do?”

“I say we try the ear thermometer first. I don’t know about you, but I wouldn’t appreciate having a thermometer shoved up my butt while I was fast asleep.” Charles chuckled, expecting Sally to join in. She always laughed at his little jokes, but today, now, she just nodded solemnly.

Charles fiddled with the packaging, and then turned the device over several times before finally finding the ON button. He held it to Morgan’s ear, watching the light flash. It beeped. “99.1. Is that high?”

“I think that’s fine for his age,” Sally said. “I remember them saying to call when it’s over, uh, 100?”

“All right. So, no fever. Just tired. Did he throw up again?”

Sally shook her head and chewed on her nail.

“Okay.” Charles started pacing. Probably just a stomach thing—maybe that damn frittata. Should he mention it? Sally seemed so on edge already.

“Why don’t you go to the store and get some things?” she said. “We need more milk, toddler formula, and his favorite Goldfish crackers.”

“Do you think we should take him to the doctor? Just in case—”

“It’s Saturday,” she said. “We’d have to go to Urgent Care. It’d probably take hours.”

“Ah, yeah. You’re right.” He scratched at the stubble on his chin.

“We can call the nurse line. See what they say.”

“Great idea.” He instinctively reached to his back pocket, realizing he was still in his boxers and a T-shirt. “I’ll go get my phone.”

“It’ll probably take a while to get through. I’ll call, you go to the store. And by the time you get back, we’ll know what to do.”

“Uh, sure. Okay.” Charles crouched down and gently pulled her and the snoring Morgan in for a hug. Sally mumbled something into his chest. When he pulled away, his shirt was wet from her tears.

"Hey, hey, look at me." He grabbed her chin, tilting it up. "It's going to be okay. Kids get sick all the time." Somehow his words seemed to make it worse. She yanked her face away, her expression turning stony and distant.

"I'm sorry," he said, even though he didn't know what he'd done wrong. True, they'd never experienced Morgan being sick before—he'd never thrown up before—but it was bound to happen eventually, their little boy catching some bug. He couldn't understand why Sally appeared so distraught over it.

"I'll be back soon," he said and stood. "And, well, call me if the nurse wants us to bring him in right away." He waited for her to respond but she buried her face in Morgan's hair, whispering words he couldn't make out. But he could hear the panic in her tone.

Chapter 6

Sally

Days two and three

Sally sat cross-legged on the kitchen floor, banging together stainless-steel measuring cups, trying to elicit a response from Morgan. She then tried the metal spatula against a skillet, knocking them rhythmically before resorting to banging them on the linoleum floor, pounding and pounding until they left a mark. She screamed into the noise. Morgan usually loved Sally's impromptu musical jams. But today, this morning, he sat in front of her, staring right through the ruckus as if she were invisible.

All those times spent trying to get him to *stop stop stop* crying, and now all she wanted was to hear his howls, the stamping of his feet, to see the beet-red face that came from a three-hour tantrum. Anything but this maddening silence.

"Please," she begged.

She held out the measuring spoons, bound by a silver ring, and lightly tapped them against his nose. His arms hung limp by his sides; his eyes remained empty.

"I'm so sorry," she whispered, collapsing to the floor. She hurt her little boy, the baby she'd promised to keep safe the minute the nurse placed him in her arms: *I'll never let any harm come your way.* She'd never once thought that she, his very own mother, would be the real danger in his life.

Charles returned from the grocery store. "Did you call the nurse line?" he called from the living room.

"Yes," she lied, picking up the scattered measuring cups, the skillet and spatula. Using her foot, she tried to rub clean the black scuff marks, but they didn't budge.

"What'd they say?" He heaved the grocery bags onto the counter. "I got extra laundry detergent, by the way. In case we're dealing with a stomach-flu type of situation."

"The nurse said, uh, to watch out for a fever or other symptoms. You know, give it a couple of days, see if his system fights it ... whatever it is." Sally swallowed, then hoisted the milk jugs into the fridge.

"What should we do for now?"

"Sleep. Keep up fluids. Avoid loud noises." It sounded like something a nurse would say. Her dream of becoming a nurse had started back during her first semester—her *only* semester—at UNC-Greensboro. If she hadn't been derailed by her mother's death, she'd be the one on the health line, advising fretful parents on what to do next. Instead, here she was, attempting to pass chemistry for the third time while burying herself beneath a pile of lies.

Charles pulled Morgan off the floor. "We'll see if we can fight off this bug, okay little man?"

He seemed to buy it, for now. But if Morgan didn't improve, he'd know something was up. He'd eventually ask: *Who is this quiet, even-tempered child? This isn't our son.*

And what would Sally say in return?

✦

Morgan napped while the washing machine filled the house with a grating noise (thank goodness Morgan could sleep through anything). Sally always washed Charles's crisp work shirts every Sunday afternoon, all five of them, even though he constantly rebelled—*Who the hell cares what I look like?* But corporate, they maintained a strict dress code, even if Charles worked behind the scenes. She'd then ferociously cleaned the entire house from top to bottom, standing on the rickety stepstool to knock down ancient cobwebs in the corners of the living room, scrubbing the toilet for over twenty minutes in hopes of eradicating those stubborn stains (it didn't work), and polishing every window until each one sparkled and shined. In the end, she was dripping in sweat, her hands reeking of bleach and disinfectant. Her heart beating way too fast.

Morgan had nibbled a bit here and there over the weekend—a handful of Goldfish crackers, a chunk of banana, a blueberry yogurt cup, not much really. He drank a couple of bottles, so at least he was staying hydrated. But his body already felt lighter, his diapers needing to be fastened tighter, his once-snug onesies now loose and roomy.

Sally tried to keep Charles distracted, encouraging him to attack those wild, unruly weeds in the garden, to mow the lawn, to take the car to the car wash. Now she sat at the kitchen table, her hands clasped together, feet firmly planted on the floor. Mr. Moops meowed and pawed at her ankles. He was Beth's cat, a sweet old thing with cinnamon-brown fur, piercing orange eyes, and a long bushy tail, his mouth stuck in a permanent pout.

"Why do we still keep him? He's so old and fat and annoying," Charles constantly complained. But Sally couldn't bring herself to give him up. It wasn't Moop's fault that Beth abandoned him. He didn't do anything wrong. Besides, Sally loved snuggling with him and Morgan on the couch during story time every night, the way Moopsie spread across their laps, vibrating with pure joy—even when Morgan squeezed him too tightly.

A plan. She needed to come up with a plan. Charles now insisted on a doctor's visit, which seemed natural, expected. What parent wouldn't take their sick kid in?

"Did you call the nurse again? He's been sick for almost two days now. We should take him in tomorrow, don't you think?" Charles had said earlier while Morgan watched endless episodes of the brightly colored *Little Baby Bum.* Morgan usually didn't have such patience for TV marathons. Charles kept touching his forehead, offering sips of milk.

"Let me call again," Sally had said, disappearing into their room.

It wasn't clear if Charles suspected *her*. In his eyes, what could she possibly do wrong? She'd given him a baby. Beth and Charles had tried—for years. In the end, the doctors had told Charles his sperm were slow swimmers, "dwindling in numbers."

That's why they didn't use protection. Sally believed it was safe, or at least safe enough. She kept telling herself: *next week*. She'd go to the doctor next week and get the pill, like she used to take back when she fooled around with Jeremy in the backseat of his mom's Toyota Corolla. But next week never came, and then everything happened so fast: the positive pregnancy test, Morgan's heartbeat pulsating across the screen, Charles's sobs (*happy crying,* he reassured her), followed by him breaking Beth's heart. Basically, an unstoppable tsunami headed directly toward his settled, ordinary life. Her life, too.

Time passed like the snapping of fingers and next thing she knew, she was sprawled on the hospital bed, grunting and bellowing every swear word possible while Charles cradled one of her legs, watching in shock as Morgan crowned away. Eighteen hours and a failed epidural—the miracle of birth was downright ugly. Charles proudly beamed, though. He'd only wanted one thing in life: to be a dad.

Sally, on the other hand, had never given motherhood much thought. She'd figured it would happen much later in life, after she was settled in a career. But Morgan had another plan. He latched onto her breast, suckling instinctively, and she exploded into a fit of exhausted tears: *I'll always love you.* It took her by surprise, the rush of immense adoration and devotion.

Now, on the kitchen table, she spread out her stash of cash, which she kept hidden in empty tampon boxes in her underwear drawer. Behind all her lace and satin and more practical cotton undies was her own secret. Saved up tips from Denny's, plus that tainted fifty-dollar bill, earned over two years ago—a spontaneous lap dance in the shadowy hallway at the Gray Lion (such a stupid name). She'd only gone that night because her friend Jenny, visiting from college, had scored fake IDs. It was Jenny's idea to do the lap dance for money. That was right after Sally's mom had passed away, before Charles. Sally had only made one mistake *after* Charles, when he still lived with his wife. That drunken night in Raleigh. She didn't like to think about that night.

She was saving this cash for a rainy day. Or a plan B moment, like right now.

$546—she counted it twice. How far could they go on that? And to where? If she took the Volvo—she'd have to, it had Morgan's car seat—they'd be traceable. Unless she changed the license plate or traded it in for another car? Charles might be suspicious of her now, but it'd surely raise a red flag if she fled in the middle of the night with Morgan. Could they take the bus? But again, to where? If only her mom were still alive, she'd know what to do. That festering cancer had burrowed deep into her bones, scraping away her energy, her thick hair, withering her boisterous laugh down to a croak. Sally's only solid rock in life, until she met Charles.

The doorbell rang and Sally jumped. Who could it be? She grabbed a nearby tea towel and tossed it over the cash before smoothing back her hair and heading to the door.

A cheery-faced Girl Scout stood on their porch, wearing the iconic green vest with about a dozen badges sewn in neat rows. Sally's muscles relaxed as she saw the wagon of cookies on the sidewalk. Although her mom never had time to take Sally to fun afterschool activities like Girl Scouts, they bought a decent stash of Thin Mints every year and stored them in the freezer to enjoy together late at night over cold glasses of milk.

"Wait right here," Sally told the girl, then closed the door, rushed to the table, and grabbed a twenty. Briefly closing her eyes, a thickness forming in her throat, she remembered the way her mom dunked each cookie into milk three times before popping it into her mouth. Sally opened her eyes and grabbed another twenty and headed to the door. The young girl beamed with gratitude before wheeling her wagon onward to the next house.

Once she got all eight boxes of Thin Mints secured in the freezer, Sally turned back to her money—now only $506. She flung off the towel and hastily rolled the bills, shoving them back into the tampon boxes.

Without a foolproof plan, some way to disappear from the sharp and relentless eyes of the law, she was stuck.

And she wasn't leaving without Morgan.

She grabbed one of the blueberry muffins Charles had bought yesterday, gulping it down in a few bites, oblivious to the taste. She had no choice but to take Morgan to the doctor. Maybe, hopefully, it wasn't that bad. He was close to fourteen months old. Surely it wasn't as bad as shaking a newborn, what with their delicate, fragile brains, that soft spot gaping open. Perhaps Morgan only had a minor concussion. You can recover from a concussion, right?

Charles's mother had stayed with them for three months when Morgan was born, since Sally was a "young and inexperienced mother" (his mother's exact words). At the time, Sally felt so offended, as if they didn't think she was capable of taking care of a baby. But now, with nobody to turn to, she wished Nancy had just moved in with them, permanently.

If she'd been here, if anyone else had been here, none of this would've happened.

✦

"Are you sure you're okay doing your shift?" Charles asked. "You could be carrying Morgan's germs."

Sally stood in their bedroom, a peach towel wrapped around her. Charles always stayed home on Sunday evenings while she worked her regular shift at Denny's. It was a slow night for Uber, and he treasured the one-on-one time with Morgan.

"Well, it's probably going around. Remember, I had to cover for Greg on Friday because he was sick." Sally turned away from Charles, and pulled on undies, secured her bra. She yanked on her elastic-waisted black slacks, the only suitable pants that fit after having Morgan. No matter what she did, the stubborn post-baby weight refused to budge. "For all we know, you could have it too."

"I feel fine ... so far." Charles tapped his knuckles on the wall: *Knock on wood.*

The TV blared from the living room. Morgan was watching a counting video starring Elmo. Sally slipped on her black dress shirt, focusing intently on each button.

"And what about the doctor?" Charles asked. "Did you make an appointment yet?"

Sally headed into the bathroom. Charles followed. "The nurse told me to call his pediatrician first thing in the morning," she said, dragging a brush through her damp hair. She'd never called the nurse line, not even once.

"What should I do for dinner?" Charles asked. "I don't want to, y'know, make him sicker."

"I've prepped a bottle in the fridge. You can try grilled cheese? Or a pouch, but go for the lighter colored ones. We don't want another plum fiasco—that stuff stains." Sally flicked on the hair dryer. "And if all else fails, there's some Thin Mints in the freezer, but just give him one."

"Okay, okay," Charles said, his voice straining over the hair dryer. He paced the bathroom, wringing his hands.

Sally clicked off the dryer. "You'll be fine," she said, her voice surprisingly calm. "All toddlers get sick." The new plan: Head to the doctor tomorrow, have Morgan examined, and wait to see what happens next.

There was no other option.

Charles scooped up the rumpled towels, removed the bath toys from the tub, and rolled up the bathmats.

"What are you doing?" she asked.

"Clearing a path. In case of a barf emergency. I figure a bath is the best plan—for everyone." He stood, surveying his work. "I should change into yard clothes. I don't want to ruin my nice clothes." He hurried out of the bathroom.

Sally inhaled sharply, bracing herself on the edge of the sink. She thought about the money in the tampon boxes. Should she slip it into her purse, just in case she needed to bolt when the cops showed up? Would they show up at her work?

But she couldn't leave without Morgan.

Just calm down, she told herself. *It's going to be okay.*

With a click, the hair dryer whirled up again. She watched as her blond hair fluttered in the wind, ignoring the sickening flutters in her stomach.

✦

At work, Sally tossed her purse into her locker, her hand shaking as she turned the key. She fastened the black apron tightly around her waist, tying it in double knots, and then secured her name badge over her left breast.

She busied herself with cleaning and organizing the trays, the list of symptoms of Shaken Baby Syndrome playing on repeat: *difficulty staying awake, poor eating, vomiting.* Morgan had actually thrown up! But she knew not to trust Google, not entirely. It always displayed the worst-case scenarios, when most things in life turned out just fine. Except, well, in the case of her mother—all those things did happen, and at a shockingly fast rate.

"How's little Morgan?" Robin asked. She secured her apron, smoothed back her strawberry blond hair, then proceeded to fiddle with the coffee machine.

"Oh, he's actually a bit sick," Sally said.

"Do you think he caught what Greg had?" Diana asked, appearing out of nowhere. She unloaded a tray of clean coffee mugs, her tight black curls bouncing. "My little Nicky got it, whatever it is. Sniffles, barfing, the works."

"Oh no," Sally said. "Morgan's only thrown up once ... so far."

"Is he with the sitter again?" Robin asked. Her jewel-blue eyes focused on Sally.

"No, Charles is home tonight."

"Ah, that's good," Robin said, giving the coffee machine a firm slap. It spurted into action. "I don't know how you can trust those babysitters."

"What do you mean?" Sally asked.

Diana leaned in. "Did y'all hear about that babysitter? She got pissed because the kid wouldn't go to bed, opened the window, and hurled him onto the lawn. Second floor. True story—the neighbors saw it all. The video's gone viral."

"No shit," Robin breathed. Hot steam billowed up from the machine. "That's messed up."

"Is the kid okay?" Sally asked. A tray slipped from her hands and landed directly on her foot. She bit her lip to keep from crying out.

"Yeah, I think so. A broken leg or something," Diana said. "Not too bad."

Robin raised an overly plucked eyebrow. "See? This is *exactly* why you shouldn't trust these sitters. Tell me, you got good references on this one?"

"Alyssa would never do anything like that," Sally said, her mouth going dry. She wiped the tray before returning it to the stack.

"That's what they said about this girl, too," Diana said. "Straight-A student, star of the basketball team, even volunteered at the children's hospital. You never know what someone is capable of until it's too late."

"And just because the kid wouldn't go to bed? Shit, she must've been a real whack job, beneath it all," Robin said, hands on hips, eyes on the coffee dripping into the clear pitcher.

"Excuse me," Sally mumbled. She headed straight to the bathroom, hearing the girls speculating behind her about how she was going to spew, just like Greg.

The bathroom was empty. She hurried to the last stall, the spacious handicapped one, and locked herself in. She could already hear the shock: "Wow, that Sally. Seemed so sweet. I never saw it coming."

She must've been a real whack job, beneath it all.

Then it struck her: Alyssa. She watched Morgan Friday night, the day it happened. They didn't have any of those fancy Nest cameras. There were no witnesses. Morgan couldn't even talk yet. *This is* exactly *why you shouldn't trust these sitters*—that's what Robin had said.

A wave of heat washed over Sally. She sank onto the toilet seat. Her stomach churned. *No, no, no.* She couldn't do that. No way. Alyssa was thoughtful, dependable, coming to babysit at a moment's notice, even cleaning up around the house. So devoted to Morgan. And Morgie … well, Morgie adored her in return.

What the hell's wrong with you?

She emerged from the stall and splashed cold water on her cheeks, careful not to smudge her mascara. She stared at her reflection: Slight dark circles framed her skittish eyes, her pale lips trembling. But still, she looked somewhat composed, just a little frazzled—like a fretful mother, someone visibly worried about her little boy's health. Not like a child abuser.

Stick to the plan, she told herself. It could be something entirely unrelated. Maybe he just caught Greg's nasty bug after all? She didn't have to resort to anything crazy—not yet.

She straightened her apron, polished her name tag with a paper towel, applied a new coat of pink lipstick, and pressed her lips together for it to stick.

It's all going to be okay.

She slipped the lipstick back into her apron, took a deep breath, and returned to her shift.

Chapter 7

Mandy

Day four

Mandy hit the snooze button with too much force, sending the beeping clock crashing to the floor. She used an old-fashioned alarm clock in an attempt to halt her late-night phone addiction, with her phone safely "hidden" in the kitchen. It didn't help; her sleep was forever ruined by the memories of her precious Zack, his cold, unmoving eyes returning night after night. The clock continued its maddening blare. Reaching over, she yanked the cord. Just five more minutes, she begged as her head sank back into the pillow.

Monday. That meant Print Solutions, her latest temp job. She'd done two weeks with the company back in March, tucked away in the call room while someone recovered from some kind of surgery. Then they called her before Labor Day, an opening in data entry—could she do spreadsheets? *Yes, always say yes.* She'd returned last week, crammed in a cubicle between Charles and Ingrid, pulling an all-nighter to learn the latest version of Excel. Sleep? Who needed sleep?

She sighed. All these piecemeal jobs, they were barely enough to support her and Alyssa. Oh wait—*Monday?* She had another interview today.

She flung back the covers, toes searching for her bunny slippers. In the kitchen, Alyssa was already up, wearing a snug crop top, frayed shorts, red hi-top All Stars with no laces, shark tooth earrings, and that purple pony necklace she never took off. Who did she think she was—a badass punk or a little girl?

"You can't go to school like that," Mandy snapped. "Go and change."

Alyssa slumped in a chair and shook corn flakes into a bowl. She dumped on two heaping spoons of sugar, then grabbed the milk carton. Only a trickle came out. "Mom, we're out of milk again." She pushed the bowl away in disgust.

Mandy knew better than to start the morning with a battle. But a threadbare shirt exposing her daughter's belly button? She had to draw the line somewhere. "Alyssa," she said, more softly.

"So." Her daughter's lips smacked. "When are we gonna invite that new guy over?"

Mandy stopped, holding the tea kettle, steam fogging her glasses.

"Y'know, the hot man who lives right below us?" Alyssa pressed on. "Remember, we saw him yesterday. In the parking lot?" She beamed. "Did you see the size of his bicep?"

"Oh jeez, can you drop this already?" Mandy sighed. "I have another interview today."

"Whatever," Alyssa said, disappearing into her phone.

As if she'd invite some random guy over. And do what? Sip chilled wine on the couch? Strike up a conversation about the handmade blanket she kept draped over the rocking chair? She could talk about how she knitted it between Alyssa's colic attacks, while Ian wasted away the days with dead-end projects, shady investments, failed rock bands, and the daily "this is my best idea yet!" But guys didn't like it when you badmouthed your exes, it made them feel uneasy. She read that in ... what? *Vogue*. Not that she ever bought those magazines, she only read them at the doctor's waiting room.

"Go and get changed," Mandy tried again, watching the coffee granules dissolve in her mug.

"We should make him muffins. It's the neighborly thing to do." Her daughter's eyes remained glued to her phone, which emitted a steady stream of bird chirps and bee-like buzzes.

She must see my loneliness, Mandy thought. Maybe she's even thought of sex by now. Not had it, of course. But thought of it, yes. Probably.

"Muffins? Don't be absurd," Mandy said. "Now, please. Go. Change."

"Mom, just chill," Alyssa said, rolling her eyes. "Unless school sends me home, I'm not changing."

"Listen, Alyssa—"

Alyssa bolted up and grabbed an energy bar from the wicker basket on the counter. "Sorry, gotta run, Jess is here. I'll be home late … babysitting, then studying for that chem exam. Don't save dinner." She had the audacity to kiss her on the cheek. "Love you, mean it, bye!"

"Wait—" Mandy shouted as the door slammed.

She drummed her fingers against the chipped tortoise-speckled mug Alyssa had made in fifth grade, pottery class. She blew on the coffee and took a tentative sip. Lord, *another* interview.

To think, she'd only had two semesters left to get her Master of Social Work, back at Northwestern, before Ian popped by her college apartment right after Christmas break, snowflakes clinging to his shaggy bohemian hair. Twenty-six minutes, that was all it took for her dream of a real career to slip by, like sand sifting through her fingers. The busted condom, the fear rippling across his face. She'd brushed it off—*What are the chances?* She wasn't even near ovulation. Ah, but those eggs, they were determined little suckers.

But without Ian, she reminded herself, she wouldn't have Alyssa. (Still, she was already stockpiling birth control brochures for Alyssa, for that day *long* in the future.)

Also, without Ian, she wouldn't have to carry the crushing memory of baby Zack.

She rose to her feet and shook her head. She knew better than to waste time contemplating the *what ifs* in life.

✦

Mandy shuffled into the bathroom. She frowned at the mirror. Was that gray in her roots? She was seven months shy of turning forty;

far too young to go gray. She made a mental note to buy more dye—Rosy Copper, a subtle red tone that supposedly complemented her fair complexion. Slipping off her glasses, her hands moved quickly: a dab of foundation (with extra moisturizer, thanks to her twelve-year cigarette addiction, cracking her skin, staining her teeth, luckily revitalized with whitening treatments), a touch of mascara—Onyx, and a streak of lipstick—Rain (where did they come up with these names?). She wiped her glasses on her nightgown, slipped them on and studied her reflection. Not too bad. She added a touch of blush. She imagined the interviewer beaming: *You've got real potential.*

But if you had potential, her inner voice said, *you wouldn't be a temp scrambling at every interview that popped up.*

Ignoring the negative self-talk, she opened her closet. She really should've asked Alyssa to help her pick an outfit for today's interview. As much as she despised her daughter's own style, Alyssa possessed real talent when it came to helping her poor mother keep up with fashion trends. Mandy settled on a navy-blue blouse and a cream-colored linen skirt after googling "what is the best color to wear to an interview?" Both needed pressing, but she suspected the iron was at Jess's house. She slipped on a pair of silvery shoes, the ones that resembled ballet slippers. Alyssa had demanded she buy them: "They're fire, Mom." That was teen code for *hot.*

Mandy drove to the Nordstrom interview and rehearsed her answers in her head: *Bra fittings? Sure, I can do that. Customer service? I'm a natural.*

At a red light, she flicked on the radio and sighed. She still held out hope that something long-term would manifest at Print Solutions, especially if Charles buttered her up to the boss. She couldn't wait to see him today, to see if he'd heard anything about the report she'd done on Friday.

Fingers crossed this was her lucky break.

Chapter 8

Charles

Day four

Monday morning. Charles slumped at his desk and once again contemplated turning in his resignation. Do something meaningful, he thought, something with purpose, like leading outdoor adventures for troubled teens. He'd recently seen the ad in the paper and, with a twinge of excitement, had started filling out the online application, even uploaded his resume. He could do it, go off into the woods for ten days straight, deprived of all technology, whipping disgruntled adolescents into shape. It'd be like his hunting excursions—the addictive stillness of the woods, the night sky peppered with stars, the unforgiving ground reminding him to never take modern comforts, like soft beds, for granted. He'd been a devoted Boy Scout growing up—earning the prestigious rank of Eagle Scout. Yes, he'd make a strong, dependable leader.

But what was he thinking? He couldn't tolerate being away from Morgan and Sally for that long.

Maybe he could try law school. That was the original plan, when he was plowing through undergrad back at ECSU in Windham—a bachelor's degree in Political Science. Ah, such youthful ambition. But before applying for grad school, his brother, Danny, pulled some strings at Print Solutions and Charles accepted the job, moving down to North Carolina. It seemed like the logical, safe thing to do—moving closer to family. But, of course, Danny then up and moved to LA. *That bastard.*

The cubicle next to him remained empty. As much as Charles wanted to be alone, to hide in his work cave, he liked having that perky temp around—her fresh, optimistic energy. Hopefully she kept her word about those spreadsheets. He hadn't heard anything from the boss yet.

Poor little Morgie still seemed out of sorts. No interest in food, or playing, or anything really. Crying out in pain or discomfort when he woke up, when he was dressed, even when Charles gave him a goodbye hug.

"I'll call the doctor. Don't worry," Sally had reassured Charles as she pushed him out the door, shoving his briefcase into his arms.

"Call me right away, okay?" Charles had said.

"Yes, yes!"

Morgan hadn't thrown up again, nor did he have any other symptoms—no fever, no runny nose, not even a cough. He just seemed unusually tired, even though he was sleeping more than usual. And in pain. Meanwhile, Sally alternated between acting weirdly subdued, almost mute, to being absurdly freaked out and manic—like how she'd insisted on pulling down all the window curtains after her shift last night, complaining they hadn't been washed since she'd moved in. And then he woke up in the middle of the night to find her quietly sobbing by her dresser, rummaging around in a drawer.

"You okay?" he'd asked.

"Yes, I'm *fine.*"

It had taken Charles a long time to learn that "I'm fine" meant a woman was definitely not fine. Why didn't they just give men a manual? It would make the whole dating/relationship thing a hell of a lot easier. He'd normally press: *What'd I do? What'd I say?*

But it was some ungodly hour, and his brain was mush, so sleep won that battle. And in the morning, she seemed fine—humming while she diligently rehung all the curtains.

The morning dragged on. Whenever anyone walked by, Charles started typing or shuffling papers or rearranging pens, acting like he was doing important stuff. He refilled his coffee mug four times.

Shortly after 11:30 the temp finally slid into her cubicle.

Charles stood, leaning over the partition, a little jittery from all the caffeine. "So, hey, Mandy, right? Did you finish my report on Friday?"

She blinked up at him, her lipstick smeared, hair windblown. "Yes, of course. Did the boss like it?"

"I haven't heard anything. Usually no news is good news, at least around here." He paused. "You want me to put in a good word, don't you?"

"Uh, yeah." She shifted her weight in her chair. "To be honest, I'm a bit desperate for a job. I have a kid to support, on my own."

"Ah. I got a kid too."

"Oh really? How old?"

"He'll be fourteen months at the end of this month. A little boy—Morgan. Such a firecracker. Until ... well, he's sick. Threw up on Friday."

"Poor little guy. Is it flu season already?" She turned on her computer.

Charles rested his arms on the partition and spun his watch around his wrist. He shared the basics: the weird lethargy, the lack of any serious symptoms, and how something felt "off."

Mandy suggested food allergies, which led him back to that slimy, undercooked frittata. He wondered if Sally ever bothered to check expiration dates. He often found Tupperware containers shoved to the back of the fridge, full of mysterious green and black and white fuzzy items, like science experiments gone wrong. He usually tossed them directly into the trash.

"My baby," Mandy continued, facing him and smoothing out her frizzy hair, "she had colic. She'd cry and cry, sometimes for hours on end. Nothing seemed to help. I was so sleep-deprived and my husband, well now ex-husband, was so useless and—" She stopped abruptly, adjusting her glasses. "Let's just say it was hard."

"Yeah, Morgan cries a lot too," Charles said. "I know it gets to Sally. It gets to all of us."

"But trust me," she said with a smile. "They grow out of it."

"Thanks. I'm going to try calling Sally again. See if she managed to get an appointment."

He wanted to believe Sally could handle this, he really did. But part of him worried that she'd get too overwhelmed, or fear she'd look like a bad mom. As if Morgan getting sick was her fault. Unless it was the frittata, but there was no way Morgan would be sick for days from spoiled eggs. Could food allergies make you lethargic? Maybe.

He shot a quick glance over his shoulder to make sure his boss wasn't hovering, then opened a browser, typing in *toddler acting lethargic, not eating, no fever.*

The first hit: **Emergency Symptoms Not to Miss.** He quickly scanned the article, stopping on the description of lethargy: *If your child barely responds, stares into space, and is difficult to wake up, seek medical attention immediately. Note: If your child is sick, expect more sleep than usual, but for your child to be alert once awake.*

Alert? Since Saturday, Morgan seemed chronically tired, even after a full night's sleep. The article offered nothing about potential causes or explanations. He went back to the search page, clicking on **Causes of Lethargy in Toddlers.** Stuff about falls and head injuries: *If worried about concussion, take your child to a dark room to see how their eyes react to a bright light. If both pupils don't contract immediately ...*

Charles leaned back in his chair, exhaling slowly. *Symptoms of concussion include confusion, vomiting.* Was something else going on? Did Morgan fall and hit his head? Was it while Sally was distracted, or even, he shuddered, when Alyssa was there? He never liked leaving Morgan with babysitters, especially before Morgan could even talk. What if a sitter locked him in a closet for hours? Wasn't Alyssa only fifteen? Barely a kid herself. Maybe he should get those security cameras, the kind you can view from your phone or computer. But that wouldn't help now. Sally would've told him if Morgan had taken a tumble. He was always stumbling around, his chubby legs still getting used to the concept of walking. It must have happened with Alyssa. Leave it to a teenager not to fess up.

He grabbed his phone, tapped on Sally's number, and headed down the hallway.

"Everything okay?" Mandy called after him.

He turned the corner, almost running now, and reached the door to their floor's one balcony, shoving it open. A guy hovered in the corner, a curling puff of smoke drifting from his glowing cigarette. Sally finally answered.

"Sally? You okay? How's Morgan?"

"We're at the doctor's office now. In the waiting room."

"Did he throw up again?" Charles leaned over, trying to catch his breath.

"No, he's been quiet all morning. Just a little fussy."

"Fever?"

"No."

"Have you checked his eyes? I read this thing online ... well, it was about lethargy, which took me to a part about concussions. He didn't fall or anything, did he? I mean, he could've bumped his head. Maybe when he was with Alyssa? Have you checked his pupils? Have them check his pupils. You make it dark first ... they'll know how to do it, of course. Just ..." He glanced at the smoker, who snuffed out his cigarette and raised his eyebrows before heading back inside. "Just make sure they really check him, okay?"

Sally was quiet.

"Did you hear me? I'm just ... I don't know. It could be anything, really. I don't mean to freak out. Damn Dr. Google, you know?" He inhaled deeply, the remaining trail of smoke tickling his lungs. "Look, do you want me to come down there? I can leave work right now."

"No. It's okay," Sally said, her voice hushed. "I gotta go."

"Sally—"

She hung up.

He exhaled, slipping his phone into his back pocket. He gripped the railing of the balcony as the sun beat down. Sweat dripped down his forehead. If it was that damn babysitter, if she hurt Morgan or there was an accident or ...

The door swung open. "There you are," Mandy exclaimed, slightly out of breath. "I was looking everywhere for you."

"You didn't have to come out here. I'm okay."

"You didn't seem okay." She scanned the balcony. "I didn't know you were a smoker."

"I'm not."

She closed her eyes, taking in a long breath, a reminiscent smile on her face. "Me and cigarettes, we go way back." Her eyes fluttered open and she shook her head. "So, what happened? Any update on your son?"

Charles peered over the railing's edge. A couple argued below, he could tell from their body language—the man's exaggerated gestures, the woman's brittle posture. "It's just so weird," he said. "Like something happened, but I don't know what."

"Did your wife take him to the doctor?"

"They're there right now," he said. "I guess, I hope, we'll get some answers soon."

"Gum?" Mandy held out a stick of Wrigley's sugar-free, mint.

"Sure." He unwrapped it slowly.

"Gum is my go-to, whenever I'm stressed. Which is a lot." She stepped beside him. "I'm sure everything will be fine. It's probably some harmless bug."

"You're probably right." Charles blinked up at the sun. "It's just, well, he's never been sick before. But every kid gets sick, right? I mean, eventually." He rolled the silver wrapper into a tight little ball, tempted to drop it on the feuding couple below. They'd blink, their fight halting to a stop, looking at each other in confusion: *Did you do that? No, it wasn't me.* He shoved the ball in his pocket.

"Oh yes," Mandy said. "And getting sick just helps strengthen their little immune systems."

Charles nodded, drumming his fingers on the railing.

"Let's go back inside," Mandy said. "I need to show you a few tricks so you can be an Excel master, too. Assuming the boss liked my work on Friday." She held the door open.

He stepped back inside, the wave of cool air causing his skin to ripple with goose bumps.

Chapter 9

Sally

Day four

Sally slid her phone into the diaper bag. Charles's concerns centered around Alyssa, not her. But could she—*they*—really pin this on Alyssa? What would the consequences be?

Last night at work, Robin had said that other babysitter, the one who'd shoved the kid out the window, would probably be banned from working with children again, but would likely go on with her life—attend college, get a job, have her own children.

"In fact, the whole thing might be wiped from her record once she turns eighteen," Robin said. And she knew her stuff, she was studying pre-law.

If blamed, Sally concluded, Alyssa could eventually put this all behind her. As opposed to herself being convicted and having Morgan ripped from her arms. *Would it be forever?* She absentmindedly squeezed him until he cried out and squirmed in her lap. Right there, thumbtacked to the wall in the doctor's waiting room, a poster read: NEVER SHAKE A BABY!

But I didn't, she told herself, trying to rewire her memory from last Friday afternoon: *We were playing, coloring, stacking blocks, and then I left him with the babysitter. I don't know what happened after that ...*

"Morgan?"

Sally blinked. A nurse wearing Mickey Mouse patterned scrubs towered over them.

"We're ready for you now."

Sally balanced Morgan and Elmo in her arms, following the nurse down the long corridor, as if marching to trial.

The nurse weighed him, checked his temp—*98.9, normal*—then led them to the Tiger Room, which had a dozen smiling orange tigers plastered on light yellow walls, surrounded by decals of fluffy trees, tropical birds, and winding rivers. Morgan usually pointed at the animals, excitedly blabbering "ti-hur!" or "burrr," but today he remained silent.

The nurse clicked on a laptop, her nails a glittery sky blue, perfectly manicured. "So, what's going on?"

Taking a deep breath, Sally rambled off the symptoms: *tired, not eating much, not acting like himself.* She bit her lip, rubbing Morgan's back.

"How long has this been going on?"

Sally couldn't say early afternoon on Friday, that would point directly to herself. "The babysitter said he threw up Friday night. He's been out of it all weekend." Her eyes shifted to the floor. *What am I doing?*

The nurse asked more questions: *Fever? Cough? Runny nose?*

Sally shook her head.

The nurse typed, then smiled gently at Sally. "Dr. Reynolds will be here shortly. It's probably that bug going around."

There's always a bug going around, Sally thought. Come in any time of the year with a baby and they'll always speculate about some "bug."

The nurse left. The clock's hands ticked onward. Morgan breathed softly, his mouth slightly agape. A large tiger stared at Sally with dark, scornful eyes, as if growling: *I know what you did.* She switched her focus to the laminated poster above the sink that had detailed instructions, complete with illustrations, on how to properly wash your hands: *Rub vigorously for 20 seconds.* Who had time for that?

"Good morning, or, gosh, it's already past noon," Dr. Reynolds said as she entered the room. "I hear little Morgan's not feeling well." She lowered herself onto the spinning stool, flipping open her laptop. She had long gray hair pulled into a loose braid, a white blouse splattered with red lilies, and pink-rimmed glasses, dangling on a rainbow-beaded chain. "Did he catch that bug going 'round?"

Sally wiped her sweat-slicked palms on her frayed athletic shorts. "Maybe. He did throw up, on Friday night." Why didn't she say he fell down the basement stairs? She could claim it was an accident: *I looked away for a second, I swear it was only one second!* It was every mother's worst nightmare, the things that can happen in the blink of an eye.

Except there were no bruises, no scrapes, no cuts to back up that kind of story.

Reynolds slipped on her glasses. *Clickety-click* on the keyboard. "Mm-hmm," she acknowledged. "Any indication of ear pain?"

"No."

"Any fevers?"

"No."

"Sore throat?"

"No," Sally said firmly, trying to stop the question-and-answer game. As if Morgan would tell her if he had a sore throat. Besides, didn't the nurse take down the same information? What were they doing on there—playing Wordle?

Reynolds peered over her glasses, her eyes turning dark, just like the tiger's. "Any other symptoms?"

Sally swallowed. She longed for a drink. "He's sleeping a lot. Fussy and whiny, crying out here and there, but not his usual screaming fits. That's a good thing, believe me, but it's worrisome. He's not eating much, either." The lineup of symptoms hit hard: *This is bad.*

But maybe, she hoped, it was like a bad bump, something that would heal with time. Little kids were robust, sturdy. They bounced back from tumbles and falls. And yet the thought stabbed at her: *What if Morgan never laughs again?*

Reynolds studied Sally, then her eyes drifted down to Morgan, fast asleep in her lap, his arms wrapped around Elmo.

"No crying bouts? That *is* unusual, especially for Morgan. We all know he has quite the set of lungs on him."

Sally forced a weak laugh.

"When did this all start?"

Ignoring her erratic heartbeat, Sally looked directly at the doctor. "It started, uh, Friday night, when Morgan was with the ... with his babysitter." It sounded so obvious, such a weak lie. *It wasn't me, I swear.*

Reynolds's fingers sped over the keys, a barely perceptible shake of her head. Sally imagined the words: *suspected child abuse.* Was there a special button they pressed to secretly call social services, like banks use when they're getting robbed?

A wave of nausea washed over Sally. What exactly did she tell Charles when he came home on Friday? Didn't she say Morgan had been sick? No, no she didn't. She said he'd skipped his nap and went to bed early. But Charles had commented on *her*: "You look rough. Are you getting sick?" Would he put it together? She felt like she was trapped in a sticky web, an unstoppable force squeezing in, restricting the air flow to her lungs. A gasp for breath. She was tempted to toss her hands in the air and shout: "Take him! Take him now!"

Sally licked her dry lips, pushed a wisp of hair out of her eyes, and looked out the window, a glimpse into the world below—people studying parking meters, pushing strollers, carrying bags of groceries. Such predictable, stable lives.

The doctor continued typing, alternating rhythm with the clock—*click-click, tic-toc, click-click, tic-toc.* She finally looked up. "Did you give him any medication?"

Sally spun her wedding ring, her placeholder ring. The smooth edges, the small diamond, shiny and glimmering. "Baby Tylenol. On Saturday, I think. Sunday afternoon, too. He seemed in pain, I figured it was a new tooth. A molar?" She shifted in her seat, Morgan's limbs loose and floppy in her lap.

More typing. "3.75 milliliters, at least four hours between doses?"

"Uh, yes," Sally said, nibbling on her pinky nail.

Reynolds firmly closed the laptop and pulled off her glasses, letting them clank against her blouse's metallic buttons. "Let's take a look and see what we can find."

Sally nodded.

"We're going to need to wake him up."

"Oh, yes. Of course." Sally pushed Morgan up, giving him a gentle shake. "Come on, my little snuggle bear."

Reynolds gathered her equipment—stethoscope, ear monitor, tongue depressor. "He *is* unusually quiet. Aren't you, little guy?" The doctor gave his cheek a little pinch. Morgan stared at her stethoscope, not even attempting to grab it.

"Do you think it's just"—dare she say it?—"a bug?"

"Maybe." Reynolds cleared her throat. "Let's make sure Elmo's okay first," she said to Morgan, crouching in front of him and pushing her stethoscope against his doll's furry chest. Sally expected Morgan to giggle at that, but he just frowned and rubbed his eyes.

Reynolds gave a little sigh before setting Elmo aside and checking Morgan's chest, back, ears, throat. "Everything seems fine so far." She dug her fingers inside his mouth. "I don't feel any teeth coming in. But that doesn't mean one isn't ready to break through. Those new molars, they sure can turn our sweet babies into little beasts." She chuckled, reaching over to flick off the light and holding a pen-like light up to Morgan's face, moving it back and forth as if trying to hypnotize him.

"So far so good." Reynolds switched back on the humming overhead light.

Sally exhaled, unclenching her fists and studying the nail imprints left in her palms. Based on what she'd read, and Charles too, the eyes indicated brain-related trauma. Broken blood vessels, pupils not dilating, all that. Even though she hadn't noticed any of those things, hearing the official confirmation was a relief.

Does this mean he's going to be okay?

"Let's get him onto the table."

Sally pulled her clingy shirt away from her moist skin. Morgan stared out the window. "Come on, my little pea," she said. Usually Morgan thrashed, kicked, and screamed at this, trying to hurl himself airborne like a fish out of water. But now, he sprawled out, limp and compliant, staring helplessly at them. Sally's stomach tightened. She just wanted him back—to go back to Friday, rewind it all, keep hugging him instead of...

Reynolds lifted his gray dinosaur shirt, a smiling T-Rex shouting "Roar On!" She pushed and poked his belly and groin area. "We'll run a CBC—complete blood count. That'll check for anemia, bacterial infections. Has he been low in iron before?"

"Um …" Sally pressed her hands together. "I don't think so."

"I'll do a complete metabolic panel as well, check his kidney and liver function. Highly unlikely there's any problem there, but might as well cover all bases. A thyroid test wouldn't hurt, either."

"Okay," Sally said. She grabbed Morgan's small hand and gently squeezed it.

Morgan cried out, wincing, and rolled toward the wall.

"Oh, my poor baby." Sally leaned over, trembling as she kissed his cheek.

"There seems to be some pain or discomfort in the upper right part of his belly. It could be liver, or gallbladder," Reynolds said. "I need to check the other side."

Sally helped position Morgan onto his back. *His liver? Gallbladder?* Was something else going on, something unrelated to the … the incident?

"This side seems fine. Why don't you scoop him up?" Reynolds lowered herself onto the stool, the wheels creaking as she slid back to her laptop.

Sally settled Morgan on her lap, smelling his downy hair—a fruity citrus scent. She wrapped her hands around his chest, his heartbeat pulsating against her fingers, steady and strong.

"Here's what we're going to do." Reynolds's sharp eyes turned soft, concerned. "The nurse will do his blood draw. The lab's pretty quick, the results should be in by tomorrow. In the meantime, I'm going to put in a referral at the hospital for an abdominal scan to look at that area in case it's organ related. We'll see what comes back and take it from there. How's that sound?"

"So …" Sally blinked. The room was spinning, the colors blurring into a neon swirl. "We go to the … the hospital next?"

"First you wait for them to call. They'll squeeze you in today or tomorrow."

Sally released an agonized exhale.

"I know this is a lot to take in. We'll figure out what's going on, I promise." Reynolds took Sally's clammy hand in hers. "For now, keep pushing the fluids, let him rest, and call if his symptoms get worse."

Sally nodded. Morgan shifted in her lap, his face contorted with pain. Her phone rang—Charles. She feared another disturbing list of worst-case scenarios; she'd read enough already. She leaned over and swiped the call to silent.

Morgan clung to her as she made her way out of the office, down the flight of stairs, out to their station wagon. He cried out as she secured his car seat straps.

"I'm sorry, sweetheart," she murmured, rubbing his forehead. "Mommy's so sorry."

Standing up, dizzy under the heat, she looked through the mist of tears at the nearby businesses—a bank, health food co-op, drug store, everyone walking at a fast clip. If only she knew of some place to go, someone who could help, someone who would understand: *Something's wrong with my baby. He was crying nonstop, and then I shook him and made it worse.* She chewed on her nails. Not even Charles would understand that she'd lost it.

"It's going to be okay," she said, half directed at Morgan, who was already snoring gently, his head slumped against the car seat pillow, drool pooling onto Elmo's face.

She slid into the car and focused on her breathing—*in, out, in, out.* Her phone rang—Charles, again. She let his ringtone fill the quiet, the upbeat melody of "Butterfly Dance." When the music stopped, she switched the ringer to silent and started to drive home. She would wait for the call from the hospital and do whatever they told her to do.

But what if they found damage caused by her, damage too subtle to be picked up by Dr. Reynolds's exam? Could she risk more poking and prodding, and all the questions that would follow? She could just keep driving.

No, she told herself, gripping the steering wheel tighter. She needed to do what was best for Morgan. Even if it meant losing him.

Random memories flashed by: the time she flew headfirst over her bike, her mom tenderly applying rows of Curious George Band-Aids to her fresh wounds. Pulling Morgan into their bed, those delirious early days when his days and nights were reversed, his warm body squirming beside her milk-laden chest. Mashed bananas—the first food they fed Morgan, his mouth open like a sightless bird, a helpless creature who trusted his mother with unwavering devotion.

Her boy trusted his mother to do the right thing—always.

Exit 31B approached, but she kept driving, whizzed right past it, blinking into the slanting sun, the trees closing in as she continued west on Highway 54. Morgan slumbered in the back, unaware of the tears streaming down his mother's face.

Chapter 10

Charles

Day four

Charles stared at his phone. He'd called Sally four times now and still no answer. It was turning into the longest Monday ever.

He tried a few texts:

Where are you?

Are you OK?

Call me.

Why was he still at work? His son was sick, for Christ's sake. He should've taken the day off, gone in with them to see the pediatrician. But he knew he was overreacting—kids get sick all the time.

"No word about your son yet?" Mandy asked. She appeared in his cubicle, without warning, like an office ninja. It made him jump. "Sorry—didn't mean to scare you."

"No, it's okay." He checked his phone again. "Nothing. They were in the waiting room around noon. That was about four hours ago."

"Maybe her phone died? Happens to me all the time. That's why I carry a spare charger." She smiled, tucking a flyaway strand of hair behind her ear. "Maybe call the pediatrician?"

"I don't have the number," he said. "Sally's always the one who takes care of those things."

Mandy pulled out her phone. "What's the name of the clinic?"

"It's … um … Oak Wood Children's Clinic?"

"Wait, what?" Her eyes brightened. "You live over in Oak Wood too?"

"Yup."

"Cool. We could maybe carpool," Mandy said. "Here. It's ringing." She thrust her phone at him.

"Oh, okay," Charles said, flustered. He put the phone to his ear. A chirpy voice answered.

"Hi, this is Charles Haywood. I'm calling about my son, Morgan. He was there this afternoon, with my wi—um, his mother, Sally. I haven't been able to reach her. Are they still there?"

"Let's see. Morgan Haywood?"

"Yes, that's him."

"Actually, we got a few of his blood tests back already. Let me transfer you to the nurse. Hold on a sec."

Charles spun around in his chair. Mandy had disappeared. He stood, peering into her cubicle. He scanned the rest of the office, looking for a flash of her auburn hair.

"Mr. Haywood?" a voice asked.

"Yes, I'm here."

"This is Sarah, the nurse who saw Morgan earlier."

"Sorry to bother you. I haven't been able to touch base with my, er, partner yet." Damn it, he never knew how to refer to Sally.

"It's not a problem. I was about to give you guys a call anyway," Sarah said. "Morgan's blood results came back showing a slight iron deficiency. Now look, anemia is pretty common in kids, especially at Morgan's age. Usually a switch in diet clears it right up."

Charles stared at his computer, the screen saver a swarm of blue and yellow fish swimming in circles with a low bubbling sound. "Wait, so all of this is because of *low iron?*" He thought of Morgan's limp body curled up in his lap, sucking his thumb, ignoring the world around him.

"It's just one thing we've found, so far," Sarah said. "I know Dr. Reynolds ordered more tests. Not everything came back yet."

"Oh." Charles pushed his glasses up his sweat-slicked nose. "So, what do we do next?"

"I'll send over some info about iron-rich foods. And we'll reach out once we get the rest of the results in."

"All right."

"I hope he feels better soon."

"Thanks." Charles clicked off the phone. The background picture showed Mandy cradling a chubby baby in a white snowsuit with fluffy, pillow-like clouds surrounding their smiling faces. He set it down, carefully, feeling guilty for taking a small glimpse into her personal life.

He picked up his own phone and scrolled through the messages. Nothing from Sally. He called again.

"Hello?" she answered, sounding small and meek.

"Jesus, Sally," he said. "Where the hell have you been? I've been trying to get a hold of you all day. Did your phone die? Are you guys back home? How's Morgie?"

"Morgan's okay."

"Where are you?"

"We're at the zoo."

"What?" Charles choked. "Did you say the *zoo*?"

"Yes. The zoo." She paused. "By the monkeys, actually. Pumpkin, do you see that monkey with a banana? Morgie, look, look! He's eating a banana. Do you see?"

"Sally. Sally!" Charles shouted. "Why would you take him to the *zoo*? That's what, an hour away? He's sick. Why aren't you guys at home?"

A nearby co-worker stood up, peering at him with a concerned look. Charles cleared his throat and lowered his head.

"Don't you think you guys should stay home?" he whispered. "Until we know what's going on?"

"We needed to get out," Sally said. "Morgan needed an adventure, some cheering up. The doctor said the fresh air would do him good. Do you remember his first food? Mashed bananas! Doesn't that seem so long ago now?"

"Sally." Charles sighed. "I just talked to the nurse, the one you saw this morning."

"Oh?"

"She said he's low on iron. Anemia."

"Huh," Sally said.

"Did they say anything else when you were there? Did they check his eyes, you know, his pupils?"

"His eyes were fine."

"Anything else?"

"Uh … it's hard to remember. They talk so fast, you know. Using all that doctor lingo." Sally laughed. "I have no idea how I'm ever going to survive as a nurse."

Charles felt like banging his head against the wall. He should've gone with them, or at least grilled the nurse for more info. Sally had a great knack for details until a bad mood hit. Then everything turned to shit.

"Was there anything"—he swallowed—"concerning?"

"They said something about ordering blood tests, wanting to check his liver. Or was it gallbladder? Thyroid, I think." She commented on the monkeys again, to a most likely annoyed and overly exhausted Morgan. "But the anemia thing, that sounds like something. That could explain his tiredness, right?"

"Yeah, I guess so." His fingers hovered over the keyboard, tempted to google *anemia in toddlers*. "It just seems odd. Everything coming on so suddenly. One day he's fine, the next day he's not. Wouldn't anemia be a long, drawn-out thing?"

Sally didn't respond.

"And the pediatrician didn't say anything else?"

"Look, I gotta go," Sally said. "They're about to feed the lemurs. Morgan loves the lemurs."

"Sally, you don't seem ok—"

She hung up.

"Damn it!" He opened his call log, then scrolled to find the children's clinic. It took a solid minute to remember Mandy had made the initial call from her phone. He typed in Oak Wood Children's Clinic, tapped the number, and waited. After a few rings, it went to a chirpy voicemail greeting. He ended the call and slammed his phone onto his desk.

His computer dinged. An email from nurse Sarah with an attached document: *What to Do with Iron Deficiency.*

He slid his glasses up his forehead and rubbed his achy eyes. Somewhere in the background the whir of a copy machine kicked in, the monotonous sound of pages chugging out. The nurse had sounded so calm. Why get worked up over nothing?

Still, he couldn't shake the feeling that something happened last Friday. To Morgan. It couldn't have been Sally—she always told Charles everything, like if Morgan bumped his knee or landed too roughly coming off the slide. She'd even called him at work once, during an important meeting she knew about, to report that she'd accidentally nicked Morgan's finger while trimming his nails. Then came the squirrel incident—she'd cried hysterically for days over that. "It wasn't your fault," Charles had tried reassuring her. "Squirrels are everywhere. It's better you didn't swerve to avoid him." But Sally had been inconsolable for days, completely consumed by guilt.

He knew his Sally, she would've called the second Morgan got hurt. Unless, he thought, something happened when she turned away? But she would've heard his cries, his pain, and texted Charles right away: *Something's wrong with Morgie.*

Alyssa. It all came back to the babysitter. She'd started in the spring, after he saw her flier displayed in the staff room, with a personal message scrawled in the corner, in Sharpie, something like: *The daughter of a fellow employee.* And a smiley face. A signed name? Did he know this employee?

Without thinking, he grabbed his phone and bolted out of his cubicle, dodging a group of co-workers carrying stacks of papers. He pushed open the door to the break room, letting it bang against a trash can.

"Oh hey, Charles. How's it going?" It was Joyce from accounting.

"Fine, fine," he mumbled, heading straight toward the bulletin board. He scanned the random notes and fliers: a Ford truck for sale, a litter of new puppies—Labrador retrievers with golden fur (Morgan would love a puppy, but Sally insisted no, she was allergic), details about the upcoming staff picnic. Nothing, nothing, nothing about babysitting.

"How's little Morgie?" Joyce asked.

"He's great." Maybe he'd texted a picture of the flier to Sally? He scrolled through his texts, selfies of Sally and Morgan sharing an ice cream together, a pic of a onesie that said *I'm cuter than Dad,* until he found something from March 14: Alyssa's first name and phone number. That was it. Damn, he didn't even know her last name. His heart sank. Sally was the one who'd called, did the interviewing, checked the references.

"Whatcha looking at?" Joyce waltzed over to him. "Those puppies? Makes the heart melt, don't they? I'd take them all home, for my grand-babies. But the youngest one, little Jamie, he has a thing for yanking tails. Can you believe he dislocated my cat's tail? Had to rush him off to the emergency vet. Let me tell you, that was one helluva bill—"

"Do you remember seeing a babysitting flier here? Back in March," Charles said. "It was an employee's daughter, a teenager named Alyssa."

"Alyssa? Haven't heard the name. But then again, not everyone's that open," Joyce said. "Like Susie, over in HR. She's got twins who just started kindergarten, but she never talks about them. Looks at you like you're a nut if you ask about them, as if you're gonna kidnap them." She shook her head. "I mean, who doesn't want to talk about their kids?"

"Uh-huh." Charles took a step toward the door.

"But March? I was off with my family in the mountains, spring break. Did I tell you about spotting a bear, right outside our window? It could've eaten us alive."

"Oh wow." *Closer closer closer* to the door. "I really need to get back to—"

"I'll let you know, though. I'll ask around." She gave him a wink and a nod.

"Great, thanks. Nice chatting." He ducked out the door before she could say another word. Christ, he hated this place.

Back at his desk, Mandy's phone had been replaced with a yellow Post-it note: *Hope everything's OK with your son. See you tomorrow. — Mandy :-)*

A smiley face. Like the one on the babysitter flier. But plenty of people used smiley faces, it was the era of emojis. Or was the proper term emoticons? Mandy said she had a son, a baby, right? He couldn't remember. She looked a tad too young to have a teenager but then again, he was terrible at gauging a woman's age.

He sank into his chair and swiped to contacts until he found *Alyssa—Babysitter*. He skimmed over their text exchange from Friday night, about Morgan throwing up.

His last text to her: **OK. Let me know if anything changes.**

What an idiot. He should've canceled everything, immediately. Isn't that what you're supposed to do when your kid's sick? Instead, he and Sally both continued working while their poor baby suffered at home, with only the babysitter to help.

Just drop it, he thought. Go home and cook some iron-rich foods, give Morgan a bubble bath, read a few stories before bed. But he couldn't help himself. His thumbs moved quickly, independently from his body, frantically typing out a message to Alyssa: **Did anything happen on Friday night? Besides Morgan throwing up? He doesn't seem like himself. Did he fall or hurt himself?**

He paused, then added: **Did he hit his head?**

It seemed over the top. The nurse or doctor would've noticed if something was suspicious, they were trained to look for that kind of stuff. Morgan had no visible bumps, bruises, or scrapes. But throwing up? The nonstop lethargy? How his face clenched in pain, pushing away his favorite foods, with that lost, lackluster expression in his eyes. Low iron? It didn't add up.

Charles hit *send*. His phone made a little swoosh sound, confirming that the accusatory text was delivered to a teenager—a kid, really—who may or may not know anything about his son's condition. And if Alyssa did know something, if she harbored some terrible truth, was she really going to fess up via text?

Chapter 11

Alyssa

Day four

Alyssa stared at the bubbling pot of noodles, the cheese pack on the counter. Her phone chirped. She had a soft bird tone for babysitting families, allowing her to respond discreetly, even in the middle of class. (Jess got a buzzing bee, her mom got the *Jaws* soundtrack.) She couldn't afford to miss a potential job—she was saving for a car.

Jess got her license in January, literally two days after turning sixteen, and then declared: "We should buy a car. Together. When you get your license in November. We'll do joint custody. Like, you get the car Monday, Tuesday, I'll get it Wednesday, Thursday. And we'll alternate every weekend."

"That's stupid," Alyssa said. "We hang out all the time anyway."

"Yeah, but we'd have our *own* car. Not my mom's junky Mazda. We could get something dope, like a hybrid or a Tesla."

"You're insane. Do you know how much a Tesla costs?" Alyssa rolled her eyes. "You'd have to flip a million burgers for that."

"Hey, I'm due for a raise at Burger King any day now."

"Wow. An extra 25¢ an hour."

"It adds up." Jess folded her arms across her chest. "And I can always ask my dad for the rest."

Jess's dad worked as a big shot lawyer in New York, living in a swanky high rise in Manhattan (Alyssa and Jess had visited last spring break). He loved spoiling Jess with extravagant birthday gifts—like the latest iPhone or another set of AirPods (which Jess was prone to losing within several weeks)—but deprived her the rest of the year with some lame excuse about learning to "make it on her own." Jess was super lucky, though. Alyssa's dad never sent anything, not even an obligatory birthday card, since he'd disappeared over ten years ago.

Alyssa pulled out her phone. Elodie, the seven-year-old she was babysitting, happily smeared paint on an oversized canvas: an outer-space-themed masterpiece.

"I don't care what anyone says," Elodie said, defiantly, "Pluto is still a planet."

Alyssa nodded her agreement while scanning Charles's text: **Did he hit his head?**

The water bubbled over, hissing and spurting. "Shit!" She lowered the heat, frantically stirring the foaming mess.

"Mama says no swearing," Elodie said.

"Sorry," Alyssa said, grabbing a towel. "The mac-n-cheese is almost ready."

"I want to eat in the living room," Elodie announced. "While watching *Frozen.*"

"Uh, sure." Alyssa drained the noodles, the steam fogging the window.

She sent Charles a quick response: **Nothing else happened, just Morgan throwing up.**

Should she ask questions? Charles had said that Morgan didn't seem like himself. Her body stiffened. Should she tell him she'd thought the same exact thing on Friday night? Oh God, did she make it worse when she—

"I'm hungry!" Elodie screeched.

Alyssa forced herself not to think about it as she slopped a serving of sickly orange mac-n-cheese onto an Elsa plate. Jess would know what to do.

✦

Jess picked her up, promptly at 6:30 p.m.

"I got Chipotle, burritos. Figured we should head to my place and get this chem shit over with."

"Okay," Alyssa said, shoving her backpack to her feet.

"What's wrong?" Jess said, pulling out of the driveway before Alyssa even fastened her seatbelt.

"I got a really strange text."

"From that new guy downstairs?"

"No, he's another story," Alyssa said. "Did I tell you he left at three in the morning?"

"What were you doing up at that hour?" Jess turned onto the highway, rolling down the windows. The breeze whipped through their hair.

"I just had this sense. I looked and there he was, getting into his car."

"It's no crime to go for a drive in the middle of the night." Jess screeched up to a light and scrolled through Spotify, clicking on Grace VanderWaal. "But here's what you should do: Buy a burner phone, set up GPS-sharing, slip it into his car. Then, we follow him." She flashed a mischievous smile.

"Okay, sure." It was always best to go along with Jess. "Now, can we please focus on what happened today?"

"What happened today?"

"I got this strange text from Charles."

"Hmm. The pudgy Uber driver?" Jess turned on her blinker, cutting someone off. She ignored the series of angry honks that followed.

"Eh, I think of him more as stocky."

"But he's still kinda cute and cuddly, like a slightly balding teddy bear. Nice eyes."

"Yeah, whatever." Alyssa scrolled to a picture of Morgan, his four jagged teeth, the startling blue eyes. "Don't you think it's weird that both Charles and Sally have brown eyes and yet Morgan's are blue?"

Jess raised an eyebrow. "Whatcha implying, detective?"

"I dunno. Genetics, right?" Alyssa zoomed in on the picture. "Dominant versus recessive."

"I didn't pay attention in Bio. You're the brainiac." Jess licked her glossy lips. "If you hadn't skipped first grade, we wouldn't be friends."

"And my life would be depressingly boring."

"Okay, tell me about this sketchy text."

Alyssa read it aloud. "*Did he hit his head?*" she repeated.

"Well damn." Jess exhaled, speeding through a yellow light. "He thinks something happened, like, while you were there."

"For real?" Alyssa stared at her phone. Then, in a whisper: "What kind of babysitter do they think I am?"

"Did anything happen?"

"No, of course not." Alyssa leaned back, crossing her arms. "He definitely didn't hit his head." She filled Jess in on the gist of Friday night.

"Nothing else?" Jess pulled into the Cedar Park complex and cut the engine. "C'mon, I can tell you're leaving something out. Did he jump out of his crib or something?"

"What? No." Alyssa kicked open her door, grunting as she lifted her backpack. "He was in his crib pretty much the whole time."

"Maybe he jumped out, hit his head on the floor, and then climbed back in?"

"Okay, the kid's like one. He's not a Cirque du Soleil acrobat."

They walked up the steps to Jess's townhouse. Just Jess and her mom—like Alyssa and her mom. Except that Jess still had a dad, someone to visit during school breaks, to treat her to scrumptious five-star dinners and magical Broadway musicals, to maybe buy her a car.

"Here, catch." Jess tossed a foil-wrapped bundle.

They headed upstairs, then sprawled their thick chemistry books on the gray carpet, next to the purple stain—the unfortunate grape juice incident from years ago. Jess's mom, Claire, had tackled it with baking soda and Dawn dish detergent before swearing and giving up.

After inhaling their burritos, Alyssa read off her response to Charles and then said, "He didn't write back."

"The mystery continues." Jess moved on to straightening her fuchsia-tinged black hair. "You know what you should do?"

"Look under their bed? I actually did." Alyssa shook her head, feeling ashamed. "Oh, and there's a third bedroom, locked. You gotta teach me how to pick a lock."

"Oooh, that's something!" Jess's eyes opened wide. "Probably a room full of drugs. Or piles of cash. Like *Breaking Bad.*" Jess pointed the hair straightener at her. "Liss, you're babysitting for Walter White."

Alyssa rolled onto her back, groaning. "You and the drugs." She peered up at the ceiling, a faded unicorn poster pinned to it. When had they put it there? When they were eight or nine? She remembered balancing on the step stool, thumbtacks raining down.

"Did you see any bumps? Bruises? Was the kid really okay?" Jess squinted into the mirror above her dresser, plucking her eyebrows.

Alyssa rested her head on the chemistry book, an uncomfortable pillow of the Periodic Table. "It was late, so it was hard to tell. He did seem out of it, but he'd just thrown up."

"If you text him—Charles?—too many questions, it'll look like you're trying to cover your ass." Jess studied her eyebrows, turning to Alyssa. "Are they even?"

Alyssa nodded.

"And what about the mom?" Jess tossed her tweezers into her camouflage-patterned make-up box and pulled out a circular palette of eyeshadow. "Could something have happened with her, like, before you got there?"

"I don't think—" Alyssa paused, remembering Sally's disheveled hair and red, splotchy cheeks. The way the house was eerily quiet when she'd arrived, as if it'd been shaken to stillness.

"Purple or silver?" Jess tilted the palette toward Alyssa.

"We're supposed to be *studying*."

"Silver it is then," Jess huffed, turning to the mirror.

"I guess things did seem a little off," Alyssa said, flipping through the pages of her book. "Sally, Morgan's mom, was a hot mess. Like maybe she'd had a fight with Charles? But she's really sweet. I can't imagine her ever doing anything to Morgan."

"I say ignore it and move on."

"But—"

"Let's take a break. My brain already hurts. Let's get some milkshakes. Might as well put my Burger King discount to use." She fluttered her silver-streaked eyelids, her lips pursed in a pout.

"Jess! We haven't studied at all. I need to pass this exam to maintain my GPA to impress Ms. Beastly so she'll write me a recommendation for that fancy conference next summer, which I *really really really* need to get accepted to a good college otherwise I won't ever become a doctor and I'll be left juggling a bazillion boring-ass temp jobs just like my mom." She released a dramatic sigh. "The exam's on Wednesday. Need I remind you, today's *Monday.*"

"Oh my God. Just chill." Jess rolled her eyes. "It's only September. Even if we fail this one, we've got all year to pull it together. I promise." She grabbed her purple velvet wallet. "C'mon, my treat."

✦

They slurped down milkshakes at Burger King, then Jess dropped Alyssa at home, smacking her moist, raspberry-scented lips against her cheek: *Don't worry. This'll all blow over.*

Alyssa dragged her feet up the stairs, staring at the closed blinds of the new guy's place. *Luke.* What was in his black duffel bag? Stinky gym clothes? Top secret CIA files? Those CIA agents, they had to live somewhere. It would be just her luck he picked right beneath their apartment.

She tiptoed to her room. Her mom was probably soaking in the tub with eucalyptus or tea tree oil or whatever, the typical ritual after another interview. Alyssa struggled to keep track of her mother's scattered career path, jumping from office to office: a call room, data entry, receptionist, *boring, boring, boring.*

They'd lived in this apartment for close to ten years now. Alyssa remembered their old duplex, over on Bridgewater Road, when her dad still lived with them. He'd walk her home from preschool while her mom worked at the Food Lion across town. There were brief snippets from that time, like a clipped trailer of a movie: Alyssa eating stale Cheetos from the bag, her hand covered in orange dust. Sipping her mom's diet sodas, the fizziness making her stomach gurgle and pop. Her dad's ear-splitting snores blending with the nonstop lineup of TV shows—yucky kissing, deafening gunshots, ads about foaming toilet bowl cleaners.

Then her dad would shake her awake from her boredom-induced slumber. She'd rub her eyes, the flickering TV casting a strange glow across his tightened face.

"We gotta go," he shouted. "Now!"

He carried her out to his pickup truck, not bothering with socks or shoes or the required potty break. There was often the promise of McDonald's—a hot Happy Meal, maybe a milkshake. She loved chocolate. But did he keep his word? She couldn't remember.

What she did remember was sitting in his pickup truck at some rundown shack, alone, searching for the promised golden arches in the distance. *Where's Daddy?* Shivering, she discovered a half-eaten box of raisins under a pair of his grease-slicked overalls. She scrunched up her nose. They were hard and shriveled, beyond acceptable raisin standards. But hunger won over and she sucked on them until they softened, her growling stomach grateful for anything.

Jess's response to these stories was always the same: "Drugs. Sorry, Liss, but your dad was a legit dealer."

"Maybe." Alyssa would never know for sure. Her mom went all feral at any mention of her father, quickly changing the subject. Once she broke a plate.

He might as well be dead, Alyssa thought. Maybe he was.

✦

Alyssa popped a Midol for her throbbing headache, then leaned against her pile of pillows, journal balanced on her lap. She couldn't stop thinking about Morgan. She loved the little guy, even though she'd only known him for about half a year. He'd changed so much in that time—learning to crawl, babbling a few words, and most recently, taking brave, unsteady steps.

She reached for her pen and wrote:

Monday, September 10:

Something's wrong with Morgan. I don't know what. But something was definitely off when I got there. Charles's texts are so vague. I want to ask what's going on, but Jess told me not to text them anything more. "It'll just make things worse," she said.

But what if she's wrong???

It gnawed at her. Any decent babysitter would say *something.*

She snatched her phone off the nightstand, thumbs quivering as she typed out the message: **Just checking in. How's Morgan doing?** She hesitated. It was 1:05 a.m. It'd be super weird to text Charles after all this time had passed, and at this hour. With a sigh, she quickly deleted the message.

The towering oaks scraped at her window as creepy shadows danced across her walls. The air conditioner hummed its gentle hum. She shivered. Maybe she should tell someone about what happened that night. About Sally—so strained, a bit unhinged. But who to tell? And gosh, she didn't even know what was wrong with poor Morgie. It could be nothing.

Leaning over, she delicately placed her journal, pen, and phone back on the nightstand, and then snuggled deep under her daisy-printed comforter, as if its warmth and heaviness would shut out the mystery of Charles's text: *Did he hit his head?*

As she slept, she zoomed ahead to Beastly's chemistry class—to exam day. She sat bathed in sweat as the exam's words and letters swirled in red before fading away completely. She lurched for the door, tripped, then was tumbling down the school's front steps with Morgan in her arms. Someone shouted, "Don't let him hit his head!" and she protectively cradled his head while her own went *thump thump thump* against the concrete steps. She collapsed on the pavement like a limp rag doll, Morgan's dull, glass-like eyes staring up at her.

Next, she crouched in a crammed, icy-cold cell, with only dry, moldy raisins to eat. *I made sure he didn't hit his head,* she whispered. But nobody listened.

Chapter 12

Sally

Day four

The monkeys swung freely, their sausage-like fingers wrapping around thin branches, bushy tails swishing, the trees creaking under their weight. They had always been Sally's favorite. She owned every Curious George book growing up. And the doll, too.

Sally's mother used to take her to this very zoo—the Asheboro Zoo—when they moved here from Charlotte. Such a promising time: her mom's cancer in remission, an exciting job at UNC-Greensboro, Sally starting fourth grade at a new school with new friends (she was thrilled to ditch the snooty ones back home). Her mom allowed Sally to tag along while she oversaw bustling conferences, glittery weddings, college orientations, a squawking walkie-talkie forever glued to her hand.

Sally never knew her dad. Her mother used a sperm donor with her then partner, Gwen. The dreaded cancer made its debut appearance shortly after Sally's seventh birthday. She sat by her mother's side, holding her hand, as the chemo machine tried to work its magic, one, two, then three times a week.

Her mother's hair fell off in thick clumps and Sally dutifully swept it away. Sally rushed in for the middle-of-the-night barf sessions and held a sick-smelling bowl to her mother's thin, gray lips. Gwen, who vowed to be the loving wife, who had even insisted Sally call her Maw-Maw, couldn't stomach it. *Through sickness and health.* What bullshit.

The heat seemed slightly more bearable today. Morgan sat in his umbrella stroller, the one they kept in the car for impromptu excursions like this. He hugged Elmo, gazing listlessly at the monkeys, who chattered back at them.

Sally hoisted herself onto a stone wall and sipped her iced latte as families strolled by. She imagined she looked like an ordinary mother, enjoying a lazy Monday afternoon in the sun with her sweet boy. Nobody knew her secret.

Morgan lifted a hand, one shaky finger pointed at the monkeys, and she jumped down from the ledge. Her baby was coming back to life, emerging from his hibernation. She desperately pawed through the diaper bag, she needed to snap this: *Morgan's okay!* Charles's face flashed silently across her phone's screen, a goofy picture of him hanging upside down from the monkey bars in their backyard.

She hesitated before answering. "Hello?"

He filled her in: the talk with the nurse, Morgan's iron deficiency. He didn't mention the referral for the abdominal scan. Apparently nobody informed him about it? She noticed a missed call from a local, unknown number.

Anemia? Could that really explain all of this? Perhaps she didn't do anything wrong after all. Morgan had just pointed—*pointed!* That had to be a definitive sign he was okay.

It only happened once, she told herself. It wasn't like she rattled his brain for days on end. *It was one little shake.* She wasn't a child abuser. Not like that psychopath who beat his toddler with a baseball bat or that deranged babysitter who flung a kid out the window. Those were the real whack jobs, the real dangers to society.

"Let's go see the lemurs," Sally announced after hanging up on Charles. Morgan looked up, his face once again slack, his eyes distant.

"It'll be fun." She rustled his blond hair, ignoring the wave of flutters in her gut.

After the lemurs, they headed to the popsicle stand next to an arched walkway. Lush green vines intertwined over it with towering sunflowers on each side. Kids reached into the oval fishpond, even though the sign said not to. Tall shrubs created a barrier between them and the busy street. A nearby cluster of moms hugged and chatted, pushing sleek strollers. She should've gone to that local mom's group, that playgroup. Bonded with other women, made some actual friends.

Sally lost most, no, *all* of her friends when she'd moved in with Charles. Oak Wood was a solid hour from her mom's apartment in Greensboro, where she'd stayed for almost a year after her death, walking past the lifeless dresses and stacks of untouched books, a pair of bifocals still perched on the coffee table as if her mother was simply out running errands. Charles had come to town for some work conference and gosh, if it hadn't been for her clumsiness with those ice cream pints, where would she be now?

Beth moved out, Sally moved in—her slim body still able to fit snug, skinny jeans since, according to the Bump app, Morgan was merely the size of a plum. And then poof: Her friends vanished. They were engulfed in their sophomore year of college, living it up with keg parties and reckless sex. Why would they come to see her? They couldn't Uber or taxi or bus their drunk asses back to Greensboro or Raleigh, not that far. And, sadly, none of her friends took their higher education to Oak Wood, even though it had one of the best liberal arts colleges in the country.

Plus, now she had a baby. It might as well have been the plague from the way her friends avoided her. And, of course, she couldn't make the trek to see them, not with Morgan's restrictive nap schedule and apocalyptic meltdowns. She spied on their lives from afar: Spring Break pics in revealing bikinis with bronze tans and toned bellies, one steamy boyfriend after another, winning local sporting events—the shiny medals and trophies flooding her Instagram feed.

Sally remembered those early days, rubbing pasty cream over her cracked nipples, steadily rocking Morgan in his bassinet as she clicked from one enthralling post to the next, before deleting all her social media profiles and creating a new one: *Sally Haywood.* It wasn't her legal name, she didn't have a marriage certificate (yet), but it felt reassuring to see her new role—pretend wife, devoted mother—become Facebook official. Her only friends now were people from her recreated life: her job at Denny's, Charles's family, plus a few aunts and uncles, nobody she could really trust or confide in. Just people, strangers really, who sent sparkly Christmas cards with pictures of awkward cousins in braces and dogs in matching plaid outfits, with phony phrases like *Family is LOVE* or *We Wish You the Best.*

The best? Really?

Morgan tentatively held the melting strawberry-lime popsicle, staring at a squirrel bounding across the pavement. "Come on, pumpkin. Just try it," Sally encouraged, gently pushing the popsicle toward him. She didn't usually give him sweets, she tried to reserve them for special occasions, but she'd do anything to see him smile again, to hear the magical cadence of his laugh.

"Ma-ma," he said, quietly.

Dropping down, she peered into his blue eyes. "What? What do you want?" Had he said anything this whole time?

"Ma-ma," he repeated, reaching out.

Quickly, she unbuckled him and pulled him into her arms as the popsicle fell to the ground. He cried out in pain. "Shhh, it's okay," she whispered, carrying him to a nearby bench.

He pawed at her chest, tugging at her shirt. "Ma-ma."

He wanted to nurse; that was his sign. She'd weaned him over a month ago, right before he turned one. He'd lost interest, she'd had another bout of angry mastitis, so she tossed in the towel, switching to toddler formula.

But now, he wanted the comfort.

Without pause, Sally lifted her shirt, yanked down her snug bra, and let him latch on. He nestled right in, his warm breath moist against her bare chest, his satisfied gurgling sounds. He suckled as if his life depended on it—for reassurance that everything was okay in the world. She doubted there was any substantial milk left.

Her phone vibrated in her pocket. She pulled it out. It was the same unknown number.

"Hello?"

A curt woman from the hospital needing to schedule the scan.

"Yes, yes," Sally said. "We'll be there."

"Please arrive fifteen minutes early to fill out paperwork."

"Yes, yes, we'll be there." She clicked off, not even remembering what time or place she'd just agreed to.

A flock of pigeons landed nearby, heads tilted inquisitively toward Morgan's abandoned popsicle, which had become a little puddle of pink goo by now. Morgan's face rested between Sally's breasts, eyes closed, his breathing soft and steady. She didn't move in fear of waking him. Around her the crowds packed up, everyone heading home to happy, wholesome households, to hearty dinners, to peaceful, guilt-free nights.

She watched them leave, asking herself: *What happens next?*

Chapter 13

Charles

Day five

Charles's eyes wandered across the backyard as he held the sprinkling garden hose. The shrubs needed trimming, the roses had lost their vibrant color, the gardenia had seen better days. This had once been Beth's domain, kneeling in the dirt with her worn leather gloves, a floppy straw hat protecting her face against the sun's UV rays.

He bent down and examined the bell pepper plants. Morgan liked to tug on them, vigorously, and now they drooped, with only a few sad peppers thriving to fruition.

Imagine if Beth could see him now—gardening! She wouldn't believe it. And a baby. She'd wanted—they'd both wanted—children so desperately. The doctors blamed Charles's sperm, so defective they couldn't figure it out with the egg *right there*, ripe and ready in the petri dish. How embarrassing, and yet, somehow, with Sally it worked out. It did cross his mind, briefly, that she could've slept with someone else. He was still with Beth at the time, and Sally was living in her mom's apartment in Greensboro, doing God knows what. So many unknowns. But he trusted Sally; she'd been nothing but an open book since he'd met her.

And then, of course, came the wrath of Beth after she discovered the affair. He turned to the cops: *She stole my money!* But, as the police explained, they were still married so her withdrawal of cash from their joint account was no more of a crime than Charles's adultery.

"What about filing for divorce?" Charles asked.

The cop's response: "That's between you and her."

"But I can't find her!"

"Well, in North Carolina you can get what's called a simple absolute divorce," the cop explained. "It's all legal, even if the spouse can't be located."

Well, damn. Filing a divorce without Beth even knowing? That felt beyond shitty.

Then the nosy Joyce at work caught a whiff of his sticky situation and gave him a card—a friend of her uncle's, a private investigator. "He's the best," she said. *Everyone always thinks their guy is the best.* But he took the card and kept it tucked in his desk drawer in their third bedroom, which used to be his home office, now overtaken by Sally's exercise balls, untouched yoga mats, and boxes of pastel-colored swatches from her failed baby bootie business on Etsy. He pulled the card out periodically, tracing its edges, working up the courage to track Beth down. Get a proper divorce. Or ask if she still loved him. Of course she didn't—she loathed him. Did he miss her? It was complicated.

But truth be told, the thought of confronting her terrified him. She blocked him on social media, her family refusing to answer his calls. He feared what would happen if he tried to find closure.

✦

Charles carefully plucked a ripe pepper from its vine, adding it to the bowl with the puny others, along with a few plump tomatoes. The sun peeked over the neighboring houses, already direct and sweltering at this early hour. The houses on either side were somber, neighbors he once grilled burgers and clinked Bud Lites with before they retreated to their private lives after Beth left. Now they shook their heads disapprovingly behind tightly shut windows.

Back inside, he set the bowl of veggies on the kitchen counter and wiped his soiled hands on his jeans. "I'm not going to work today," he announced.

Sally stirred oatmeal on the stove, the vent on full blast. Morgan watched a *Wheels on the Bus* compilation in the living room, rhythmically sucking his thumb, an untouched bottle balanced in his lap.

"Okay," Sally said, not looking up.

Charles poured a mug of coffee. He pushed aside a stack of bills and catalogs on the table, settling into the chair. "What do you know about Alyssa?" he began. "What's her full name?"

"Um ... Alyssa Hoyt." Sally opened the fridge, disappearing behind the door. "She's going to be in, uh, *The Wizard of Oz*? We should totally buy tickets."

"Did you call her references? Y'know, when you hired her."

"Yes, of course," she said. "She'd completed a babysitting course through the Y. CPR, First Aid, all that stuff."

"Who are her parents?"

"Her parents?" Sally slammed the fridge door shut and heaved a gallon of milk on the counter. "Miranda, I think? Her dad's not in the picture. I don't really talk to babysitters' parents."

"Sorry." He sipped his coffee. "I wasn't sure how it worked."

She took a tentative nibble of oatmeal and scrunched up her nose.

"I'm just worried that—" He stopped, glancing over at Morgan. He never used to have the attention span for TV, not this much. "This just seems like way more than anemia. Don't you think?"

Sally turned off the stove. "Why don't you feed him breakfast? I'm gonna take a shower."

"What? Did I say something wrong?" Charles pushed back his chair and stood.

"I'm just tired. And I'm way behind in my homework for that chemistry class I'm taking."

He wrapped his arms around her for a hug, but she stiffened. "Okay, go take your shower. Study. I can handle breakfast."

She nodded. He heard her sniffing as she shuffled down the hall.

Sighing, he walked over to the pot of oatmeal, a burnt smell wafting up. He opened the cupboard and found a packet of instant oatmeal. Oats were top of the list of the iron-rich foods nurse Sarah had sent over.

Once the microwave dinged, he walked into the living room. "C'mon Morgie, it's time to eat." He lifted his boy off the couch. His body felt light, and yet heavy at the same time, as if he lacked the basic energy to engage his muscles. Charles pushed his hair back, looking into his eyes: tired, distant, droopy.

Perhaps they needed a second opinion. Or to be direct and call Alyssa. She'd responded to his text with a brief message, a reiteration that nothing else happened besides Morgan throwing up. If that *really* was the truth, she should've written more, asked questions, showed some concern. But perhaps she was shocked, as if he was accusing her of something. Well, he kind of was. Then again, she could be busy. Their babysitters often fell off the radar, later rambling excuses about cramming for exams or attending soccer games out of town. Such lame excuses since teens these days were glued to their phones 24/7.

And what about Sally? He couldn't figure out what was going on. She seemed ready to crack, to burst open like an egg on concrete, her emotions oozing and sizzling under the merciless sun. It seemed best to simply tiptoe around it all.

Morgan took a few bites of oatmeal, his head nodding forward then jerking back as sleep tried to take over.

"How about some juice?" Charles offered.

He'd call the doctor that afternoon. All the results should be in by then. If he didn't get any concrete answers, he'd take Morgan somewhere else. Even if it meant waiting for hours at Urgent Care.

✦

Charles sprawled across the couch, laptop balanced on his lap. A Rolling Stones documentary played on TV while Morgan napped, his steady breathing crackling over the monitor. Sally had run off shortly after breakfast, rambling about needing tampons and new jeans. *Jeans?* She hadn't worn jeans since halfway through her pregnancy with Morgan. And who'd want to wear jeans in this heat? Clearly she needed a break.

He plowed through his backlog of work emails. There was one from his boss deeming Friday's spreadsheet "well done." She never doled out praise, so that meant something. He started typing his response: **Actually, the temp took charge with that one ...**

His phone rang. A local, unknown number, which he'd normally ignore, but perhaps it was Morgan's doctor with the final results. He kept postponing calling the clinic himself because Morgan seemed in better spirits, even laughing at lunch time, a sweet high-pitched giggle that caused Charles to sigh with relief. Perhaps Morgan's strange behavior was simply a result of iron deficiency after all.

"Hello?"

"Good afternoon. May I speak to Mr. Haywood?"

"This is he."

A clearing of the throat. "I'm calling from Oak Wood Hospital. We haven't been able to reach Morgan's mother. We've tried several times. You're Morgan Haywood's father, correct?"

"Yes." He was confused. *The hospital?*

"We received a referral yesterday from Dr. Reynolds at Oak Wood Children's Clinic, for Morgan. Some ... er ..." He heard the sharp clicks of typing. "Abdominal pain, possible liver or gallbladder issues. Morgan had an ultrasound appointment this morning but didn't show up. I assume you want to reschedule?"

Charles bolted up, setting his laptop on the coffee table. He strode to the window in two great bounds. Their driveway was empty. Sally had been gone for hours now.

"Um, she ... Sally ... she hasn't been feeling well." Why was he lying for her? More importantly, why had she lied to him?

"Dr. Reynolds's notes recommended doing it within a day or two," the voice continued. A gentle tone, caring and professional. "We've just had a cancellation so we can squeeze Morgan in first thing tomorrow morning, at eight. Will that work?"

Charles paced. What day was it? *Tuesday*. What about work? Could he miss another day? He had to.

"Yes, yes," he said. "Eight o'clock. We can do that."

"Check in at the front desk, they'll instruct you where to go. And please arrive fifteen minutes early to fill out paperwork."

"Okay." Charles looked for a pen to jot down the details.

"And if his symptoms get worse, bring him into the ER," she said, then hung up.

He stood there, grasping a pen. Dr. Reynolds wanted Morgan to get a scan at the hospital. And the nurse, when he'd called yesterday, didn't think to mention it? And Sally—what the hell was wrong with Sally?

He stared at his phone, his stomach twisting. Who to call? Sally? Dr. Reynolds?

Sally. He had to know why she'd kept this from him before calling the pediatrician and sounding like an idiot—the clueless dad left in the dark.

"Hey," Sally answered.

"Sally." He stepped outside into their backyard. "I just got a call from the hospital."

Silence.

"They said you missed an appointment this morning. For Morgan."

More silence.

"Is this true?" he asked.

Finally: "Yes."

"What the hell? Why didn't you tell me? He's my kid, too. You can't make all the decisions here." His voice crept higher, anger starting to boil. He needed to stay calm, he didn't want things to escalate. "I asked you for all the details, for everything that happened at the doctor's visit. You didn't think to tell me about this?"

He heard nothing but her breathing.

"Did you just *forget*? Did you think it wasn't important?" He kicked a swing, watching it wobble and twist, the chains creaking. "Morgan's doctor—his goddamned pediatrician—said to take him to the hospital, something about possible liver or gallbladder issues? Jesus. And what do you do instead? You take him to the zoo, you go off shopping, you ignore everything." He shook his head. "What's going on?"

"I did tell you they wanted to check those things—liver and gall-bladder. Yesterday, when you called me at the zoo."

"Yeah, but you didn't tell me they'd scheduled an actual hospital appointment. Why didn't you take him this morning?"

"I was afraid," she whispered.

"Afraid? Of what?"

"It's just that ..." She paused, blowing her nose. "They kept poking and prodding him. They were hurting him. I didn't want to drag him from place to place, putting him in machines, having him examined to no end."

Charles lowered himself onto the swing, grabbing the slick chain with one hand. "But why not talk to me? Tell me your concerns? Why *lie?*"

"I didn't lie."

"But you didn't tell me everything."

More silence, her jagged breathing rising a decibel higher.

"I feel like something's going on. You don't seem ..." Charles took a deep breath. "You don't seem like yourself."

"I'm trying," she said, even quieter.

"Really? Not taking our son to the hospital is trying? What? Trying to be a bad mother?"

"You don't mean that." She was sobbing now. "I can explain. Let me explain!"

"Okay, okay," he said, inhaling deeply. The sun pierced his eyes. His throat clenched. "Just come home. We'll talk it through." He wanted it to make sense, to believe in her, to trust she was doing the right thing.

She went silent again.

"Sally? Are you there? Can you hear me?"

"I'm here."

"Can you drop whatever you're doing and come home right now?"

"Why are you screaming at me?"

"I'm not screaming." He exhaled loudly. "Please. I—I just ... We need to be on the same page. Something's wrong with Morgan. He's not okay." He stood and started pacing. "Just come home so we can figure this out, okay? Together."

"I ... I need some time ..." she stammered.

"Time?" he asked. "Time for what?"

"Please, just stop yell—"

"What could possibly be more important right now? You've been gone all day! Morgan's sick, for Christ's sake!" He could feel the tension pounding in his head, like a blood vessel ready to pop. "You need to come home. Now."

"I can't—"

"Fine," he snapped. "Don't come home then."

He ended the call before she had a chance to respond. With shaking hands, he slid open the back door. The house was silent. Morgan slumbered on.

After setting his phone on the counter, he leaned forward and rested his forehead in his palms. His breath wheezed out in spurts. Had Sally simply plummeted into a crazed state of denial? What else could explain her bizarre behavior? Although, he should've seen it coming after the way she'd dealt with her mom's death. "She'll just love this," Sally had said when he bought her a new woven rug, after spilling wine on her old one. He was confused at first—*Who? Your mother? But she's ...?* He eventually chalked it up as a coping method. Sally, he now realized, didn't know what to do when faced with a crisis.

And here they were, dealing with something serious. Their sweet boy needed a scan. Abdominal pain. That explained the random crying out. Liver or gallbladder? Neither sounded good. Did he actually accuse Alyssa of this? He shuddered. No way was this her fault. Yet still, he couldn't shake the inexplicable feeling that *something* bad happened last Friday.

The doctor. He needed more information. He grabbed his phone, searched the call history, and pushed the button. The receptionist answered and told him Dr. Reynolds was currently with another patient.

"Please have her call me back," he said. He didn't want to talk to a nurse or another doctor, he needed to hear the facts directly from Morgan's pediatrician.

He then called Sally five times in a row. He didn't mean for things to get so out of control. He texted her: **They rescheduled Morgan's appointment for 8am tomorrow. Please come home. We really need to talk in person.**

"Shit!" He slammed his hand on the counter. What if she took him seriously and didn't come home at all? How was he going to get Morgan to the hospital without their car?

He sighed, then added: **I'm sorry.**

This wasn't Sally's fault.

He didn't know whose fault it was.

✦

Throughout the night, Charles constantly reached over, instinctively, to Sally's empty side of the bed. He checked his phone. The doctor never did call back. And Sally had sent one lone text before midnight: **Got called into work. I'll be home in the morning.** Christ, he hoped she meant it.

He knew Sally was trying her best. She didn't expect any of this—this new life that was hurled at her so quickly, so unexpectedly. But, then again, he didn't either.

He had loved Beth. Truly. But Sally possessed this magical force, pulling him in so immediately, without warning. And like a starved, desperate man, he'd grabbed onto her as she soothed, satisfied, and placated.

Sex with Beth had become a prescribed, lackluster event: *I'm ovulating. Today.* They were quick and efficient, with no foreplay, no silky lingerie, no scented candles, no hot whisperings in the ear. Just pull down your pants, get to business, NOW.

"But wait!" Beth would shout. "It's better if I orgasm." She meant the chances were better. For conception. Make a baby—that was their only goal.

Eventually the sex got phased out. He remembered standing in that sterile room at the fertility clinic, with a small screen TV, a stack of porn magazines, an empty cup on the counter, his boxers and jeans bunched around his ankles as he awkwardly aimed for the little plastic cup, praying his product was potent enough to make a new life, to save his marriage.

But sadly, it wasn't.

Back at home, Beth glued herself to the couch, surrounded by mounds of crumpled tissues, listlessly stroking her cat, Mr. Moops, who seemed equally devastated by the unfortunate turn of events.

He tried to entice her out of the darkness. "Want to go see a movie?"

"No."

"Bowling?"

"No."

"Should I order takeout? Chinese?"

"Just stop."

Meanwhile, their coffee table piled up with brochures about egg donors, sperm donors, adoption—local or international?

Charles crawled to Sally, falling into her flesh, into the satisfaction of real sex—their steady rhythm, deep sighs, fingernails clawing up his back. He'd forgotten what it could feel like. It was always good, even now. Even with Morgan in the next room, with both of them drained and exhausted and overtaxed.

He knew the whole situation seemed like a cliché—a middle-aged man letting his desire get the better of him, chasing after a woman half his age. But he cared about Sally. Really. And without Sally, he wouldn't have Morgan.

He blinked at the clock on his nightstand. It radiated 2:57. They'd never had a big fight before. He hoped she'd found somewhere to sleep, somewhere safe. Maybe with one of her co-workers? If it wasn't for Morgan and not having a car, he'd be out there searching for her.

But maybe having space would do them good. Maybe she just needed some alone time to come to terms with their boy being sick.

I miss you, he texted.

And then: **I'm so sorry.**

And after half an hour: **I love you.**

Nothing. He got nothing back.

He dreaded what tomorrow would bring.

Chapter 14

Sally

Day five

"Fine. Don't come home then."

Charles spewed those words, like hurling a glass of ice water in Sally's face. She stared at her phone, still warm in her hand. Her heart clenched into a tight fist.

She'd fled the house about six hours ago, distracting herself with stress shopping—stretchy jeggings, a pleather purse from Forever 21, a forest-green corduroy jacket for when the weather turned cold. She stopped to refuel at Starbucks and that's when her phone rang. The time had come: Charles suspected her. But to what extent? Did he simply think she was an irrational, neglectful mother *or* did he know the brutal truth?

She took a sip of her iced latte, her lips thick with froth. What did she expect? For Morgan to suddenly wake up—healthy, unscathed, full of giggles? And then what? Return to his vigorous screaming fits—hours. How did he have energy to wail like that for hours on end?

Charles called and called. He texted about the hospital appointment being rescheduled for tomorrow morning, and then begged for her to come home so they could *talk*.

She gripped the table, as if the floor was dissolving beneath her, as if she was about to tumble into a dark abyss. Like that night her mother slipped away, the last beeps lulling Sally to sleep. She allowed her heavy, exhausted eyelids to flutter shut, just for a minute, and then without warning or a final goodbye, her mother's soul was wrenched away.

Her phone gave a double beep: Charles's apology. But could she really believe it? Nothing good would come from heading home. He would grill her about the missed hospital appointment and why she didn't tell him. Lying took everything out of her. It wouldn't take long for him to uncover the truth, shove her out the door, and demand full custody of Morgan. It'd be easy, right? She was a damaged, unfit mother, a simple case for the courts.

Should she just run away right now? Her breathing escalated. But her stash of cash was back at home—now $661 after her Friday and Sunday night tips, minus the Girl Scout cookies. She usually deposited most of her tips into their joint account to help with bills, but this time she hid it all.

She could leave the cash behind, rack up their credit cards instead, let Charles deal with the bill. No, that's what Beth did. Charles was a good man; he didn't deserve that. And besides, she couldn't leave without Morgan. But how could she sneak away with him if he needed medical attention? *Liver or gallbladder.* She should've taken him this morning, when he had his original appointment, if she had only written down the details.

She had no valid excuse, nothing to offer Charles.

She shook her head, hair falling into her face. She needed a motel. Sleep it off. Set her alarm and figure out what to do in the morning. "Everything'll look better tomorrow," her mother used to say.

Maybe Morgan would wake up and be fine. Like yesterday, when he pointed at the monkeys. That seemed like a good sign, right? She warmed at the memory of him saying *Mama* and nursing again.

Nobody had declared this an emergency. Even Dr. Reynolds had said the scan was checking the boxes, just being safe. But still, she needed to take him in. Then, once Morgan received proper care, life could go back to normal. Unless they found evidence that she did this. They'd shake their heads: *Sally? But she was so sweet.*

Then she'd lose Morgan.

Her heart ached, a sharp, throbbing pain. Thick tears dripped down her cheeks. A stranger touched her shoulder. A Starbucks employee in a green apron approached her, rambling off a series of questions, their eyebrows knitted in concern. Sally didn't respond. Her phone rang and rang, sounding far away, like it was locked in a box buried underground. Somehow she ended up in the car, abruptly turning right and left at random, squinting into the afternoon sun.

Her phone rang again. Work.

"Another emergency shift?" she asked, balancing her phone on the steering wheel and switching it to speaker. A car blared its horn.

"Hey Sal! Any chance you could come in tonight?" Her boss, Krista, paused. "I know it's probably a stretch, unless Charles is home?"

Why not? It'd give her some normalcy, a break from whatever this was. And she'd get a hot dinner—one of those sizzling egg and veggie skillet dishes, maybe a buttered English muffin. Bacon. Her mouth watered. Had she eaten all day? As if on cue, her stomach growled.

She could ask one of her co-workers if she could crash at their place. "Charles and I got into a horrific fight," she'd say. Except, well, they never fought. Not like this.

"You won the husband lottery," the girls liked to coo when Sally showed off her latest gift or raved about Charles's delicious pasta alfredo recipe, passed down from his grandmother (although he rarely had time to cook these days).

Robin had recently left a violent relationship and now slept with a butcher knife under her pillow (protected by a leather sheath, of course). Diana lived with her parents, along with her three-year-old son. Neither seemed like an ideal host for an emergency sleepover.

"I can be there by five," Sally told her boss, pulling over in front of a gated subdivision. A purring SUV sped past her. After hanging up, she realized she'd left her shopping bags, abandoned on the floor of Starbucks. She couldn't muster the energy to go back.

Sally powered through her shift with renewed gusto, pouring steaming coffee, clearing plates with chunks of soggy waffles floating in lakes of syrup, making tedious small talk—*Yes, it's like a second summer out there, isn't it?* She'd haphazardly applied makeup in the bathroom, stuff she'd dug up from the dredges of her purse.

"You okay?" Diana asked.

"Yeah, just tired," Sally said. "Morgan's still sick."

"Oh, poor little nugget."

She rehearsed the words: *Do you have room for me to crash tonight? A couch, the floor, whatever. I don't want to be an inconvenience.*

Would it be too much to ask? They never hung out, besides at work. But still, they were Facebook friends, that had to count for something. Tearing at her nails, she imagined their questions: *What happened? What'd he say? What'd you say next?* Women wanted to dig deep, paint the scene, figure out how to help.

What about calling one of her old friends, like Jenny over at NC State? She could drive an hour to spend the night on her couch, if her roommates agreed to letting her stay. But Jenny would also press for details. Every lie took more and more mental power. Eventually she would slip up.

And the truth? Diana or Robin or Jenny—could any of them handle it? *I shook my baby so hard he passed out.* Nobody wanted to hear such a revolting confession. Nobody wanted a criminal sleeping under their roof.

A motel looked like her best option. Or sleeping in the car. But she needed to be alert and functioning tomorrow; she needed to get Morgan to the hospital.

"Have a good night," Robin said, slinging her leopard-print purse over her shoulder.

"You too." Sally focused on wiping down a grease-splattered table.

"I'm staying on. Doing the full night's shift," Diana said. "Mom's watching Nick."

"God, you're so lucky," Sally said, "having parents around to help out."

Diana shrugged. "Eh. She's always telling me what I'm doing wrong."

"Nobody's perfect," Sally said. Certainly Diana was a better mother than herself. Everyone was. Except that dad who beat up his kid. Or that babysitter who threw that innocent kid out the window. That girl was worse than Sally, hands down.

Although, according to an online interview, the babysitter claimed she didn't do it. The kid had behavioral issues and was pushing back against the bedtime routine. He screamed bloody murder, hurling objects at the young babysitter. She cornered him, speaking in gentle tones, when the kid opened the window and threatened to jump. She desperately clung to his pants before he slapped away her hands and fell in front of a swarm of gaping neighbors.

Well, dang. If that's really what happened, Sally thought, that girl was definitely *not* a criminal. And that made Sally a—

"A bad mother," Diana said, twirling one of her ringlet curls around her finger. "That's what she calls me. A bad mother."

"What?" Sally said. "Your mother actually said that?"

"Yup. Right to my face."

"You're a great mom," Sally said.

But really, what did she know? She'd never hung out with her; she'd never even met the boy. Diana could be berating him every night, banishing him to his room over the silliest reasons: "You put your shoes on the wrong feet. Shame on you!" It didn't take much to push an exhausted, overworked, single mother over the edge. Sally wasn't single, but at times it felt like she was—balancing on the brink of disaster every day.

✦

Sally fumbled with the plastic card, jamming it repeatedly into the slot over the doorknob. The light kept flashing red.

"Damn it," she hissed.

"Insert it slowly." A stranger passing by.

The door opened. "Thanks," she mumbled.

Motel 6. She surveyed the room. A jail cell would be smaller, she told herself. But would they arrest her? Or just take away her rights as a mother, limiting her to supervised visits with a rigid social worker perched on the couch, making sure she didn't lose it again: *We know the type. Once an abuser, always an abuser.*

Sally flung the Food Lion bag of snacks onto the flowery bedspread, then set the cheap box of wine on the nightstand. A dull ache spread across her lower abdomen. Her period was definitely on its way, her first period since having Morgan. Her OB had said it might not return while being on the mini pill—the progesterone-only birth control, supposedly safer for breastfeeding—but now, maybe, the random nursing session from yesterday had messed up her hormones. Or, more likely, all the stress.

She texted Charles that she'd be home in the morning, then silenced her phone, shoving it into the nightstand drawer. She struggled with the wine box's spigot and eventually ripped it off, tilting the box to her lips, guzzling and gulping. She tossed the almost-drained box to the floor and moved on to devour two Little Debbie chocolate cupcakes and a bag of Fritos before flinging herself face down on the bed.

Oh, if her mother were to see her now. She tried so hard to push Sally, staying up late drilling tricky SAT questions, marking up her essays with a thick red marker, shaking her head when Sally's grades dipped below the B level. *You gotta dream big, sweetheart. Don't settle for less.* It worked: Sally graduated near the top of her class, won countless medals for track and field, snagged the crown at a local beauty pageant, and even received a full scholarship to UNC-Greensboro. She couldn't help but wonder how many of her accomplishments came from her own abilities versus her mom's devoted, relentless guidance. Because once her mom disappeared from the equation, Sally failed at everything.

Literally everything.

"I'm sorry."

After the sobs ran dry, she shed her clothes and stepped into the shower, furiously unwrapping the white bar of soap—a bland, sterile smell. Hot water burned her skin as she scrubbed and scrubbed, as if trying to wash away her actions, eradicate the memory of grabbing Morgan. The words came in a hush: *You don't deserve to live.* She dropped the soap, the urgency racing through her. She didn't have a razor, and the image of all that blood made her head spin. Pills? What did people use? She had Tylenol in her purse. How many would do the job?

No, no, stop! It was one thing to run away, but to throw a suicide at Charles, on top of abandoning him with a sick, possibly brain-damaged toddler? *Unthinkable.* She turned off the shower and quickly dried off, then headed back into the main room.

She paced, damp hair clinging to her face, her naked body shivering. She felt like a caged animal, like that majestic tiger they saw at the zoo, strutting in his enclosure with such intense, fierce eyes. A danger to the world. He had to be locked away, to keep everyone safe.

Just yesterday they leisurely meandered through the zoo, the sun shining bright and vibrant, a comforting warmth. Her breasts ached at the memory of Morgan suckling. She craved his weight curled in her lap, his hands pawing at her. Would he miss her if she ended up in prison? He was young, way too young. In a matter of months—*or even weeks?*—she would be wiped clean from his memory, a faded past that no longer mattered.

✦

Sleep didn't come. She missed Charles's gentle snores and steady warmth beside her, the reassuring sound of Morgan's breath crackling over the monitor. The motel room started spinning, like an amusement ride revving up, one she didn't want to be on. Why did she drink so much?

Standing, she flung open the curtains, peering into the desolate parking lot. The moon shone between branches, a foreboding shimmer, as if it, too, knew of her horrific secret. If there was a heaven, her mom floated up there, staring down. Judging her? Feeling sorry for her? Probably both.

"I really messed up," Sally said, expecting some reassurance, a whimsical spirit or a protective angel to whisper back. To tell her what to do next. But all she saw was her own reflection: splotchy cheeks, gnarly hair, sunken eyes.

Her stomach churned, hot liquid burned her throat. She raced to the bathroom, coughing, and leaned over the toilet just in time. With long, wrenching spasms, her stomach emptied, a foul stench. She tugged at the toilet paper, swiping at her mouth with shredded pieces. And then her body quaked again, more gagging; the remainder of her Denny's dinner, Fritos, and chocolate cupcakes floating in the toilet bowl.

She sank to the cold floor, clutching the edge of the toilet, waiting to see if her stomach settled. She blinked in and out of consciousness. Did she catch that bug? Shit, there was no bug. This was her own doing.

She pulled down a stack of fluffy white towels, crisp and citrus-scented, and wrapped them around her trembling body. Pull it together, she told herself. She tried to hum, a nameless tune her mother used to sing to calm her, but it didn't help. The memory of her own screams grew louder and louder.

Stop. Stop! STOP!

She tried to get Morgan to stop. Her hands. His closed eyes. The silence that followed.

She did that.

Chapter 15

Charles

Day six

Morgan sat in his baby swing, legs kicking as delightful squeals rolled across the wind. But then he flew up, up, up, like a bird. Defying all sense of logic. Charles watched him falling, fast. *Hold on!* Where'd he go? Charles ran in circles, breathless, looking up, looking down. He was standing in a field, spiky bushes scratching his bare legs. He bellowed Morgan's name, then paused, listening for his tell-tale scream. A vibrating sound rumbled and spurted. A lawn mower? Who mowed their lawn in the pitch-black of night? They were going to run over Morgan!

Charles's face was wet. Cold, sticky, gross wet. *Where am I?* In the pond adjacent to their subdivision's playground? What idiot decided to put a pond there? A deep fear gripped him, the endless worry that Morgan would chase after a waddling goose, and accidentally tumble into the deep, murky water. It only took a second for something catastrophic to happen.

You had to be vigilant with children, *always always always.*

"Morgan!" he shouted again, but the sound came out muffled, as if a scarf was suffocating him. A warm, fuzzy, slightly itchy scarf. Like something Sally had lovingly tried to knit.

Now he couldn't breathe. *Am I drowning?* He clawed at the space around him but felt nothing. No water. Just an open void.

His eyes fluttered open and he struggled to inhale. Mr. Moops lay sprawled across his face, licking his cheeks, mewling for his breakfast.

"Get off," Charles muttered, shaking his head. The cat let loose a fierce meow before springing to the floor and hobbling to take cover in a nearby slipper. Charles scraped the fur out of his eyes, blinking. Why was the cat limping? He reached for his phone. Nothing from Sally. It was almost six o'clock. He tried calling—no answer.

What if she didn't show up in time? He needed a backup plan. The neighbors had young grandchildren. He often saw them on the trampoline, their gleeful faces and wild limbs springing up and down beyond the fence. They were bound to have an extra car seat. But how to phrase the question? "Sally took off. We need a ride to the hospital." It sounded so extreme, so dire.

But why she'd leave? they would ask with judging tones, remembering how Beth had left first.

Because I'm a jerk, he thought. Sally's young, she's doing the best she can. We all make mistakes.

But why'd she lie about the hospital appointment? That one had him stumped.

He could call Jack. He also worked for Uber.

Coffee first. No, he thought. Morgan. Go check on Morgan.

✦

Morgan was sleeping curled in a ball, his chest steadily rising and falling. So serene. Charles stroked his soft blond hair. He thought of his own faded baby pictures, the ones his mother kept framed on the walls in their Victorian-style home in Connecticut: little Charles with cherub cheeks, a dimpled chin, an inquisitive expression.

"He has your eyes," his mom liked to say. But that was it—*he didn't.* Morgan's eyes glistened like a vivid, crystal-blue lake; Charles's were a dull, muted brown.

He let Morgan sleep and slipped out to call Jack.

"Hey, sorry to bother you so early," Charles said, clearing his throat. "I need some help."

"What's up?" Jack said, his voice laced with sleep.

"Don't panic. We're okay. But Morgan has an appointment at Oak Wood Hospital. Sally … uh, had to go out of town, unexpectedly, and took the car. It's not an emergency, not really. We just need a way to get there." He swallowed. "By eight."

"Eight a.m.?" Jack asked.

"Yes." He paused. "This morning."

A deep inhale. "Yeah, sure. I can come get you."

"You have a car seat?"

"Yeah, I've got a toddler seat. He'll fit."

"Oh man, thanks so much," Charles said. "I owe you one."

"I'll be there by 7:30, 'k?"

"We'll be ready." Charles exhaled. He hung up and immediately texted Sally that he'd found a ride. **Unless you can be here before 7:30?** he added.

He tapped his screen, waiting to see if the little dots appeared, proof that she was typing back. Zilch. A mix of panic, worry, and anger fused in his stomach. Where the hell was she?

✦

Charles steered Morgan's stroller through the hospital's automatic doors. The main foyer was bustling, brightly awake at such an early hour. He dodged wheelchairs, clusters of medical staff in scrubs, women waddling with swollen bellies, carefree children darting in and out while dragging worn teddy bears and tattered blankies. Morgan yawned. Elmo rode on his lap, facing outward as if to take in all the sights.

A short, frumpish nurse with pink polka-dotted scrubs led them to a bare, windowless room, similar to the stark examination rooms he'd taken Sally to when she was pregnant. He remembered how the technician slid a wand over her lubed-up belly, and the shock and anticipation he felt as a blurry blurb danced on the screen—their little bean.

The nurse took Morgan's vitals and chit-chatted about the weather. "When's fall going to come?"

Charles stared at her, trying to find the right word for *My son might be dying and you want to talk about the weather?* Instead, he mumbled, "Yeah, this heat is ridiculous."

Then she left.

Morgan didn't seem to mind the waiting. He stared at Elmo, glanced up at Charles, and then studied the clock. Charles checked his phone. Should he call Sally again? He'd never yelled at her before. This was uncharted territory.

He texted her: **We're at the hospital now. Room #38. Waiting for ultrasound.**

She probably stayed up late, bitching her heart out to one of her co-workers. "What an asshole," her friend would say, generously pouring more wine. He imagined her knocked out on their couch, struggling with a wicked hangover.

A firm knock rattled the door. A lanky man entered with spiked brown hair and a tattoo wrapped around his wrist—a green lizard, the same shade as his eyes. He looked like a teenager, a hint of peach fuzz sprinkled across his upper lip. No way was he the actual doctor.

"Morgan Haywood?" the man asked.

"Yes, that's us," Charles answered.

"I'm Dr. Frederick."

Charles stifled a groan.

The doctor stared down at a clipboard. "Looks like we're doing an abdominal scan. Reported pain in the upper right quadrant."

"Sounds about right." Charles bent over to lift Morgan out of the stroller. "Apparently he's anemic too. And, well, he hasn't been himself. It's like something happened ... last Friday." Morgan rested his heavy head on Charles's shoulder.

Frederick pointed to the examination table with his pen. "Let's take a look."

The door swung open and a smiling woman entered, toting a wicker basket piled high with colorful toys, dolls, and books. "Hey, I'm Lucy, with Child Life," she announced. "I'm here to help make the hospital experience better for your little one." She smoothed back her flaming red hair. "I assume this is Morgan?"

Frederick acknowledged her with a curt nod, then turned to Morgan. "How you doing, little guy?" He lifted Morgan's pajama top, the one with fire trucks, and pushed on his belly in a circular motion. Morgan let loose a high-pitched wail.

Lucy stepped toward him, waving a squeaky doll in the air. "It's okay, it's okay," she said in a sing-song tone. Morgan looked at her, bewildered and confused. A few tears slipped down his cheek as he continued to whimper.

"You can pick him up," Frederick instructed. "There's a tender area on that right side. Hard to say what could be causing it. We'll start with an ultrasound—it's less invasive. We prefer not to expose children to radiation unless absolutely necessary." He grabbed his clipboard. "I'll leave you guys with Lucy. The technician will be in shortly."

Charles situated Morgan on his lap. He'd hoped, all along, that it was nothing; that Morgan's pain was something harmless, like a new tooth.

"Do you guys need anything?" Lucy asked. "We have snacks, pouches, juice, Goldfish crackers—"

"Could I get some water?" Charles croaked.

"Yes, of course." She placed the basket at Charles's feet. "These toys have all been sterilized, just for Morgan. And if there's anything else he wants, let me know. We even have iPads with age-appropriate apps."

Morgan stared at the toys with a disinterested gaze.

"Just the water for now, thanks," Charles said.

"Sure thing," she said and left the room.

The technician entered next. "How's everyone doing today?"

"Fine," Charles said. What else could he say? *On the edge of my seat here, wondering what the hell's wrong with my boy!*

The technician tapped at the keyboard and the machine blinked to life. He had gray wisps in his hair, a few wrinkles etched around his eyes, a proper grown-up mustache. Charles felt relieved having someone older, a real adult in charge.

Morgan accepted it all—in the stroller, on Charles's lap, on the table, back to the lap, on the table again. Charles never took him to his pediatric appointments, but from his experiences of changing diapers he knew this was atypical. Most diaper changes resembled a wrestling match, with a heel usually landing smack in the middle of Charles's face. But now, Morgan lazily sprawled out, like a sloth basking in the sun.

"Hey, mister," the technician said, tickling Morgan's chest. "This won't hurt at all."

Morgan didn't protest as the wand slid effortlessly over his belly, down to his groin area, up to his rib cage. Lucy returned, positioned herself at the foot of the bed, and began reading a book about the alphabet tumbling out of a tree.

The technician worked in silence, leaning over occasionally to type, to click on the mouse, to squint at the screen. There was no small talk, no complaining about the wretched, sticky September weather.

Charles squirmed in his seat. He wanted to ask questions—*What are you seeing? Is everything okay?* But his jaw locked, too scared of what the answers might be.

Once, during one of Sally's ultrasounds, a similar silence had filled the room. The technician had stopped talking and started frantically clicking away, the creases on her forehead deepening. She excused herself without a word, leaving them alone for ten minutes—which felt like an eternity. The doctor then told them they couldn't get a clear image of Morgan's heart. *Something's wrong with his heart?* they gasped. But a week later, at the follow-up, the technician exclaimed, "Oh, now we can see his heart!" And it turned out fine, Morgan was healthy. All that worry for nothing.

"He's such a perfect patient," the technician commented. "Most kids scream their heads off. Or try to grab everything."

Charles let out his breath and unclenched his fists. Finally, the guy was talking. "He's not normally like this," Charles said. "He usually thrashes about, like a wild alligator."

"A lot of kids lose steam when they're sick," Lucy said. "I see it all the time."

"But he's been like this for *days*," Charles said, more dread welling inside.

"We're just about finished here," the technician said.

Charles studied his face, trying to see if he could decipher anything. A frown? A smile? Nothing. He must be a good poker player.

"You can wipe him up." The technician handed Charles a wet wipe. "Dr. Frederick will come back to discuss the results."

And with that, he left. Everyone coming and going; nobody telling him what the hell was going on. *Liver? Spleen? Appendix?* What was wrong with Morgan?

Charles lifted his boy into his arms, his body limp, frail. Morgan released a pained moan. "It's okay," Charles whispered. He glanced at the screen, the keyboard, hoping to find answers, some clue.

Lucy turned on the iPad and Morgan crawled down to her lap, his thumb back in his mouth, eyes drooping.

Something must be wrong for them to be taking this long, Charles thought. He took a long breath, spinning his watch around three times. And waited.

✦

Dr. Frederick finally returned, after a twenty-minute wait. They had been there for almost two hours.

"Well, we didn't find anything organ related," he said.

"Oh," Charles said. "That's good news, right?"

Frederick frowned. "His pain seems quite significant, especially for a child his age. Some kids exaggerate pain, just for attention." He glanced down at Morgan, now fast asleep in Lucy's lap. "But not for someone as young as Morgan."

"So, what could it be then?"

"It's hard to say." Frederick set his clipboard on the counter. "We found an area that looked like a fracture, but we couldn't get a clear image to confirm it."

"A fracture?" Charles's stomach seized.

The doctor hesitated. "Let me check the area again." Charles helped Lucy to her feet. She gently lowered the slumbering Morgan onto the table.

The doctor pushed on Morgan's belly again, slowly venturing up his side and over his ribcage. Morgan's eyes sprung open, his mouth forming into a wide O-shape, a sharp scream piercing the room.

"I know, I know," Lucy said, handing him Elmo and smoothing back his sweaty hair. "Nobody wants to wake up to poking and prodding like that."

The scream hit Charles like a punch to his gut. Something was definitely wrong.

Frederick exhaled, looking distressed. "It could be bone related. The pain goes up the side, over his ribs."

"Bone? Like a *broken bone?*" Charles settled back into the chair with Morgan in his lap. "Wouldn't he be in a lot of pain if he had a broken bone?"

"Well, clearly he *is* in pain," Frederick said.

"I meant ..." Charles trailed off. Lucy slinked back, solemnly studying the floor.

Frederick cleared his throat, picking up the clipboard and flipping through the pages. "Did he have a fall recently? Stairs? Playground?"

"No, not that I know of." Charles wrapped his arms around Morgan. "And we don't have stairs, except to the basement."

"Perhaps it happened with someone else?"

"Well, he was with the babysitter on Friday night," Charles said. "She said he threw up—she swears that was all." The panic returned, the urge to hunt down Alyssa: *Did you do this?* "But his behavior literally changed overnight."

Frederick fiddled with his name badge, stretching it out on the retractable cord, and then letting it snap back into place. "It does seem like there's a few things happening here," he said. "I'd like to go ahead and do an X-ray, even though it exposes him to radiation. It's really the only way to see what's causing the discomfort."

"Yes, yes. Of course."

"From there, we can look into other options," he said. "We may need to do a CT scan, to see if there's a possible head injury."

Head injury? Christ. His mind flashed back to the Google searches. Initially he thought he was acting overly paranoid, but what if his gut had been right all along?

"First, let's find Morgan a pediatric X-ray room," Frederick said, heading toward the door. "And please, notify Morgan's mother. She needs to be here."

"I understand," Charles said. "She had to work today, but I—I'll get her to come in." He struggled to take a breath. Why was he lying? Because he couldn't tell the truth about their fight, not with the way Frederick stared at him. As if this, Morgan's unexplained misery, was his or Sally's fault.

✦

They settled into a marine-themed X-ray room. Gigantic blue whales, sparkly rainbow-striped starfish, and smiley octopi with long tentacles and opaque eyes covered the walls.

The nurse instructed Charles to strip Morgan down to his diaper and place him on the examination table. The technician opened a tube, which looked like a PVC pipe, and snapped it around Morgan's slender, naked torso, his arms stuck in an upward position, as if he was being arrested.

Morgan looked confused, almost on the verge of panic, but once again, he didn't fight back. He resumed his blank, lifeless stare, as if he was floating peacefully with the whales.

"Wow, such a dream patient," a nurse cooed.

"He's not normally like this!" Charles seethed, his blood pressure rising. How many times did he need to repeat this? Nobody seemed concerned that his baby, barely a toddler, acted so damned compliant, so placid. They had to know this wasn't typical behavior from a one-year-old.

Charles snuck a quick glance at his phone. Sally had finally responded saying sorry, she'd overslept, she needed to head home to change, then she'd come to the hospital. He blew out a gust of air. Thank God! She was okay.

Her texts seemed curt, to the point, with no acknowledgment of Charles's middle-of-the-night declaration of love. He braced himself for the storm to come—a furious and fuming Sally. Or perhaps a guilty and ashamed Sally? She did leave them in a bind, after all. It nagged at him, that she would abandon them without a car. But then again, she could say, "You told me not to come home."

But Sally, I wasn't serious.

"We're all done," the technician said. A nurse released Morgan from the suffocating tube.

"Mama," Morgan said in a hushed tone, his eyes flitting around the room.

"Mama's coming," Charles said, delicately lifting him off the table. Morgan winced, latching on to his thumb, sucking with vigor. "She's coming," Charles repeated, trying to hide the worry in his voice.

Chapter 16

Sally

Day six

Sally rolled over, her head banging against a hard surface. She opened her eyes, slowly, blinking against the harsh, blinding light. A piercing pain vibrated behind her eyes. Was that a … toilet?

Her stomach lurched and she coughed, a sudden spell of dry heaves. She felt cold and achy as a weird, unnerving chill spread across her skin. She struggled to remember.

Then it came: the fight with Charles, dragging through her Denny's shift, checking into Motel 6, chugging that cheap box of wine. *So much wine.* And then throwing up—twice?

The hospital. The hospital! Oh crap, she had to get Morgan to the hospital. His appointment at eight o'clock.

What time is it?

She tried to untangle herself from the towels but a dizzy wave made the room flicker out of focus. She needed her phone. Pushing against the cold tiled floor, she grabbed the edge of the sink and clawed her way to standing, avoiding looking in the mirror, scared of what she would see.

Stumbling into the room, she shaded her eyes from the warm light streaming through the window. The clock read 10:04. *Oh no no no.* Her one chance to redeem herself, to drive Morgan to the hospital. To be a responsible mother.

She downed two Tylenols without water, her throat scratchy and coarse, then scrolled through Charles's messages.

They managed to get there without her. An X-ray? That sounded bad. Sally pulled on her wrinkled clothes, ran a wet washcloth over her face, and attempted to detangle her hair with shaky fingers.

✦

Outside, she blinked under the searing sun, a Styrofoam mug of the motel's lukewarm coffee between her hands. A plan. A plan. What next?

Go home, grab her money, and run? But she needed to know Morgan's diagnosis—it could be something benign or totally unrelated to what she'd done. She longed to see him, to hold him again before ... She shook her head, trying to dispel the image of handcuffs on wrists.

Charles seemed calmer, at least in his texts. Hopefully that meant he wouldn't interrogate her anymore. But still, she needed her money, just in case. She'd rather be on the run than locked away in prison. Then, when it was safe, she could sneak back and grab Morgan. Never mind the details, she'd figure that out later.

She messaged Charles saying she needed to go home to change first. She held her breath, waiting to see if he texted back with shock—*Change? No, get here now.* But he didn't respond.

In the car, someone else moved her body, making the next decision for her; a puppeteer taking control of her weakened limbs, turning the wheel for Whispering Wind Drive.

✦

The house felt eerily vacant. She touched the picture frames, lightly, in fear of watching the memories disappear before her eyes, as if this life had been one big hoax. The pictures from their faux wedding and Hawaiian honeymoon reminded her of her past beauty—toned, tanned, such luscious hair. She touched her greasy hair and cringed. She hadn't washed it last night because she hated motel shampoo, and now there wasn't enough time.

She quickly changed into a pair of navy-blue leggings and a billowy yellow tank top, long enough to cover her squishy curves, then dug out her cash from the tampon boxes. After applying deodorant and dabbing lotion on her face, she slipped both bottles into her purse and surveyed the room, her and Charles's room. Previously Beth and Charles's room. How long would it take for Charles to replace her? He would probably beg for Beth to return, as if Sally had been a mere blip, an anomaly in his life's trajectory.

"At least she gave you Morgan," she imagined Beth saying, cradling Morgan in her arms while Charles leisurely sipped a glass of merlot. Beth would be everything that Sally could never be, plus more.

Sally took a deep breath, forcing the tears down. She would come back for Morgan. She promised.

As long as I can avoid getting arrested.

Her stomach churned. She made her way into the kitchen, pulled out a box of Thin Mints from the freezer, and quickly downed four cookies, then five, then one more. She stared at the dirty dishes—she should leave a clean house for Charles. But what was the point? She could scrub and scrub and scrub, but the dishes would just pile up again. They always did.

How she longed to crawl into bed, yank the covers over her head, sleep the day away, awake to her mom's heart-shaped buttermilk pancakes, the house filled with gentle humming and sweet aromas. Or to have Morgan curled beside her—healthy and happy, like his old self.

But was he ever happy? He sure did scream a lot.

She slipped a small, framed picture of Morgan into her purse, the one from the JCPenney photoshoot: Morgan embracing that rubber duck with all his might.

As she was heading toward the front door, Mr. Moops came slinking out from under the couch, meowing in protest. He reached up and rested his front paws on her shins. Biting back tears, she leaned forward to scratch him behind his ears, his favorite spot.

"Sorry, little guy. I don't know for sure if I'm leaving, but if I do, you have to stay here." She swallowed the lump in her throat. "Take care of Morgan until I figure out what happens next. Okay?"

Moops rubbed his head against her legs, purring his agreement.

✦

Sally struggled to locate Morgan and Charles. They were no longer in room 38. Her texts kept coming back with an error message, thanks to the hospital's impenetrable brick walls.

The front desk directed her to one unit, then another. Now she waited in a spacious waiting room, her brown leather purse at her feet, watching as people chatted around her.

The cramps kept coming in waves. She leaned forward, clutching her stomach, breathing through clenched teeth. Her periods were never this intense before. But obviously, bodies can change after having a baby.

A nurse appeared, lightly touching her shoulder. "Ma'am?"

Sally bolted up, a bit too quickly. The room started to spin and swirl; bright stars flickered and danced in her vision.

"Morgan's done with his X-ray," the nurse said. "I can take you to his room."

Sally nodded, swaying.

"Are you okay?" the nurse asked, reaching out to help steady her.

"Yes, I'm fine." Sally winced, briefly leaning into the nurse.

"Just this way."

Sally stumbled after her, focusing on the nurse's pink polka-dotted scrubs.

Charles jumped up when she entered the room. "You're here! Oh, thank God." He wrapped his arms around her. "Sally, I'm so sorry. I didn't mean to fight. I was so worried about you." He pulled back, placing his hands on her shoulders. "Are you okay?"

Morgan dozed in his stroller, Elmo tucked under his arm. Sally sighed with relief, glad Charles remembered to bring along the beloved doll.

"I'm fine," she said. "I can't believe I overslept and left you guys scrambling for a—"

"Shhh, let's not talk about that now," he said. "Sit. You look exhausted."

She lowered herself into a chair. "What's happening?"

"They couldn't find anything on the ultrasound but he's still in pain," he said. "They think it might be bone related. That's why they did the X-ray."

"Bone?"

"Yeah, bone." His face tightened. "Like a broken bone."

"But how?"

"They think maybe he fell?" Charles rubbed his eyes, pushing his glasses askew. "I don't know. Maybe something happened with Alyssa?"

Sally's mind spun. *His rib?* All this time, she'd been worrying about his head—a concussion, brain damage, whiplash. Or worse, she shuddered, a broken neck. But he'd be screaming like crazy if it was that extreme.

"The doctor will be here soon with the results." Charles sighed. "Hopefully he'll have some answers and we can all go home."

"How's Morgie handling it?" she asked, her insides roiling from the lingering hangover. She swallowed.

"He seems okay enough. Just not himself. Quiet, not really responsive." Charles shook his head. "They keep praising him for being the most compliant patient ever. I tell them this isn't how he usually is, but they refuse to listen."

"I missed him," she said, choking back tears. She yearned to scoop him up, to feel his warmth against her breaking, cracking chest. But her eyelids grew heavy, a strong wooziness taking over. She tried, with every ounce of will, to hang onto the sound of Charles's voice.

"I really didn't mean what I said ..."

She nodded, resting her head against the wall.

"... It just didn't make sense, you know what I mean? Not telling me about the ..."

Her lips parted, but no sound came.

"We're okay, right?"

Charles's hand, soft and firm, squeezed her arm. She tried to find comfort with her family sitting beside her, everyone drawing from the same air, their hearts pounding in unison, but she knew, somehow, that something bad awaited her: being chopped away, a tumorous part of the family that no longer belonged.

Chapter 17

Charles

Day six

A knock stopped Charles mid-sentence. He'd been rambling to Sally, trying to gauge their status, but her eyes remained shut.

"Is this Morgan's mother?" Dr. Frederick asked. He dragged a stool over.

"Yes," Charles said.

"You need to wake her up," Frederick said with a frown. A definite frown.

Charles grabbed Sally's shoulder, giving it a firm shake. Her eyes fluttered open.

Damn it, she fell asleep. Did she even hear a word he said?

"I'm Dr. Frederick," he said to Sally, not even offering to shake her hand. "I have the results from Morgan's X-ray."

"Oh?" She rubbed her eyes.

Charles searched the doctor's face. Bad news, it had to be bad. Doctors always announced good news right away. But dreadful news, they drew it out with tortuous suspense.

Frederick interlaced his fingers, looking at Charles, and then at Sally, his face somber. Charles's stomach dropped.

Here it comes.

"Morgan has a fractured rib," Frederick said.

Charles blinked.

"It appears to have happened about four, maybe five days ago. We'll have to do another scan in two weeks. With young children we often can't see certain fractures until the bone starts healing." His penetrating green eyes stopped on Charles. "This fracture, however, was significant enough to show up on the X-ray. But honestly, there could be more."

"His rib?" Charles racked his brain, thinking of that dream, the ominous sound of the lawn mower. Did someone hit Morgan with a car? But when? Alyssa didn't have her license yet, he always saw that punkish friend picking her up.

"Yes. His right rib is fractured," Frederick said. "This, of course, explains his pain."

Morgan's random shrieks, his sudden resistance against hugs, the deafening screech when Charles tightened his car seat straps that morning. *Maybe it's a new molar*—that had been Sally's guess. How could they have been so ignorant, this unaware? What kind of parents were they?

"But ..." Charles looked helplessly at Sally.

"How did this happen?" Sally finished for him.

"Sometimes it's something minor, such as slipping in the tub or rolling off the changing table," Frederick said. "Can you think of any such incident that's happened this past week?"

"No, nothing like that happened with me," Charles said, studying Sally.

"What? You think this happened with *me?*" Her gaze snapped to Frederick. "No. Absolutely no."

"Are you sure?" Charles said. "I mean, it could've happened at the park or, you know ... if you were distracted by your phone—"

"We didn't go to the park," Sally said curtly.

"In the backyard? Did he jump out of the swing?" Just recently, Morgan had attempted to stand up in the baby swing attached to their jungle gym. He was getting to that age, pushing limits and taking risks, seeing what he could get away with.

"I was watching him," Sally insisted. "The *whole* time."

"Well, it's impossible to watch him *every* second," Charles said.

Frederick tapped his pen against the clipboard, mouth slightly agape, his face pivoting between Sally and Charles as if watching a heated tennis match.

"This doesn't make sense," Charles said. "Why isn't there a bruise or something?"

"Toddler's bones are very fragile," Frederick explained. "We've seen them crack while receiving CPR, without the slightest bruising."

"But …" Charles scanned the room, as if the answer was scrawled on the walls, the blue whale ready to spurt it out. Someone out there knew what had happened. "Are you sure?" he asked Sally again. "It only takes a second for an accident to happen, especially if you were staring at your—"

"Stop it! I wasn't on my phone," Sally snapped. "What about Alyssa? You were the one who saw her Friday night. Did she seem nervous or anything?"

"Um, now that you mention it …" Charles turned to the doctor. "She did rush away awfully fast. Said her ride was waiting." And what about her short response to his accusatory text? She didn't seem concerned or upset, not like a sweet, caring babysitter should.

"And what?" Sally asked. "You didn't think to tell me that part?"

"I didn't … I never thought …" Charles stammered. "But wait a minute. You didn't tell me about the—"

"Listen," Frederick interrupted, his voice turning a tone deeper. "We need to talk about Morgan's condition. We want to make sure there aren't other injuries. We'd like to get him in for a CT scan as soon as possible, to check for possible head trauma. And then we'll need to monitor him for at least twenty-four hours. He'll also need to minimize movement, to allow the rib to heal. It'll take about six weeks to fully recover, granted it's just the one fracture."

Charles exhaled, his chest caving in.

"I know this is a lot to take in." Frederick fiddled with his name badge again, then clasped his hands in his lap, the lizard tattoo quivering on his wrist. "And I need to let you know that, well, when it comes to children and broken bones, especially incidents that are unexplained"—his eyes flicked to the floor—"we're required to call in CPS." The doctor paused, then added: "Child protective services."

"Are you serious?" Charles said.

"Unfortunately, yes." Frederick took a breath, his eyes meeting Charles's. "A detective from the Crimes Against Children unit will come to question you, both of you. And, of course, anyone who's cared for Morgan in the past two weeks."

"A *detective?*" Charles asked, his arm hairs bristling.

"You see, this is what we call a 'non-accidental trauma.' Meaning there's not a specific incident, such as Morgan falling at the playground. So … well …" Frederick shifted in his chair, rubbing at the back of his neck. "We need to look further to see if it's a result of, um, abuse."

"Abuse?" Charles said. "Christ, who would try to break Morgan's rib? An accident must've happened with Alyssa, the babysitter. And she was too scared to tell us." Charles glanced at Sally, hunched over and gnawing on her nails.

"The detective will reach out to the babysitter," Frederick reassured them.

"But Morgan … he'll be able to go home after all the monitoring?" Sally asked. "If he's doing okay?"

"Not exactly," Frederick said. "He won't be released until the detective and social worker deem one, or both of you, safe."

"Wait, so you think …" Charles swallowed. "You think that Sally and me … we're not safe parents?" Just saying the words made his stomach lurch, bile rising to his throat.

"Look," Frederick began, sitting up straight, "this is our usual procedure. Required by law."

Charles struggled to take it all in. A fractured rib? Possible head trauma? All the worst-case scenarios coming true. Did this really happen with Alyssa?

"Why don't we transfer Morgan to another room? Get him all settled in," Frederick said, his tone turning cheery, as if he'd just suggested they go out for ice cream sundaes. "Your case worker will be here shortly. She'll be able to answer any questions you may have."

Charles pushed Morgan's stroller out the door while Sally shuffled beside him, quiet and sullen. Morgan had a broken rib. *His goddamned rib!* Perhaps Morgan flung himself out of his crib, Alyssa raced in and tripped in the dark. The weight of her body slamming against his—that kind of force could snap a bone, right?

Breathe, he told himself. He needed to make a note of all the possibilities, fire them off to their case worker. *A case worker.* Christ, was this happening?

"Right this way." Frederick opened the door to a vibrant room—each wall painted a different shade of green with a papier-mâché sun hanging in the corner. Stacks of toy bins lined the walls, along with a cushioned rocking chair and a crib on wheels.

"Go ahead and get comfortable," Frederick said. "The nurse will come to discuss pain med options for Morgan."

"And what about the babysitter?" Charles said. "Should I call her?"

"The babysitter?" Frederick's eyes widened, his peach fuzz twitching. "Oh, no. An officer will be in touch with her directly. Just take it one step at a time, okay?" He nodded, then quietly left the room.

Charles fumed, pulling out his phone. He started composing a text to Alyssa, the words pouring out like a bursting dam: **Morgan's in the hospital. An accident on Friday. The police want to talk to you. Please, I need to know what really happened.**

His finger hovered over the *send* arrow, but he stopped himself. What the hell was he doing? He thought of Alyssa's smile, the way she apologized on Friday night, supposedly over not starting the washing machine. But what if she was sorry for something else? What if she was terrified to tell the truth?

He shook his head. Even if it was an accident, it was wrong to let Morgan suffer for days—*for five days!*—with a broken rib. How could she not have told them? Unless she didn't know the extent of his injuries? No, she should have said something, no matter what.

He added: **You're not going to get away with this.** He read through the full draft, his stomach tightening. He set down his phone, not sure if he should send it or not. He cracked his knuckles, rolled his shoulders, and exhaled loudly. Maybe he should call her instead? Let her know the full scope of the situation.

Sally leaned over to check on Morgan. Charles watched as she smoothed back his hair, gently kissed his forehead, and studied his eyes.

A solid knock announced a nurse at the door.

"I need one of you to come fill out some forms," the nurse said.

"But I already filled out a bunch of paperwork this morning," Charles said.

"That was for the scan," she explained. "Morgan needs to spend the night, and with that comes more forms to sign." The nurse shrugged in apology.

Charles gave Sally's shoulder a quick squeeze. "I'll go," he said.

When he returned, he found Sally slumped in the chair, sobbing. Morgan lay soundless in his crib.

"Hey, come here." Charles pulled her to her feet.

"His rib?" she cried. "But how?" She leaned into him, the delicate scent of her vanilla-infused lotion wafting up. He wrapped his arms around her, wanting to ask where she'd stayed last night, if she was okay, why she'd arrive so late, but his throat glazed over.

"I don't know," he said. "I really don't know."

She buried her face into his chest. "It wasn't me," she whispered.

"I know, I know," he said. It had to be true, Sally not knowing what happened. Even if she was distracted by something, he knew their kid. Whatever happened—a tumble out of his crib?—their boy would've put those powerful lungs to use, letting the neighborhood, the entire world, know of his misery. This alone would've forced Sally to call Charles, to beg for backup.

But still, *something* happened last Friday. The X-ray confirmed it.

"We failed." Charles released a defeated sigh. "We failed to keep Morgan safe."

"I know," Sally whispered. "I know."

Chapter 18

Mandy

Day six

Mandy glanced at the time—almost noon.

She'd spent the morning filing a fresh stack of papers, neck tense, wrists aching from the drum of typing. No sign of Charles, just like yesterday. Did he even tell the boss about her hard work last Friday, kicking butt with her efficient Excel skills? She took pride in her ability to take any talent or skill and manipulate it overnight: *Just fake it 'til you make it.* She clung to a thread of hope that Nordstrom would offer her that job. She knew nothing about fashion but heck, she'd learn—Alyssa could teach her. But then again, wasn't the future of brick-and-mortar retail doomed?

She grabbed her purse and headed toward the elevator, hoping to avoid the lunch-break crowd. Nope, they all had the same idea, cramming into the elevator like a pack of hyenas with high-pitched yammering and forced laughs, strong colognes, and icky perfumes. Someone shoved Mandy to the back, a sharp heel jabbed her foot. Damn these ballet flats, she thought. She didn't care how cool Alyssa said they were, they belonged in the trash.

Downstairs in the food court, she decided on Oki Sushi. Such a midday luxury, the white-hot wasabi a nerve-tingling reward after her productive morning. It took her mind off the temptation of a cigarette—the ever-present threat, especially when work turned stressful. When wasn't work stressful?

She waited in line, holding her tray with a salmon roll and Diet Coke, thinking about that quirky woman Joyce, from accounting. Her poodle-like perm and shrill voice. She appeared in her cubicle first thing that morning, with an awkward grin, and proceeded to dig into Mandy's personal life. Husband?—*No.* Kids?—*Yes.* Then out of the blue, Joyce blurted out Alyssa's name before Mandy had the chance. How'd she know? Then, this was the strangest part, she handed Mandy a creased Post-it note with Charles's name and number.

"What's this for?"

"He's looking for a babysitter," Joyce explained. "For his son."

"Oh." Mandy stared at the note. "Okay."

It irked her, the whole interaction, but she brushed it off as Joyce being the office gossip. She knew the type, one lurked in every office. Something in their blood made them need to feast on the misfortunes of others, then regurgitate the drama to anyone willing to listen. Mandy tried to avoid staff break rooms, no matter the office.

She tapped at her purse, Charles's number tucked safely within. She felt a giddy rush—butterflies? For a brief moment she thought about texting him, to ask about his son; children were a great lead-in for breaking the ice. Flushing, she shook her head. He's happily married, she reminded herself.

But is he?

She stepped up to the counter, balancing her tray, and pulled out her wallet. Then her phone rang. Alyssa. When did she ever call instead of text? Balancing the phone between her ear and shoulder, she scribbled on the receipt. The woman behind the counter scowled at her.

"Hey sweetie," Mandy answered.

"Mom," Alyssa said, her voice a strangled croak.

"What's wrong?"

"Mom, the kid I babysit for, he's in the *hospital.*" Her voice broke.

"What? The hospital? Who's in the hospital?" Mandy abandoned her tray on a table and stumbled outside.

"It's that boy." Alyssa took a sharp inhale. "The one I babysit for. Morgan."

Mandy reached out to a lamp post for balance. "Morgan?" Where had she heard that name before?

"I got this text." A gasp, a sob. "An accident happened, on Friday night. He—his dad, Charles, said the police want to talk to me. Me. Mom! They think I *did* this."

"Wait." A rush of dizzying heat coursed through her. "Morgan's the boy you *babysit?*"

"Yes," Alyssa groaned. "But I didn't do anything. I swear!"

"Okay, okay. I believe you. Where are you now?"

"At—school. In the bathroom. I'm missing my chem exam. I just ... I don't know what to do."

Mandy took a long breath as the threads collided: Morgan. Charles. Alyssa. Morgan was Charles's son? *How did we not make this connection?* Alyssa must have told her the details at some point, shared their names, but Mandy was likely distracted and, besides, she couldn't keep track of *all* the families her daughter babysat for. But Joyce, upstairs—did she know about this?

"Listen," Mandy said. "Head to the principal's office. Tell them I'm coming to pick you up."

"But what about the chem exam?"

"Don't worry. You can retake it later."

"Just get here as soon as you can."

✦

Mandy paced the elevator, now empty. She needed to retrieve her keys from her desk. *An accident happened.* What kind of accident? Charles never mentioned anything of the sort.

Terror raced through her, a flashback to the panicked calls she used to receive from concerned neighbors: *Ian's letting Alyssa swim in the pool, again. By herself!*

The elevator door slid open. Mandy stood paralyzed, for a brief second, the door starting to close. She bolted forward and walked briskly to her desk. But ... Charles? Accusing her daughter of something? He seemed so benign, so non-confrontational. So pleasant, that's what Mandy thought when they'd first met.

Were they—she and Alyssa—even talking about the same man?

Chapter 19

Sally

Day six

A broken rib. It had to be from *her*—from Sally's shaking. Was she really that strong? The memory barreled through her: her fingers wrapped around Morgan's torso, his flailing body arched in protest, the uncontrollable panic pulsating through her blood. Then she closed her eyes and the trying-to-be-patient mother disappeared, some other creature—*a monster*—taking over: a part of herself she never knew existed.

Biting her lip, she studied Morgan's hospital room. She thought about all those gentle parenting blogs she'd read, the endless advice on what to do instead of lashing out. None of those blogs ever talked about what to do *after* you've lost control.

She watched as Charles furiously typed on his phone, his face distorted in disgust. She knelt in front of Morgan, amazed at how calm and peaceful he remained, completely unaware of the complicated drama unfolding around him.

If he could talk, would he turn me in?

Charles left with the nurse, his phone forgotten. Sally couldn't resist: She stood, picked it up, and entered his password. Her pulse quickened as she read his unsent message to Alyssa, telling her about the hospital, the police. **You're not going to get away with this.** Scrolling, she saw his earlier text from Monday, asking if Morgan had hit his head.

A chill shot through her. Charles mentioned his doubts about Alyssa here and there—just like she half-heartedly did—but now she held the proof in her hand: Charles believed in Sally. It was their word against Alyssa's. She felt a stab of guilt as she set down his phone. *Poor Alyssa.* But what other option was there?

She heard a little swoosh sound and froze. Morgan looked at her. She unlocked Charles's phone again. Her stomach dropped—the last message somehow went through. *Oh shit!* Hearing the door creak open, she dropped the phone and turned. The nurse wanted to discuss pain meds for Morgan.

"It'll probably make him sleepy so let's get him settled in the crib," the nurse instructed.

Morgan continued staring at Sally as she picked him up, as if he knew what she'd just done. As if he desperately wanted to plead, *Don't blame Alyssa.*

"And I just need to set up this monitor." The nurse dragged a rolling stand into the room. "We refer to it as an E-sitter."

"An E-sitter?" Sally eyed what looked like a video camera.

"Yes." The nurse fiddled with the device. "Since the authorities are involved, we have to monitor Morgan around the clock."

Sally stepped back, as if the camera was a python ready to strike. She lowered Morgan into the crib, watching as the nurse positioned the camera's angle directly at them. Was it so she wouldn't hurt Morgan again? So she wouldn't take him and run? Or, she shuddered, to catch her confession?

After the nurse left, Sally collapsed in the chair, the sobs erupting once again.

And when Charles returned, he pulled her into his embrace, holding her tenderly, as if she still belonged on the loving parent team. She waited for his worried eyes to switch to a look of revulsion and disbelief: *How could you?*

But he doesn't think that, she reminded herself. *He blames Alyssa.*

They sank into chairs and waited. Charles started to rant, "I mean, Morgan was asleep when Alyssa arrived. Did he climb out of his crib and fall? Can he do that? It seems like the most logical explanation. I just can't believe she didn't tell us. And how could we not have noticed? And that ridiculous doctor? He's like Doogie Howser with tats. I think we need another opinion, don't you?"

"A broken bone's a broken bone," Sally murmured. "What's another doctor gonna say?" She glanced at the E-sitter and then at Charles's phone on the counter. What if Alyssa texted back? She should've deleted the entire thread.

"Yeah, but—"

"I'm hungry," she said, standing up. "I saw some vending machines in the lobby. Do you want anything?" She grabbed her purse and a plastic water bottle Charles had handed her at some point, then bolted toward the door.

"But Sal—"

In the hall, she paused, leaning against the door, taking several labored breaths. It's going to be okay, she told herself. With all the chaos going on, Charles would just assume he'd accidentally sent the text. But what about Alyssa's reaction to the accusations? She shook her head, trying to focus on the main goal: *I need to keep Morgan.*

"Excuse me, Ms. Haywood?"

Her eyes snapped up. "What?"

"I'm Detective Rodney Jameson, with the Oak Wood police department," a portly man said, thrusting his hand toward her. "And this is Ms. Elaine Flynn, your social worker. Do you mind if we ask a couple of questions regarding your son, Morgan Haywood?" Beside him, the slender woman also extended her hand.

"Oh," Sally said. They were here, already.

"You are Morgan's mother, correct?" the detective asked.

Sally slowly nodded before tentatively shaking each hand.

"It won't take long," he said, smiling.

"Uh, okay," Sally said. "Let me just ... let me tell Charles so he doesn't worry." She looked past them, briefly, over their shoulders and down the hall, her nails already tapping against her teeth.

✦

The detective led the way to one of the hospital's private conference rooms, down the hall and up a flight of stairs. It was a spacious room, clearly designed for conferences and staff trainings—not for child abuse interrogations.

"Go ahead and take a seat," the detective said. Jameson, was it?

Sally settled into one of the smooth leather chairs and slung her purse—her getaway money and Morgan's framed picture safely stashed inside—over the back. The detective and social worker sat across from her, the long, polished table looming between them.

"First, I'll need your ID," Jameson said. He had wispy grayish-brown hair, wildly overgrown eyebrows, a craggy mustache.

Sally pulled out her wallet as the tight-lipped social worker smoothed down her long chocolate-toned hair, straight bangs framing her sharp, cutting eyes. The woman's bracelet jangled with every move.

"Ah, I see you kept your maiden name," Jameson said as he examined Sally's license.

"We're not technically married." She saw a flicker of judgment, or speculation, flash across the detective's face as he slid her license back.

"I find it easier to record than to document everything on paper," he said, placing a black recorder on the table. "You okay with that? That way I can focus on the conversation and avoid repeating questions. This old brain ain't so good at multitasking anymore." He chuckled, tapping his pen against his bald spot dramatically.

"I'm going to do it the old-fashioned way," the social worker said, eyeing him and hoisting up her pen, as if in competition.

Sally stared at the recorder, the words right on her tongue: *Do I need a lawyer?* No, that would only make her look guilty.

But Sally, a voice said, *you are guilty.*

"Yes, that's fine," Sally said. They seemed friendly enough, nobody whipping out handcuffs or reading off her rights. She wiped her sweaty palms on her leggings.

Jameson pushed the recorder's button and stated the preliminaries: date, names, location. "I know this is a tough situation, Sally. Can I call you Sally? I imagine you want to get back to tending to Morgan. I get it, I'm a parent too. A teenager, so at the opposite end as you, but let me tell you, she's full of trouble."

Sally forced a smile.

"Oh, before we get started … do you need anything? Besides water." He motioned toward the water bottle in front of her.

"I'm fine."

"All right," Jameson said. "Let's start with last Friday. That's the approximate date of Morgan's rib fracture, and right before he started displaying symptoms."

Sally shifted in the chair, briefly chewing on a chipped nail before placing her hands flat on the table. She rambled off Friday's events, carefully avoiding Morgan's meltdown and her attack. Was it an attack, though? If not an attack, what the hell was it? She couldn't say self-defense—he was a *baby*.

"Did you see anyone that day? Friends? Neighbors?" Jameson did all the talking, the social worker silent beside him, her harrowing eyes glued on Sally.

"No." God, if only they'd gone to that playgroup …

"Did Morgan seem sick or out of sorts before you left for work?"

"He was a bit tired but mostly his normal self." Her eyes drifted down to her lap, trying to ignore the guilt surging through her. "He threw up with the babysitter. She texted us about it."

"How quickly did you come home after that?"

"I, well, I didn't have my phone on me—I work at Denny's. Friday nights are pretty busy. So, yeah, I didn't know anything until my shift ended. And Charles didn't think it sounded serious enough to cancel his last client."

"So …" Jameson took a long slurp from his Styrofoam cup. "Charles arrived home first?"

"Yes," Sally said with a nod. "He paid Alyssa and she … he says she raced off. *Quickly*."

"And how long was Charles alone with Morgan before you came home?" He scratched at the stubble on his chin, jowls wobbling.

"What do you mean?"

"Charles was alone with Morgan, correct?"

"Yes, but Morgan was *asleep*."

"I'm just gathering facts," Jameson said. His unruly eyebrows arched—what she'd give to take tweezers to his face.

"Uh, maybe an hour or two? I can't remember," Sally said. The social worker—Ms. Something Flynn?—moved slightly, her chair creaking. She never once took her eyes off Sally.

"Does Charles have a history of violence or mental illness?" Jameson asked.

"What? Are you serious?" As much as Sally didn't want them blaming her, she most certainly didn't want Charles to end up as the scapegoat. Morgan meant everything to him.

"These are standard questions, Sally. I'm not implying anything here. Just gathering—"

"Gathering facts. I get it." Sighing, she studied her jagged nails. "No, Charles has always been ..." But *could* she turn it against him? Wouldn't they believe the mother over the father? It seemed more plausible than blaming the babysitter. Flynn leaned in, her relentless eyes probing deeper, a hint of—of what? Encouragement? As if, maybe, prodding Sally to admit Charles was the abuser.

"Yes?" Jameson asked.

"He's not home often. He works a lot—two jobs, in fact. And ..." The air in the room grew heavy, thick, her skin moist. She swallowed. She needed to get the story straight, whatever story she was going to tell.

"And?"

She exhaled, then, "No, he's not violent." She couldn't turn Charles into a villain. Not with this hangover, the lack of a proper meal, her body aching from a night passed out on Motel 6's unforgiving bathroom floor, her bladder ready to explode. And besides, Charles was a good man. He loved Morgan more than anything.

"Okay." Jameson cleared his throat. "Please tell me, why didn't you take Morgan in once he started feeling sick?"

"I called the nurse line on Saturday," she lied. "They told me it was okay to wait until Monday." Would they go as far as checking her phone records?

"And why'd you miss the hospital appointment on Tuesday morning?"

She squirmed. What would Charles tell them? She assumed his interview was next.

"Sally?"

She blew a strand of hair out of her eyes. "I was worried about the poking and prodding. He seemed … Morgan was exhausted. I felt like he needed a break."

"But surely you were concerned," he scoffed. Sally noticed a thick gold band on his ring finger. A wife? Really? How could any woman let him leave the house with those eyebrows?

Flynn's bracelet clanked against the table as she changed position, her eyes turning a shade darker. Doubt?

"Morgan's doctor said it was possibly organ related," Jameson said, a quick glance to his notepad. "He didn't seem to be getting better. Why weren't you worried?"

"I don't know what I was thinking. It was a mistake." The words tangled and twisted inside her head: *It wasn't me. I hurt my baby. I didn't hurt him. I shook my baby. It wasn't me. Me. Not me.*

"And where were you this morning?"

"I haven't been feeling well," she mumbled, instinctively touching her stomach. The tremors still came in waves, unpredictable, sometimes lasting a minute or longer, halting her breath before fading away.

Jameson studied her, his face a blank slate. Sally unscrewed her water bottle, took a few sips.

"Your husband, I mean, Charles, told Dr. Frederick you were at *work* this morning," he finally said.

She gnawed on her lower lip and fiddled with her earrings—wide-eyed owls, sterling silver, a gift from Charles, something they couldn't afford but he bought anyway—then shoved her hands between her clenched thighs. "Yeah, I was supposed to go to work. But, uh, I called in sick."

"I'll need the name and number of your manager."

"Yes," she said. *Just cooperate.* "Of course."

"Sally," he said.

"Yes?"

"Has Charles ever hurt or threatened you in any way?"

"No, never." Her eyes watered at the thought of it.

"You can tell us anything, okay?" Jameson offered a cordial smile. "You can trust us."

She nodded.

Next, he asked about her physical and mental health: Clinical depression? Drug addiction? Medications? "Have you experienced suicidal thoughts recently?"

She thought about last night, the scalding steam wearing down her reserve—*razor or pills?* "No," she lied, licking her lips.

"Last question, I promise," he said. "Morgan's walking, yes? Running? Climbing up on stuff?"

"Yeah," she said. "He only started a few weeks ago. He still wobbles, a few harmless tumbles here and there."

Jameson eyebrows jumped at "tumbles." He jotted something down in his notepad. "Okay, I think I've got enough for now."

"But ... but ..." Sally stammered, then swallowed hard. She dug her nails into the chair's armrests. "What about Alyssa? The babysitter. She was with Morgan on Friday night. He was different after ... after she was there," she said carefully.

"Don't worry, we plan to meet with her this afternoon." He dug through his briefcase and pulled out a notepad and pen. "I need your babysitter's full name and address, your work details, and a few personal references—anyone who can vouch for you as a mother."

A drop of sweat trickled down her back. "What?"

"Parents, friends, neighbors. Basically, anyone who hangs out with you and Morgan on a regular basis," he said. "Again, this is our usual procedure. We'll ask the same for anyone who's cared for Morgan over the past couple weeks." He slid the notepad across the table.

"I don't have friends. My mother, she passed away."

The detective blew out a gust of air, his fingers trailing over his mustache. "Sorry to hear that. Just try your best, okay?" He glanced at the social worker, exchanging a coded conversation with their eyes, a slight nod, and furrowed eyebrows before turning back to Sally. "Ms. Flynn would like to ask a few questions in private." He then stood, packed up his briefcase, and left the room.

At the mention of her name, the social worker shuffled over to Sally's side. Her demeanor shifted, like a veil lifting: shoulders relaxing, eyes softening, as if she was now a supportive therapist ready to take on the weight of Sally's troubles.

"You can be honest with me," she said.

"I've already told you everything ..." Sally let her voice drift, glancing at the framed picture on the wall: three pastel-colored tulips, a bronze sunset, a tattered straw hat. Her stomach tensed, followed by a fresh wave of cramps.

"It's going to be better for everyone if you come forward. We can help, whether it was you or Mr. Haywood—"

"You don't need to call him that." Sally inhaled sharply. "Charles is fine."

"Sure, of course." Flynn smiled. "And does that mean you prefer Sally over—"

"Sally." She knew she'd never officially become Mrs. Haywood, not after what she'd done.

"Got it. And please, you can call me Elaine."

Yeah, right, Sally thought. *We're not friends.*

"Now, there may be some parenting classes, a few supervised visits," Flynn continued. "But you're not going to lose Morgan."

Sally's body turned ice-cold. She knew the social worker was trying to box her in with lame reassurances, whatever it took to get her to confess. Like in the movies, where they promise the criminal freedom for cooperating, then turn the tables at the last minute: *Just kidding. Here's twenty years in prison.*

"I don't know what else to say. Something must've happened with Alyssa—the babysitter," Sally said, forcing her voice up a notch. "I'm sure it was an accident and—"

"Look," Flynn cut her off. "I really need you to be honest. If Charles hurt you, or threatened you, I need to know. We can help protect you."

"Nothing hap—"

"Morgan can't go home with one of you until we figure this out. You know that, right? We can't hand him back to you guys until someone comes forward, until we have a plan. As of right now, this looks like a direct result of someone hurting him. Intentionally." Flynn took a deep breath, her glitzy bracelet jingling again. "And, of course, we need to prevent it from happening again. Because abuse like this usually isn't a one-time ordeal."

We need to prevent it from happening again. Sally nodded, biting down on her nails, hard. She took another swig of water, squeezing her thighs as her bladder protested.

"We never want to separate children from their mothers. That's not our goal." Flynn scooted closer. Sally could smell her overwhelming perfume, a rosy undertone. She closed her eyes.

"Please, Sally. Let me help you."

Just say it, she told herself. Go on: *I shook Morgan. I broke his rib.*

"I know you love Morgan," Flynn continued. "Losing control can happen to anyone, even the best of parents."

Shit, what did this woman know? She appeared so flawless, so in control—designer clothes, silky hair, a diamond-charmed bracelet. Her eye shadow, a subtle mauve, matched her nails *and* her shoes. Sally imagined this woman returning to a sophisticated life after this, a life with a spotless kitchen and plush carpet, martinis with olives, a white leather couch—immaculate, unstained. This Elaine Flynn, she had no idea what it was like to listen to a red-faced baby howl for hours on end, pulling out your hair in frustration, every neuron exploding, tortured by your complete inadequacy, your inability to soothe and comfort your own baby.

Shut up!

Stop! Stop! Stop!

Sally cupped her hands over her ears as Morgan's screeches rattled deep inside, even now, even after all these days of punishing silence. The truth she kept avoiding hammered into her: *I've destroyed my baby.*

"Sally, you seem really upset and I want to—"

"Are we done?" Sally dropped her hands, ignoring the single tear rolling down her cheek. "I really need to pee."

Flynn sighed. "We'll be in touch to schedule a follow-up appointment, okay? In the meantime, here's my card. Call anytime, day or night." She lightly touched Sally's arm. "Really, I'm on your side."

Sally bristled at her touch. She snatched up the card and shoved it in her purse. "Where's the bathroom?" She'd held on long enough—the contents of her rumbling stomach ready to explode, her bladder on fire.

"Down the hall, to your right."

Sally stood, the room briefly flashing to black, then a foggy, diluted white. She inhaled sharply, searching for the outline of the door.

"Do you need help?" The social worker's voice was edged with concern. Everything swirled into a blur, with one infinite worry on repeat: *I'm going to lose Morgan.*

Chapter 20

Charles

Day six

The detective and social worker whisked Sally off to her interview around one o'clock. Shortly after, Charles left Morgan with the bubbly childcare helper and went outside. He needed to move their station wagon. Sally had parked in the short-term section, only valid for two hours, and now, with the state of Morgan's condition, it looked like everyone was going to stay the night.

He called his mom on the walk, speeding through the details: *Rib. Babysitter. Possible head injury.*

"Slow down," his mom said. "What happened? Who cracked a rib?"

"Morgan! Morgan has a fractured rib. There was a babysitter Friday night," he said. "It must've been an accident, something she was too scared to admit."

"Goodness gracious," she said. "Have you talked to her, this babysitter?"

"The police are supposedly going to talk to her. They're with Sally now." He didn't want to tell his mom—or anybody—about texting Alyssa. The last message, the really nasty one from this morning, had been a mistake. He'd finally decided to call her, clicked on her name, and then discovered the long message had accidentally been sent. *Dammit.* And saying anything more was bound to make it worse. "I think they'll want to talk to me next. They think—" He glanced at a man in green scrubs and waited for him to pass. "Mom, they think *we* did it."

"Oh no, honey. This is terrible," she said. "How's Morgie doing?"

"As okay as he can be, with a cracked rib. They gave him some pain meds. They want to do a CT scan next." Charles paced the grassy patch in front of the parking garage. "Mom, it just doesn't seem real. A broken rib?"

"Oh my. I can only imagine," she said. "And what about Sally? What does she think about this all?"

He took a deep breath. "Well, she's in some kind of shock. She didn't even tell me about the ... never mind. It's just—"

"I'm going to come down there," she cut in. "Let me help you guys."

"No, no, no. You don't need to do that. I just wanted to keep you in the loop and—"

"Charles, listen," his mom said, her voice firm. "This is *serious.* You don't need to deal with this alone. And Sally, it sounds like she needs some support."

"I don't know how this happened," he said, his head heavy with disturbing images: mysterious hands smacking his boy, shoving him down the basement stairs. "I mean, he was asleep when the babysitter arrived. And Sally swears she didn't see him fall or anything."

"Let me see what I can do. There's that daily nonstop on Delta, around five o'clock. Just try to stay calm, okay?" she said. "Obviously it was an accident. Like when your brother broke a metatarsal bone in his foot. He was pulling frozen chicken out of the freezer and the darned package slipped. Imagine my shock when they did the X-ray and said it was *broken—*"

"Mom, I know crazy things can happen. But breaking a bone in your foot and breaking your rib are two very different things. I'd get it if Morgan fell or ... I don't know." He fished his keys out of his pocket. The sun beat down on him. "But we can't come up with any logical explanation, so they're left thinking we abused him."

"I'm sorry, dear. Sadly, this is what happens with kids and broken bones." She sighed heavily. "And Sally and the babysitter, they were the only ones with Morgan on Friday?"

"Yes. I've asked Sally multiple times. She swears *nothing* happened."

He could hear the judging click of her tongue.

"Mom. Sally would never hurt Morgan," Charles snapped. "Never."

"Oh honey, I'm not implying that. But if an accident *did* happen—"

"It was the babysitter. Look, I'm exhausted. I had to wake up early to get Morgan to the hospital by myself—" He stopped.

"What do you mean, *by yourself?"* his mom probed. "Where was Sally?"

"I can't get into this right now," he said, ducking into the parking garage. "Just call if you get a flight, okay?" He switched off before she could respond.

✦

Charles stumbled into the bathroom. He set his glasses on the counter and splashed cold water on his face. He felt trapped in a dream, a never-ending nightmare. Drying his face with a stiff paper towel, he tried to shake off the detective's gruff words from his interview—no, his *interrogation,* that's what it was.

"Were you actually there when Sally called the nurse line on Saturday?"

Christ, why would Sally lie about that of all things?

"I see that Sally made an appointment with the hospital to bring Morgan in on Tuesday morning. But she missed that appointment. Was there a reason for this?"

Detective Jameson presented a friendly facade—"Just some routine questions, that's all"—but Charles felt unsettled, an acute trepidation slinking up his spine: *Don't trust this man.*

"And you didn't even know about the hospital referral, is that right? That's what the hospital gathered when they called you on ..." Jameson paused, flipping through his notepad. "Tuesday afternoon. Around 3:30 p.m."

Charles couldn't remember exactly what he said in response, his voice warbled, stammering, "She ... we ... Morgan had been through so much already."

"You do realize that was neglectful behavior, right? Your son was in pain, the doctor urged you to take him to the hospital, and you guys chose not to go?"

"Uh, well, I ..."

Why didn't Sally tell me about the hospital appointment?

The questions continued in quick succession, like rapid fire. The detective's forehead etched with worry lines, the social worker rigid and mute beside him.

"Does Sally have a history of mental health issues, violence, or substance abuse?"

Jameson reassured him these were standard questions; the same for everyone. He kept pausing to smile, like they were old college buds catching up over some brews.

Charles flashed to his early days with Sally, when Beth trotted off on weekend business trips and he rushed over to indulge in guilty sleep-ins with his young lover, only to discover Sally sobbing in the bathroom late at night, hysterical over her dead mother, an empty bottle of wine at her feet. Experiencing grief after losing a parent was to be expected, he knew that. But for how long? It seemed a bit extreme after eight months.

Charles struggled to pick the right words. "Sally, she's had some struggles. But she's always pulled through."

"And would you say she's been a good mother?" Jameson asked.

His answer was a resounding *yes.* Morgan had changed Sally for the better. He saw the way she read story after story to him at bedtime, on the random nights he was home. How she rushed to his room to soothe him during his middle-of-the-night wakings, refusing to try the cry-it-out sleep-training method. She even taught Charles how to rephrase words to be more aligned with the gentle parenting movement—"Don't say 'no, you can't have that.' Instead, offer an alternative he can have."

Where would he be now without Sally, without their precious family?

"No signs of violence? Yelling? Falling apart?" Jameson tried to expose the flaws in Sally, some glaring sign that she'd unraveled, become unhinged.

No, Charles had never seen her yell or snap or even raise her voice. Cry, yes. Scream? *Never.*

"Would you say Sally's been overwhelmed lately?"

She had that frazzled, exasperated look on Friday, when he arrived home from work. Maybe Morgan had another epic meltdown, causing Sally to take reprieve in the bathroom? He'd found her in there once, trembling behind the shower curtain while Morgan watched *Sesame Street* in the living room by himself. She said she needed a break, a moment to compose herself.

The more Charles talked, the worse he seemed to make it. "Do we need to get lawyers here?" he asked at one point. As if on cue, the detective smiled with a light-hearted, breezy chuckle.

"Don't worry," Jameson said. "Nobody's being accused of anything."— *Yet.*

Next came the worst part, the questions about his time with Morgan: "So, you got home at 11:15 and Sally just after midnight." Jameson stroked his chin, deep in thought. "That gave you about forty-five minutes with Morgan. Alone."

Charles now paced the bathroom, watching the tremors in his hands, his breathing sporadic. What did he tell the detective? He had watched *Lost,* drank the rest of the merlot, ate a blueberry muffin, loaded the dishwasher. "I swear, this happened under Alyssa's watch!" But without an alibi, a proper witness, the detective and social worker's eyes simply narrowed in suspicion.

They finished "the interview" by informing him they needed to do a house visit, to assess the safety of Morgan's living environment.

"Just to check for problematic areas," the social worker explained, "such as easily accessible swimming pools, unlocked doors to the basement, stuff like that."

"We don't have a pool."

She ignored him, scrolling through her phone's calendar with an optimistic smile, as if they were making a date to have coffee and waffles. "I drive past your place on my way home so can do later today, around five o'clock?"

He shuddered at the thought of the two of them prying into closets, snooping under beds, judging their stained carpet. At least Sally had done all that crazy cleaning this past weekend. But what about Mr. Moops? He'd forgotten to leave out any cat food. "Sure, five today. I'll be there." Did he have a choice?

Before they released him, he managed to ask what would happen if Alyssa refused to confess. "You're left blaming us, right?"

Jameson let loose a shallow cough while Flynn rearranged her bracelet. She explained that her job was to ensure that Morgan received proper care and attention. If they discovered sufficient evidence that they weren't safe parents, he'd be removed from the home, with requirements such as supervised visits and mandatory parenting classes. "In the meantime, it's worth contacting a relative to act as a temporary safety provider," she said. "That way Morgan can go home after the doctors are finished monitoring him. As long as we approve of the home environment." And with that, Jameson clicked off the recorder.

Now Charles was shaking his head at the unfairness of the situation. *But we didn't do anything wrong!* The fury erupted as he slammed his fist into the bathroom wall. "It was the babysitter!" he shouted, continuing to pound the wall. "It was the goddamned babysitter."

He stopped and unclenched his fist. His fingers seared with pain. His knuckles were splattered with bruises.

✦

He hurried back to Morgan's room, desperate to hug Sally. Together, they'd take Alyssa down.

Morgan sat on the floor beside Lucy, watching her stack neon-colored blocks into a teetering tower.

"Where's Sally?" Charles asked.

"She went for a walk," Lucy said, "to get some fresh air."

"She left Morgan alone?"

"No, I've been here the whole time."

"She couldn't wait until I got back?" Charles spun around, expecting it to be a prank, for Sally to jump out from behind the curtains.

"She seemed antsy. I told her I had things under control." Lucy smiled up at him. "I find it helps anxious parents, getting out in the sun."

Charles pulled out his phone.

"This room's reception is hit or miss. It sometimes works over by the window"—she nodded her head toward the streaming light— "but the lobby is your best bet."

"You're okay with him?"

"Of course!" She gave Morgan a little tickle. He looked mildly annoyed, clutching a bottle to his chest.

Charles stepped out, holding his phone in the air. Lucy was right—the signal didn't kick in until he was in the lobby. He tapped on Sally's picture and waited.

Voicemail. *Christ.* He shoved his phone into his back pocket. A weird knot formed in his gut, something gnawing away. Why would Sally decide to go for a walk *now?* Right in the middle of a child abuse investigation? But he'd gone outside to move the car so obviously they weren't on lockdown.

He walked to the vending machine and impatiently tapped his fingers on the window. Maybe a candy bar would help. Snickers. He shoved in his credit card.

Where the hell are you, Sally?

The candy wrapping crinkled in his hand as he took a bite. He glanced at his watch—3:08. When was Alyssa's interview? He hoped she'd quickly crack under the detective's pressure and they could leave this whole mess behind.

He returned to Morgan's room and waited. Waited for Sally to come back. Waited for more examinations. Waited for his mother to arrive, if she managed to catch a flight, armed with endless advice and judgment.

Charles shook his head. Never had he needed Sally more, the warmth of her body, her intoxicating scent—coconut, vanilla—her honey-sweet voice. "It's okay," she'd say. Or he'd say. Or they'd whisper together, embracing each other like their lives depended on it.

"Did you get a hold of her?" Lucy asked as he returned to the room.

"Yes," he lied. "She's outside, just as you said."

"I'm gonna run to the bathroom," Lucy said, rising to her feet.

"Yeah, sure."

Charles stared out the window, hoping to catch a glimpse of Sally lounging on the grass below, doing a bendy yoga pose, finding her inner calm, or indulging in an ice cream cone, chattering away to random strangers. Anything.

Christ, Sally.

He obsessively checked his phone again.

"Mama?" Morgan whispered.

"She'll be back soon," Charles said. He spotted the car keys on the counter, where he'd put them after moving the car. Without thinking, he scooped them up and shoved them to the bottom of Morgan's diaper bag. Just in case they questioned Sally's whereabouts. He needed an excuse ready: *She went to pick up my mother.*

He lowered himself next to Morgan and added a bright yellow block to the unsteady tower. "It's going to be okay," he said, pausing to lightly touch his son's cheek. "Mama's okay."

The tower crumbled, as if struck by an earthquake. Blocks scattered across the floor. Morgan didn't even flinch.

Chapter 21

Sally

Day six

Sally settled into a gray plastic chair at the Greyhound station, firmly holding her paper ticket. One and a half hours until departure. How long until Charles noticed she wasn't coming back?

He would never understand. All he desired in life was a happy family. He'd even recently brought up the idea of having more kids, on Morgan's first birthday at the end of July.

"We survived the first year," Charles had said. "Everyone says that's the hardest year of all."

"It hasn't been that bad," Sally lied, opening the cake box—a wide-grinned Elmo with fluffy red frosting.

"So, you ready to do it again?" His eyes twinkled with giddy anticipation.

"You really want another baby?" Sally watched as the cake crumbled under the knife, as thoughts of having friends—any semblance of a social life—flitted away.

"Of course," he said. Such certainty, such conviction. "Don't you?"

"Uh ... maybe?" Sally gulped at the thought of more restless nights, leaky nipples, those ugly, scraggly lines etched across her jiggly stomach. *Abs.* She used to have rock-hard abs, back when she spent every afternoon pounding the track at Northwest Guildford High. "But shouldn't we wait until Morgan's a little older? He just turned one." She held up the rainbow candle, which they'd blown out together, Morgan's exhale more like a mouse's squeak.

"Yeah, but my brother and I, we were close in age—only twenty months apart," Charles said. "We loved it. I don't want Morgan to grow up an only child. That's boring." He slid a slice of cake onto a Big Bird plate.

"But I grew up as an only child," Sally said. "And I turned out mostly okay." She remembered asking her mom about it when she was seven. She even wrote Santa asking if he could bring her a baby sister for Christmas: *I want her to have blond hair and blue eyes.* Her mom had shared a knowing glance with Gwen and simply said, "We'll see."

Instead, Santa brought cancer.

"Yeah, but it'll be great for Morgie to have a playmate," Charles said.

"So you're thinking maybe one more?"

"Or a few."

"A few?" Sally accidentally knocked over a stack of Cookie Monster napkins.

"Sure, why not? You're so young," Charles said. "Having a big family would be fun."

Fun? She reached down and crumpled the napkins in her hands.

Yes, of course she cherished the good moments with Morgan—when he babbled into an old paper towel roll, clanked measuring cups together like musical cymbals, or helped pop the bubble wrap, jerking with surprise at each *snap, pop.* She loved the sweet snuggles, and his endless obsession with *Green Eggs and Ham* (he insisted she read it to him at least five times a day). Sally clung desperately to those fleeting moments, when the screaming paused long enough for her to peacefully sip tea, or when he played quietly by himself, allowing her to tackle a few dishes, even vacuum up the layer of cat fuzz.

But several children? What if they were all screamers?

She couldn't remember what she'd said in response. Something like *I'll think about it.* Whatever she said, it made Charles smile.

Now, with an exhale, Sally looked around the Greyhound station. She didn't have to worry about more babies, not with this one-way ticket to Colorado. She originally picked California but then the pimply-faced boy in the ticket booth demanded ID. *Oh crap.* So, right on the spot, she devised a new plan to throw the authorities off her trail: Bus to Colorado, hitch to Cali. If anyone decided she was worth hunting down.

She knew Charles would mourn with despair—at first. He would probably cry. He loved her, or what he believed to be her. But once he learned the truth—*Wait, Sally did what?*—his sadness would turn to outrage.

Closing her eyes, she sank further into her seat. She needed to leave before the storm erupted.

✦

Sally dozed, snapping back to reality when she heard loud honks outside. Two buses halted, brakes screeching, inches away from crashing. A quick glance at her phone—thirty minutes to go. A mother dragged two kids by their wrists through the terminal, barking orders to sit in the row across from Sally. She slapped the older boy's hand. "Stop picking your nose!" The kid scowled, arms crossed.

Sally wanted to tell him, *At least you have a mom.*

This boy reminded her of that scrawny kid from second grade. Jimmy Roberts. His mom took off in the middle of the night. They all knew about dads who left, like Misty Gordan's father in kindergarten. But mothers? They were supposed to be forever.

"What kind of mother abandons her babies?" Sally's mother had said as they stared at the four disheveled Roberts kids lined along the curb, picking at scabs, their eyes sullen, dejected.

A year after that, Sally's second mother, Gwen, left.

And then, years later, Sally's own mother died.

Now, here she was. Abandoning her precious baby.

The truth stung: *Mothers aren't forever.*

✦

Sally couldn't believe she had managed to slip out of Morgan's hospital room without a glitch. Nobody tried to stop her, to hold her back. Of course, nobody knew she was planning on leaving for good.

Flynn's comment had pushed her over the edge: *We need to prevent it from happening again.* The plan, blaming Alyssa, was flawed because the real problem, the obvious threat, was Sally. Even if she managed to successfully get off the hook and avoid jail time, once they returned home there was one thing she knew for certain: Morgan was not safe.

I'm not a safe mother.

After the exhausting interrogation and her emergency bathroom break, Sally had dragged herself back to Morgan's hospital room, dreading what needed to happen. If she loved Morgan, and she did, she needed to protect him at all costs. Gnawing on a nail, she hugged Charles before Jameson took him to his interview, and then tried to unravel the logistics—the Greyhound station, the best bet for getting out of town, out of state. But dang, the walk in this heat? Brutal. And she couldn't use Uber, Charles would know, somehow. A taxi. Her insides shuddered again. The room's colors turned into a snowy blizzard. She gripped the crib's railing, taking slow, deep breaths.

"Why don't you take a walk? Get some fresh air?" Lucy suggested. "There's a nice flower garden next to the parking deck. The gardenias are just lovely this time of year."

"Great idea," Sally said. It was a sign from the universe: *Now is the time.*

She waited for the cramps to subside, scanning Morgan's room for her stuff. All she had was her purse.

Leaning over, she playfully tousled Morgan's hair. "I'll be back soon, okay?" She kept her voice steady, light. Like an ordinary mother, getting some fresh air.

She stood, headed toward the door. She fumbled with the handle, turning it right and left, but it refused to budge. She considered giving up—*you're making a mistake!*—when the door flung open, the bright hallway pulling her out like a strong magnet. The door slammed shut behind her.

Once a mother, now a ...

A failure? Deadbeat? Criminal?

A child abuser.

She clutched her purse to her chest, holding her breath, and walked straight for the elevator. She pressed the down arrow, the doors opened, and she stepped inside, letting it swallow her whole.

At the bottom, her face streaked with tears, she immediately pounded the number five. *He's my baby. My baby.* She couldn't just leave! She rode the elevator back up to the fifth floor, alone, counting the passing floor numbers. But just as the elevator dinged, she remembered Morgan's face—the slow fluttering of his eyelids, his head cocked to one side, his raspy gasps for air. She had it in her to shake her baby that hard. To break bones.

What if next time I don't stop?

✦

Her bus's departure time crept closer. No plan—just a lump of cash, minus the taxi fare and her bus ticket. She could buy a surfboard, let her hair go wild with dreadlocks, the fierce ocean smoothing away this painful past, like a hardened rock turning to dust. Or, she could get a job, attend nursing school, return in a few years, be a better mother. *In a few years?* Who was she kidding? She couldn't disappear from her son's life and expect to wiggle her way back in whenever it suited her. Just like giving a baby up for adoption, Morgan no longer belonged to her.

She stood, feeling lightheaded and dizzy once again, the room spinning too fast. Hunger? She wandered over to the vending machine, a crumpled bill in her hand, and eyed up the chips, her stomach a mix of nerves, a hint of the delirious hangover still lingering. She slid the dollar into the machine, punched a few numbers. Nothing happened. Slapping the smudged plastic wall, the chips wiggled, teasing her, refusing to fall.

Maybe the CT scan would show nothing, no brain damage. Maybe she was overreacting. Maybe the broken rib was the only damage she'd caused. Broken bones, they could heal. They could mend.

But Flynn's voice returned: *Abuse like this usually isn't a one-time ordeal.*

Sally rested her head against the vending machine and pulled out her phone. She had silenced it and switched off the GPS after leaving the hospital. There were several missed calls from Charles. She clicked on the text messages.

Where are you?

Uh-oh. He knew. She braced herself for the slew of angry texts to follow: *How could you?* and *I hate you.*

But instead: **Everything will be okay.**

Really? She beat up their baby, lied about it, then left. How could life ever be okay again?

And finally: **I love you.**

Charles still believed in her. *For now.*

She numbly pressed her finger against her phone's power button, watching the screen flicker to black. Holding it over a nearby trash can, hovering, she squeezed her eyes shut. But she couldn't do it—it contained her only connection to Morgan, besides the picture frame in her purse. He might forget her, the sweet times annihilated from his long-term memory, but she couldn't bear to lose him, not entirely.

She tossed her phone into her purse and watched a bus driver outside flick his cigarette butt to the pavement, using his boot to squash out the flame. She pounded on the vending machine with clenched fists. "Give me my goddamned chips!"

Morgan would despise her for leaving. And then, eventually, he'd hear the full story: *She shook you, hard enough to break a rib.* Then he'd hate her even more. "My mother abused me, and then left. What a piece of shit." She took a deep breath and continued her attack on the vending machine.

The guy behind the ticket booth came to help.

"I'm just really hungry," she sobbed.

He unlocked the vending machine door and handed over the bag without a word.

She gobbled them down too quickly, almost choking. Then came a strong wave of nausea, followed by another. Gagging, she made it to the bathroom in time. Dancing silver-white stars clouded her vision.

Stabbing pains dug into her gut. Even her back throbbed. *Flush*—the heaved-up chunks disappeared. Looking down, she noticed her leggings, the entire crotch area, was soaking wet.

She fell to the floor, as if in slow motion. Or did someone help her down? But she never heard the door open. The tile felt cool, almost refreshing, against her flushed cheek.

Is Morgan going to be okay? Can I really leave?

The sharp pains began to subside. The world dimmed to dark. A chilling, desolate darkness. And then everything was still.

Chapter 22

Alyssa

Day six

Charles's text came at the worst time possible. Alyssa should've waited until after the exam to look. She should've stashed her phone in her backpack. But once she caught a glimpse of the word *hospital,* she couldn't resist reading the rest, her heart hammering away like a caged bird.

It happened at school, her aching brain sifting through the elements of the periodic table as she dragged herself down the hall. *Aluminum=Al, Magnesium=Mg.* Was she supposed to know the atomic number too?

She'd stayed up until 1:30, flipping through copious notes, googling terms she couldn't decipher, her mom bringing a steady stream of hot cocoa with mini marshmallows. Then she awoke at dawn to a clamber and crash outside. Their new neighbor—she still referred to him as Luke—was wrestling a recycling bin to the curb. He unlocked his car and tossed in that mysterious duffel bag. What was in there? Their eyes locked, briefly, before he sped away.

Now she stared at Charles's text, the hair on her arms prickling. The final sentence made her almost drop her phone: **You're not going to get away with this.**

Get away with what? Her fingers quivered as she typed: **What are you talking about?** But she didn't hit send. She stumbled through the crowd of students, a backpack knocking into her, a random elbow jabbing her rib. She ducked into the nearest bathroom. The last bell rang, the deafening sound clamoring in her ears as students stampeded down the hall. She imagined her classmates settling in, clicking mechanical pencils, wiping sweaty palms. Jess probably at home, feigning sickness. Alyssa was pissed at her for bailing on last night's study session and hadn't talked to her since.

Trembling, Alyssa unlocked her phone and tapped on her mom's number.

✦

All her mom had to say was "family emergency." Nobody pushed for details, not with Alyssa's tear-soaked face and her mom's wide-eyed expression. Mrs. Phillips, the principal, reassured Alyssa she could make up the exam later.

"Did he say what's wrong with Morgan?" her mom asked as they turned out of the high school's parking lot.

"No. Just that he's in the hospital." Alyssa tugged on her necklace. "Some kind of accident."

"And Morgan's dad, Charles—he said the *cops* are involved?"

"Yes. And there's more." Alyssa opened the thread. "*You're not going to get away with this.*"

"Jesus," her mom whispered. "Charles texted that?"

"Yes, Mom! He thinks I hurt Morgan. But how?" Alyssa stared at her mother. "Why would anyone purposely hurt Morgan?"

"It's gotta be a mistake."

"Try telling that to the cops," Alyssa said, watching as the trees whizzed by in flashes of swirling green and brown.

Inside their apartment, her mom latched the deadbolt. Alyssa dropped her backpack to the floor. Oh, how the chem exam would've been so much better than *this*.

"You saw no signs of anything?"

"Nothing obvious," Alyssa said, "except Morgan throwing up. I dunno, he kinda stared at me like he didn't recognize me."

"Do you think the parents could've hurt him?"

"They're super nice. I just can't imagine it."

"So weird." Her mom started banging pots and pans in the kitchen. "You hungry? I can heat up a can of soup. Chicken noodle?"

"No," Alyssa said, ignoring her rumbling stomach. She flopped on the couch, her mind reeling through every crime movie she'd ever seen: those two-way mirrors, a team of officers on the other side watching the suspect's every move. Would they hook her up to a lie detector?

"Here, drink some water." Her mom handed her a glass brimming with ice.

Alyssa took a long drag. The cold shot right to her brain.

"This whole thing is insane," her mom said. "You babysat Morgan on Friday. Today's Wednesday. Why would they blame you?" She paced the living room, unwrapping a silver-foiled stick of gum.

Alyssa's phone buzzed.

Jess: **u didn't show up to exam. u ok???**

Jess actually went? Wow. Alyssa wanted to forward Charles's most recent text, wait for Jess's shocked reaction: **WTF!** And then: **it must be drugs.** Instead, she pulled a hand-knitted blanket over her head.

"You need to change." Her mom yanked down the blanket. "Ripped jeans? You look like a rebel."

"Leave me alone."

"No," her mom snapped. "This isn't up for debate."

Alyssa watched her mom brush aside the window's curtain and peer out at the parking lot.

"Do you think the cops are coming *here*?" Alyssa asked.

"I don't know." She turned, the lines between her eyebrows deepening. "Go take out those pigtails, brush your hair. Just fix yourself up, okay?"

"*Fine,*" Alyssa groaned.

Inside her room, she struggled to button her floral dress. She ran a brush through her hair. Applied clear lip gloss. Slipped on her strappy tan sandals, the ones saved for special events, like Aunt Susan's wedding last summer. Sitting on her bed, hands neatly folded in her lap, she ignored her pounding headache and tried not to move in fear of wrinkling her dress.

✦

The detective called her mom at exactly 1:51 p.m. Alyssa stood in her bedroom's doorway, watching as her mom's face twisted with worry, her tone turning serious. "Yes, yes. I understand." A pause. "Actually, she's home from school already—yes, okay. Four o'clock. Do we need a lawyer or anything?"

A grim silence followed.

"Okay, we'll be there," her mom said, ending the call.

"Am I in trouble?" Alyssa asked.

"He made it seem like you'd be helping them out," her mom said. "Just some routine questions about the Haywoods."

"Huh." Alyssa sat on the couch. "Did he say what's wrong with Morgan?"

"No, he didn't give any details." She sighed, sitting next to Alyssa. "I just don't know about this."

"Mom, avoiding them will only make me look guilty," she said as a tight panic swelled inside her. "You know that."

✦

Alyssa's first experience with the police occurred at a young age, when she witnessed them grilling her dad on the front porch. This became a routine part of their lives, Alyssa timidly peering through the screen door, nervously waiting to see if they took her daddy away.

Then, as if following in his footsteps, she got busted for shoplifting when she was nine. The grocery store's security guard caught her, not an official cop, but still—he was tall and gruff and made her cry.

"Why were you stealing *shaving cream*?" her mom had asked afterward.

Alyssa knew enough to never mention her dad, even back then. She'd wanted to send something for his birthday, even though she didn't know where he lived. She had her heart set on a sparkly orange tie, her dad's favorite color, but Food Lion didn't have many options—nothing luxurious for forgotten fathers. She clung to a memory of him shaving, leaning into the foggy bathroom mirror, slathering white foam onto his face; a sweet, strong smell, his face buttery smooth afterward.

Now she inhaled the muggy afternoon air and stared at the reflective doors of the Oak Wood Police Station. This wasn't a stern scolding about the morality of stealing, shoving a bottle of shaving cream under her tank top, skipping out of the store as if nothing was amiss.

A little boy is in the hospital, she thought. *And Charles thinks I had something to do with it.* And what about Sally? What did she think?

A receptionist with frizzy hair ushered them to a stiff leather couch inside the lobby, and then brought them drinks—a Coke for Alyssa, coffee for her mom. Alyssa crossed her legs, the leather releasing a loud, smacking sound. Her mom fiddled with her keychain while blowing on her coffee.

A short man with a protruding gut approached them. He looked like a Santa employee, sans the white beard and velvet red suit. "Alyssa? I'm Detective Rodney Jameson."

Alyssa stood, shaking his hand. He had stubby, calloused fingers, like a hobbit hand.

"I'm Mandy—the mother."

"Thanks for coming down. We really appreciate it," he said.

"Are you sure we don't need a lawyer?" her mom asked.

"If you want a lawyer, that's fine," Jameson said with a heartwarming chuckle. "But we're not accusing Alyssa of anything. This is just to get her side of things. It shouldn't take long."

"Hmmm," her mom said, shifting her weight.

"Only guilty people need lawyers, Mom," Alyssa said, standing up straight.

"She's right," Jameson said, his eyes twinkling. "How about this: Mandy, you come down to the room with us. She doesn't have to answer any questions she doesn't feel comfortable answering, and you guys can leave any time."

"I think it sounds fine," Alyssa said.

"Great. Follow me."

Her mom seized her arm. "We can demand a lawyer, you know," she hissed.

"I just want this over," Alyssa whispered. "He seems nice. And besides, I didn't do anything."

Her mom inhaled sharply as they followed the detective. "You have to stay calm," she instructed. "Tell them everything from that night. You never know what'll help solve the case."

The case. *Who hurt Morgan Haywood?* It could be a movie. Or at least a miniseries on Netflix. Something she and Jess would binge watch, but only if it was happening to someone else.

"And don't look at your phone. Silence it. Now." Her mom spat on her fingers and smoothed down a flyaway wisp of Alyssa's hair.

"Maybe I should go in alone," Alyssa said, shying away from her mother's touch.

"What?"

"You're making me nervous. I'm already sweating!" She tugged at her itchy polyester dress.

"You can't handle this alone." Her mom peered into the room where the detective was already seated.

Alyssa crossed her arms. "Mom, I'm almost sixteen."

"You're still a minor."

"He hasn't accused me of anything."

"Not yet," her mom snipped.

"I think I'll be able to concentrate better if I'm by myself." She could see her mom, butting in after every question, trying to finish her sentences. Or shooting her looks, a disapproving shake of the head.

"No, I don't like this," her mom said, her lips tightly pursed.

"I'll stop if it seems like too much, okay?"

Her mom pulled her in for a suffocating hug. "Alyssa, this is a pretty big thing."

"He just said he's not accusing me of anything," she said. "It's fine. Really."

Her mom released her from her death grip, hands settling on her shoulders. "I swear, at times you act like you're the adult here, treating me like the ki—"

"I just want to help, okay?" Alyssa smoothed out her dress. "Morgan's in the *hospital*."

Her mom shook her head and stepped back. Alyssa took a deep breath and entered the interrogation room. By herself.

✦

The room looked like an exact replica of a movie set—a single table, two chairs, and a mirrored window, which had to be see-through.

She sat in her chair, sliding her phone under her thigh, and placed her Coke on the table, watching its condensation drip. She noticed subtle rings from previous drinks, scattered across the table like a sloppy geometry project.

Jameson asked for her info—full name, address, date of birth—and then cleared his throat. "So, you go to Oak Wood High?"

"Yes."

"Fifteen. A sophomore?"

"Junior. I skipped first grade."

His bushy eyebrows arched. "Impressive. You must be super smart."

"I guess." She always hated the attention this elicited, the way her kindergarten teachers proclaimed her a genius after finding her plowing through chapter books and memorizing the multiplication table.

"My daughter," Jameson continued, "she's a senior there. Heather Jameson. You know her?"

"No, I don't think so."

"She's into athletics, soccer. What's your favorite subject?"

"Uh, chemistry." Why'd she say that? She was practically failing that class.

"Oh wow. Cool. You want to be a scientist or something?"

"A doctor."

"Ah. What field?"

"I don't know yet." She traced her finger along the faded rings on the table. "Maybe pediatrics?"

He studied her quizzically before slowly nodding. "All right then, let's start from the beginning." He interlaced his fingers behind his head, leaning back. "When did you start working for the Haywood family?"

"About six months ago, in March," Alyssa began. "But, um, can you tell me what happened to Morgan? Is he okay?"

"He has a fractured rib and a possible concussion."

"What? His *rib?* A concussion? But ... I held him. He didn't even scream." She shook her head. "Wouldn't he have screamed if ... I mean, I checked him over after—"

"After what?"

"After ... he threw up. I ... I made sure he was okay."

Did I hold him too tightly?

"We're trying to understand what happened," Jameson said. "Please, tell me about last Friday, September 7, while you were there."

Alyssa stared down at her Coke, willing herself not to look at the mirror. One glance and someone on the other side would proclaim: *Guilty. Totally guilty*! "I texted both Charles and Sally, right after Morgan was sick." Surely they had access to the phone records, right?

"Did you notice anything unusual about Morgan's behavior?"

"Uh, yeah. He definitely wasn't his usual self," Alyssa said. "Like, he seemed *really* out of it. Quiet. Like he didn't recognize me. But I thought it was ... well ... he was sick. 'Probably a little bug'—that's what Sally said. And not to wake him, that he'd had a rough day."

"A rough day?" His eyes flickered with interest. "She said that?"

"Yes."

Jameson flipped open his notepad, scribbling like mad. He looked up. "Did you use the changing table?"

"You mean when I changed his diaper?"

"Yes."

"Of course." She methodically rubbed the slick pony pendant around her neck.

"Did you strap him in?"

"What? Um, no, but I was like, uh, standing there the whole time." She looked directly at the detective. "I didn't let him fall, I swear."

"Do you have any history of mental illness? Substance abuse? Alcohol?"

Alyssa froze. Maybe Charles and Sally noticed the red drops in the Big Bird cup? She only drank half a cup but stupidly didn't rinse it out. That's something they'd tell the cops: "She's only fifteen and was *drinking.*" It was too late to test her blood level. She jerked up straight. "No."

Jameson's eyes narrowed in. No good would come of admitting to the wine. *It was just a few sips.* Alyssa kept her eyes locked on his, willing herself not to blink, like a ruthless staring contest. He finally nodded, taking a long, sustained glug from his coffee. He wiped his mustache with the back of his hand, then asked about Sally and Charles as parents. She told him she'd never seen them yell, shout, or bicker, not even raise a voice. "I've always liked them," she added.

"How were they this past Friday?"

"Sally seemed a bit high strung, I guess. She looked like she'd been crying. Charles ... he seemed the same as always, I guess." She took a sip of Coke, the fizz burning her throat. Should she mention the frenetic way Sally searched for her keys? Was that really a clue? Her own mother turned into a similar tornado when getting ready for work. What about Sally's alcohol breath? No, that would bring the topic back to her own drinking.

"Have you ever noticed any unexplained bruises on Morgan in the past?"

"No."

"And the state of the house? Does it seem like a safe environment?"

"It's messy, clutter everywhere. And in the basement, there was a—" But what if the playpen wasn't there anymore? "Never mind," she said, playing with the tab on her Coke can, bending it back and forth.

"What was in the basement?"

She glanced at the mirror, she couldn't help herself. She saw herself staring back, the color drained from her face.

"It's confidential, what we discuss here." His voice remained soothing, reassuring. She liked him, and yet she doubted him. What if Sally and Charles were standing behind that window, listening to every word? She felt sick.

"I once found a playpen set up down there, with Morgan's favorite doll, Elmo. And a bottle of milk. It was like Sally—*or Charles?*—kept him down there. And, well, a gun. Charles's hunting rifle. That was back in March, I think, so, yeah, I dunno ..." She exhaled. What if they said she was making it all up?

"Hey, Alyssa," Jameson said. His round eyes gleamed. "It's okay. You're doing a great job."

She nodded, another quick glance at the foreboding mirror.

"The social worker's doing a house visit later. I'll make sure she checks the basement."

"What's going to happen?" Alyssa asked.

"What do you mean?"

"Is Morgan going to be okay?" She crinkled the Coke can in her hands. "From the injuries?"

"Unfortunately, we can't share those details with you."

"Is Sally or Charles ... or whoever did this ..." She swallowed. "Are they going to jail? Even if it was just an accident?"

"You don't have to worry about that."

Alyssa tugged on the hem of her dress. Hopefully they'd find the playpen behind the tower of boxes—open, with a bottle of milk, a clear sign of negligence. Case closed. But what if they found absolutely nothing? Who was going to believe her against Morgan's own parents? At least the detective seemed to be on her side, for now. But if they *did* accuse Sally or Charles, then Morgan would lose a parent. Or both parents.

"I know this is a difficult situation, Alyssa. I really appreciate you helping out." Jameson pushed a notepad and pen toward her, asking for references: past babysitting jobs, teachers, anyone who could attest to her maturity and responsibility. "We're also going to need your mother's consent to run a background check."

"But why?" She reluctantly took the pen. "Does this mean I'm a suspect?"

Jameson laughed, as if it was such an absurd thing to say. "Don't worry. It's just a formality, really."

Would that shoplifting experience show up? She was nine!

Jameson pushed his chair back and stood. He smiled down at her, like a warm-hearted Santa pretending to be a hard-ass detective. "You really did a good job. Do you need another Coke?"

"Uh, sure." He left and she sat alone, even though she knew she wasn't alone—eyes peered in on her, still. She could feel it. She knew from the crime shows. Looking for any sign, any action that proved her guilt. *The abusive babysitter.* She stared at the blinking red light in the corner, recording her every move, each bead of sweat.

Someone had hurt Morgan with enough force to break a rib. To hurt his brain.

She pressed her palms together, resting her forehead on her fingertips—*Please help me. Please help Morgan.* This wasn't happening. She couldn't get blamed for this. Not after she'd worked so hard to claw her way to the top of her class, the counselor reassuring her that a promising future lay ahead. What would her mom do if she failed?

She couldn't hold back any longer. Hot, burning tears spilled down her cheeks as she shook with fear and disbelief.

✦

Another officer escorted Alyssa to the lobby and she saw her mom animatedly talking to someone. Stepping closer, Alyssa realized who it was. *Luke.* She'd captured at least a dozen pictures of him on her phone—next to his Prius, the streetlight silhouetting his muscular figure, the ever-present duffel bag. She blinked. Now here he was, *laughing* with her mom.

"Oh, sweetie!" Her mom turned toward her. "Are you okay? What did they say?"

Alyssa stared at Luke, trying to connect the dots.

"Hello, Alyssa," he said, extending his hand. "I'm Simon."

"Can you believe our downstairs neighbor is a detective?" her mom said.

A detective? That explained the middle-of-the-night excursions. The black duffel bag—probably filled with a bulletproof vest, holster, guns, bullets. What a small town. Too small. Luckily, he wasn't assigned to her case. *Why do you have pictures of your detective on your phone?* Try explaining that.

"Hi," Alyssa said, coldly.

"Listen," Simon said to her mom. "Take my card. If you run into any issues, call me." He pulled out a pen. "This is my personal cell."

What a sly way to give his number. He lived right below them, he could just bang out a message with a broom, tapping out his lusty feelings via Morse code. Her mom wouldn't have a clue, though. She'd be like, *What the hell? Why's our neighbor making such a ruckus?*

"Oh, sure. Thanks," her mom said, tentatively grabbing his card.

Simon. What a weak, pathetic name. "Can we go now?" Alyssa asked.

"Are they finished with everything?" Her mom tossed her Styrofoam cup into a nearby trash can.

"Yes. I'm innocent until proven guilty. Let's go." Alyssa headed for the door.

"It was great finally meeting you," Simon shouted after them. To her? Or her mom?

✦

At the car, her mom stopped. "I'm sorry."

"Whatever. You were busy flirting up a storm while I was being interrogated for a crime I didn't commit." Alyssa slid into her seat.

"Honey, I wasn't flirting. I explained the situation and he offered to help. He knows people."

"You're telling everyone I've been accused of child abuse?" Alyssa scoffed. "Great."

"He's our neighbor," her mother said, turning on the car.

"You know that everything you told him can be used against me?"

"No, Alyssa. That's not how it works."

"How do you know how it works?" Alyssa snapped. "Besides, I was the one who wanted to meet Lu—I mean, Simon. To make him muffins. But *you* resisted, you thought he was a serial killer. Remember?"

"He knows a good lawyer, if it gets to that. I trust him."

"I don't need a lawyer." She wanted to add: *I said too much. If they lock Charles and Sally up, it's all my fault.*

"What do you need? We can go to Denny's, get pancakes ... No? Okay. What did that Jameson guy say? I should've gone in with you. Were you scared?"

Alyssa stayed quiet.

"I'm sorry," her mom repeated. "I just—"

"Mom, stop," Alyssa said. "Morgan's in the hospital with a broken rib and a possible concussion. That's how bad this is."

"What? A broken rib?" Her mom choked on the words. "But—*how?*"

"Someone must've ... I dunno ..." Alyssa leaned against the window, praying for this day to end. Wishing she'd never babysat last Friday night.

✦

Back at home, Alyssa locked herself in her room. She blasted Justin Timberlake's "Say Something" to drown out her mother.

Jess texted: **u ignoring meeeee?????**

How to even begin? She flipped over her phone, as if that'd make this whole messed-up situation disappear.

Sitting perched at the bay window, she tugged on her fuzzy, rainbow-striped socks. She stroked Snoozy, a worn stuffed turtle from her dad, and went over every detail from Friday night.

A broken rib and a possible concussion.

As the sun started to fade, the ominous rays turning to lava red, she waited for a rush of cop cars to surround their apartment complex with flashing lights and deafening sirens—Simon heroically leading the team. Of course, he would; her fantasy crush disappearing in a tragic plot twist. Because, in the end, who was going to believe the teenage babysitter? Jameson's good-natured attitude now seemed like a big act—*You're doing a great job.* Yeah, right. He wanted her to relax, to let down her guard. She'd seen enough crime shows on Netflix. She should've known better.

She dragged the ends of her hair through her grinding teeth, trying to remember exactly what she'd told him and if it would be enough to implicate her.

She wrote in her journal:

I'm innocent. I didn't do anything wrong. I didn't hurt Morgan. But innocent people get locked away. It happens all the time.

Chapter 23

Charles

Day six

Charles fumbled with the key, unlocking the door to their house.

"Detective Jameson will be along shortly," the social worker said as she pushed past him.

"So, do I just come in? Or wait out here?" He didn't know if his presence would taint the results. "I really need to check on the cat."

"Yes, come in." She paused to survey their living room. "Just keep everything as it is. I'm going to take some pictures."

"Got it." He stepped inside and gently closed the door.

"Sally's back at the hospital with Morgan?" She switched her phone to camera mode.

He assumed the hospital staff kept her briefed. But no one at the hospital even registered that Sally hadn't returned.

"Yes," he cautiously replied.

Flynn nodded, seemingly satisfied by his answer.

Taking a deep breath, Charles walked into the kitchen. He cracked open a tin of cat food for Mr. Moops. The noise lured the cat from his hiding spot under the couch.

"Has your cat always had a limp?" Flynn asked, crouching to take his picture.

"Uh, well ..." Charles watched as Mr. Moops gingerly approached his bowl, his right front paw tucked under his body. "He's always been overweight and sluggish but he's due for a check-up at the vet soon so ..."

Flynn didn't respond.

"Coffee?" Charles asked as he turned on the machine. Flynn moved swiftly, snapping pictures of the TV, the kitchen table, Morgan's high-chair, even the expired contents of their fridge. Pausing only to tuck a strand of sleek hair behind an ear.

"I'm fine, thanks." Her voice rigid, like those automated bank robots. "Can you explain these scuff marks on the floor?"

He squinted to where she was pointing, then, kneeling, he ran his hands over the cluster of black marks on their linoleum floor.

"What the—?"

Flynn leaned over and snapped a picture, before shaking her head and heading down the hall. She asked him to unlock the third bedroom.

"We keep it locked because there's financial documents, credit cards, the title to the car," Charles said, even though she hadn't asked. He pressed in the key. "Wouldn't want a babysitter snooping in there to ... you know ..."

She never made eye contact. Charles despised everything about her: the expressionless face, the curt tone, the way she held their son's fragile future in her hands—one simple declaration and Morgan would be whisked away to foster care.

He dragged himself back to the kitchen and studied the mysterious scuff marks again. Could it have been the babysitter? Did she drop something? He shook his head and rubbed his eyes. The coffee brewed. Just last Friday morning, Morgan's cheerful laughter had permeated their breakfast, inquisitive eyes exploring the room, a seemingly ordinary day ahead. And yet, Charles hadn't appreciated it; he'd failed to pause, to fully soak in the gratifying joy of a normal life.

What the hell happened that day?

After filling his mug, he sat at the table and wrote his boss a quick email—he needed another day off. He checked his texts, something from Danny, his older brother in LA: **Mom says Morgan was abused?!? Call me.**

His heart constricted, his sore hand pulsating from when he'd slammed his fist into the bathroom wall. Who else was his mom blabbing to?

He noticed a missed call from her, which probably didn't ring due to the hospital's poor reception. He listened to the voice message, but the words were garbled and distorted, as if she were driving through a tunnel. He tried calling, no answer, then shot her a text even though he knew she didn't like texting: **What's going on?**

And still, nothing from Sally. She'd left, supposedly for a dose of fresh air, during his interview at two o'clock. Relax, he told himself. That was just a few hours ago; she could still be out blowing off steam.

He opened his pictures to distract himself and scrolled to a few weekends ago, their family trip to Flowers Park. He stopped on Sally, her hair golden and goddess-like under the sun's radiance, those almond eyes—exotic, sexy. Glossy pink lips puckered like a model. Morgan nestled on her lap, devouring a mint chocolate chip ice cream cone, chubby fingers coated with stickiness. His heart melted at the image.

"I need to head down to the basement."

Charles's head snapped up. Flynn hovered a few feet away, eyes glued to her phone. "The basement?" he asked. "But Morgan never goes down there."

"It's in my instructions."

"Oh, okay." He stood. "Do you need me to … are you okay by yourself?"

"Jameson is supposed to be here by now. Just wait up here."

"Alrighty." He busied himself with unloading the dishwasher. Waiting. Always waiting. Morgan's CT scan was scheduled for tomorrow morning. The doctors continued to voice their concerns about possible brain trauma: "His overall vitals are good, but he has some verbal and visual impairment, possible reduced brain processing. We want to be very thorough."

Charles had clenched his fists at the update, ready to fire off questions: *What did Alyssa do to him? When can Morgan go home? Is he going to be okay?* But he worried what they would ask in return, such as, *Where is Sally right now?* They already thought the worst about her.

"Charles?" Flynn's voice floated up.

"Yes?" He met her at the basement door.

"I thought you said Morgan never goes down here."

"That's right."

"Then why is there a playpen?" she asked, out of breath from climbing the steps.

"What? Oh, that. I think, well, Sally meant to donate it. I guess she forgot."

"But it's set up inside the storage closet. With a sheet. And *this*." She held up a bottle of crusted, coagulated milk.

"What? The closet?"

"It's one thing to use a playpen down there. But in a storage closet with no ventilation and a stack of cleaning supplies? What if Morgan had climbed out?" She tapped on her phone and pressed it to her ear. "Excuse me, I need to see what's the hold up with Detective Jameson."

The storage closet? He bounded down the steps and sure enough, the playpen was crammed next to brooms and a moldy mop, a bottle of bleach tipped over. He'd seen the playpen before, behind a stack of boxes, but had barely registered it amid the clutter of other unused items. Now, in the dim light, he slowly approached it, as if it caged a feral animal.

Flynn was right, there was a sheet inside. He reached over, feeling a groove from someone snuggling within. His hand quivered as he yanked it back. Did Sally really put Morgan down here and close the door?

Above he could hear a car pulling up, then a door slamming. Charles frantically searched the basement; he needed a place to hide. To duck behind the freezer, to pretend this wasn't his life. Wake up when it was over.

No, he needed to face the truth. At the steps, he glanced back once more. The playpen. The dingy, lonely basement. The thought creeping in: *Do I even know Sally at all?*

But by the time he reached the top of the steps, he'd changed his mind. Sally would never resort to this. Maybe putting Morgan in his crib, stepping outside for a breather during one of his manic episodes—that seemed believable. But dragging a howling Morgan down to the basement and locking him up in the closet?

Hell no.

Flynn and Jameson were waiting for him in the kitchen.

"I've never seen that set up before," Charles said. The words just trickled off his tongue.

"Excuse me?" Jameson asked, setting his Starbucks cup on the counter. He pulled a notepad from his breast pocket.

"*Sally* didn't put that playpen in the closet," Charles corrected himself. "It must've been Alyssa."

Jameson and Flynn looked at each other, eyebrows arched.

"Let's sit down." Jameson jerked his head toward the table.

Charles nodded in compliance.

"Now, do you think Morgan is capable of climbing out of that playpen?" Jameson asked.

"Maybe," Charles began, trying to make sense of it. "Morgan recently started crawling up on everything, pulling himself onto the couch. He even tried to stand in the baby swing, the one out back. So, yes, it's possible he could've climbed out of it."

Jameson scratched his chin, a quick glance at the glass sliding door. "You swear you never saw the playpen set up? You guys never used it?"

The cat clawed at Charles's ankle. He discreetly tried to push him away. "We never used it. Maybe Sally couldn't figure out how to collapse it? But we definitely didn't move it to the closet."

"So, you think the babysitter—Alyssa—put Morgan in the basement? In the closet?" The detective's eyes bore into Charles. "Why would she do that?"

"I don't know." Charles paused. His left eye itched but he didn't dare scratch it. "Maybe Morgan was crying too much? He has a history of these long crying spells. Alyssa probably got overwhelmed, couldn't handle it. Maybe she set up the playpen, put him in the basement so she could have a break." His lungs tightened as he plowed on. "Then, perhaps, Morgan climbed out? Fell right onto the hard concrete."

"Or tried to climb the stairs," Jameson added.

"Yeah, maybe ... if the closet door wasn't latched." He could see it. Morgan possessed a surprising strength, a stubborn will. He wouldn't have tolerated being trapped in the basement, not for long. And if the door had been latched shut? He felt sick at the thought, his son rummaging through bottles of toxic cleaning supplies in the dark. Who would leave him alone like that?

"Morgan hurting himself in the basement is a plausible explanation. One of a few," Jameson said as he exchanged another glance with the social worker. Flynn's mouth twisted, but she remained silent.

"However, there's no knowing if it was under Sally's or Alyssa's watch," Jameson continued, closing his notebook. "We're going to need to look into this further."

"Okay," Charles said, tapping his fingers against his coffee mug. Flynn's eyes shot down to his bruised knuckles. He immediately dropped his hands to his lap, wringing them under the table. "I should really get back to Morgan. Unless you have more questions—"

"No, we're done here." Jameson stood, sliding the notepad into his chest pocket. "Please tell Sally we'll need to ask her some more questions. It's getting late now so how about tomorrow morning?"

"Oh. Morgan's CT scan is at ten a.m."

Jameson nodded. "Let's plan on after lunch then. How about two?"

"Two. Got it. Yes." Charles cleared his throat. "And um, what about Alyssa? Have you guys talked to her yet?"

"Don't worry," Jameson said as he opened the front door. "We're going to do a thorough investigation here."

Flynn stopped. "Before we go, we need to lock up that hunting rifle in the basement. It's a risk for everyone, especially with Morgan climbing stuff. And you have underage babysitters going down there."

Charles's muscles stiffened. "I—yes, of course." He wanted to add: *Please don't take Morgan away from us.*

"Let me grab a gun lock from my car. I can handle this," Flynn said to Jameson. He shot Charles a stone-cold look before brusquely turning to leave.

✦

After securing the rifle out of sight, Flynn left with a curt goodbye. Charles locked the door behind her. He leaned his head against it, breathing hard. Then, like a bolt of lightning, he flew down the hall to their extra room. The office/Sally's Etsy project-craft-exercise space. He wrenched open the drawer to his rickety desk and found it—the card from Joyce. A private investigator: *the best.* It was meant to expose Beth. But now, studying the number, he wondered how far he'd go to get Sally back.

If, in fact, she was truly gone.

Chapter 24

Sally

Day six

Sally awoke in a pool of blood. Dark, red, sticky blood. She last remembered seeing her leggings soaking wet, then collapsing to the floor. The Greyhound station.

"Oh God."

Switching to autopilot, she yanked wads of toilet paper off the roll, sopped up the mess, dabbed at the blood on her purse, then frantically dug inside—the money, the money! Whew, it was still there. Had anyone even noticed her sprawled out in here?

The time. What was the time? She fumbled through her purse again, trying to remember what happened to her phone.

A swirl of pain caused her to double over. She yanked down her leggings, dropped onto the seat, listened to a whooshing sound. More blood? Yes, more blood.

Breathe.

There at her feet sat the remains of her Greyhound ticket, blood-soaked and turning to pulp.

"Help," she cried out weakly. Shaking, she continued digging through her purse and pulled out the social worker's creased card. *We never want to separate children from their mothers. Call anytime, day or night.*

No, Sally told herself. That woman was not on her side. And yet, she didn't know why, she shoved the card back into her purse. Her fingers then found the shape of her phone. Who to call? Charles? A cab? Maybe go back to the motel?

But look at that blood.

"Help," she whispered again. The tears dripped onto her phone, her hands trembled. She swiped at the wetness, struggling to turn the damn thing on. The time glowed 4:44—one minute before her bus's scheduled departure. She tried standing, but her muscles locked up. A series of beeps came through, more texts from Charles. She couldn't bring herself to read them. An email notification from her chem teacher—an upcoming quiz this Friday. Shaking her head, she held the delete button, watching the message vanish. Talk about a waste of money. Then she noticed a flashing voicemail, from Charles's mother, Nancy. What did she want?

"Hey, Sal, I'm going to board soon. I can't get a hold of Charles. Arrival time is 7:06. Should I rent a car? Call me."

Wait, she was coming here? Sally tried to click out of voicemail but somehow hit the *call* button.

"No! No, no, no." She frantically pushed every button. The keypad froze; the call kept ringing.

"Hello?" Nancy answered, bright and alert.

Sally sighed, putting the phone to her ear. "I ... I'm sorry. You're at the airport?"

"Oh Sally!" Nancy exclaimed. "I've been trying to reach you guys. Yes, I'm at Bradley. We're about to take off. Can you guys pick me up? Or I can rent a car."

Sally chewed on a nail, then remembered the blood. Shuddering, she pulled her hand away.

"So, what do you think?" Nancy asked. "I can grab dinner, too. What's that pizza place you like? Mellow Mushroom? I know how disgusting hospital food can be."

"Oh, um ..." Sally took a sharp inhale, the room spiraling again, darkness closing in.

"Sally?"

"Yes, I'm here," she whispered.

"Are you okay?"

"Uh, no," Sally said, meekly. "I think I need help."

"Okay. Are you at the hospital?" Her voice sounded so composed, so calm. Did she even know the extent of what was going on?

Sally wanted to beg, *come help help help meeee.* Oh, to have Nancy's arms take her in, smooth back her damp hair, reassure her that everything was fine. But no, she couldn't tell her anything. Nancy would drag her directly to the nearest hospital, like any concerned person would do. And then the repulsive detective, the snooty social worker, and poor, innocent Charles—they'd all come to ask questions. More questions, endless questions.

"I need to go," Sally murmured. *The plan. The bus. Colorado. California.* "They're at the hospital, Oak Wood Hospital." She pushed the red button to end the call. It worked. Silence.

Nancy called back. Again. And again. Sally slipped her phone into her purse. Stood up. The toilet flushed automatically, causing her to jump. She rummaged through her purse, found an emergency tampon, ripped off the wrapper with her teeth and inserted it.

She made it out of the stall. Washed her bloody hands. Took a rattled breath. Studied her reflection in the mirror, the bruise across her cheek. She remembered the sickening *smack* sound, her face hitting the floor. Clenching her teeth, she smoothed back her hair with splashes of water. Holding the wall, she inched along, pausing before pulling the door open.

Chapter 25

Mandy

Day six

Mandy paced outside Alyssa's locked door, offering bribes: *Dinner out? Your favorite movie? Ice cream sundaes?*

Alyssa cranked the music louder.

Mandy gave up. What terrible timing, earlier today at the police station with Simon—laughing about that kooky lady from their complex, the one who wore duct-taped flip-flops, no matter the weather, walking a dozen writhing, hissing cats on leashes. Simon seemed to have a knack for calming Mandy's agitation with humor. But *that* was the moment Alyssa was released from her interview. Mandy berated herself for not pushing harder to go in with her.

Defeated, she headed into the kitchen. She loaded the dishwasher, watered the plants, and scanned the refrigerator for a dinner plan. Blowing out a gust of air, she stood and closed the door. An idea suddenly came to her and she couldn't drop it.

Grabbing her keys, Mandy shouted over the deafening beats and blaring lyrics: "I'm going to pick up a pizza!"

Simon had advised her against this, confronting Charles. *Don't,* he'd said. *It'll make things worse.* She ignored his warning, her car whizzing across town to Oak Wood Hospital.

Simon's words still troubled her: *These things happen all the time.*

"What?" she had asked him. "Babysitters getting accused of hurting children?"

"Babysitters getting caught up in ..." He scanned the police station lobby, stepping in closer. "It's an easy out for parents. To blame someone else."

In this case, the someone else happened to be her daughter.

"You're wise to be worried," Simon added.

And now Alyssa was shutting her out, not sharing the intricate details from the detective's interview. Were they treating her like a suspect? Her daughter had always been strong-willed and fiercely independent, even from an early age. But God, Mandy thought, I'm still her mother.

What was I thinking, letting her deal with this on her own?

She barely knew Charles, yet she knew him. She saw the way his face lit up when he talked about Morgan. That left, who? The mother? But what kind of mother breaks her baby's ribs?

Alyssa still didn't know Mandy worked with Charles. Or *had* worked with him—surely she'd be booted out after this. Unless she successfully patched things up, convinced Charles to stop blaming her daughter. Did Charles even know Alyssa was her daughter? If so, he didn't reach out to her.

But then again, why would he?

✦

The doors swooshed open to Oak Wood Hospital. Mandy gulped as she stepped inside. Hospitals made her jittery, the memories of losing Zack slamming into her, making her claw desperately at the past, wishing she could've done something differently.

She had tried to hide her second pregnancy from her crazed husband, after he demanded an abortion. But Ian wasn't foolish—he figured out soon enough that she'd skipped the appointment. At first he conceded, helping repaint Alyssa's old crib powder blue with little, dotted white clouds. *For our son.*

But then Mandy came home one afternoon to find the crib shattered, a hammer lying in the middle of the rubble.

"It's either him or me," Ian demanded. "You can't have us both."

"What do you expect me to do?" Mandy cried, rubbing her beach-ball sized belly. "Ditch him in a dumpster?"

"We can't afford another child," Ian said. "There are plenty of people who want a baby."

"I can't give away our *baby*. We'll find a way," Mandy pleaded. "We can move in with my parents, back in Illinois."

"To Buffalo Grove?" he spat. "You gotta be kidding."

"But we'd be close to Chicago, to the music scene. Your music career could boom."

"My music career is over." The unspoken part: *Thanks to you and Alyssa.*

And so it went, their fights spanning hours, days, weeks. Why did she stay? Well, on that particular day, she didn't. She waited until Ian passed out in his recliner, then drove straight through the night to her parent's house. *Where's Daddy?* Alyssa asked from the back seat, weary-eyed and distressed. *It's okay, sweetie. He's staying home to watch over the house.*

They had six peaceful days before Mandy's body seized, amniotic fluid gushing onto her parents' porcelain-tiled floor. She delivered her son at twenty-eight weeks, and he lived for three days, hooked up to a spider web of tubes.

Zack.

It took time, but Ian came crawling back. He always did. "I'm sorry. I'm taking my meds now. I'm ready for us to start over."

Mandy tried to push him away—*Lies! Lies! Lies!*—but he was relentless.

"It does look like he's stabilized," her dad said.

"It's amazing what those medications can do, isn't it?" her mom chimed in.

Mandy agreed to give it another shot. She believed Ian; or, more like she *wanted* to believe him. It took another three and a half years to realize she was headed down a one-way tunnel, with a train barreling directly at them.

An announcement blared over the hospital's speaker: Visiting hours for non-family members were ending in thirty minutes, at 7:30 p.m. Mandy shook her head to break the trance; the way Zack appeared during times of crisis, like a grenade—one little flick and her insides exploded. Her fingers rubbed together, trying to conjure a cigarette. *Stay strong.*

She rode the elevator to the children's unit on the fifth floor and approached the check-in desk. She knew they wouldn't easily give out Morgan's details—not with a suspected child abuse case. She decided to take her chances.

"I'm here to see Charles Haywood," she explained. "He's with his son, Morgan Haywood."

"Your name?"

"Mandy." She paused. "A co-worker."

"Go ahead and sign in." The nurse nodded down to the register. "I'll see if someone answers the phone."

Mandy filled out her details. But then she felt an unsettling chill. Charles had sent those vengeful texts to Alyssa. Why would he want to see the suspect's mother? Go home, she commanded herself. Tend to Alyssa, even if she's refusing to talk. She's in shock.

"Mandy?"

She looked. Charles stood in the hallway—dark circles under his eyes, hair ruffled.

"What are you doing here?" he asked.

Without thinking, she rushed toward him and pulled him in for a hug. "Are you okay? How's Morgan?"

"How'd you know we were here?" He stumbled backward.

"Charles," she began, "there's something I need to tell you."

His face softened. "Come, you can meet Morgan." He grabbed her arm and led her down the hall.

"But wait," she tried. "I need you to know that—"

"I really need a familiar face right now."

"I understand," she said, confused. Didn't he have other people to rely on? Friends and family?

Morgan sat in a highchair with a bowl of soup in front of him. A redheaded woman swayed beside him singing the "Itsy Bitsy Spider" with animated hand gestures.

"You must be Morgan's mother," she said, her hand extended. "I'm Mandy."

The woman looked up, perplexed.

"Uh, no. That's Lucy," Charles said. "She's part of the childcare staff here."

"Oh, gosh," Mandy said. "I'm sorry."

"This is Morgan." Charles leaned over and kissed the boy on his head.

Mandy knelt, staring into his watery blue eyes. "Hey there, little guy. I heard you haven't been feeling well." He looked healthy enough. No casts, no bandages, no beeping machines. What she would give to see Zack like this—in a highchair, eating soup. *Alive.*

"How exactly did you find us?" Charles asked. "Did that nosy Joyce say something?"

Mandy stood, straightening her skirt. "It might be a shock to hear this but—"

Morgan splashed his hands in the soup, red tomato juice spraying across the floor.

"Oh no!" Charles said.

"I'll get a towel," Lucy said, bolting to the bathroom.

"Where's Morgan's mother?" Mandy asked as she surveyed the room.

"She, uh, went to pick my mother up from the airport," he said. "She's flying down from Connecticut. To help out."

"Do you need anything?" Mandy ventured. "I was going to pick up some pizza."

"I have to wait for a phone call from my mother. She's landing soon," Charles said.

"But you just said your wife is picking her up," Mandy said.

"I'm going to rinse this out in the sink," Lucy said, holding up the soaked towel, averting her eyes as she ducked away.

"Oh, yes, right." Charles ran his fingers through his thinning hair, glancing out the window.

"I'm sorry to barge in like this," Mandy said. "Maybe I should go."

"Let me walk you out," he said. "Lucy, I'll be back in a few minutes."

"Sure, no prob," she chirped from the bathroom.

Charles held open the door. Mandy headed into the hall.

"What was it you wanted to tell me?" Charles asked once they were in the waiting room.

Mandy looked directly in his eyes. "Alyssa's my daughter." Quick and rapid—like ripping off a Band-Aid. "Alyssa is Morgan's babysitter."

Chapter 26

Charles

Day six

"What?" Charles shook his head. Mandy was Alyssa's *mom*? How did he miss that? They'd only worked beside each other for a week, but still.

He expected to feel a burst of outrage as she stood there, defending Alyssa—"She'd never hurt anyone. She's a responsible babysitter and gosh, she just adores Morgan. You have to believe me here ..." He expected to grab her tiny frame, to shake her to oblivion: *How could your daughter have done this?* Because, well, he'd blamed Alyssa all along. Who else could be responsible for breaking Morgan's rib?

Instead, he stared at Mandy, stupefied. Her chest puffed out, bony chin held high. He studied the zigzagged part in her auburn hair, stark roots poking through—a dirty blond with subtle streaks of gray. The little things you notice when standing close, when really looking at someone.

He finally cut her off. "Why'd you come here?" Weren't there laws against mingling with the opposition? Although he'd technically started it by sending Alyssa those texts. Did Mandy know about them?

"To tell you that Alyssa didn't do this," Mandy said, her tone steady, even. "And to make sure you're okay. That Morgan's okay."

He exhaled, a rock-like weight crushing his lungs. "He has a broken rib."

"I know," Mandy said, hushed.

"He could've fallen. It could've been an accident. But nobody's saying anything, which makes it look bad. Really bad." He locked eyes with her. "And Alyssa was there, you know, the day it happened."

Mandy flinched but didn't look away. "I know. But you have to believe me that—"

"If Alyssa didn't do it ..." One of them had to be the culprit—Alyssa or Sally. There was no other option.

"I hope you get some answers soon," she said.

He lowered his head. *What sort of answer would make this better?*

"When's your wife coming back?"

He looked past her, to the large glass windows, darkness sneaking in along the edges of the sky, the light blue fading away. It was going to turn chilly soon; Sally didn't have a jacket. She was out there, without a car. Alone. Where the hell did she go? He yanked out his phone, hoping, praying for some clue. Nothing. He slipped his phone back into his pocket.

"Your wife. Is she okay?" Mandy adjusted her glasses, her stormy-brown eyes scanning his face. "I can help. Just let me know what you need." Her demeanor switched to warmth, like the alluring glow of a fireplace.

"I don't know," Charles said. He needed to blame *someone*. Perhaps if he projected enough malice and contempt toward Alyssa, Sally would sense it was okay to come back. As if she was cowering in a nearby broom closet, waiting for Charles's declaration of love, his solid resolve in her innocence.

But maybe he didn't want Sally to come back? The thought horrified him.

The overhead speaker warbled out an announcement: *Visiting hours are now over for non-family members.*

Mandy awkwardly embraced him again. "Please, just ..." She released her arms, averted her eyes.

"It's time to go," he said, snapping to reality like a drunk sobering up. He couldn't be friends with her. "Jesus, Mandy. Alyssa's a suspect."

Mandy's cheeks flushed red. "But—"

"Please. Leave."

She opened her mouth to speak but her face hardened shut. She shook her head, sighed, then whispered, "I just wanted to ..." She didn't finish. Charles watched her turn and walk away, his pulse racing. Then he walked to the window and pressed his face against the cool glass. He watched the blur of cars below, the glow of the ER sign, a line of ambulances parked along the curb. Should he go look for Sally? The childcare provider told him earlier that she needed to clock out at 8:30. Did his mom manage to catch a flight? If so, he would have to backtrack his story about Sally going to pick her up.

He headed to the vending machine and selected Ritz crackers, white-dusted donuts, pretzels, two candy bars, a chilled Dr Pepper—might as well stock up. The items landed with a *clunk clunk clunk.* He sat and gnawed on a donut, not tasting anything. Then his phone rang.

"Mom? Did you get a flight? What's going on?"

"Hey sweetie. Didn't Sally tell you?" she said. "I got a rental car and I'm here. She told me to go to the Oak Wood Hospital."

"Wait, stop. You talked to *Sally*?" He lowered his voice. "When? What did she say?"

"She said she needed help. I assumed ..." Her voice crackled in and out. "Is she not there with you?"

"How did she sound?"

"What do you mean?" Her voice slipped up a notch. "Did she leave or something?"

"I—I'll explain." He stood. "Where are you now?"

"Just walking up to the hospital's main entrance."

"Okay. Wait right there. I'll come down to meet you."

✦

"How's little Morgie?" Charles's mom asked after they hugged. She tried to smooth out her silver hair, a few static strands standing straight up.

"Rough flight?"

"I'm *fine.*" She waved her hand dismissively. "Had to leave in a rush to catch that nonstop. Didn't even have time to say goodbye to your father. But don't worry, he's prepared to drive down if needed."

Charles looked around, pulling his mom off to the side. "Look," he began, "Sally's gone. Just up and left. Right in the middle of this madness."

"Oh dear," his mom said. "But I talked to her."

"What exactly did she say? Did she tell you where she was?"

"No. I assumed she was here, with you. She said she needed help. I thought that meant you guys needed help."

"Shit."

"Where's Morgan? Who's watching him?"

"The hospital provides a childcare person. She has to leave soon, though." He glanced at his watch. "Let's get you checked in. If anyone asks, just say Sally picked you up and went to grab dinner, okay?"

"Charles," she protested. "Shouldn't we tell someone she's missing?"

"Not until I know why she took off. I really should be out there looking for her."

"Go," she commanded. "I'll stay with Morgan."

"Let me help get him settled into bed first," Charles said, the sliding doors parting for them. "He's probably freaking out right now, being in a new place. I'll sleep here with him tonight, on the recliner. And you can go to the house after … after I find Sally." His voice caught on the last words.

If I find Sally.

✦

Charles stopped at Denny's and peered through the windows like a creeper, then the local bus station, Greyhound, even Amtrak—which was closed. He considered flashing Sally's picture: *Have you seen this woman?* Or calling the cops. But he dreaded the outcome, the accusatory headlines: *Mother Flees, Abandoning Injured Son in Hospital.*

The airport. He sped there; it only took thirty minutes without traffic. Scanned the unoccupied check-in lobby, the Starbucks with a barred gate, the baggage claim area, one belt churning, surrounded by a small crowd of disgruntled travelers. It hit him, his absurd stupidity—it was almost 10:30. Sally had been missing for about eight hours. If she came to any of these places, she'd be long gone by now.

The sound of the conveyor belt dragged him back: giggling as they retrieved their bags at the Kahului airport, an interlude of steamy kisses, his hands caressing her not-yet-noticeable bump. Their honeymoon. Well, *pretend* honeymoon since they never officially tied the knot. Not yet. That trip to Hawaii—five luxurious days snorkeling, devouring fresh coconuts, cuddling by the breezy shore—inspired their baby's name. Morgan for a girl, after Charles's grandmother.

And if she's a boy? Sally had asked.

Still Morgan, Charles had replied. *It works both ways.*

His phone chimed. He frantically unlocked it. His brother: **Do you need me to fly there? Mom says this is serious.**

Charles wrote back: **It's under control.**

Standing, he scanned the baggage claim area again, as if he'd skimmed over Sally the first time. His mother's only clue—*She said she needed help.* What did that even mean? If Sally really needed help, why didn't she respond to his calls, his texts? Unless this was Sally's way of retaliating after their fight last night? A shiver bolted through him. She never did share the details of where she had stayed.

He headed back to the parking lot, his feet leaden. He unlocked his car and slid in, his breathing thin and shallow. Was Sally's disappearance a sign of their imminent breakup?

Slamming his palms into the steering wheel, the horn released a series of deafening blasts, shattering the evening's stillness.

"Dammit, Sally!" he cried out. "I need you." Then, more quietly, "We all need you."

Chapter 27

Alyssa

Day six

A mug of chicken noodle soup warmed Alyssa's hands while she watched a reality show about renovating attics into posh bedrooms. The front door opened and she jumped.

"What took you so long?" Alyssa asked, glancing over her shoulder.

Her mom set a Domino's box on the dining table, car keys rattling in her hand.

"What did you do?" Alyssa stood.

"Nothing. Why do you think I did something?" She flashed a weak smile.

"You look guilty." Alyssa sauntered over and opened the pizza box. Plain cheese. She grabbed a lukewarm slice.

"Get a plate," her mom said. "Don't be a slob."

"Okay, something's up. Tell me," Alyssa said with her mouth full.

Her mom's eyes glazed over as she jingled her keys.

"Mom!"

With a sharp inhale, she flung the keys onto the table, then sat down. "I went to see Charles, at the Oak Wood Hospital."

Alyssa almost choked on her pizza. "Charles? As in, *Morgan's* dad?"

"Yeah."

"But why?"

"I know him, Alyssa."

Alyssa sank into a chair, speechless.

"We work together," her mom continued, "at that print shop. Where I've been working as a temp. He must've seen the babysitting flier I put up back in March—when I first worked there." She pressed her fingers into her temples.

"You knew Charles? All this time? And you didn't tell me?"

"I didn't make the connection until—"

Alyssa threw the half-eaten slice into the box. "You're friends with him, aren't you?"

"No." She paused. "Not exactly."

"How could you still be friends with him after he said those things to me? God, Mom, what the hell's wrong with you? He thinks I abused his baby." Alyssa sprung to her feet. "You think I hurt Morgan, too, don't you?"

"No, no, of course not. I know you'd never do anything like that. Not on purpose …" She shuffled around the table, arms open for a hug. "Honey, you can tell me anything."

Alyssa slapped her hands away. "So you think it was an accident? Under my watch?"

"Well, accidents do happen. It's better to come forward now and admit—"

"Oh my God. You don't believe me."

"Sweetie," her mom began, "your eye's doing that twitchy thing it does when you're lying. Please, tell me if—"

"Stop," Alyssa snapped. "I didn't do it! Nothing happened." She stormed to the fridge and flung open the freezer. The swoosh of chilled air stung her hot-flushed face.

"Okay, I'm sorry. I just needed to check." Her mom hovered next to her. "You want to know what I really think? Morgan's mother is missing. I think something happened with her. And I think Charles is …"

Alyssa dug past the Weight Watchers frozen meals and pulled out a pint of strawberry ice cream. She grabbed a spoon and leaned against the fridge. "Go on."

"Either he's covering up for her—*but why?*—or he's in denial."

"Or he's the guilty one." Alyssa popped off the lid. "So, why do you think Sally's missing?"

"She wasn't at the hospital with Morgan. Charles made up some excuse about her going to pick up his mother, but I didn't buy it. He seemed, I don't know, all antsy and nervous." Her mom opened the drawer and grabbed another spoon. "Like he's hiding something."

"We should call the cops," Alyssa said. She chiseled into the crystalized ice cream. "Maybe she's on the run."

"Maybe." Her mom leaned in, leveraging out a spoonful.

"There's always been something odd about them, about that house." Just saying it now, an electrifying tingle traveled up her spine.

"Like what?"

Alyssa wandered to the couch. Her mom followed. Holding the icy pint between them to share, Alyssa rambled off more details—the playpen, the gun, how weird Sally acted on Friday, the cluttered mess. "Does that make her a bad mother?"

"The messy house, no. But the playpen in the basement?" Her mom tapped the spoon against her lips.

"It was hidden behind a tower of boxes. Like, way in the corner. And there was no reason for it being down there, such as somebody needing to use a washing machine or something."

"You told the detective about it?"

"Yeah," Alyssa said. "He said the social worker's doing a house investigation."

"Okay. I'm sure they'll look into it."

"But don't you think we should tell someone Sally's missing? Like Simon." She tugged on the ends of her hair, eyes concentrated on her mom. "You have his number."

"You mean right now?"

Alyssa nodded.

Her mom hesitated, swiping at her phone. "Alyssa, it's already after eight."

"That's not too late." Alyssa set the empty pint on the coffee table and pulled her mom to her feet.

✦

Simon's apartment was a smaller version of theirs—leather loveseat, oval mahogany coffee table, an empty bookshelf. Minimalistic. Not at all what Alyssa expected. But then again, Simon was nothing like she'd expected. She'd devoted hours to the obsession, the exhilarating fabrication: mysterious druggie, bad-boy criminal, cool CIA agent, zooming in on every feature of his chiseled face. But nope. Just an ordinary, law-abiding detective. *Boring.*

He appeared ambivalent, or maybe secretly enthralled, by their impromptu visit. He politely offered drinks—lemonade for Alyssa, white wine for her mom.

I'd actually prefer the wine, Alyssa almost said but caught herself. She shuddered when she remembered the Big Bird cup, her small indulgence of wine on Friday night. Would Jameson find out?

Her mom quickly filled Simon in on everything.

"I told you not to go see Charles," he said.

"I know, I know. I couldn't help myself." Her mom clasped her hands in her lap, shoulders hunched like a reprimanded child. They shared the loveseat while Simon paced.

"I really shouldn't be talking to you guys about this, you know," he said.

"But you're not officially on the case," her mom said.

"We're just concerned if Sally's missing," Alyssa added. "And thought this might help. This information."

"You have no proof, though," Simon said. "She could've gone to the airport, to pick up her mother-in-law, just like Chris said."

"Charles," Alyssa corrected him. "And can't you go, or call? See if she's back at the hospital?"

His eyes narrowed, head cocked. "Why exactly are you so concerned?"

Alyssa shot her mom a helpless look. Her mom gave a reassuring nod.

"I—I ..." Alyssa stammered. "I don't know. I care about her. I want to help, I guess."

"But why?" he asked. "If she's really on the run, don't you think that means she—"

"Wait a minute. What if she's running from Charles? He's the one who sent those horrible texts. I think ... oh my God. Sally could be in danger." Alyssa desperately looked at him as the idea, this theory, became crystal clear. Her ice cubes clattered in her glass.

Simon exhaled, then lowered himself onto the coffee table. His breath carried a hint of alcohol. "Look Alyssa, this is what I can do. I'll go down to the station tomorrow morning. I'll talk to Detective Jameson, he's the one on the case, and see if there's anything we—"

"But it'll be too late by then," Alyssa said. She envisioned a terror-struck Sally quivering in the backseat of a taxi while Charles breathed threats over the phone. Or worse, flinging herself off a high-rise building. "You hear these disturbing stories about battered women and how nobody believed them and how their husbands appeared to be oh-so-wonderful and then they suddenly go missing or are murdered and everyone's like, 'Why didn't the world listen? Why didn't somebody help?'" Alyssa paused to catch her breath. "Someone hurt Morgan. We need to find Sally to find out if it was Charles. What if he's about to hurt someone else next?"

Simon stared at her as if she were a raging lunatic. "I can see you're really concerned. It's just that ..." His eyes darted away, searching her mom's face, before snapping back. "Well. You're my only source for this theory and you're still a—"

"A suspect," Alyssa finished.

"Until we—they—get more evidence, yes." Simon gave Alyssa a patronizing look.

The words, Simon's obvious doubt, smarted like a bee's sting. Alyssa stood.

"We appreciate your help anyway," her mom said. His help? But he didn't do a damn thing. Alyssa watched as her mom busied herself with clearing away their glasses.

"Sorry to meet under such circumstances," Simon said.

Alyssa seethed, flinging the door open. Outside, she paused under the beacon of moonlight, breathing in the night's crisp air.

Her mom poked her head out. "Actually honey, I'm going to have a word with Simon, okay? In private. I'll be up shortly."

"What?" But her mom had already closed the door. She shook her head, pulling out her phone. Jess. Of course, Jess would know what to do. She might be clueless when it came to factoring polynomials and logarithmic equations—that's where Alyssa saved the day—but now, with this shit storm brewing, she'd know exactly what to do.

Alyssa: **i need u to come over nowww**

Jess responded immediately: **omggg i thought u ghosted me**

Alyssa: **sorry plz come ASAP**

She paused, then added: **ur not gonna believe it ... more trouble from charles**

✦

Alyssa brought Jess up to speed in record time, omitting certain parts—like how much wine she'd consumed last Friday night. The two of them sat cross-legged on the couch. Alyssa was just finishing the story when her mom returned.

"Big yikes," Jess said. "It definitely sounds like Sally's nuts. Like, she got high, swung a bat at Morgan—like that dad, did you read about him? They were drug dealers, by the way. Crystal meth. Then Sally acted like nothing happened. Now she's on the run. Understandably so." She nodded, seemingly confident with her dramatized synopsis.

"I doubt it," Alyssa said, taking a sip of hot cocoa. "I never saw drugs in that house—and remember, I even looked under their bed." Her mom raised her eyebrows at this.

"But what about the playpen? With milk in the basement? That's so sus," Jess said.

"Sus?" her mom asked as she settled into the creaking rocking chair.

"Suspicious," Alyssa said.

"Jeez." Her mom shook her head. "Why can't you girls just speak normal?"

Alyssa ignored her. "It doesn't seem like Sally. Either it was a total accident, like, I dunno, a slip in the kitchen? Falling down the basement stairs? Or else Charles—"

"A slip in the kitchen wouldn't cause that much damage," her mom butted in. "And a fall down a flight of stairs—wooden, right?—would've caused a ton of bruising."

"Yeah, and apparently eighty-two percent of infant rib fractures are caused by child abuse," Jess said, tapping on her phone's screen.

"But Morgan's not an infant," Alyssa said. "And really, why isn't anyone blaming Charles? Do I need to repeat what he wrote me? Sally said nothing to me, at least so far."

"That's true. It could totally be him." Jess chewed deliberately on a mini marshmallow. "But let's talk about Simon. Your hunky neighbor's a detective? That's so *sick.* Did you see his gun? Oh, wait." Jess's eyes shot down to the floor. "Do you think he can hear us?"

Alyssa imagined Simon balanced on a stepladder, a glass pressed between his ear and the ceiling. Surely he'd have more advanced equipment than that, though. Or maybe—*nooooooo*—did he plant a bug on them? And what on earth happened with her mom and Simon behind his closed door?

"Don't be ridiculous," her mom said. "Now girls, I think everyone needs a good night's sleep." She rolled up the mini marshmallows and secured the bag with a wooden clothespin. "We can touch base with Simon tomorrow and take it from there."

"But I'm positive Sally would never hurt Morgan. And if she didn't do it, that means Charles ..." Alyssa swallowed the lump in her throat. "Am I the only one who thinks we need to find Sally tonight?"

Jess gave her a sharp jab in the ribs. "I think you're right, Mandy. We'll figure it out in the morning." She winked at Alyssa.

"Uh, can Jess spend the night then?" Alyssa asked, already aboard Jess's train of thought: the rope ladder tucked in her closet, the ticket to their escape plan.

"Of course. Just let your mom know, okay?" Her mom opened the dishwasher.

"On it," Jess said, already texting away.

✦

They locked the door to Alyssa's room. They had conducted an experiment years ago, testing how far their voices could travel through the apartment. The result: the safest location to share secrets was in the depths of Alyssa's closet, behind the lineup of blouses, dresses, and puffy winter coats.

"Whatcha thinking?" Alyssa whispered in the dark.

"We follow the most logical trail. Places like the train station, the bus. Airports are tricky with extra security."

"I doubt she'd still be there." Alyssa unlocked her phone. "It's already after ten. Most places will be closed."

Jess flashed her phone. "The Greyhound station closes at midnight."

"And what? We hope for a guy and flirt our way to answers?"

"You got a better idea?"

"We can try calling her," Alyssa offered. "Like, on her phone?"

"Uh, someone on the run isn't going to answer a call from her babysitter."

"We'll have to wait until my mom falls asleep. That doesn't give us much time."

"But it's something. You want to do something, right?"

"Yeah." Nobody else was taking this seriously—Sally lost, alone, possibly in danger. Was Charles even who he said he was? Alyssa needed to know exactly what happened last Friday. With a sigh, she pushed aside the Tide-scented blouses and long dresses, expecting her mom to be waiting, hands on hips: *Gotcha.* But luckily for them, her mom remained clueless to their scheming. As usual.

Jess unraveled the rope ladder. "Little did your mom know how her preparedness would eventually backfire," she said with a chuckle.

Alyssa tugged on her Nikes, double knotted the laces. She zipped her black jacket up to her chin. "What'll we do if we actually find Sally?"

"Beats me. I'm just in for the ride," Jess said with a shrug. "I've watched enough crime shows. Now I get to live one." She leaned out the window and tossed the ladder below. It hit the wall with a clatter and a *bang, bang, bang.* "Shit!" They froze, eyes on the door. Nothing.

"Why don't you go check on your mom?"

"But I'm wearing a jacket and sneakers."

"She won't notice."

"She notices everything. Believe me."

Jess gave her a firm push. "Just go."

"Fine." Alyssa cautiously opened the door and tiptoed into the dimly lit hall. Her mom's door was ajar, her slumped body illuminated by the lamp's soft glare. On the nightstand sat the bottle of Ambien. Ah, Alyssa thought with a smile. *She'll be out for hours.*

"We're good," Alyssa told Jess as she nestled her bedroom door closed and flicked the lock.

"It's showtime." Jess climbed out the window and effortlessly slid down the ladder, and then darted into the lurking shadows of the night.

Alyssa took a deep breath, secured her phone into her jacket's pocket, and blindly followed after her best friend.

Chapter 28

Sally

Day six

Sally scanned the Greyhound lobby, her breathing labored. That mother was still there with her unruly boys, who were now fighting over a bag of Cheez-Its. Sally teetered toward the terminal's monitor. Her bus's status showed "departed." Damn. The oversized digital clock above glowed 4:58. What were her options? She could buy another bus ticket—*just get me outta here*—slapping more bills on the counter. But the puny ticket guy would ask what happened to her Colorado ticket. Plus, he'd notice her soiled leggings—despite their dark color, it was obvious. She needed to cover up.

Eyeing the two boys, she casually sauntered in their direction. They bounced from chair to chair, while their mother ignored them, absorbed in her beeping phone. She noticed a black hoodie draped over a nearby chair.

Sally couldn't believe she was even thinking of stealing. Her mother always taught her to take the high ground, do the right thing. Be a moral person. *Well Mom,* she thought, *look at me now.*

She watched the boys out of the corner of her eye, waiting until they landed on the floor in a brotherly tackle-wrestle embrace, Cheez-Its flying. In one swift movement, she tucked the hoodie under her shirt.

Without hesitation, she plowed ahead, ignoring the quick stab of guilt. She saw her mom's wide eyes—the sad disappointment.

Sorry, she mumbled under her breath.

✦

Sally stumbled down the road and ducked into an alley. Breathing heavily, she leaned against the brick wall, waiting to see if the boys were trailing close behind, screaming their heads off. They looked like screamers. Or if the guy behind the counter would come yank away the hoodie with a judging *tsk, tsk,* slapping her on the wrist. What was the penalty for stealing clothes?

Once her breathing stabilized, Sally pulled out the hoodie. The arms were long enough to tie around her waist, but the bloodstains were still visible from the front. She stepped into it and pulled it snug around her hips, like a makeshift skirt. From there, she tied the arms in front.

No way she could embark on a cross-country trip now. She'd soak through the seat once the tampon wore out. She'd stupidly forgotten to buy more at Food Lion last night. Was that terrible fight with Charles just last night? And because she didn't go home, she'd skipped her daily birth control pill. Maybe that was what caused her hormones to go awry?

Heading back to the Motel 6, or any motel, sounded the most appealing. She could lock the door, sink into a soft bed, pull the comforter over her head, or take a long, soothing bath. Anything to make the whirling stop. But what if she passed out again? Nobody would notice, until house cleaning discovered her blood-soaked body.

What she would give to call her OB-GYN right now. To cry, *Is this normal?* But surely everyone was on high alert, notified that she was on the run, a flight risk. Isn't that what they called it? The cops were probably swarming the Greyhound station right now, getting a statement from those young boys. They'd add stealing to her list of offenses—just a hoodie, but still, a crime's a crime.

She stepped out of the alley, waiting to see if anyone pounced. A car honked, a man spat on the sidewalk, a Greyhound whizzed past. She mustered the courage to wave down a yellow taxi.

"Where to?" the driver asked.

"The nearest department store," she wheezed. "Or grocery store."

✦

Sally hit reset at Walmart.

Pink floral underwear, tampons, a bottle of Midol for the wretched stabbing in her gut. She needed new pants. No time to search for style or price; she grabbed something displayed near the front, first a pair of shorts—it was a scorcher out there—but no, it'd be colder in Colorado, if she made it that far. She selected a pair of size ten Khaki pants with a drawstring waist.

She thought of Diana, her co-worker, who always bragged about how her body sprung back into shape after having Nick. *Sprung.* As if she had been a stretched-out slinky, one that miraculously contracted back to a more pleasant size afterward.

"What's your secret?" Sally once asked her.

Diana shrugged. She forgot to eat, that was it. Talk about unfair. Sally tried it all—starving herself for an entire day, doing every YouTube core workout, the keto diet, even trying to run again—but the fierce hunger and the unshrinkable flab won that battle.

Fingering the pants, she opted for a size twelve instead, what with this period bloat. *Muffin top.* She always hated that phrase, even though Charles said he liked the extra squish—"More to hold and love." With a grumbling stomach, she made her way to the food aisle. She scanned the packaged cereals and protein bars, finally grabbing a box of Clif Bars—cool mint chocolate. Extra protein. Healthy, right? Dinner, done.

While checking out, Sally noticed a plastic box on the counter, a picture of a bald girl wearing a rosy pink shirt and gold-studded earrings plastered on the front. Donations for St. Jude's Children's Research Hospital. The girl seemed to be looking directly at her with sparkly blue eyes and a hopeful smile. A surge of heavy grief coursed through Sally.

Imagine those poor parents, being told your child might die from cancer.

The cashier handed her back a $10 bill and some loose change, and Sally shoved it all into the box, hoping her miniscule contribution made a difference.

In the restroom, she changed into her new pants, then rolled the bloody leggings up with the stolen hoodie, like an oversized burrito. She stuffed it deep into the trash and piled paper towels on top. Then she remembered it might get cold at her new destination, so she scooped out the hoodie.

Outside, she downed the entire pack of energy bars, the foil crinkling in her hands, crumbs dribbling down her shirt. She felt better, more alert, the sugar rush kicking in. But her insides still rumbled. It was only a matter of time before she passed out again. She needed to get somewhere safe—fast.

She scrolled through her contacts, hoping to stumble across the perfect someone, loving arms, a reassuring voice, a step-by-step plan that could carry her away from this disaster.

But who? Who wouldn't ask questions? Who wouldn't take her directly to the hospital?

Sally suddenly thought about *her*.

No, she couldn't.

Not after what *she* did to Sally's mother.

No, nope, never.

And yet her fingers typed in her name, studying her Facebook profile. A tanned face with a few crow-like wrinkles, the same wry smile, a dyed platinum-blond pixie cut making her look ten years younger. Did she still have that teasing laugh, the way she'd chuckle when Sally flipped over the wrong squares on Memory, a quick tussle of the hair—*Next time. You'll get it next time.*

She had been her mother's partner, Sally's second mother: *Gwen.* But then cancer hit and Gwen split. Sally hadn't seen her since she was what, eight? Would she even answer to Sally's call for help? Or worse, would she turn Sally in? Was there another option? Her location said Charlotte—a little over two hours away.

Sally sent a quick message: **I really need help. Right now**. She leaned against a lamppost, steadying herself as another dizzy wave steamed through her. A few people stared quizzically in her direction as they pushed their overfull carts. She managed a feeble smile in return.

How long until Gwen saw her message? Older people weren't on Facebook all the time. If she even saw her message. What if she'd blocked Sally?

A motel. There had to be one nearby. She called a taxi, waited.

Her money was rapidly disappearing. $105 for a one-way ticket to Colorado Springs, wasted. Pants, tampons, Clif Bars, Midol—all with her precious cash. Helping the cancer kids, but that was important. Two, now *three* taxi rides. Another motel. She'd never make it anywhere at this rate.

"Sally? Is that you?"

Sally whipped around, shading her eyes against the sun. A woman sporting a Duke Blue Devils shirt was heading straight toward her, a canvas Walmart bag swinging in each hand. She had a toned physique, shoulder-length chestnut hair, a determined look. Was she with the authorities?

It was too late. There was no time to run.

"It's Annie West," the woman said, pushing her sunglasses up to her forehead and offering an eager smile. "Kelsey's mom."

Sally continued to stare, her mouth dry, her face impossibly hot.

"Kelsey West? She was a grade below you, but you girls competed together on the varsity track team, during your last year. Remember? Back at Northwest Guildford High."

"Oh."

"Gosh, you won so many awards. Kelsey always looked up to you. What are you up to these days? Do you still run?"

Sally rubbed her forehead, quickly scanning the parking lot. Where the hell was her taxi?

"Kelsey's just started her junior year, here at Duke. She finally made the varsity team."

"That's great."

"I heard you had a baby. How old?"

"He's one. Charles—"

"Oh, that's an adorable name! Kinda old fashioned, but I love it."

"No, Charles is my, uh, partner. My baby ... his name's Morgan."

Annie lowered her bags and dug through her purse. "I've just gotta get a pic of us. A selfie! Kelsey won't believe it. Do you live nearby? Maybe you two could meet up and go for a run or—"

She was interrupted by two sharp beeps. The taxi was finally here.

"Sure. Yeah. Have her call me," Sally said, forcing a smile. "Sorry, but this is for ..." She turned and wavered toward the taxi, then paused, resting her head against the car's tinted window.

"Sally," Annie said, "are you—?"

Sally couldn't remember what she said next. She crawled into the backseat. The car lurched forward. Looking back, she saw Annie West—Kelsey's mom—giving a half wave, a baffled look on her face. The taxi's air conditioning blasted, arm hairs fluttering, sweat drying to numb skin. A staticky radio station warbled out an old Britney Spears song—something Sally remembered listening to while training.

I'm going somewhere, Sally repeated, like a mantra. That was all that mattered.

Chapter 29

Mandy

Day seven

The upbeat melody of Mandy's cellphone startled her from a deep sleep. She usually charged her phone in the kitchen but must've forgotten. She struggled against her covers and swiped her phone to answer. "Hello?"

Someone from the high school, inquiring as to why Alyssa was absent.

"Oh, sorry," Mandy mumbled, noticing her alarm clock on the floor, unplugged. She must have gone back to sleep after the alarm went off. "She's not feeling well. She and Jess are both here sick. Uh, food poisoning."

She clicked off. It was already after nine. She shook her head and then remembered taking Ambien last night, which always had a zombie-apocalyptic effect the next morning. Tiptoeing her way to the kitchen, she veered around the creaky floorboard by the bathroom to avoid waking the girls.

The morning's rays streamed in as she methodically scooped, poured, stirred her instant coffee. The caffeine began to wake her brain, sweeping away the cobwebs of medicated sleep. She called her boss at Print Solutions, telling her she needed to tend to her daughter but she'd be in soon.

God, what a day yesterday: Alyssa's interview at the police station, taking a spontaneous trip to confront Charles at the hospital, and then barging into Simon's apartment, unannounced.

Her cheeks flushed at the memory of her meltdown.

"What's really happening here?" she'd asked Simon after Alyssa left.

"Honestly, I don't know. I'm not privy to the case. But"—his eyes switched to a foreboding look—"given the amount of time Alyssa was in the interrogation room, it looks like she's being treated as a suspect."

Mandy lost all composure at that. She burst into tears, right there in Simon's kitchen, blubbering apologies as he awkwardly handed her a box of tissues.

"It's not the end of the world," he said. "You just need a good lawyer, to stay strong. You can fight this."

She struggled to believe him while he mixed her a Mojito and set out a bag of Tostitos, a can of bean dip. She ravenously dug in, realizing she hadn't taken a single bite of the pizza upstairs.

Afterward, at the door, she apologized again for her sudden breakdown.

"Hey, I get it," he said. "I grew up with four sisters. Plenty of drama—and tears—to last a lifetime." He pulled her in for a hug and she succumbed, glad to have somebody on her side.

Now she studied Alyssa's picture on her fridge, last year's school shot. Alyssa's smile wide and bright, her eyes sincere and honest. Mandy traced her daughter's face—*if there's one thing I did right in my life, it's this, right here.* A cutting chill sliced through her: Who would accuse this innocent girl of such a crime?

It weighed on Mandy, the way Alyssa fervently defended Sally's innocence while Mandy believed the opposite—that Sally was guilty.

Well then, who did it?

Her toast popped and while buttering it, she tried to focus on Simon's advice: Get a lawyer. She shuddered. That sounded outrageously expensive. Should she call Ian? The courts had demanded he pay child support but of course he'd scoffed at the responsibility—following one whim after another, Argentina, Iceland, New Zealand, she couldn't keep track.

No, she would have to ask her parents for the money.

After swallowing down the toast, she headed to her room to get dressed, but then paused in front of Alyssa's door. Might as well check if the girls needed breakfast before heading off to work. She gently turned the doorknob. It didn't move. She jiggled it harder.

Locked!

Alyssa often locked her door when she wanted privacy, but first thing in the morning? Mandy gave a gentle knock. Nothing. She knocked harder, a surge of panic racing through her. She pounded hard, with both fists, calling out Alyssa's name.

No answer.

She bolted down the hall and dug through her nightstand drawer until she found a paper clip. Stumbling back to Alyssa's door, she unraveled the paper clip and jammed it into the slot, repeatedly. She'd once watched a YouTube video on how to do it and yet it was surprisingly difficult.

Click. The door finally opened.

The room was empty, the bed neatly made with corners tucked in, sunshine-yellow pillows fluffed. Her eyes fell upon the open window. Trembling, she stepped closer—the rope ladder? Her legs buckled as she gripped the windowsill. She bellowed their names, then waited for a response, as if they were simply frolicking in the backyard.

Her pulse pounding, she raced to the kitchen for her phone, called Alyssa, then Jess. No answer. She looked out the window. The guest parking spot sat empty; they'd taken Jess's car.

She dialed 911. It rang once but she hung up. Alyssa was a suspect in a *child abuse investigation.* Disappearing like this would look really bad.

She dialed Jess's mom. It went straight to voicemail. "Hey, Claire. How's it going?" She tried to sound casual. "Just wondering if the girls are there? I got a call from school and they're not there. I'm sure it's no big deal but give me a call. Okay, bye."

Her hands shook. They went searching for Sally. Of course they did. Why didn't she see this coming? Mandy knew nothing about the woman. Did she have a job? Family nearby? What if Sally didn't actually leave and was still at Oak Wood Hospital with Charles? She fished through her purse until she found the folded Post-it note Joyce had given her at work yesterday. Charles Haywood. She smoothed it on the counter and sent him a text: **This is Mandy. I'm sorry to bother you.**

She hit send, then continued: **Alyssa's missing. I believe she went searching for Sally. I know this is crazy, but do you have any idea where they could be?**

Her insides coiled. What if Charles used this as evidence against them—against Alyssa? Why did she keep thinking she could trust him, especially after their terse conversation last night? And really, what evidence did she have that Sally was in fact missing?

Still. Charles might know something.

She sent the message and slipped her phone into her robe's pocket. She opened the front door and bounded down the steps in her beige nightgown, her oversized bunny slippers bouncing on her feet. Hand poised over Simon's door, she paused. Alyssa could be hurt, she could be lost, or she could've found Sally. Either way, Mandy needed to do *something*.

Simon opened the door, a smile arching across his face. "Mandy, what a surprise."

Mandy choked out the words: "Alyssa and Jess are missing."

"What? Are you serious?" He stepped aside, motioning for her to come in. "When did this happen?"

She mumbled something inaudible. He gave her a quick hug, then squeezed her shoulders. "Hey, hey. It's going to be okay. Let's figure this out. Do you think they went looking for that Sally woman?" He walked over to the counter, poured cream into his coffee, plopped in two sugar cubes, then gave it a good stir.

"I think so. She was all they could talk about last night."

"Maybe as some heroic act, being a good-hearted Samaritan?" He clanked the spoon against the rim of his mug. "Or, perhaps, she's on the run herself. Afraid to admit something?"

"No. Alyssa has nothing to hide." She frantically picked balls of fluff off her tattered robe. "But will this make her look guilty? I mean, more guilty?"

"It doesn't make her look good, that's for sure."

"Goddammit."

"But—" he began, filling a second mug.

"I don't want any."

"Trust me, you need it. Cream? Sugar?"

"Fine." Mandy sank into the couch and pulled her robe across her chest. Her phone dinged. A reply from Charles: **I hope we find them soon.** And there it was: *them.* Confirmation that Sally was also missing.

"Here's another thought," Simon said, setting a steaming Garfield mug in front of her. "Perhaps both of them are guilty."

"Both of them?"

"I'm just speculating here. Maybe something happened when Alyssa showed up on—did you say Friday night? Sally confided in her and Alyssa promised to cover it up," he said, pausing to shrug. "Believe me, I've seen it all."

"What? No. Alyssa would've told me if that happened. Besides, Sally ran away first."

"Well, that's just speculation." He took a long draw from his coffee. "We don't know that for a fact."

"Actually, Charles just confirmed it." She held up her phone.

He took her phone and squinted at the message. "You're texting *Charles*?"

"What else was I supposed to do?"

"I don't know. Call 911?"

"I started to, but then I freaked out." Mandy grabbed her mug but her hands continued to shake, hot coffee sloshing over the rim. She quickly set it back down, biting her lip, and dried her scalded hands on her robe. "I didn't want to make things worse because, well, she's a ..."

"Suspect."

"Yeah, that."

"You've tried Alyssa's cell? Her friend's? Her friend's parents?" He took his seat on the coffee table and handed back her phone. "How about the Find My Phone app? GPS tracking?"

"I've called everyone. I never set up GPS tracking on Alyssa's phone. I never needed it before." She stared at her phone, willing it to ring. "Can you do it now? Do you know how?"

"I'd need a court order to do something like that." His fingers grazed the faint hint of stubble on his chin.

"God, why didn't I see this coming? She was so determined to help—to find Sally. And I just went off to bed like nothing was going on."

"Hey, these things happen. All the time." He drummed his fingers on his knees, his forehead rippling with worry lines. "Let's make an official report. We need to make sure she's safe—that's the top priority here. I'll check in with Jameson, see what he's dug up on this Sally. In the meantime, go drive to her favorite hangouts, like the mall, movie theater, the pool, roller skating rink—do they still have those? You get it, wherever teens chill these days." He stood. "There's no point in jumping to conclusions yet."

"No." Mandy sprung to her feet and firmly grasped Simon's arm.

"Excuse me?"

"She's not going to be at any of those places, I know it. She went looking for Sally. And we *can't* get the police involved. I mean, the other police. They already think the worst." She took a long, exasperated breath. "I can't have Alyssa's future ruined over this. I can't."

"Mandy," he began, looking down at her tight hold. "You know I can't just look the other way here. I'm a detective. It's my job to—"

"Please," Mandy said, stepping closer, moving her hands to his shoulders. "Just ... please. Help me find her." Her insides tightened as she saw a glimpse into her daughter's grim future. "*Without* the police."

Simon took a deep breath, appearing to mull it over.

She dropped her hands. "I'm sorry. I know it's a lot to ask. I just know Alyssa. She didn't do this. She didn't hurt Morgan. And the last thing I want is for that detective to add 'runaway teen' to his list of evidence. You even said it wouldn't look good ..." The words tapered off as the tears took over.

"Oh Mandy," Simon said, handing her the box of tissues again. "I have a weak spot for crying women." He sighed and dragged his fingers through his hair. "Look, I'll come upstairs with my laptop. We can do a little digging around. Discreetly, of course. And look up the license plate number, check for accidents and such."

Mandy's hand fluttered to her mouth as she stifled a scream. She imagined the car overturned in a ditch, Jess's and Alyssa's bodies seizing and twitching and oozing blood. She didn't even hug Alyssa last night, didn't say *I love you,* didn't brace herself for this possibility, the chance her daughter could …

No, she told herself. Don't go there.

"But after an hour, we need to call the station, okay?" Simon said, his voice firm.

Mandy nodded solemnly in agreement.

✦

Simon set his laptop on Mandy's kitchen table while she ducked into her room to change.

"We need Sally's full name," he shouted out.

"I don't know her full name," Mandy shouted back.

"You don't?" He coughed. "You sent your daughter off to babysit for a family without knowing anything about them?"

"Alyssa has always been super responsible, independent. Jess drove her to all the jobs. I wasn't involved in that part of her life," Mandy said as she sat beside him. A heavy knot twisted in her gut. "But her husband is Charles Haywood. So she must be Sally Haywood."

"If she has the same last name." Simon's eyebrows furrowed. "Women these days, they don't always—"

"Hold on." She opened the Facebook app, carefully avoiding the friend request button. That was the last thing she needed, awkwardly befriending the prosecution. Sure enough, Sally Haywood. It had to be her—she held a baby, a younger version of the boy she'd met yesterday at the hospital. Sally's youthfulness startled her; she looked the same age as Alyssa. It didn't seem possible that this naïve, sweet-looking woman could crack Morgan's rib.

Alyssa's words hit her: *Why isn't anyone blaming Charles?*

"We need to dig through Alyssa's socials," Simon said. "Reach out to her friends—"

"Alyssa doesn't do social media. And she has no other friends. She and Jess, they're like misfits. Peas in a pod. They cling to each other, in their own secret world and—"

Her phone's ringing cut her off. She answered with a desperate "Hello?"

"Good morning. This is Detective Jameson. Is this Mandy?"

"Yes. This is Mandy." She mouthed *Jameson* to Simon. He shook his head, his eyes saying: *You're screwed.* Or more like: *We're screwed.*

"We need to ask Alyssa a few more questions," Jameson continued. "When will she be home?"

He knew, he knew she was missing. But no, he wouldn't sound so casual, so nonchalant. "Uh, Alyssa will be home this afternoon, after *school,*" she said.

"Can you guys come down to the station again? Say around 4:30?"

"Yes!" She grabbed a tissue and dabbed at her damp armpits. "We'll be there." She ended the call and turned to Simon. "More questions for Alyssa."

"We're digging ourselves in deeper here, Mandy," he said. "They can help."

"We'll find her."

"Try calling Jess's mom again. Might as well exhaust all the leads we can."

Chapter 30

Charles

Day seven

"We need coffee," Charles said.

"But Morgan's CT scan is soon," his mother protested. She'd just arrived at Morgan's hospital room, along with Lucy, right on the dot at 8:30—everyone prepared for another long day.

"The nurse said she'll meet us here in an hour. I really need coffee." He smiled at Lucy. "You okay with him?"

"Yes, of course." Lucy dumped out a new bin of toys. She didn't ask about Sally; most likely sensing the impending doom.

It'd take an idiot not to feel the tension in this room.

Charles led his mom down the hall, through the waiting room, and across another hall to the hospital's cafe. They ordered coffees, then settled into their seats.

"Any news from Sally?" his mother asked. She neatly unfolded a paper napkin and spread it across her lap.

"No." Charles rubbed his eyes under his glasses. A cramp in his neck pulsated, probably from sleeping on the recliner in Morgan's hospital room. "We have until two to find her. They need to ask more questions."

"I called her this morning, no answer. I tried sending a text but gave up."

"Where could she have gone?" It shamed him to admit he didn't know her co-workers' names. Did she have any other friends?

His mom blew on her coffee, sat back, and licked her lips. "Charlie, honey," she said, her voice rimmed with intent. "I think it's time you tell the police she's missing. Come clean. It'll help clear you as the *responsible* parent."

"And what about Sally?"

"Sweetie, you know Sally's young and inexperienced. She must've had some kind of breakdown. Why else would she run away like this?" She focused on twirling her coffee with a little wooden stirrer, then took a delicate sip.

"So, you think Sally hurt Morgan."

"I'm not saying that."

"It sounds like you are."

She looked up, eyes scrutinizing. "Well, dear, we know *you* didn't hurt Morgan. And it seems highly unlikely a babysitter would—"

"What, you think Sally hurt her own baby?" His voice pitched higher. "That she locked him in the basement closet when she couldn't deal with him? Then what? Beat him until she broke his rib and caused permanent brain damage, then fled before anyone could accuse her of anything?"

His mom shifted in her seat. "Well ..."

"Why does it keep coming back to Sally? She couldn't break anyone's rib if her life depended on it."

"Honey, I think you should focus on Morgan. Get through this CT scan, see what the doctors say. Let's pray he can go home soon. And"—she dabbed at the corners of her mouth with a napkin—"let the police and social worker deal with Sally. That's their job." She said it as if Sally were vermin, the cops the exterminators.

"Of course I'm focusing on Morgan! Why the hell would you even say that?" He took a deep breath, noticing a few inquisitive stares pointed in his direction. "Look," he began, lowering his voice, "I don't want Morgan to lose his mother. I want to know what happened. And until I can talk to Sally face-to-face, I can't blame her for this. I just can't."

She sighed, scrunched up her napkin, then stood. "Why don't you stay here and finish your coffee." It was a command, not a question. "I'll get Morgan ready. You've got some time." She squeezed his shoulder before turning, her heels clanking out a steady rhythm as she disappeared down the hall.

Charles took a sip of his coffee, bitter, lukewarm. He'd forgotten to grab sugar. He gulped it down anyway, the acidity assaulting his tongue. His phone chimed.

It had to be Sally. Finally.

But no, a text from an unknown number. He tapped on it.

Mandy? What the hell did she want? He waited, a surge of hope. Maybe Alyssa had finally confessed? Having confirmation of Alyssa's guilt would be a godsend right now.

He gaped at the next message. Alyssa. *Searching for Sally?* But how did anyone know Sally was missing? Unless ... did Sally reach out to Alyssa? He shook his head, he didn't have time for this. He needed to get ready for Morgan's CT scan, the moment of truth: if there was internal brain damage from whatever the hell happened. The worry wedged in his throat.

He looked at his phone again. This ruined everything. Alyssa out searching for Sally, some act of redemption. If she found her, which seemed impossible, the cops would shower her with praise: *Heroic Babysitter Chases Down Abusive Mother.*

Or the other scenario: the cops discovering *both* Sally and Alyssa missing—halting the case in its tracks. It might buy him more time. Time for what? To call that P.I., to find Sally. But did she want to be found?

He longed to ask Mandy: *Why the hell is Alyssa doing this?*

He cleared his empty mug and headed back to Morgan's room. They'd arrived at the hospital a little over twenty-four hours ago, and in that time, Morgan had an ultrasound, an X-ray, various brain and sight and hearing and verbal tests, and blood pricks. Next up, a CT scan. At only one year old, he'd had more tests than Charles had had in a lifetime.

Please let there be nothing. Please let his brain be unharmed, he begged. To whom? A God? Sally? The universe?

In the end, was it his fault? Yes, it was. For trusting Alyssa? For not demanding that Morgan see the doctor sooner? But why would Sally run away?

He paused, then typed out his response to Mandy: **I hope we find them soon.** The simple truth: *Let's find everyone and figure out what the hell happened to Morgan.*

"We're just about ready," the nurse said, standing in front of Morgan's door. Morgan sat in his wheelie-crib, firmly grasping the bars, ready to be whisked off to yet another invasive procedure, more poking and prodding and zapping in the endless search for answers.

Charles leaned over the crib's railing and cupped Morgan's face in his sweaty palms. "You got this, little buddy," he said. Morgan stared at him with a vacant expression.

"Mama?" he mumbled, pulling away and shoving a thumb in his mouth.

"Mama loves you," Charles managed to say. He gently kissed his boy on the forehead. "She loves you." He fought back warm, burning tears, hoping the words still held a hint of truth.

Chapter 31

Mandy

Day seven

Mandy peered out the door's peephole and watched as Claire paced her front steps like a predator ready to pounce. She was an older version of Jess: red glossy lips and gold eyeshadow sparkling in the morning sun; jet black hair—cut and styled into a fashionable bob; the same piercing, stubborn eyes. They'd never hit it off as friends, Mandy and Claire, even though their daughters insisted, pushing them together for years until finally giving up.

Mandy took a deep breath and opened the door.

"What's going on?" Claire demanded, searching the room before her eyes landed on Simon. "Where's my daughter?"

"Claire. I'm Simon." He walked over and extended his hand.

"*Detective* Simon," Mandy added. He shot her a look: *Don't.*

"A detective? Shit." Claire pushed her way in. "Mandy, you call me and say they're missing and that's it?"

"They—" The words stuck in Mandy's throat.

"They snuck out in the night," Simon finished.

"What do you mean they *snuck out?* Last night?" Claire flicked a tanned wrist upward and tapped on her gaudy metallic watch. "It's just past ten and I'm only hearing about this *now?*"

"I left you a voicemail, first thing this morn—"

"Did you get into a fight with Alyssa?" Claire asked. "Is that it?"

"What?" Mandy shook her head. "*Jess* is the one behind this. They took her—*your* car! Alyssa would've never left on her own—"

"Oh, c'mon. Jess has never run away before."

"Neither has Alyssa," Mandy snapped.

"Hey, hey, hey." Simon wedged himself between them. "Everyone needs to calm down. Take a deep breath. It's been less than twenty-four hours. And now that Claire's here I can do a search on the license plate—she took your car, right? Mandy, why don't you make everyone some coffee?"

"Yeah, Jess has my car," Claire said, sighing as she sat down at the kitchen table. "I work from home—I'm a bookkeeper—so I let her take it most days. Luckily I was nearby at that cafe down the road. My friend dropped me off here. If I'd known, I would've come much sooner and ..." She paused, drumming her sparkly, gold-tipped manicured nails on the table. "Are they ... do you think this is serious?"

Mandy switched on the electric kettle, not listening to Simon's response. She spooned coffee granules into three mugs, remembering one of Alyssa's final sentences: *We need to find Sally.* Alyssa believed Sally's life was in peril and how did Mandy respond? By dismissively shushing them off to bed, popping an Ambien, slipping into a coma-like slumber.

She brought the mugs to Simon and Claire, then walked back to the kitchen window. She stared out at the parking lot, blinking against the sun. Claire's phone rang.

"Derek, hi," Claire said. Her ex, Jess's father up in New York. "Yes, she's missing ... No, I didn't push her away ... Yes, there's a cop here."

Mandy felt a hand on her shoulder and jumped. She turned.

"What's the deal with Alyssa's father?" Simon asked.

"Ian? No. Alyssa would never go to him."

"Runaway teens often—" He stopped, a quick glance in Claire's direction. "I think it's time we consider ..." He spoke cautiously, as if attempting to defuse a bomb. "The *possibility* that Alyssa knows something about Morgan's accident. She was terrified, no doubt, too overwhelmed to come forward. That'd be enough to make any teen run away." His gaze dropped, as if to study the intricate pattern of her linoleum floor.

"I already told you, Alyssa had nothing to do with Morgan's accident."

"But maybe she didn't realize Morgan was hurt. Like a quick tumble down the stairs. It could happen to anyone."

"No," she said firmly. But then she saw a flash of Alyssa crying herself to sleep, harboring such an unbearable secret. She gasped at the thought, tears springing to her eyes.

"Hey, it's okay," Simon said, already armed with a tissue. "Sometimes it's hard to see or believe that the people we love could do—"

"Stop," Claire spat into her phone. "We *weren't* fighting."

Simon sighed, massaging the bridge of his nose with his forefinger and thumb. "I checked all the hospitals and car accident reports. Nothing there. I can check on a few more things but I think it's time we notify the—"

"I have no idea why she'd do this," Claire said, still on the phone. She turned and stared at Mandy, eyes flickering with fear and blame. As if this was all Mandy's fault.

Maybe it is.

The room was closing in. Mandy struggled to breathe. She pressed Alyssa's number again and again, then tapped on the volume button, turning it up.

"Mandy?" Simon said. "Did you hear what I said?"

She pushed her glasses into place, a revelation snapping into focus. With renewed gusto, she grabbed her purse and keys. "I have one more lead. Just give me thirty minutes."

"Wait, what?" Simon said. "Do you need me to come with you?"

"No." Mandy opened the door. "I need to do this on my own."

✦

The children's unit at Oak Wood Hospital was swarming with visitors toting balloons, bouquets of fresh flowers, boxed lunches. The sterile smells and flickering lights once again dragged Mandy back to the hospital, that other hospital in Buffalo Grove almost thirteen—no, fourteen years ago. *Zack.* Her son had lived for three brief days. She lost him. She couldn't lose her daughter too.

She groaned when she saw the long check-in line ahead.

Rocking side to side, she continued hitting redial—listening to her daughter's deadpan voicemail: *Why oh why leave a message when you can text instead?* Alyssa had to be with Sally and Sally had to be with Alyssa. And Charles … he was the missing link. He had to have a clue, an overlooked answer, something he didn't feel comfortable sharing over text.

The line inched forward.

She felt bad abandoning Simon with the irate Claire, but she knew in her gut she had to do this. Together, with Charles, they could solve the mystery, figure out where Sally and Alyssa were hiding out. Hopefully it would work. She found Simon's card in her purse and sent him a quick text: **Sorry to rush off. I'll explain soon.**

Her eyes floated up and there, up ahead, she saw Charles pushing Morgan in an umbrella stroller, a gray-haired woman shuffling beside them. Morgan's grandmother? Morgan peeked out from under a blue-starred blanket with weary eyes, a tattered Elmo balanced on his lap.

A nurse spoke to them. Mandy squinted, trying to interpret her face, the soundless words. Charles and the older woman listened with bleak expressions, heavy eyes, solemn nods. Were they crying?

Bad news. It had to be bad news. But what? Morgan already had a broken rib. Mandy stood still, uncomfortably spying on their misery, taking in such palpable grief. Sweat shone on Charles's forehead. Then she remembered the other part of Morgan's prognosis, what Alyssa shared after her interview: *A possible concussion.*

It struck her. The plausible truth.

Years ago, she had held a squirmy, pink-cheeked Alyssa close to her chest, swaddled in a red-poppy-patterned blanket, while the postpartum nurse firmly told her: "If you ever feel angry or out of control, put your baby in a safe place. Leave the room to calm down. Don't ever hold your baby while you're mad."

Why? Mandy had innocently wondered. The nurse simply handed her a brochure: **Never Shake a Baby.**

Mandy watched as Charles, Morgan, and the grandmother disappeared down the hall. The nurse paused, a deep sorrow painted across her face, before heading down another corridor.

Someone nudged Mandy. "You're next."

She reached out to steady herself on the desk. Why didn't she see this, think of this before? Could it be? Could Sally have—?

"Ma'am?" a voice called, from faraway, as if echoing through a hollow cave.

She had to leave. She couldn't show up *now*, not with Charles facing a gut-wrenching diagnosis. What if he tried to pin this on Alyssa? The heaviness dragged her down and once again, she saw Zack—his wrinkled lips sucking on the plastic tube, his frail body convulsing—the deadly seizure two hours after surgery, his balled-up fists swinging in the air, desperately trying to cling to a fading life. Mandy leaned over, gasping, as tears spilled down her cheeks.

Another voice, "Do you need help?"

Her phone silently vibrated in her hand.

"H—Hello?" she answered.

"It's me. Simon."

"Did you find them?"

"I—"

The phone cut out. Mandy held up the screen. Blank. She pushed the power button. The battery, it must've died. Oh God, she'd forgotten to charge it last night. She dropped to the floor, dumping her purse's contents, and shoved aside her wallet, tampons, tubes of crusted lipstick, searching for a power cord. She always carried a power cord. Why didn't she hear the warning beeps? Unless, in her frenzied state to crank the volume up, she'd accidentally turned it down?

"No, no, no." She shoved everything back into her denim purse. Did Simon have good news or bad news? Or no news at all?

Mandy frantically pushed the elevator button several times and waited. After a minute, she turned and pushed through the exit door, holding her breath as she raced down five flights of stairs. Outside, she inhaled the humid air, her heart exploding.

Please be okay, she pleaded to her daughter. She hoped that her voice, her love, resonated loud enough to keep her only child alive.

Chapter 32

Alyssa

Days six and seven

Jess unlocked her mom's black Mazda. Alyssa stopped in her tracks, waiting to see if the *bloop-bloop* stirred the dead. Nothing. It seemed too easy, sneaking out, being reckless. Except, Alyssa told herself, we're not being reckless. The goal of this mission: save and protect Sally.

"Greyhound first?" Alyssa asked.

"That's where I'd go if I wanted to disappear," Jess said, balancing her phone on the steering wheel as she selected a Spotify playlist.

Alyssa punched in the address on her phone.

"So." Jess licked her lips. "You really think Sally is innocent?"

"I'm pretty sure." Alyssa remembered Sally's red-rimmed eyes from Friday—the fear, the tremors, the tear-stained cheeks. "Like, she's running from Charles. Guys like him, all chill and stuff, people never see it coming."

"Like that guy in Colorado. The one who strangled his pregnant wife. And killed his two little girls. Did you know they were from North Carolina?" Jess shook her head in disgust. "Everyone thought the guy was like the best dad ever. What a sicko."

"Exactly," Alyssa said. She thought about her own dad, how he dragged her on those secret missions, abandoning her in his cold truck for all of eternity. Was he *all* bad, though? She remembered the sweet moments, his hands firmly secured around her wrists, spinning her faster and faster until the world transformed into a colorful swirl: *I'm flying!* Or catching her at the bottom of the world's longest slide. "Don't worry, I won't let you fall." A solid promise, one he did manage to keep.

"Find a pic of Sally," Jess instructed her.

Alyssa typed in *Sally Haywood.* They were already Facebook friends.

"Wow, look at those lashes," Jess said, leaning over. "Extensions?"

"All natural, I think."

Jess pulled into the Greyhound station. She flipped down the mirror and applied mascara with two quick strokes, followed by a thick coat of vibrant red lipstick. She puckered her lips before grabbing Alyssa's phone. "Let's do this."

A teenager with angry acne sat behind the counter, swiping at his phone. The lobby was empty, apart from a guy in a flannel shirt and ripped jeans and mud-splattered hiking boots sprawled across a bench, using his backpack as a pillow.

"Hey," Jess said. She flicked open the top two buttons of her shirt and rearranged her boobs. "My cousin's run away and we're trying to find her. Have you seen this girl?" She held up Alyssa's phone.

The guy kept his eyes glued on his phone. "Call the cops."

"Bro, we really don't want to involve the authorities." Jess leaned over the counter. "We're hoping we can figure this out, just between the two of us."

His eyes widened as he took in Jess's cleavage. Alyssa rolled her eyes.

"What's in it for me?" He set down his phone, cracking a grin.

"$10?" Jess offered.

"$30."

"All we've got is $20." She slid the bill across the counter.

"Okay, fine." He snatched the bill and grabbed Alyssa's phone. "Yeah, she was here, earlier today. Got real mental with the vending machine."

"And?" Jess prodded.

"She had a ticket for ... Colorado? But she didn't board. Bolted outta here around five-ish or so."

"That's it?" Jess said. "That's all you got?"

"That's all I saw."

"Well, damn!" Jess said, slapping the counter.

"Let's just go," Alyssa said.

"Wait," the guy said. He came out from behind the counter. "I did … well, I noticed one more thing."

"Yes?" Alyssa asked.

"She looked like … her leggings. They were, um …" He looked over at the guy on the bench, still passed out. "They were soaked. It was hard to tell but it looked like blood."

Jess and Alyssa locked eyes, as if to say *period leakage?*

"Way worse than *that*," the guy added, his pimples turning a shade brighter. "I started to come around, to check if she needed help, but that's when she ran. I checked the bathroom and found a few streaks of smeared blood on the floor. It didn't seem sus enough to call the cops so I just let her go …" He shrugged, then shoved his hands into his pockets.

"Oh my God, she's legit hurt," Alyssa said. "We really need to find her now."

"She couldn't have gone far," Jess said, already sprinting toward the door.

Alyssa glanced behind her to see the ticket guy saunter back to his station.

"Liss! Let's go!"

✦

Jess flicked on the headlights as they squealed out of the Greyhound station. "You were totally right on your hunch that she was missing."

"It was actually my mom's theory."

"Ah, well. *She* was right. Now, let's start by calling all the nearby motels. They won't tell us the room number, but they'll connect us if she's staying there."

"And then what?" Alyssa asked.

"One step at a time." Jess pulled into the Burger King drive-through, ordered using her employee discount, and pulled around to the front.

She unwrapped a greasy burger, took a bite, then started googling motels.

Alyssa blew on a hot fry. “This is never going to work.”

“Hello?” Jess said into her phone. “Yes, I’m looking to speak to Sally …” She raised her eyebrows expectantly at Alyssa.

“Haywood. Sally Haywood,” Alyssa said.

“Uh-huh. I understand,” Jess said while nodding. “Sorry to bother you.”

“We’re wasting our time.” Alyssa downed her milkshake, too fast. *Brain freeze.*

“Just chill. We know they don’t have a lot of money, or at least they don’t act like it, working for Uber and Denny’s. She probably picked a budget place, like Super 8 or Motel 6. Next, she picked one close by, to save on taxi fare. So, we’ve got like ten places. Easy peasy.” Jess continued scrolling, her face scrunched up in that concentrated look, the one Alyssa only saw emerge when she struggled to understand algebraic equations or the periodic table.

“The chem exam,” Alyssa said. “Did you actually go?”

Jess snorted. “Yeah. Talk about a total shit show. Ended up filling the bubbles at random while Beastly stomped around the room like a deranged drill sergeant.” She fiddled with her nose ring. “Wait. Maybe Sally checked in under her maiden name? To be less traceable?”

“But don’t you need proper ID to get a motel room?”

“She could’ve used an old one.” Jess’s teeth glowed under the luminous moon.

“You really think of everything.” Alyssa opened Facebook again, clicking on Sally’s profile. “It just says Sally Haywood, no maiden name.” She paused on a picture of Sally and Charles, his arms wrapped around her. Strong hands. The kind of hands that could break ribs.

“Okay, let’s think.” Jess ran her fingers up and down the steering wheel. “Any clues at their house? A diploma hanging on the wall?”

Alyssa squeezed her eyes shut, scanning the stored memories of the Haywoods’ house—the dirty carpet, the pesky cat doing figure eights between her legs, the stack of fly-ridden dishes piled in the sink. The playpen. That freakish dead rabbit and its haunting eyes.

"The fridge. Maybe a postcard?" Jess prodded. "An appointment reminder?"

Twirling and twisting the ends of her hair, a blurred vision started to sharpen into focus. An obituary, pinned on the fridge next to one of Morgan's splattered finger paintings.

"Anything?"

"I think ..." Alyssa tapped her closed eyelids. "Her mom died of cancer. Anita Steele? I'm positive. Well, like 93.7 percent sure."

"Sally Steele." Jess skimmed the results, then held up her phone. "This looks like her."

A couple of years younger, thin cheekbones, but without a doubt it was Sally—the same delicate eyes, her signature sun-streaked blond hair, those model-like lashes. "Wow, she was a star athlete at Northwest Guilford High," Alyssa said. "I never knew she was a runner."

"Interesting. And there's something here from a beauty pageant. So skinny! Sally Steele—totally sounds like a movie star's name."

"Yeah. Much better than Haywood." Alyssa scratched at her head. She couldn't help but wonder why Sally didn't share anything from her past. It wasn't like they were besties or anything, but still. "I wonder why she changed it?"

"Love does crazy shit." Jess scrolled to the next motel on the list. "You can try calling too, you know."

"You're doing a pretty good job yourself, *detective*."

Jess scowled at her, stealing a fry. After the seventh or eighth call Alyssa yanked the phone out of Jess's hands. "I'm getting tired of this," she said.

"Yes, we have a Sally Steele here," a voice echoed on the other end. "Let me put you through."

"Hang up!" Jess shouted.

"Oh my God," Alyssa shrieked as she ended the call and tossed the phone into Jess's lap as if it'd bitten her. "Was that really—did we just ...?"

Jess studied her call log. "The Budget Inn, over by Walmart."

"Shit, are you serious?"

"Unless there's another Sally Steele out there?"

"Ahhhhhh! I didn't think it was possible!" Alyssa screeched, pounding her fists on the dashboard.

"I knew she wouldn't go far."

Alyssa trembled with a giddy disbelief. Sally hiding out, right here in town. She'd run away and they'd tracked her down. It felt impossible, all of it.

Now, hopefully Sally will spill the details and we'll have proof that Charles is a dangerous maniac and I can clear my name, retake the chem exam, and pretend like none of this ever happened.

✦

Jess and Alyssa stepped out of the car and surveyed the sketchy parking lot. The Budget Inn.

"What's your plan?" Alyssa asked. "We're too young to rent a room."

"I know."

"You better figure it out fast." Alyssa had vague memories of this dilapidated motel, or one that looked exactly like it, waiting in her dad's truck while he bounded up the stairs. He was gone for hours and when he returned, he shoved a small paper bag under the seat. *Drugs?* She shivered.

"The rooms are accessible from the outside," Jess said. "Sally would've requested a ground unit, being in pain and all."

"We assume she's in pain."

"If you were bleeding enough to soak your pants, you'd be in pain."

"Why do you think she's bleeding so much?" Alyssa asked.

"Miscarriage?"

"Or an attack from Charles?" Alyssa felt a wave of nausea. "Why didn't I speak up sooner?"

"You had no way of knowing. It could've been self-harm." Jess's eyes narrowed in, green lasers analyzing, dissecting. "She could've cut herself, like on her thighs. Remember Lydia, in the seventh grade? I saw the scars when we changed for gym class."

Alyssa wrapped her arms around herself. "Sally doesn't seem like a cutter."

"There's probably a lot you don't know about that woman." Jess pointed in opposite directions. "How about you go right and I'll go left?"

"Are you kidding me?" Alyssa stepped closer and latched onto Jess's arm. "No way, I'm not splitting up. Not here, not at this hour."

"Okay, okay. *Chill.* We'll go together."

"What exactly are we looking for?"

Jess switched on her phone's flashlight. "If she's bleeding, there's gotta be a spot somewhere. On the sidewalk, the door handle—"

"Wait." Alyssa stopped. "We're going to shine our phones at every window and door? At *midnight*?"

"You got a better idea?"

"I—"

Jess didn't wait for her to finish. She tiptoed toward the first row of rooms. Almost half of them had curtains wide open—dark and lifeless. But two rooms had slivers of light glowing around the curtains' edges.

"I say that one." Jess pointed.

"What makes you think she'd leave her light on?" Alyssa jumped at a rustling in the bushes.

"Imagine this: stumbling into a motel room, flicking on the lights, passing out on the bed."

Alyssa tried to picture it but the stream of questions rushed in: Why did Sally stay so close to town? Why didn't she reach out to the cops if Charles was threatening her? What if she refused to open the door for them?

Jess knocked. A man with a flimsy towel wrapped around his hairy waist flung the door open. "What?" he sneered.

"Sorry," Jess said. "Wrong room."

The man slammed the door in her face.

"You're going to get us killed," Alyssa hissed.

"If we don't do anything, Sally's going to die."

"Then let's call the cops. We know she's at this motel. We can give an anonymous tip—"

Jess knocked on the next door and pushed her ear against it.

"Jess!"

Jess put a finger to her lips: *shhh*. She knocked louder.

They listened. Sure enough, soft footsteps padded closer.

"Gwen?" a tired, weary voice called out.

They looked at each other, shrugging.

Jess cleared her throat. "Yes, this is Gwen," she said in a deep voice.

The deadbolt unlatched; the door creaked open. And Sally's pale, swollen face peered out.

Holy shit, we found Sally.

Chapter 33

Sally

Days six and seven

Sally collapsed on top of the mustard-yellow bedspread, her head—pulsating, vibrating—sinking into yet another motel pillow. The painkillers stilled the incessant, inexplicable pain.

She fell into a fitful sleep. She was pushing a trolley through an airport terminal, piled high with suitcases. She noticed a stroller up ahead—Morgan's stroller, surrounded by sniffing dogs. A crowd began to gather. A suitcase fell over and clothes tumbled everywhere. "Shit!" She paused, then hurried on without it, plowing through the crowd.

Finally, she reached the stroller. It lay on its side, empty. The dogs fought over the Elmo doll like a tug-of-war. It burst open, white fluff flying everywhere, Elmo's bright-white eyes rolling across the floor with a disturbing clunking sound.

"Where's Morgan?" Sally cried, dropping to her knees and clawing at the stroller. A loud wail filled the space—"My baby! My baby!"—her voice raw and brittle. Nobody offered to help. They peered on in horror, possessively guarding their purses and suitcases, cautiously inching away but too mesmerized to scatter. Someone even spat at her. The dogs ran off with the remaining Elmo fluff hanging from their jowls. Sally tried crawling into the stroller, but it was too small. An officer kicked her, then hoisted the stroller above his head before disappearing into the disorderly crowd.

"Help!" Sally bellowed from the floor. Nobody listened. Nobody cared.

A steady knock stirred her out of the dream. She jerked up, dripping in sweat. Blinking, it took a moment to orient herself, for the memories to flood in: Morgan's screams, her hands squeezing his torso. Leaving the hospital. The bus station. Bleeding. Walmart. That cancer girl's innocent eyes begging for help.

The pounding returned, a little louder. Both from the door and from inside her muddled head. Reaching down, she felt the dampness between her legs. She looked—the bedspread stained with blood.

"Noooo," she moaned.

The knocking didn't stop. She clambered out of bed, then focused on the motel's door. "Gwen?" she called out. Who else could it be?

A pause of silence.

"Yes, this is Gwen," the voice responded.

Sally wobbled across the floor and unlatched the lock. Her heart wild and unhinged. *She came?*

✦

How could she have been so stupid? Gwen never responded to Sally's pleas for help. But who would've thought Alyssa had the wits and gumption and resources to hunt her down? And why?

"It's okay, we're here to help," Alyssa announced. She waltzed right in, followed by a punkish teenager with purple-pink streaked black hair, a silver nose ring. *Click.* The lock latched.

Sally shook her head, her tangled hair falling into her eyes. They didn't belong here. This was not part of the plan. *Leave,* she tried to say, but no sound came.

The girls stood there, looking dumbfounded. The air conditioner kicked in, the buzzing whir slicing the silence. Then the girls guided Sally back to bed. A cold hand brushed her forehead as her eyes clouded over, the voices swirling together.

"She's burning up."

"Oh my God—is that blood?"

"She's not looking good."

"Shitshitshit. Jess, what do we do?"

Sally's eyes squinted open. The nose-ring girl—Jess?—disappeared. The spinning returned and Alyssa's face distorted, doubled, then tripled, her mouth opened wide, eyes brimming with shock.

"I got some towels," Jess said.

"We need to do something," Alyssa said. "I'm calling 911."

"Noooo," Sally mumbled, trying to sit up. "They can't know ... they'll ask questions ..." The girls were surprisingly strong, pinning her down. They draped a cool, damp rag across her forehead. Her stomach stirred, the excruciating stabs digging deeper.

"Sally," Jess said. "This is serious. We can either call 911 or drive you to the hospital."

"No ambulance ... my insurance doesn't cover ..." Sally trembled. Alternating cold chills and heat waves seized her muscles.

"And what about *Charles*?" Alyssa said. "He'll find her."

"Let's drop her at the ER, give them fake names. I think Durham Regional is close."

Their voices drifted away. Sally moaned. Pain meds, she needed more meds. With a shaky finger, she pointed to the nightstand, the Midol bottle flickering in and out of focus. And then Morgan appeared, his angelic blue eyes peering up at her. "Mama." She reached out to him, trying to block the sharp memory of his screams.

"I'm sorry," she whispered. "My baby. My baby."

The girls ignored her.

"We don't have much time," Alyssa said. "This is ... holy shit. There's *so much* blood."

"It's time to sit up, Sally," Jess instructed.

Sally slapped the girls away, searching the room for her boy. He was right here, she saw him. They forced her to her wobbly feet, then tied a white sheet around her waist, like a makeshift toga.

"I can't." Sally muttered. "Morgan. Where'd he go?" The room blurred, colors dissipating, the sounds screeching to a halt. Then came the now familiar blackness.

✦

Sally opened her eyes. She was in the back of a car. Every bump made her insides jostle. She released a throaty growl. A hand squeezed hers. Then, the car stopped. A clatter of noise outside, like the dream at the airport.

Is this another dream?

Someone lowered her into a wheelchair. She tried to protest, arms flailing, but a calm voice instructed her to relax. Staring at a streetlamp above, she watched, transfixed, as it split into a million spots, blinding bursts of dancing golden light.

They passed through sliding glass doors. A rush of cold air. Harsh lights, a sterile sickening smell, pristine floors, white walls. The hospital. They were at a hospital.

Morgan, she squeaked. *Where are you?*

She was wheeled to a room with pale pink walls. She closed her eyes, listening as the panicked voices swirled around her.

"… blood loss …"

"… critical …"

"… let's move her …"

"Sally? Can you hear me?" The voice bounced off the walls. "We need your consent to give you a blood transfusion. Do you understand?"

She opened her mouth but only a whimper came out.

The cold air paralyzed her, goosebumps rippling across her body as they tugged off the bloody toga-sheet, leggings, underwear. Clicking, whirring sounds, more voices—mumbled, desperate. A stabbing pain in her arm. Drifting off… waking up. Something cold and hard pushing into her aching belly. She tried to lift her head, but a firm hand forced her down, rubbing her forehead. "It's going to be okay."

But they were wrong; nothing about this was okay.

The room grew dark. Shadows danced around her, more bodies, more voices. The hypnotic beeping sounds luring her into a sedative trance.

"Mom …" she mumbled. And just like that, her mother appeared: thick, luscious hair, rosy, plump cheeks, the lavender essence—so familiar and pacifying. She slid in beside Sally. *There, there, it's going to be okay.* Her presence felt like an extra layer of skin, a shield of armor ready to defend Sally, to offer unconditional protection.

I missed you, Sally sobbed, stroking her mom's hair.

All the voices and beeps and clicks trickled to silence. Her mom vanished. "No, no, no, don't leave me," Sally begged. She tried to open her eyes but couldn't—they were drained, lifeless. She couldn't even move her hands.

Am I dead?

Chapter 34

Sally

Day seven

Sally's dreams continued, convoluted and distressed: Morgan red-faced and teary-eyed, his high-pitched wails ringing in her ears; Sally curled in a ball, naked, shivering; Charles pacing and shouting. What was he saying? Sally's hands wrapped around Charles's torso, her fingers squeezing and pushing, shaking. Charles's head lolled to one side; Morgan tugged at her pants. *Stop.* Did he just talk?

Next, Sally was running outside, a heavy backpack thudding against her back, Morgan screaming in his stroller. She tripped over a rock and went sailing through the air, her head slamming into the pavement. Looking up, she watched as the stroller rolled down the hill, picking up speed, heading directly to a glistening lake below.

"Help!" she screamed, paralyzed. Too late.

"Sally? Can you hear me?"

Her eyes snapped open. A machine stood next to her, flashing with rhythmical beeps. A clear tube stuck out of her arm, a liquid bag suspended above. The hospital.

"She's awake," a voice said.

Sally coughed. Someone handed her a glass of water. She took a few sips.

"Sally." A nurse blinked into focus. "You're lucky your nieces brought you in when they did. You've lost a lot of blood. We had to do an emergency blood transfusion." The nurse fiddled with the tube and replaced the bag.

Nieces? Blood transfusion?

Alyssa stretched her arms overhead as she rose from the couch in the corner. She took a tentative step closer. The other girl joined her. Jess?

Sally struggled to sit up but the nurse placed a hand on her chest.

"You need to rest," the nurse said. "We did an ultrasound, and the baby is okay, for now."

"The baby?" Sally croaked. Did she mean Morgan?

"We need to know how many weeks along you are," the nurse continued. "And the name of your current OB."

Sally blinked. "What?"

"You do know you're pregnant, right?"

The words didn't make any sense. Sally instinctively touched her stomach—a strap snug across it with a bulging monitor. No. No. *No!* She took the pill, religiously, every single day.

"Um …" The nurse looked at Alyssa, and then Jess. "Let me get the doctor."

Once the nurse left, Alyssa leaned in. "Sally." Her color drained, like she'd seen a ghost.

"Why'd you tell them my real name?" Sally's eyes lingered on the door. How much did they know? How long before the cops barged in?

"We were going to give them a fake name, but you blurted *Sally* right when we arrived," Jess said. "Don't you remember?"

"Huh?" Sally rubbed her eyes.

"You were really out of it. We tried to leave but they asked so many questions," Jess said. "We told them we're your nieces, visiting from out of town. We even gave you a fake last name. They seemed to buy it but then demanded your ID."

"We tried to protect you, thinking you were on the run from Charles," Alyssa said. "But apparently if you're in serious condition with no ID, they call the cops."

"So they know who I am." Sally tried to swallow but her throat closed up.

"But we still faked it," Jess boasted. "We stashed our wallets and phones in the trunk of the car, made up fake names—she's Stacey and I'm Claudia, from the Babysitter's Club."

"Which I thought was ridiculous." Alyssa rolled her eyes. "So obvious."

"Nobody reads those books anymore," Jess said. "It was a legit choice."

"They're *classics,*" Alyssa moaned.

"So, they called Charles?" Sally put her hand to her forehead. "He's on his way?"

"Not yet," Alyssa said. "When we gave them your ID, all we could find was the *Sally Steele* one. They asked why we'd lied about your identity. We told them you didn't want your husband to know you were here, so they flagged your chart as private or something."

"My real name is Sally Steele. We're not married, not legally. And wait, you went through my purse? Did you see an envelope with—"

A steady knock interrupted her. A slender, dark-skinned woman entered. The girls grew quiet and retreated to the wall.

"Good morning, Sally," the woman said. She had wide-set brown eyes, black hair swept into a high bun. "I'm Dr. Parvati Patel, but please, just call me Parvati."

The room's colors swirled. Sally stared at the doctor's oversized gold hoop earrings as a focal point.

"It looks like you're around twenty-five weeks pregnant," Parvati explained. "You've had a placental abruption—that's where the placenta separates from the uterine wall. It's a life-threatening situation, for both you and the baby."

The words turned to garbled static. Sally looked to the window. The blinds still closed with slender rays of light peeking in. A new day. She could open it and …

You don't deserve love. Who said that?

"Sally? Do you understand?"

She turned, her heart heavy, body spent, legs twitching. The doctor stared at her.

"But—I took the pill. Every day." Didn't she? That little packet of pink pills, lined up like diligent soldiers, ready to march to battle—to lock down her eggs, or kill the sperm. Whatever the hell they did. But then she remembered the OB's warning about the mini pill: *You must take it at the exact same time every day.*

"I see," Parvati said. A sadness spread across her face, eyes deepening. "I take it this is an unplanned pregnancy then."

Did she, this doctor, even know? Did she know about Morgan and his broken rib? What about the cops? And Charles. Where the hell was Charles?

As if reading her mind, the doctor leaned in and asked, "Sally, would you like us to contact the father of the baby?" The girls shook their heads, lips pursed, eyes averted.

"Do not call Charles," Sally said through clenched teeth.

"Another adult?" Parvati prodded, glancing at the girls. "Someone who can help with Sally's condition?"

"There's no one else," Alyssa said.

Abortion. She had to destroy this. She, of course, would never tell Charles. She'd almost done it with Morgan, had gotten as far as the procedure room, wearing a paper-thin robe, cold feet dangling over the examination table. Within seconds, he would've been sucked and scraped out, and her life—her body—would've returned to normal. Her eyes grew moist at the memory.

"Well, like I've said," the doctor continued, "we've managed to stop the bleeding for now. But we'll need to keep you here for some time, to ensure the baby—and you—remain stable. If things take a turn for the worse, we'll need to do an emergency C-section. In which case, we'll give you an antenatal steroid treatment, which will help speed up the development of the baby's lungs. This will increase her chances of—"

"Her?" Sally interrupted.

"Yes." Parvati smiled. "It's a girl."

Oh, dear God, Sally thought. *A baby girl.*

"But we want to wait as long as possible, to increase her chances of survival outside the womb—"

"Wait, you mean abortion isn't an option?" Sally blurted. The words sliced at her like a knife. How could she think about killing a baby girl? Her baby girl. But the alternative ... *another* baby? The crying, the screaming—the endless hours spent enduring those ear-shattering screams. She closed her eyes as Morgan's wails reverberated inside her, a sound she'd never forget.

"Sally, you're twenty-five weeks pregnant. That's about six months."

Her eyes fluttered open. *Six months?* "What?" She tried to sit up again, but a wave of pain knocked her down.

"You seriously didn't know?" That was from Jess, the snarky nose-ring girl.

"Look, this does happen from time to time," Parvati explained. "You were on birth control and barely showing. Plus, you have an anterior placenta. This would've dulled or completely blocked the baby's early movement. In fact, I've seen women with anterior placentas not feel a single kick until week twenty-four or later." She gave a reassuring nod. "It's not common but it does happen. Especially for first time mothers."

First time mothers. The doctor didn't know. The girls, Alyssa and Jess, must've lied. Morgan no longer existed.

How could Sally not have noticed? Those flutters and strange sensations—she kept brushing it off as gas, indigestion, hunger, stress, or a combination of it all. But she'd been pregnant before; she should've known. That was her *daughter* squirming away in there, trying to get Sally to acknowledge her existence.

How much did she drink? Downing that box of cheap wine the other night and passing out on the bathroom floor. Ruining her daughter's life before it officially started.

"Noooo," Sally groaned. She tried to claw the strap off her belly, to pull the tube out of her arm, to—

"Sally, please calm down," the doctor said, her voice turning stern. "We need to—you're in serious condition. There are options if you decide ... adoption and ..." The doctor stopped. She took a deep breath. "Can you share how you got this bruise on your face?"

Sally's hand fluttered to her cheek. "I think ... I fell?"

"Okay, okay," the doctor said, as if Sally was a young child pathetically attempting to lie. "I'll be back soon. Just try to rest up, please." She gave Sally's arm a gentle pat before leaving the room.

Sally felt lightheaded, but a different kind than before. Like floating away, ready to abandon this body, these mistakes, her failure. She turned to face Alyssa and Jess. Waited for them to say something, to explain what happened, to offer words of encouragement. Hope. Anything.

Alyssa finally spoke, "Are you sure there's no one we can call?"

"I have no one," Sally said. What would Charles do if he knew there was another baby on the way? She felt a sudden kick from within, followed by a wave of wretched pain.

Jess inched closer. "What really happened to Morgan?"

Alyssa stared at Jess, her mouth hanging open.

"He has a broken rib, Sally," Jess continued. "And everyone's blaming Alyssa. Seriously, what did you do?"

Sally bit her lower lip, still holding her stomach. She stared at the stark ceiling above, a warm tear escaping the corner of her eye. "Look, I was trying to disappear. Nobody asked you to come save me."

"That's it? You hurt him and won't even admit it?" Jess shook her head. "You had the cops interrogate my friend here!"

Alyssa grabbed Jess's arm. "Stop. It wasn't her."

"Why are you doing this? Why are you helping me?" Sally asked, studying Alyssa. "Is this some trick to, what? Turn me in? And what did you do with my money—" She stopped. Her stomach convulsed and contracted, the monitor's beeps escalating. Sally grasped the rails of the bed, watching as her knuckles turned red then white, her hoarse screams filling the room.

Chapter 35

Alyssa

Day seven

Sally's tortured screams pushed Alyssa into action: She lurched forward, arms tense, head buzzing, and pushed the red emergency button. Within moments, a team rushed in with a flurry of shouts and instructions. Bright lights flooded the room.

"You girls need to leave!" the nurse shouted.

Alyssa froze, watching as Sally writhed and thrashed and gasped for life, before Jess grabbed her and hauled her into the hall.

"We need to go home now," Jess said.

"How can you even say that? What if she dies?" Alyssa swallowed the fear filling her throat. "And why were you accusing her like that?"

"I'm sorry, it just kinda came out." Jess leaned against the wall. "I don't know, I can just see it in her eyes. She's hiding something."

Alyssa shook her head, seeing a quick flash of Morgan—his giddy laugh, his chubby little cheeks. "No," she whispered. "Sally would *never* hurt Morgan. Not on purpose."

"Okay, whatever. But you being here is bad. The fake names are only going to hold out for so long. We should split before the cops—"

"I just want to make sure she's okay before we leave," Alyssa said, leaning beside Jess, the support of the wall holding her up. She strained her neck, trying to decipher the faint murmurs coming from behind the door.

Finally, the nurse emerged. "She's stabilized. You girls can come back in."

Alyssa breathed a sigh of relief when she saw Sally—eyes blinking like windshield wipers. The beeping machines resumed their steady, reassuring pace. The team left the room in a trickle, the main doctor Parvati and the nurse staying on.

"The baby's heart rate has been sporadic. She's in distress," Parvati explained to them. "We're going to move ahead with the antenatal steroid treatment. We have to give two shots, twenty-four hours apart—"

"Wait ... what's happening?" Sally asked, her voice a hoarse whisper.

"Sally, we need to prepare for an emergency C-section." Parvati looked at the clock on the wall. Half past nine. "We'll wait as long as possible. But we're going to administer the first shot now." The nurse moved to the side of the bed, lightly tapping a needle.

"You girls really need to contact another adult." Parvati firmly squeezed Alyssa's shoulder. "Now."

"But—" Alyssa gave Jess a desperate look. Jess narrowed her eyes and shook her head.

"Look, I know you girls aren't telling the truth. Whatever you're hiding, it's okay. We want to help. If it's a domestic abuse issue ..." Parvati lowered her voice, stepping closer to Alyssa. "We'll keep Sally and the baby safe, okay? But an adult needs to be here. Maybe one of your parents?"

"We—we'll try," Alyssa said.

Parvati nodded, her smooth forehead scrunching up. "We'll be back soon," she said, then left the room with the nurse.

"Do not call Charles," Sally said after the door closed. Her face was dripping with sweat.

Alyssa took a deep breath, the fatigue creeping into the edges of her brain, her stomach grumbling. "I—can't even think straight. Maybe we should get some breakfast from the cafe?"

"Really?" Jess said. "We can just go home and—"

"It's down the hall," Alyssa insisted.

"Okay, fine," Jess said, throwing up her arms and storming out of the room.

"Wait," Sally said, grabbing Alyssa's arm. "What hospital are we at?"

"Durham Regional."

"Morgie, he's back at Oak Wood."

"I feel like we really need to …" Alyssa sighed. "The doctor, she said—"

"Don't call anyone." Sally tugged Alyssa closer. Her voice sounded weak and strained. "Please. Just help me get through this. You've helped me this far—I have no idea why—but please …" She licked her dry, cracked lips. "Don't call anyone. I'm begging you."

Alyssa looked down at Sally, taking in her watery, skittish eyes, the nasty bruise smeared across her cheek.

"Did anything …?" Alyssa blinked, fighting back her own exhausted tears. "Was it Charles? Did he hurt you? Did he hurt Morgan?"

"Just please. I need more time." Sally released Alyssa's arm. "I need to come up with a plan."

Grabbing a tissue from the counter, Alyssa turned and dabbed at her eyes. "I'll be back soon," she mumbled, shoving the tissue in her pocket as she headed toward the door, not looking back.

✦

Jess sat at a round table in the far corner of the cafe with two Styrofoam plates—toast, omelets, and shriveled potatoes. "Here. Eat," she said, shoving a plate toward Alyssa. "Luckily I had a twenty in my pocket, otherwise we would've had to trek back to the car."

Alyssa pressed her palms into her eye sockets. "I really think this is because of Charles. She looks scared, don't you think?"

"Hmm." Jess scarfed down her food, chewing audibly. "I've never met this Charles dude—only seen his pic—but he seems solid. Something's totally off with Sally, though." She pointed her fork at Alyssa. "Eat."

Alyssa stabbed a piece of rubbery egg. She swallowed it whole, then took a swig of water from a plastic cup. She examined the rock-hard, brittle toast, holding it up to the light, before letting it drop to her plate.

"And not knowing she's preggers?" Jess shook her head. "I mean, six months! Like, really?"

"She's been a bit chunky the whole time I've known her, about six months," Alyssa said. "And she always wears loose clothes so I dunno."

"It's messed up."

Alyssa exhaled loudly, pushing her plate aside. "I should call my mom. I never planned on being away all night. She's probably having a total aneurysm right now." She imagined her mom running in circles, screaming her name in vain. Discovering the ladder hanging out the open window. *Oh dear God.*

"It's nuts we've stayed this long. I wanted to go home like seven hours ago, after the blood transfusion. But you insisted on keeping me prisoner here." Jess made a pouty face and pierced a potato off Alyssa's plate. "Don't worry, I know your mom. She probably called school, made up some excuse, and tiptoed off to work."

"Still, we should call her." Alyssa used her nail to scrape at a jelly stain on the table. "And where's Charles during all this? Huh? If he's so innocent, shouldn't he be out looking for Sally?"

"Maybe he is." Jess shrugged. "Or maybe he's scared shitless of her. She creeps me out."

"What are you talking about? Only a guilty person would send those messages." The lights burned her retinas, her stomach rumbling for a real meal. She longed for the safe cocoon of her bed, her plush rainbow socks, a mug of hot cocoa brimming with mini marshmallows, even one of her mom's overbearing hugs. Nervously tapping the plastic fork on the table, she longed to go retrieve her phone from Jess's trunk. She felt naked without it.

"Maybe," Jess said. "Or maybe he's a legit worried dad, and you were the easiest target."

"So you're on Charles's side now? Is that it? I thought you were on a mission to find Sally."

"We did find her and look, we saved her life." Jess pushed a strand of hair out of Alyssa's eyes. "Now it's time to call the cops, go home before this shit turns real. One of them broke Morgan's rib. One of them is a total psycho."

"But they said she's having her baby soon—"

"And what? You want to hang around for it? You're crazy! They said it's going to be like twenty-four hours." Jess pushed back her chair and stood. "C'mon Liss, you're all sleep-deprived and loopy. It's time to split."

Alyssa dragged her feet as she searched for the right words, something to give them more time. But really, what could they do? Hide in this hospital with Sally until her baby arrived? And then what? Help her run away with a preemie? To where? Perhaps she should tell Parvati, share her suspicions about Charles—*He's a serial abuser!* The doctor seemed super nice, but Alyssa doubted she'd believe her, especially if Charles came forward insisting Alyssa was the one who hurt Morgan. Who would believe her story against Charles's version? She was just a kid. *Just the babysitter.*

✦

Back at the car, they pulled out their wallets and phones from the trunk.

"I can't get blamed for this," Alyssa said. "I can't. It'll ruin my life. After Mom's worked so hard to support us, to get me to college, to—" She stopped, noticing an iPhone in a turquoise-jeweled case, crammed in the corner. She picked it up, the screen flashing to Morgan, his four adorable teeth poking through pink gums.

"Jess," she said. "We still have Sally's phone."

"What the hell? We seriously can't get away from that woman."

"What are we supposed to do? Taking it will make us look like criminals."

"We used fake names, Liss. We're already criminals."

"Let me take it back to her. Please?"

Jess kicked the wheel of her mom's car. "Fine. Just get in, get out. I'll pull around to the front."

✦

Alyssa pushed her way into Sally's room. That look—the red, splotchy face, the frazzled expression—reminded her of last Friday night, when Sally left her with Morgan.

"You're afraid," Alyssa said. She thought of Charles's rifle in the basement. "You're scared of Charles, aren't you?"

"It's complicated," Sally said, sniffling. Crumpled tissues lay scattered across her pillow. "You wouldn't understand."

Alyssa sighed, sitting on the edge of her bed. "I'm just worried my mom will call Charles once she realizes we're missing."

"Your mom?"

"She knows Charles. She went to see him last night, at the other hospital," Alyssa said. "That's how we knew you were missing, or at least how we guessed it. Luckily, we did. Otherwise—"

"What?"

"But you know what? I'll get my mom to help. She'll know what to do."

"No," Sally said firmly. "Don't tell her anything. Not if she's *friends* with Charles."

"Well, I don't think they're friends. Not exactly." Not anymore. Alyssa considered sharing the awful texts Charles had sent. They could act as proof, showing his volatile nature. But no, Sally looked ready to dissolve into a sea of tears.

"Jess is waiting. I'll figure something out, okay? Just hang in there," Alyssa said, cringing at the emptiness of her pathetic words. She gave Sally's arm a gentle squeeze.

The door swung open without a knock. The main nurse entered, blocking the entrance.

"I was just leaving," Alyssa said, standing up.

The nurse closed the door. "Actually, I have some questions for you," she said, her eyes focused on Alyssa. "You better take a seat." She nodded toward the small couch in the corner, hands poised on hips.

Chapter 36

Mandy

Day seven

Mandy found a phone charger in her car, buried in the glove compartment beneath a leaky bottle of hand sanitizer. It still worked.

Her heart pounded as she clicked on Simon's number.

"Mandy?"

"Did you find them? Are they okay?" Mandy held the phone so hard her fingers ached.

"Sally's checked in at Durham Regional Hospital—"

"What? I thought you called all the hospitals?" Balancing the phone against her shoulder, she started the car. "Is Alyssa with her? Is she okay?"

"They said two teenagers brought her in, claiming to be her nieces—"

"Oh God. I'll meet you there." She hung up before he could finish.

✦

Mandy spotted Simon and Claire climbing the hospital's front steps. "Simon! Claire!" she shouted. "Wait!"

Simon turned and bounded down to meet her. Claire remained on the steps, her phone still pressed against her ear.

Mandy threw her arms around Simon in exasperation. "It's them, right? They're here. They're the nieces. It's got to be them, right? Are they okay?"

"Actually, there's only one 'niece' in the room right now. She won't give up her real name. I asked the nurse to try to prevent her from leaving." He patted Mandy's back before pulling away. They headed up the steps. "Only Sally's checked in. But listen, I had to call—"

"Sorry," Claire murmured to them, covering her phone with her hand. "My ex is heading to the airport. I'm trying to tell him to hold off." She put her phone back to her ear. "No, I told you, I think we've found them. Well, one—I don't know. Let me call you back." The voice on the other end protested as she clicked off.

"If it's really one of your girls, I'm going to be impressed. I might just ask them to join the team." Simon smiled, obviously trying to lighten the mood. He led them to the front of the check-in line and pulled out his badge. The woman behind the counter abruptly stood up.

"We're here to pick up the girl who brought in Sally Steele last night," Simon said, his voice sharp and authoritative.

"Room 175." The receptionist pointed down the hall.

"Simon told me what's going on," Claire said, falling into step with Mandy. "Someone's accusing Alyssa of hurting their baby? How awful. Do you know the family?"

Mandy shook her head.

"I can't imagine something like this happening to Jess. You must be so freaked out."

"Right now, I just want to find her and—"

Simon pushed open the door to Room 175.

"Alyssa," Mandy said, voice cracking. She pulled her daughter into a strong embrace, smoothing down Alyssa's unkempt hair and rubbing her back, and then, after feeling their heart beats steady, she took a step back, staring into Alyssa's tired, bloodshot eyes. Touching her face. "Are you okay? Are you hurt? You look awful."

Alyssa rambled off a list of excuses—*Sally was bleeding, we hid our phones. It was stupid, I know. I was trying to leave, I was!*—while Claire desperately scanned the room. "Where'd Jess go?"

"She's in the parking lot," Alyssa said. "She's probably turned on her phone by now."

Claire exhaled dramatically, turning on her heels. Simon whispered something to the nurse and they both stepped into the hall.

"Mom," Alyssa whispered. "Sally's pregnant. Like, six months. She had something called a placental abruption and needed a blood transfusion and everything. She—they might do a C-section. Soon." Her eyes sheened with tears. "Mom, I only wanted to help."

"I know," Mandy said as relief and anger seared through her. "But seriously, running away like that? You gave me a heart attack. You—you're grounded." Never had she uttered those words before. She never had to.

"But Mommmm," her daughter whined. "She would've died. Nobody was looking for her. We found her bleeding to death."

Mandy held the door propped open. Six months pregnant? She shuddered. Zack was born at seven months.

"She's in good hands now," Mandy said, motioning for Alyssa to follow her. She thought of Charles's grief-stricken face at the other hospital. Did Sally know the extent of Morgan's injuries?

"Wait!" Sally called out.

Mandy turned, letting her eyes settle on Sally.

"Please." Sally struggled to sit up, her face rigid with pain. "Come back."

Mandy exchanged a questioning look with Alyssa. They both shrugged before stepping back into the room.

"You ... know ... Charles?" Sally asked, her voice coming out in labored spurts.

"Charles?" Mandy blinked. "Yes, but only for a week—"

"How?" Sally asked. "And why'd you go to see him? Last night."

"I—" Mandy clammed up, studying Alyssa's face—*What did you tell this woman?*

"I need to know." Sally held herself up by the bed rails, then moaned and collapsed back onto the bed. Mandy noticed the bluish bruise on her face.

"I was concerned about ..." Mandy paused. What to say? *I went to knock some sense into your husband?* "I wanted to talk in person about the situation—"

The door swung open. Jameson barged in, briefcase in one hand, a steaming Starbucks cup in the other. Simon trailed behind him. Jameson heaved his briefcase on the counter, then turned and slapped Simon firmly on the back with a broad smile, a deep chuckle, as if they were dudes cheering on their favorite football team. "Thanks for giving us the call, Simon."

The call? Mandy's stomach dropped. When did Simon have time to call Jameson?

"Sounds like you've all had quite the adventure," Jameson said. Mandy held her breath, as if confronted by an agitated bear, waiting to see if the attack was coming for them or for Sally.

A ringing phone broke the silence. Jameson's phone, from within the leather creases of his briefcase. He cussed, rummaging, flipping it open. A flip phone? Who still used a flip phone?

"The CT scan? Yes … I understand." His eyes darted to Sally, then he turned to Simon. *Don't let them leave,* he mouthed before stepping out of the room.

"Why'd you do this?" Mandy asked Simon. "We talked about not involving the cops—"

"Wait," Alyssa said. "How did you guys even find us?"

"It turns out Jess's dad had enabled the Find My Phone app on her iPhone but forgot about it. Her last location was this hospital. I can't believe I didn't ask him sooner," Simon said, shaking his head. "Anyway, the hospital couldn't confirm any of you were here. I figured Sally had probably requested to keep her name private." He shot Sally a curious look, then turned back to Mandy and Alyssa. "So, I talked to security and yup, she was here. I had to bring Jameson up to speed. I couldn't risk my job going behind his back any further."

Mandy put her hand to her forehead. "So … what does this mean?"

"Am I in trouble?" Alyssa asked meekly.

"I don't think so," Simon said. "You girls technically didn't do anything wrong besides make up some fake names. In fact, it sounds like you saved Sally's life by bringing her in when you did." He cleared his throat. "Jameson just wants to focus on the case. On Morgan."

"Then can we go home?" Mandy asked. "We have a meeting scheduled later at the station."

"His questions should be brief, maybe he's thinking he can just ask them here?" he said with a shrug.

Mandy sank onto the couch, followed by Alyssa. She grabbed her daughter's hand and squeezed it, trying to pass a telepathic message: *It's going to be okay*. The clock above their heads ticked out the painful seconds of silence.

Until finally: "It wasn't me."

Their heads snapped to Sally's bed.

"I trusted you, Alyssa. I trusted you with my—my baby. And you hurt him," Sally said, straining to sit up. She closed her eyes, briefly, then opened them with a desperate fierceness. "You hurt Morgan."

"What? No. I—I—" Alyssa stammered. "I didn't do it." She turned toward Mandy, a desperate plea on her face.

"I know what she did," Sally said, her voice deep and guttural. "I know what you did to my Morgan! YOU HURT MY BABY!"

"No! It wasn't me. You—you know I would never hurt Morgan." Alyssa bolted to her feet.

Mandy stood, wrapping her arms around Alyssa. "Sally, you know Alyssa had nothing to do with Morgan's injuries—"

"And you." Sally pointed a shaky finger at Mandy. "You and my, my ... Charles. Conspiring behind my back. Or, what? Having an affair?"

"What?" Mandy said. "No, nothing happened—"

"Just leave."

"Please, Sally—" Mandy stopped. The razor-like sharpness in Sally's eyes made Mandy swallow the rest of her words. She looked at Simon. He moved toward them in slow motion.

"I said leave. Leave. LEAVE!" Sally growled, thrashing side to side, teeth bared. A bowl of soup crashed to the floor, orange liquid seeping into Mandy's silver ballet flats.

"What's going on in here?" a sharp voice boomed. The nurse. She charged over to the bed, positioning herself between them and Sally, a stern look on her face. "I thought you all were leaving. Come on, let's clear out. Sally needs her rest." Waving her hands, she shooed them out of the room.

They stood in the hall, blinking under the harsh lights.

"Why would Sally say that? Why?" Alyssa said, her breath coming in short gasps. "I saved her life. She asked for my help. Why—"

"I don't know, sweetie. I don't know." Mandy rubbed her daughter's back, trying to slow down her own erratic breathing. She slipped off her soup-soaked shoes and caught Simon's eyes. "She's clearly not okay."

"I'm just as shocked as you guys," Simon said, placing a hand on each of their shoulders. "Why don't you go wait in the family room. Let me go find Jameson, okay?"

Mandy nodded.

"Did something really happen with Charles?" Alyssa asked as they headed down the hall. She used the back of her hand to wipe her nose.

Mandy pulled a tissue out of her purse and handed it over. "Of course not. We just work together, that's all." Her head spun with the paralyzing realization: *Both Charles and Sally blame Alyssa. Both of them. Both.*

✦

Jameson came to the family waiting room. "Hey, I heard about Sally's little breakdown back there. You guys okay? You need anything?" He nodded to Mandy's bare feet. "New shoes, perhaps?"

"I just want to take my daughter home and get a lawyer," Mandy said tersely.

He sat on the chair beside them. "I get it. It's been quite the ordeal. But it sounds like you girls"—he smiled at Alyssa—"did a good thing, finding Sally when you did."

"So does this mean Alyssa's exonerated or what?" Mandy asked. "I mean, there's no denying that Sally is a bit unhinged."

"We still need to get the details on record. Basically, Alyssa's account of what happened last night, such as if Sally was acting reckless and so on. Now, I can ask some questions right here or we can meet at the station as originally planned, at 4:30." He studied their faces. "And if I were to guess, I'd say Alyssa wants a proper lunch and a shower right about now, huh?"

Alyssa timidly nodded, her lips breaking into a small smile.

"Can't we postpone it a few days?" Mandy said. "She's pretty shaken up."

"I wish we could. The thing is, we really want Morgan to go home as soon as possible, with at least one parent." Jameson's face softened. "Alyssa's testimony will really help us out. And it's best to debrief when everything's fresh in her mind."

"But we can't answer any questions unless we have a lawyer," Mandy said, folding her arms across her chest.

"Sure. No problem." Jameson stood. "I'll see you guys at 4:30." He gave Alyssa's shoulder a reassuring pat, then left.

✦

Claire and Jess were waiting outside the hospital's entrance, sitting on the steps. The sun blazed on, its overbearing presence the one constant in this ever-changing drama.

"Jess!" Alyssa shouted. The girls hugged dramatically, as if reunited from a war zone. "You were right, you were so right. Sally's batshit crazy! She threw soup at us."

Claire stepped toward Mandy. "Hey, I'm sorry for blaming you earlier."

Mandy nodded, letting the sun melt away the residual anger.

"Mom, I'm going to walk Jess to Claire's car. She'll drive me to where you're parked," Alyssa said, planting a moist kiss on her cheek. "Love you." The girls scurried across the lawn.

"My ex-husband's on his way, even though I told him everything's under control," Claire said, rolling her eyes. "Now *I'm* the one in trouble."

"I'm grateful you guys were able to track them down," Mandy said. "I guess it's time I enable that GPS thing on Alyssa's phone."

"Yeah, I feel pretty stupid for not having done that sooner." Claire paused, looking deep in thought. "Can I ask, do you know if the little boy's going to be okay?"

"They haven't been able to share much. Just that he's in the hospital with a possible concussion, a broken rib. I think, maybe, it was something like the shaken baby syndrome?"

"Holy hell." Claire exhaled through her teeth. "And the parents did this?"

"It's either them or Alyssa." Mandy adjusted her purse strap on her shoulder, then wiped the sweat off the back of her neck. Her fingers twitched, desperate for a cigarette, a nearby sign scolding her: *No Smoking.* "And we know Alyssa could never ever do something like that."

"So unreal. It's like that case a few years back, a baby boy who died from a brain hemorrhage. They pinned it on the babysitter. Do you remember that?" Claire waved her hand in the air, brushing away a fly. "She was toted off to jail. She fought it, of course, and later, years later, they discovered the boy had died from some weird genetic disorder. To think, all that jail time—"

Mandy stared at her.

"Oh," Claire said, pressing her lips together. "I shouldn't tell you stories like that."

"No, you shouldn't."

"Anyway, I'm sure the cops will figure it out. Sounds like that Sally is a loose cannon, right?" She gave a nervous chuckle. "Hang in there."

Mandy waited until Claire disappeared across the lawn before ducking back inside. She scanned the waiting room, then sighed with relief when she saw Simon striding down the hall, his eyes locked on her.

"Hey," he said. "I was just coming to find you."

"Same here."

"Talk about one crazy adventure," he said. "You doing okay?"

She nodded, nervously shifting her weight side to side.

"What is it, Mandy?"

"I just—what would I have done if you weren't there to help?" She blinked back warm tears. Then, without pause, she collapsed into him. He opened his arms, then squeezed her tight.

"It's going to be okay, Mandy," he said, his voice steady, reassuring. "She's safe now."

Mandy nodded, her tears soaking into his soft polo shirt.

"Go home and rest up, okay?" He pulled away, hands caressing her shoulders before reaching up and delicately thumbing away her stream of tears. "You've been through a lot."

She stood on tiptoes, heart bursting, and planted a firm kiss on his stubbly cheek. He blushed. When was the last time she'd kissed—even just a cheek kiss—a man? "You know where I live," she said, a giddy gasp of a laugh escaping her lips.

"I do."

✦

She hurried to the parking lot. Halfway there, she realized she'd left her soup-soaked shoes behind. Those ballet flats. Oh well, she hated them anyway. She texted Alyssa the parking number and climbed into her car, waiting. Her heartbeat slowly resumed a normal pace. She'd kissed Simon. Did that make her look desperate? She couldn't think about it now—she had less than four hours to find a lawyer. Did they really need one at this point?

Yes.

She couldn't risk taking any more chances. Not with both Charles and Sally pointing the blame directly at her daughter. Who knew what that couple was capable of?

Chapter 37

Charles

Day seven

"Hello?" Charles answered, switching to speaker mode as he changed Morgan's diaper.

"Hi Charles. Elaine Flynn here. Are you going to be at the Regional Hospital later this afternoon?"

"Uh, what?"

"We've moved Sally's two o'clock meeting to her hospital room," Flynn continued. "I'd really like the chance to talk to you again, either before or after her meeting."

"Her hospital room?" Charles lowered Morgan to the floor, raising his eyebrows at his mother, who was pacing the room.

"Yes, at Durham Regional," Flynn said, followed by a calculating pause. "I assumed you knew?"

Once again, he was the clueless guy stumbling in the dark. What else didn't he know?

"Oh. Yes. I'll be there." He hung up. A hospital? His stomach lurched. Christ, what the hell happened? He didn't dare ask *why* Sally was there. Besides, Flynn had sounded so calm. Clearly this wasn't a life-or-death situation ... or so he hoped.

"Honey—" his mom began.

"I need to go," he said, scooping up his keys and planting a quick kiss on Morgan's head. "Just stay here with Morgie." He barreled toward the door before his mom could fire off questions or opinions and, full of growing panic, made his way to his car and drove twenty minutes from one hospital to another.

✦

The receptionist behind the front counter refused to give any details.

"But I know Sally's here," Charles demanded. "The social worker told me."

"I'm sorry," she said. "I can't confirm that."

He leaned across the counter. "Please, can you just call her room and tell her I'm here?"

The receptionist's eyes narrowed. "I'll be right back," she snipped.

He called Sally again—it went straight to voicemail. He was tempted to bolt down the hall, bellowing her name.

After several minutes the receptionist returned. "She'll see you. It's room 175, down the hall, to the right."

Charles gave her a scowl before following where she pointed. He counted the numbers, evens on the left, odds on the right. He rounded the corner. As he got closer, he finally allowed himself to think through the possibilities: Did Sally hear about Morgan's latest update—the internal bleeding? Did she blame herself for trusting Alyssa? Did she try to hurt *herself?* He trembled at the thought. Or, had there been an accident? Pausing at the door marked 175, he took a deep breath, wiping the sweat off his brow.

He pushed the door open and gasped. Sally looked so frail—hair spread across the pillow, a bluish bruise streaked across her cheek.

"Oh Jesus. What the hell happened?" He rushed to her bed, grabbed her hand, and examined her wrist for any sign of self-harm. "Are you okay?"

Sally opened her mouth to speak.

"Charles," a voice said. "I'm Dr. Parvati Patel. Please, just call me Parvati—"

"Just tell me what's going on," Charles cut her off.

"Sally's pregnant," Parvati said. "Twenty-five weeks."

"What? Pregnant? But—but that's impossible." He faced Sally. "You were on birth control, weren't you?" Besides, his sperm was faulty. Morgan had been their miracle baby. And now this, a surprise pregnancy—defeating all odds?

Sally chewed on her lower lip. "I was on birth control. The mini pill. I never skipped it, I swear."

"And you didn't notice you missed your period?"

"I never got my period while on it. My OB—she said that was common, especially while breastfeeding."

"Oh, Sally." He noticed the monitor strapped to her slight bump. "Twenty-five weeks? Really?" Then his pulse quickened—the monitors, the IV, the doctor's concerned face. "Something's wrong with the—the *baby*?"

"She's had a placental abruption. We had to do a blood transfusion. The baby's measuring small, which could explain why she wasn't showing," the doctor said, going on to state things in complicated, technical terms. Too many words to comprehend. He heard *baby girl*. He clung to Sally's hand.

"What caused this to happen?" He blinked up at the doctor.

"The exact cause is unknown. Sometimes drug use. Sometimes stress. Sometimes—" Parvati stopped, eyeing Charles suspiciously.

"Is she, the little girl. Is she going to—" He took a ragged breath. "Is she going to live?"

"We're trying our best. We've already administered the first shot of the antennal steroid treatment. This'll increase her chances of survival outside the womb and—"

"Christ," Charles said. "Just stop." It was too much. He pulled off his glasses and burrowed his face into Sally's neck, inhaling her sweat-tinged aroma—the faint coconut and vanilla briefly stilling his frenzied brain.

"Where's Morgie?" Sally asked.

Charles lifted his head. How could he update her about Morgan now? "He's still at Oak Wood. With Mom." Oh, how his mom would squeal with delight if she heard those beautiful words—*baby girl*. The granddaughter she'd always dreamed of.

"Is he—" Sally started.

A solid knock stopped her. Charles wiped away his tears and slipped on his glasses. Jameson and Flynn swooped in and whispered to the doctor and nurse, heads bent like a football team in a huddle. The doctor's eyes lingered on Sally before she nodded and left the room, the nurse shuffling behind her.

"Sally," Jameson said, stepping forward. "We understand you've been through a lot. Do you think you have enough energy to answer a few questions?"

"What the hell?" Charles sprung to his feet. "Can't you see ... I mean, look at her! This isn't the time or place. She almost died. She—the baby—this is a critical situation, for Christ's sake!"

"I know this is hard. Really, we don't want to interfere with Sally's condition," Jameson said. He pulled out the recorder. "But the more information we get, the sooner Morgan can be released and go home."

The nerve of that asshole. Charles wanted to push for details: *How did you guys find her?* But he feared an interrogation in return, such as why he didn't notify anyone once he realized Sally was missing.

"Now, we'd like to conduct this interview in private," Jameson said, his eyes locking on Charles.

"No," Charles said. "I'm not leaving her alone."

Jameson sighed. "Sally, are you okay with him being here?"

She nodded.

"This won't take long, I promise," he said, lowering his portly body onto a stool, placing the recorder on the shelf. He leaned forward, stating the usual preliminaries—date, time, location. Charles stepped back, his eyes finally taking in the room—the black and white clock, a poster spelling out the warning signs of meningitis, the singular window, blinds fully open, the afternoon sun streaming in with hues of orange and yellow.

"I got an update about Morgan's condition, the results of the CT scan," Jameson said. "But first, I need to ask you some questions about the playpen."

Sally flinched. "The playpen?"

"The one in the basement," Jameson said. "We found it in the storage closet, with a bottle of milk. As if Morgan slept down there."

"I—I never used it," she said. "I was going to take it to the thrift store, but I guess forgot." She started gnawing on her nails, staring at the ceiling.

"Okay ..." Jameson scratched at his cheek.

"Is there a crime against having a playpen stored in the basement?" she said.

"But Sally." His tone was that of someone speaking to a small, disobedient child. "It was set up in the closet—"

"Alyssa," Sally said. "It had to be Alyssa. She's not to be trusted."

Charles felt dizzy. He leaned against the wall as the two options loomed in front of him—Sally or Alyssa. The pendulum swung back and forth, their names blinking in and out of focus. Someone took Morgan to the basement. Someone gave him a bottle of milk down there. Someone *hurt* him.

Flynn coughed, a delicate, restrained cough. She sat perched on the couch in the corner. Jameson followed Flynn's eyes as they darted to Charles. She gave a sharp, accusatory nod: *He did this.*

"Sally." Jameson took a breath. "We're concerned about your bruise. Can you tell us what happened?"

"What? You think *I* did this to Sally?" Charles swept his hand toward her swollen cheek. "I've been with Morgan the entire time. How could I have—"

The detective held up his hand like a stop sign. "Sally, I need you to answer the question." His eyes fixated on Charles's knuckles, gashed and bruised from when he'd punched the bathroom wall. Charles immediately shoved his hands into his pockets.

Sally shot Charles a helpless look. The machine's beeps increased, lines darting like a skier flying down a hill, then climbing back up. There were two monitors—one for Sally, the other for his baby. Their baby.

"Do you want us to ask Charles to leave?" Jameson asked.

"No, of course not." Sally massaged her temples. "They came to me, to my—my motel room. *She* hit me."

"Who hit you?" Jameson asked. Flynn shifted her position.

"Alyssa," she said. "Alyssa hit me."

"*Alyssa* hit you?" Jameson almost fell off his stool. "The babysitter hit you?"

"We need to file charges against her," Sally said, her voice like steel.

"Sally," Jameson started, sucking in a long breath, holding it, and then slowly letting it out. "We know from the CT scan that Morgan was ... well, they suspect someone shook him. They found internal bleeding and—"

"It wasn't me."

Charles pressed his forehead into a cabinet, the air in the room growing sticky and hot. Sally didn't seem surprised or shocked or outraged. She didn't even ask if the damage was permanent. What—*who*—was he supposed to believe? Morgan didn't break his own rib; he didn't rattle his own brain.

"And what were you doing over at the Budget Inn?" Jameson asked, flipping open his notepad.

"I needed to ..." She squirmed in the bed. "I just needed some time to myself."

"Ah. I see. That makes sense," Jameson said, a touch of sarcasm. "One more question, I promise. Alyssa said that on Friday, when she arrived at your house, you mentioned that Morgan wasn't feeling well. That he had a"—he thumbed through the pages—"a 'rough day.' Do you remember saying that?"

Sally opened her mouth, then clamped it shut, shaking her head.

"Okay." Jameson struggled to stand up, then nodded to the door. The social worker twirled her bracelet, gathered her purse, and followed him.

"Wait!" Sally called after them. "Alyssa was drinking."

"What?" Jameson stopped, holding the door open.

"I found a plastic cup. A Big Bird cup. That night, Friday night. We"—a nervous glance at Charles—"I mean, it wasn't me. I kept thinking it was strange, but figured Charles had used it. But now, after everything, I keep thinking it had to be her. Right? You wouldn't drink out of a Big Bird cup, would you?" Her eyes bore into Charles.

"No," Charles answered. "I have never used that cup."

Jameson let loose an annoyed exhale, his fingers pinching the space between his thick eyebrows. "Alright, let us have a moment. We'll be back." The door released a sustained click behind them.

"Charlie," Sally whispered. She reached out her hand. "Charlie, *please.* You need to believe me. We need to ... we're family."

He walked toward her and sat on the creaky stool. He pulled down the white sheet and wrapped his hands around her tight stomach. His throat contracted as he leaned over, pushing his ear against Sally's warm flesh, trying to listen. Their baby girl. Growing, expanding, oblivious to what awaited her. His eyes squeezed shut.

"Charlie. My sweet Charlie." Her voice floated down like a melody. She gently stroked his hair, fingers lightly scratching his scalp. "I love you. You know how much I love you. And—"

The door opened. He wearily lifted his head.

"Charles," Jameson said. "Ms. Flynn and I would like to ask you some more questions, in private. We can do it now or later, after Alyssa's interview." His eyes darkened, landing once again on Charles's tattered knuckles.

"I need some time with Sally right now. Please."

"Okay. Before we leave, I need to confirm that you—both of you—want to move forward with this statement. Alyssa hitting Sally. Alyssa drinking Friday night. Alyssa putting Morgan in the basement's closet. All of this, you believe it's correct?"

"Yes. It was Alyssa. All of it," Sally said. She reached for Charles's hand and pulled it into hers, squeezing hard.

Charles studied the stone-faced detective. Seconds of silence passed. "It *had* to be Alyssa," he finally said, his voice mechanical, robotic, one hand numb from Sally's too-strong grip, the other still curved around her stomach. He felt a flurry of movement under his fingers. A kick?

Jameson shifted his weight, smoothing out his mustache. "Alright," he said slowly. "We'll be in touch."

After the door closed, Sally said, "I didn't know you knew Mandy."

"Mandy?"

"Alyssa's mom."

"Wait. How do *you* know Mandy?"

"She was here." She started picking apart a tissue, soft flakes of white floating to the floor.

"Mandy came here? But how did she find you?"

"Alyssa. She—and her friend—they brought me here."

"Wait a minute." He watched as Sally's eyes darted around the room, her jaw locked. "Alyssa brought you in? But you said she *hit* you."

She dug her palms into her eyes. "I'm sorry ... I don't know why I lied. She didn't hit me. The bruise, it was because I fell. I passed out and hit my face at the bus—uh, on the bathroom floor."

"What?"

"I saw the way they stared at you—the detective, that snooty social worker. I could tell from their faces. They think it was you."

"Jesus, Sally." His head started to throb. "You just told a detective that a teenager hit you. After what? After she brought you to the hospital? She was—God, Sally—Alyssa was trying to *help* you."

"I did it for you." Sally's voice cracked. "They think you hurt me."

"That doesn't make it right." He looked at the door. Should he stop them? And then what? How were they going to explain the bruise on Sally's face? The coincidental bruises splattered across his knuckles?

"You need to tell me about Mandy," Sally demanded. "Why did she go to see you last night?"

Charles pulled at the tight neckline of his T-shirt, his mouth dry. He picked up the cup next to her bed but it was empty. "I work with her at Print Solutions. She's a temp. I didn't know she was Alyssa's mom until ... I swear. She was trying to ..." He stopped. Sally's eyes weren't moving, not even blinking.

"Hey, it's no surprise," she scoffed. "She's cute. Besides, you cheated on Beth with me. So it only makes sense." He could hear the rest: *Once a cheater, always a cheater.*

"Sally, no. It's not like that. Listen—"

"Never mind." She wrapped her arms around her chest. "Just forget it."

He shifted his weight, trying to make sense of it—Alyssa finding her, but how? *And why?* Mandy coming here, to Sally's hospital room. The lie about Sally's bruise—did she really pass out? And now this surprise baby.

"Sally," he said. "I feel like I don't even know you."

"It's still me."

Leaning over, he brushed a few wisps of blond hair out of her eyes and lightly traced the outline of her bruise. He longed for a moment of sweetness; a reminder of why he loved her so much. Like the night they had their first dinner out, some Italian restaurant in Greensboro, her intoxicating eyes searching his as if she could see their future together, their lives intertwining as one. But now, she recoiled from his touch, eyes skimming over, as if everything delightful between them had turned rancid.

"I need to know," he started. "I … what …" He fumbled for the right words. "Last Friday. With Morgan. Did anything …?"

"I told you. Nothing. Happened." She tugged the sheet up to her chin.

"Sally …" His thoughts fizzled out, tiredness taking over. "I need to get some coffee or an energy drink or something." He slowly rose to his feet.

Sally didn't respond. She remained frozen, like a mannequin propped up in a hospital bed.

"Is this baby …" He gulped. "Is she even mine?"

The words hung between them, suspended with the harsh reality of the situation. He wanted to take it back. But those words—that doubt—had surfaced before. He remembered the way Sally flung the pregnancy test at him, Morgan's pregnancy test, those double-pink lines glaring at him as he tried to ignore the festering doubt. But he'd shoved those suspicions to the far corners of his brain, throwing himself into the promise of a baby, *his baby.* And yet, it nagged at him, whispered to him when he studied Morgan's face: *Does he even look like me?*

Sally looked as if she'd just been struck. "Why would you even ask that? Who else's could she be? Of course she's yours."

He watched as she closed her eyes and turned away from him.

Outside the room, he slid against the wall, down to the cold floor. He pushed the heel of his hand into his chest and tried to ignore the sound of clomping feet and whirling wheelchairs echoing up and down the hall. Colors turned sharper, more vivid than usual. He waved away anyone who paused to offer a concerned look. "I'm fine," he mouthed.

Then, against his will, the dreaded thoughts surfaced: If Sally did this, if Sally really hurt Morgan, what happens next? He'd have to raise Morgan *and* this baby girl by himself. And this baby was bound to have problems from being born early. What did the doctor say? He hadn't listened; the severity of it all too raw. Whipping out his phone, he typed in "baby born at 25 weeks" and scanned the results: *Extremely premature ... lung issues, developmental delay, heart problems ... nearly eight out of ten survive ...*

Charles peeled off his glasses, letting the tears plop onto his phone.

Of course she's yours. Could he even trust Sally? But who else's could it be? How would he even know?

Don't panic, he told himself. But it was too late, doom was pouring in fast. Even if this baby girl survived—eight out of ten?—it didn't look good. None of this looked good. And what about Morgan? Christ, poor Morgan.

The CT scan, the only test where they received the results immediately, confirmed a concussion, along with internal bleeding in his brain.

"We need to closely monitor him for at least a few days, maybe longer," the doctor had explained. "Right now, the internal bleeding is minor, he's quite lucky. But we need to watch for swelling or pressure on his brain."

"And what happens if that happens?" Charles asked, dreading the answer.

"It won't be good."

"Could all of this have been avoided if we'd come in right away?"

"I mean, Morgan could've received pain relief from the broken rib much sooner. But with this type of brain injury, it's a wait-and-see situation. Now, if the bleeding increases, we'll have to drain it. As of right now, it's manageable."

"And any long-term damage?"

The doctor's eyes shifted away as he offered broad speculations: ongoing headaches, possible cognitive delays, memory problems, sensitivity to light and sound. His final verdict: "Only time will tell."

Charles's heart ripped apart at that. Someone full of rage hurt Morgan. Sally had never shown that kind of anger before—they'd never even fought. Not until the other night. Could they blame it on the pregnancy hormones? Lack of sleep? Morgan's nonstop howls pushing her over the edge? He remembered how Sally clutched his shirt last Friday, as he stood to leave for work, her doe-like eyes staring up at him: *Stay a little longer.* A slight waver to her voice, like a cry for help. A surge of guilt raced through him.

He drummed his fingers on his forehead, first gently, then harder and harder until his head ached. *For Christ's sake, Sally,* he thought. *What the hell am I supposed to do now?*

He looked up, as if the answer hovered in front of him, but the hallway was empty, chillingly empty, and quiet. So quiet.

He was all alone.

Chapter 38

Alyssa

Day seven

"Do you need anything else? Have you eaten? We can grab you a sandwich or something," Jameson said, his tone cheery and upbeat, as if this meeting was simply an excuse to indulge in yummy snacks together.

Alyssa struggled to keep her eyes open. She'd only squeezed in a few hours of sleep last night, first crammed on the short couch in Sally's hospital room, Jess breathing in her face, then a quick nap at home. Now another Coke sweated in her hands as the acid burned her growling stomach. "I'm fine," she lied.

She glanced at the familiar mirrored window, the blinking red light in the corner. A thick manila folder sat between them on the table, her name written across it in bold block letters.

A second detective joined them—Rodriguez, a wiry man with a buzz cut and a black goatee. And her mom, all twitchy faced, squirming beside her like a caged squirrel.

Her mom had spent the time between leaving the hospital and this meeting rapid-dialing lawyers, including the referral from Simon. She begged and pleaded to each one, offering insane amounts of money they didn't have, before dramatically throwing her arms in the air. "I give up! I can't find anyone with such short notice!"

Alyssa texted Jess the conundrum.

Her reply: **duh! my dad's a lawyer and he's on a flight right now!!!**

Alyssa: **can he get to the station by 4:30???**

Jess: **lemme message him. trust me, it'll take the pressure off me—the runaway rebel lol.**

"Mom! I think Jess's dad might be able to do it."

"Derek? No," her mom said. "Isn't he a patent attorney? He won't know a thing about child abuse."

"We've got no other choice, Mom." Her bones ached with fatigue; she just wanted this whole ordeal over with. Jess wrote back saying her dad's flight's ETA was 3:45. It seemed tight, but he promised he'd make it work.

Guzzling down her Coke, Alyssa watched the second hand on the clock chug its way around, the minute hand advancing in blips. 4:34. 4:35. 4:36. Still no Derek.

"Alyssa? Are you listening?" Jameson said. "We've got some delicate questions this time so let me advise you of your juvenile rights." His tone turned flat: *You have the right to remain silent, anything you say can be and may be used as evidence against you ...*

An added clause about the right to have a parent present sent a chill right to the center of her heart.

"Are you serious?" Her mom coughed. "We're not doing this until Derek gets here."

"Uh, who's Derek?" Jameson asked. "And why are we waiting for him?"

"He's the lawyer." Her mom glanced nervously at the door. "He said he'd be here."

"And I thought we're here to just confirm that Sally was ... Sally is losing it ..." Alyssa trailed off, feeling herself growing smaller.

"Hey, it's okay," Jameson said, interlacing his fingers. "Nobody's being accused of anything,"

"We have more information now," the other detective said, his voice stern and cutting. "Some stuff we need to clarify."

"Where the hell is he?" Her mom stood, tapping frantically at her phone.

"Alyssa," Jameson said. "I talked to my daughter, Heather. She says you're pretty amazing—honor student, part of the theater club. You're starring in *The Wizard of Oz,* is that right?"

"Yes." She shifted in her seat. "I'm the Wicked Witch of the West, actually."

"Huh," he said. "That means you're good at acting then, right?"

"Uh, well ... I guess so."

Her mom gave an impatient sigh, pressing the phone to her ear. The other detective drummed his fingers on the table. Alyssa rearranged her necklace and studied her Coke can.

A knock rattled the door. Rodriguez stood to open it.

"I'm so sorry. Traffic. I got here as soon as I could." Derek ran his fingers through his crew cut, his hair the same shade as Jess's, minus the neon highlights. He shook hands with both detectives, then settled in beside Alyssa. Her mom grabbed an extra chair from the corner and positioned it with Derek between them. He motioned for them to come close, his voice dropping to a whisper. "Hey, I'm here as a friend. We'll see how this goes and come up with a plan afterward. Follow my lead." He turned to Alyssa. "And don't say anything."

"All right, let's get started. And Alyssa"—Jameson flashed her a smile—"remember, you can always pass on any question. Now, we'd like to ask you about the playpen. We found it in the Haywoods' basement, just like you said—sheet inside, bottle of milk."

"I already told you all I know," Alyssa said. "I found the playpen back in, I dunno, the end of March? Early April?"

Derek put a hand on her arm, shaking his head: *Shhh.*

Rodriguez leaned forward. "Was Morgan crying? Screaming? Did you feel out of control? Did you put him in the basement's closet to have a break?"

"What?" Alyssa said. "The closet? I never saw it in the closet."

"We found fingerprints all over that playpen," Rodriquez said. "And they don't match Sally or Charles."

"But—but—" The room felt hotter than before, the air denser. "I haven't been down there in months!"

"We need to do a comparison print," Rodriguez pressed on. "You can either volunteer or we can get a court order."

"But—"

"Alyssa, stop talking." Derek's body sat erect, his jaw locked. "Next question, please."

"But I'm telling the truth," she blurted. "I have nothing to hide. I'll do the prints."

The two detectives looked at each other, a subtle shake of the head from Jameson. "Let's wait," Jameson said.

"Why'd you go to Sally?" Rodriguez asked. "To her motel room?"

"This isn't relevant to the case. The case is about Morgan, not about Sally running away," Derek said.

Alyssa stared at him. Jess must've filled him in on the details.

"Actually, Sally claims that you and Jess came to her motel room in an attempt to stop the accusations." Jameson locked eyes with her. "Sally says you hit her. Is this true?"

"I *hit* her?" Alyssa said. "She said that?"

"Can't you see how ridiculous this is?" her mom said. "Like my daughter would go and assault a grown woman? Aren't you wondering why Sally was hiding in a motel while her son was in the hospital? Seems awfully fishy to me."

"We're looking into it," Rodriguez said, deadpan. As if there was nothing suspicious about Sally up and disappearing during the middle of this investigation.

"I went to help," Alyssa said, a dull ache in her gut. A swirling pain overwhelmed her head. "I feared she was in danger and—"

"But why would you help the person accusing you of abusing her son?" Rodriguez asked. He stroked his goatee with the top of his pen. "Unless you felt guilty yourself. Guilty for what you did on Friday night."

Alyssa clenched her fists at the memory of Sally's stabbing words: *I know what you did to my Morgan.*

"I like Sally," Alyssa began. "I mean, I *liked* her, before she …" Derek put up his hand for her to stop but she shook her head. "It's fine," she told him. "I didn't do anything wrong. We found her alone in the motel room, bleeding—like a lot, so we brought her to the hospital. She begged me not to tell anyone. I thought, I dunno, that Charles threatened her, he had that gun and—"

"Then explain to me this," Rodriguez said. "Why are these people, Charles and Sally, both blaming you for Morgan's injuries if you didn't do anything wrong?"

"I ... I ..." She dug her fingernails into her thighs, gritting against the pain.

"Alyssa, you made up a *fake* name. Innocent people don't go around lying about their identity," Rodriguez scoffed. "So, what are you trying to hide? Did you sleep with Charles or something?"

Alyssa's cheeks flushed at the thought.

"Seriously? This needs to stop," her mom said. "These questions are highly inappropriate."

"I agree," Derek added. "Do you have any real evidence that Alyssa played any part in this?"

"And Sally ran away! And screamed at me in her hospital room, throwing soup and everything. Isn't that solid proof that she's hiding something?" Alyssa slammed the Coke down, froth fizzing up.

"But you took off, too. In the middle of the night," Jameson said, his teeth clicking.

"And let's not forget about your mother confiding in Detective Wilton," Rodriguez chimed in. "Regarding her suspicions about, well, *you*."

Derek shook his head in confusion. "Wait, what? Mandy, you were discussing this case with another detective?"

Alyssa slowly turned. Her mom turned pale, hands clasped together. "He's lying," she insisted. "Alyssa, I didn't say a word to Simon."

"Mandy roped Detective Wilton—their neighbor—into helping track down the girls," Jameson explained to Derek. "And in the process, Mandy shared her concerns that Morgan's injuries occurred when Alyssa was babysitting. Perhaps an accident she was too scared to report."

Alyssa ignored the pulsating beat in her eardrums. Derek swore under his breath while her mother continued to claim it was all lies.

"We've got a lot of dirt on you, Alyssa," Rodriguez said, his face turning to a sour frown as his fingers traced the edges of the manila folder. "Shoplifting, smoking pot, cheating on an exam, failing chemistry—"

"Which, by the way, you said was your *favorite* subject," Jameson interjected.

"Wait a minute," Alyssa said, breathless. "I never cheated on an exam."

"Oh, and of course, the big one," Rodriguez continued. "Drinking wine at the Haywoods' house last Friday night, while you were babysitting Morgan. Did you feel tipsy? Stumble around a bit?"

Alyssa sucked in her breath, tugging on her pony necklace, the chain cutting into the back of her neck.

"Don't say anything," Derek told her. "They're just trying to rile you up."

"Should we confiscate her phone?" Rodriguez asked. "Dig into her social media?"

She stopped breathing. "My phone?"

"Not yet. But let's start the process for a court order," Jameson said. He turned to Alyssa, placing his hands on the table as if he meant business. "Alyssa, it's time to start explaining yourself."

"Don't—" Derek began.

"Explain myself? You want to know what really happened?" She leaned forward and barreled on. "I went to help Sally because I didn't want that poor boy to lose his mother. I lost a father, did you know that? Well, I did. And it sucks." Her voice boomed in the small room as Derek insisted for her to stop. "And I loved—*love* Morgan. I do. And Sally … I saved her life. I tried to do the right thing, and this is how you guys treat me?" Then something snapped, a subtle *pang* sound. She looked down at the broken chain in her hands, the purple pony gone. The Coke can rolled across the table, bubbling brown liquid seeping into the folder.

"Oh shit!" Jameson said, scooping up the folder and shaking it over the carpet.

"I'll get something," Rodriguez said, springing toward the door

"I'm sorry," Alyssa mumbled, dropping to the floor, running her hands over the carpet. She found the pony and settled back in her seat, ignoring her mother's desperate look and Derek's head shaking.

"You actually think I broke Morgan's rib, don't you?" She squeezed the pony in her hand. "I didn't drop him. He didn't hit his head. I held him and … and …"

Rodriguez returned with a wad of paper towels.

Jameson sighed, rapidly clicking his pen. "Is there anything else you want to add?"

"No," Derek said, firmly squeezing Alyssa's shoulder. "My client has nothing else to say."

✦

Jameson ushered them to the parking lot. "Look, Alyssa. I'm really trying to help you out here. There's just a lot of pressure from the higher ups." He gave a subtle nod back to the station, then forced a smile, patting her on the back. "We'll be in touch, okay?" he said before turning to leave.

"Wow," Derek said. "That was something."

"Seriously, Alyssa," her mom said. "You really lost control in there. What were you thinking?"

"Me?" Alyssa seethed. She shoved her fists into her mom, pushing her backward. "What about you? Your suspicions? Talking about me to Simon?"

"Alyssa …" her mom began. Derek hovered beside her, silent, looking a bit dazed. Or, perhaps, thinking he made a grave mistake when he volunteered to help with this rollercoaster case. Her mom opened her arms. "Let me explain, sweetie."

Alyssa didn't want to hear it. She bolted into a sprint across the parking lot. Where could she go? She thought of her dad, the pony and broken chain secure in her clammy hands. Maybe everything about him was a lie, maybe he never did anything wrong. But how to find him?

She sped past a Shell station, a McDonald's, a Goodwill. Heaving, panting, almost knocking over a family pushing a stroller, she ran and ran, ignoring the vibrating, ringing phone in her back pocket. Eventually she spotted a grassy patch, a cluster of trees on the hill. She climbed, breathless and determined, and with shaking hands, she carefully slid the pony and chain into the depths of her pocket.

Her phone continued to ring. She pulled it out.

Mom.

She swiped the call off, then lowered herself beneath a towering white oak and studied the blurred branches above. A few leaves already tinged orange, surrounded by puffs of cloud. Once, she lay sprawled on the grass next to her dad, lazily pointing out the shapes: *Pig, duck, brontosaurus, rock.* How could a cloud be a rock?

Back then, anything seemed possible.

✦

Alyssa heard footsteps approaching. Rolling away, she buried her face in the itchy grass, stifling a sneeze. She waited for the words of comfort, her mom's lame attempts to make this better.

She could hear her mom settling beside her—she knew it was her from the subtle sighs. Above, the branches rustled, a bird shrieked and fluttered away. Somewhere below a car honked, followed by brakes screeching.

"At least we know the GPS tracking works," her mom finally said.

"What?"

"I set it up when you were asleep on the couch. Earlier."

Alyssa didn't respond.

"We'll get through this, sweetie."

"No," Alyssa said, muffled, her face still deep in the grass. "You don't believe me. You think I hurt Morgan. Jameson said ..."

"Okay, okay, I had a moment of doubt," her mom said. "Not that you did anything intentionally, but maybe you were too afraid to share—"

"I could never keep something like that to myself. *Never.*" Alyssa squeezed a fist around the grass, the sharp blades poking out between her fingers, as if they were the only thing keeping her tethered to the earth.

"I know. I'm sorry."

Alyssa felt something on her hand. She opened one eye, squinting, watching as a tiny caterpillar crawled across her clenched fingers—a fuzzy black body with orange stripes.

Her mom continued: "I saw Sally. I saw that wild look in her eyes."

Alyssa pushed herself up to sitting and gently brushed the caterpillar to the ground, watching as it crawled onto a leaf. "But everyone's against me," she said. "Sally, Charles, the detectives—all of them. Even Jameson, and I kinda thought he was nice." She pressed her fingertips into her watery eyes. "And saying that I hit Sally? Really?"

"Oh, honey. It's clear that Sally's very messed up." Her mom plucked a blade of grass from Alyssa's hair.

"They think I put Morgan in the basement. My prints are down there? For real?" The sobs took over, her entire body shaking. "I'll never be able to babysit ever again."

Her mom calmly handed her a tissue and a plastic water bottle. "Detectives, they can—and will—say anything to get their suspects to break down. C'mon sweetie, you've seen the shows. Don't believe everything they say. We're going to get through this."

"But how do you know? They'll send me to juvie and I'll miss the conference next summer and never be able to go to college or see Jess ever again. And, oh God, my cellphone!" She looked down at it. Could they really take it away? "Everyone will think I did this to Morgan. Poor, sweet, little Morgan. What if I made things worse when I—"

"Shhh." Her mom grabbed her by the shoulders, pulling her in. Alyssa succumbed, breathing in her mom's comfort, a mix of cinnamon and mint.

"We've got to believe it's going to be okay," her mom said. "We know the truth and that's all that matters."

✦

Back at home, Mandy and Alyssa ate takeout on the couch: lukewarm burgers and soggy fries with chocolate milkshakes.

Jess sent her a text: **omggg my dad said it was like a circus on fire!!**

Alyssa: **yup. they're still blaming me.**

Jess: **nooooo.**

Alyssa replied with a string of crying emojis and a breaking heart.

Jess: **don't worry, dad will kill them. btw why was simon hugging ur mom???**

Alyssa looked up, her mom now on the phone, walking in circles in the kitchen.

"Yes, she had a second interview," her mom said. "Well, they—*we* think it's the mother. They never said but... hold on." Her mom pressed her phone to her chest. "I'm going to step outside, okay sweetie?"

Alyssa reached for a soggy fry and trailed it through the pool of ketchup. She licked the grease off her fingers and typed: **WTF???**

Jess: **mom saw it at hospital, like he was gonna kisss her!!! they a unit now or what?!? gurllll he gonna be ur stepdad!**

The words spun into a blur. How could her mom even think about Simon during this mess? *Before she even knew I was okay?* She texted back a red-faced angry emoji, the one with x's for eyes.

The front door swung open. "Sweetie, Grandma's going to drive down. Tomorrow."

Alyssa stood. "I'm going to bed."

"Are you okay?"

She was tempted to let her have it: *Oh, I'm just fine. After, y'know, enduring another grueling interrogation and having my own mother think I'm a child abuser and then finding out she made a move on our downstairs neighbor while I was trying to save someone's life.* Instead, she scooped up the fast food remains and headed into the kitchen. She took one last slurp of milkshake before crumpling the cup. "I just need sleep. I've got a killer headache."

"Okay, I get it," her mom said, caressing Alyssa's shoulders. "We'll get through this. You and me."

Alyssa reached up to grab her necklace, clawing at the emptiness. She frantically dug into her pocket. Still there.

"Rest up," her mom said. "I'm meeting with Derek in the morning. He's going to help us find a good lawyer in the area to take over the case."

✦

Alyssa locked the door to her room. The escape ladder was still dangling out the window. She pulled it up, latched the window, yanked the curtains closed.

She opened her closet door and crawled to the corner where the carpet peeled back. Underneath was a wobbly floorboard, and beneath that a small box. Squinting under the light of her phone, she pulled it out. Inside was her dad's old watch, which had been his father's watch—a grandfather she never met. The golden band chipped and cracked after decades of use. That, a faded picture, and Snoozy the turtle were the only things Alyssa managed to grab in their hasty departure ten years ago. And the My Little Pony necklace, snug in her pocket.

The picture showed her at around five years old, balanced proudly on her dad's broad shoulders, him smiling with a beer in one hand, a glowing cigarette in the other. She closed her eyes, listening to his rolling laughter, breathing in his smell—burnt smoke, mustard, a potent cologne, her little fists clutching tufts of brown hair as he bounded across the yard. "How ya doing up there, li'l turtle?"

What if he'd been wrongly accused?

Curling into a ball, Alyssa pulled the watch and photo to her chest, letting the safe solitude of the closet's walls drown out the noise and chaos of her life, the detective's harsh words: *Did you feel out of control?*

✦

Alyssa bolted up, staring into the dark space, her heart bouncing in her chest. It took a moment to remember crawling into the closet. Groping the floor, she found her dad's watch, the picture, and her phone.

She tiptoed into the hall and glanced at the time—already past two in the morning. She peered into her mom's room, saw her sprawled face down, still fully dressed. On the nightstand sat a glass of red wine, the telltale bottle of Ambien.

She grabbed the glass and tilted it back, letting the wine simmer on her tongue before swallowing. After wiping her mouth with the back of her hand, she breathed in the relaxation, the dulling of her brain.

She cautiously opened her mother's closet and dug through piles of strewn clothes, discarded boots, exercise bands, piles of crap. She was searching for a clue, anything to point her in the right direction.

A box labeled *Zack.* Right on top was a framed picture of herself, age two, wearing a glittery Santa hat, her face smooshed against the clear plastic of Zack's incubator. Alyssa didn't remember much from that time, of his short-lived life. Like most of her past, only brief flashes existed: peering into the hospital's aquarium, counting the brightly colored fish. Later she asked, "Is my brother a fish?" He lived in a tank, after all, with the same beady eyes and puckered lips.

She sighed. The heavy grief lingering, always there, etched in the lines around her mother's eyes, even though she rarely uttered his name. She closed the box.

Under the bed—Jess, as always, believed that was where secrets were hidden.

Alyssa dropped to her knees, shining her phone's light underneath the bed. Clumps of dust, a lone flip-flop, a few mounds of balled-up tissues. She shook her head.

Still on her knees, she opened the nightstand and pulled out a shoe box. Inside was a long cylinder, neon pink, a tangled cord. Wait, was this—she shuddered and shoved it back. A vibrator. *Gross.*

And then she saw it on the bookshelf: a white envelope, poking out from an earmarked book titled *Raising Your Spirited Child.*

She pulled out the letter, blowing off the dust. It was addressed to her—*Alyssa.* With her father's name scrawled in the upper left corner, the postmark dated August 10. About a month ago. Her fingers traced the return address: Wyoming. Her father had sent her a letter and her mom had hidden it. Were there more?

She felt lightheaded as she stuffed the letter into her back pocket, her mind already a few steps ahead. She clicked off the bedside lamp and quietly made her way to the kitchen. She picked up her mom's keys, unzipped her wallet, pulled out a Visa card. She knew her mother, she wouldn't turn Alyssa in. Not with the whole child abuse case still open. She felt like vomiting every time she thought or heard those words—*child abuse.*

She quietly slipped outside. The stoic moon shone down, full and radiant. She hesitated. Could she do this?

It's now or never.

Nodding to nobody but herself, she headed down the stairs and unlocked her mom's Honda Civic. She grasped the steering wheel, her breath coming in sporadic spurts. She only had her driver's permit; this, this right here, was entirely illegal. The danger of it raced through her veins.

Glancing up, she jumped when she saw a hollow-eyed, disheveled Simon staring back. She lowered the window.

"Where are you going?" he asked. "You're not running away again, are you?"

"I'm, uh, going to Walgreens. My mom's got a killer headache." Somehow the lies kept tumbling out, with minimal effort. She wondered why she'd spent so many years trying to do the right thing.

These lies are the only thing saving me right now.

"I just want you to know, I don't believe Sally."

"Please, stay away from my mom," Alyssa said, flicking the window's switch, drowning out Simon's response. He stepped back onto the sidewalk, hands in pockets. The man who once seemed like a thrilling mystery, a far-fetched fantasy. If he hadn't arrived, if he hadn't tracked her down …

Who was she kidding? Alyssa knew she'd be found guilty. Sally would fight this to the bitter end: *The babysitter hurt my baby.*

She put the Honda in reverse, refusing to look back at their apartment complex, her home for the past decade. Who cared if Simon called her in? She needed to go find the one person who would understand; someone who believed in her, someone who understood how much her future mattered. Unlike her mom, who doubted her. Did her dad still love her? She nodded. Of course he did.

She thought about swinging by to pick up Jess, but knew Claire and Derek would be hovering over her like agitated hawks.

The dark, open highway loomed ahead. Alyssa's shaky foot pushed into the gas pedal. She forced her eyes to stay open, using her left hand to massage the random zaps of pain wrapping around to the back of her head. She'd have to navigate with her phone turned off. Maybe she could stop and buy an old-fashioned map? But for now, she knew enough to find her way out of Oak Wood, to get out of North Carolina. Heading west.

Wyoming.

Chapter 39

Sally

Day eight

Sally studied Charles's figure in the dark, curled on the couch, a towel haphazardly pulled over him, his gentle snores alternating rhythm with the beeping machines. He'd barely spoken to her after his short interrogation last night, about Morgan: *Did anything …?* He didn't have to finish, his wary expression said it all. He knew.

And then came his doubts about the baby—*Is she even mine?* As if she had time for an affair. Oh sure, let's just pencil that in between Morgan's nerve-rattling wails and soupy diaper changes and tending to the cat that Charles basically ignored.

The monitor's glow cast an eerie light across her bed. She ran her fingers along the IV tube attached to her arm. Charles had only expressed concern about *this* baby—who, without doubt, was one hundred percent his. The real mystery was *Morgan.* With a blink, she traveled back to that hazy Halloween party in downtown Raleigh with her old high school pal, Jenny. Charles had gone off with Beth and his nephews to a family retreat. Meanwhile, Sally slammed down the drinks, trying to drown her inner storm: the fact she'd fallen in love with a married man, with no promise of a concrete future. She dressed as a sexy nurse, the guy as Batman. The deafening music drove them down the hall, his intoxicated blurry blue eyes fixated on the missing top button on her white V-neck dress—a dress that slid so effortlessly to the floor.

Next came the missed period, then the bewilderment and dismay as she saw the double pink lines on the pregnancy test; her unspoken doubt: *Whose baby is this?* She'd slept with Charles the weekend before *and* the weekend after that Halloween party. All of it—Charles and Batman—unprotected, no birth control. She shook her head at her naive recklessness. But really, what could she have done afterwards? The guy never took off his mask, never uttered his name—or maybe he did, and her inebriated brain failed to remember. Later, she casually asked Jenny, "Who was that Batman guy?" Her friend shrugged: "Who cares?"

But was it cheating if Charles was still sleeping in the same bed as his wife?

And now, trapped in this claustrophobic hospital room while Charles seethed with doubt and suspicion, it further cemented Sally's resolve to lock away that memory, forever. Charles was Morgan's father. End of story.

She tried to push him away last night. "Go be with Morgan," she insisted. But Charles simply shook his head, quietly tending to her needs, his eyes narrowed with worry, as if she posed a danger—to herself, to the baby.

The baby's subtle squirms and kicks kept her awake. Sally cupped her hands around her slight bulge, realizing that the random flutters and tightening of her stomach had been her baby all along—or her baby mixed with stress. She was overcome with a sudden urge to wake Charles. How good it'd feel to release her guilt, to ramble off her confession: *Me, me, me. I did it.* But she'd lose Morgan. She'd lose this baby.

Her little girl, as if listening to Sally's internal debate, paused her gymnastic tumbles. A tired heaviness slowly took over, her body twitching as sleep approached. I'll come clean in the morning, she told herself.

But when the first rays blinked through the blinds, fear swelled in her throat, paralyzing her once again.

Today's Friday, she realized. One full week since …

"I'm gonna get breakfast," Charles said. He slipped on his shoes. "Gotta call my mom. See how Morgan's doing." After polishing his glasses on his wrinkled shirt, he slipped them on and looked past her, as if examining the wall. "When I get back, I think it's time we have a serious talk." His brow furrowed. "If you really did this, we need to figure out what happens next. With Morgan."

"But I didn't—"

He left the room without another word.

She saw it, crystal clear: Charles storming off with both kids, leaving her with nothing but a pile of lonely regrets.

The doctors knew about the shaking. The CT scan, internal bleeding—had she caused permanent damage? Charles looked ready to tell her, but then clammed up, throwing up a brick wall of hatred between them. She lightly dug her fingers into her stomach, seeing if her daughter kicked back. (*Daughter—I have a daughter.*) Soon the doctor would make the final decision, whether this fragile girl would be allowed more time to incubate, or if she needed to be rescued from Sally's womb, thrust into the world too soon.

The baby gave a sharp kick, her fiercest one yet, as if trying to communicate: *Go. Now.* Sally shook her head, but the pestering thought grew stronger. She took a long inhale. Could she take this baby girl and flee? Maybe. *Yes.* But where? She frantically scrolled through her phone. Gwen never responded to her plea for help. *Bitch.*

Sally tried to think it through, fighting back tears. She could get up, sneak out, find somewhere to hide, all before Charles returned. He'd win in courts, hands down, no struggle. She had to do *something*. Birth this baby on her own. She could. *YES!* Then, she wouldn't be alone. She'd have *her*—a fresh chance, an untainted beginning. No. Caring for a newborn was exhausting, burdensome, overwhelming. What if she lost control again?

You'll do right this time around.

That's right, she told herself. She wouldn't scream at this baby. She wouldn't yell. She wouldn't put her in the basement. She'd follow every gentle parenting account on Instagram, really absorbing the advice this time. She wouldn't lose it, never never never. *Never again.*

"I promise," she whispered.

Pushing past the resistance, Sally yanked out tubes and ripped off straps, breathing through bouts of raw pain. The machines flashed with angry buzzing sounds. She stood, slowly, letting her muscles settle. Leaning forward, she coughed and gagged, then threw up on the floor.

She wiped her mouth, shook her head, squeezed her phone. Just one step at a time. One step. Her daughter cheered her on: *You can do this.*

She made it to the door, somehow found the strength to open it. She took a few steps, scanning the spacious, brightly lit hall. A space to hide, a closet, or a door—an exit. She looked at her phone, only five percent charge left. Taxi? Robin from Denny's? She always liked Robin and her exuberant confidence. She was a take-charge kind of girl. Who cared about questions at this stage? She had to disappear—fast.

"Sally!" a voice shouted. "You can't be up. What are you doing?" Ugh, that damn doctor, the one who acted like she cared. Parvati. Discarding her clipboard, the doctor called out for help as she hurried toward Sally. She grabbed Sally by the wrist. "C'mon, let's get you back to your room."

"Leave me alone," Sally hissed, wrenching her arm away. The doctor stumbled backward. Sally lurched toward the glowing exit sign. The morning light beckoned her, the door to freedom, to her new life.

Outside, breathing fresh air, the sun warmed her face as she teetered down the steps, using every ounce of remaining energy to sprint across the lawn, the wet grass squishing under her bare feet. *Did it rain?* A damp, rose-scented fragrance tickled her nose. She kept running, grasping her stomach—*Hold on, sweetie!*—the cool air rippling across her naked body, her flimsy robe flapping in the breeze. She spread her arms wide, like the wings of an eagle, ready to fly, to soar far away.

A new life!

She reached the road, stumbled to a stop, wheezing and panting. A semi whizzed by. A horn blared. Her insides pulsed. She looked down—blood pooled on the sidewalk, her feet painted crimson red. *It's going to be okay,* she whispered. To her baby, to the only person who still listened. *I love you,* she said, heavy tears clinging to her lashes. *I do.*

Several people surrounded Sally and wrestled her into a wheelchair, strong arms holding her down. She screamed with a fury she didn't know she possessed, thrashing and kicking and slapping and spitting. "Let me go! Let me go! LET ME GO!" They couldn't hold her here. She *needed* to go.

A sharp stab in her arm made her freeze. She looked. A minuscule prick of blood. The gold-hooped, wide-eyed doctor held a syringe. In the distance, Charles bounded across the lawn, waving his arms, shouting her name: *Sally! Sally! Sally!* Like a scene from a movie—her lovestruck partner still cared, he still believed in her. Then it hit like an electric shock: *This isn't for me. This is for her—our new baby.* She tried to scream but her voice gave out: *This is MY baby.*

Charles's figure blurred until it disappeared completely. A warm fuzziness engulfed her, stilling her brain, halting her last chance of escape.

I'm stuck.

The motion of the wheelchair caused the final wall to crumble. She saw Morgan in her hands, his body limp, his screams drowned to an icy quiet within seconds. The words escaped from her lips in a faint whisper: "It was me."

Chapter 40

Charles

The next twenty-eight days

Charles stood alone in the NICU at Durham Regional Hospital, a steady stream of beeps counting down the days, the hours, the minutes of his daughter's life. Sally was sedated in the psych ward, whisked there after her attempted escape, after the emergency C-section. There in front of him wiggled the fragile, two-pound infant, a tiny fist wrapped around his index finger, murky hazel eyes blinking up at him.

Sally's confession on the street—*it was me*—had been whispered too faintly to mean anything. Maybe it was the breeze rustling through their hair or the squeaks of her wheelchair? Or simply his imagination? Either way, Jameson put the case on hold due to the sudden turn of events.

The name came to him immediately: *Hazel.* The nurse wrote it on the whiteboard above her incubator. Charles stroked her porcelain cheek, her head jerking toward his touch, lips parting as she sucked in air, as if searching for a nipple.

He believed, somehow, if he devoted enough love, enough nonstop attention—begging God, the universe, anyone who'd listen—this baby would live. The incessant mantra thundered within as he blinked away tears: *Please please please let her live. I'll never ask for another thing again. I promise.*

Eventually he fell asleep, his head slumped against the hard walls of her incubator, scared to step away for even a second.

✦

The doctors released Morgan from Oak Wood Hospital several days later. The social worker assigned temporary custody to Charles's mom, who took Morgan back to their empty house. Charles got a hotel room with his brother, Danny, who'd flown in from LA.

Charles and his mother walked Morgan down the corridor to Hazel's room. *Look, this is your sister.* But Morgan tensed, his face scrunched up as if he'd tasted something sour.

"No," Morgan said, his feet glued in place. Charles imagined it looked scary—a shriveled creature squirming behind plastic walls. Or, maybe Morgan knew, deep down, that she wasn't a forever sister. She might disappear, just like his mother did.

"It's okay," Charles said, scooping him into his arms. Morgan buried his face into his chest. "She knows you love her." But he knew this visit wasn't for Morgan. It was for himself—an attempt to have his two children together, to preserve this moment as a family, even as everything broke apart, like a house built on quicksand.

✦

Danny urged Charles to take Sally to see Hazel.

"You still don't know if she was the one who shook Morgan," Danny said, sitting on the hotel bed.

"She admitted it." Charles stared out the window. "I heard her."

"But still, she's Hazel's mother. This 'failure to thrive' isn't good. And once Hazel's gone, she's ..."

Sally stayed in the hospital for ten days, due to complications from her C-section and the mental breakdown. Charles walked by her door several times, close to peeking in, but then her words came hurling toward him: *It was me.* Why would she lie to him? Why would she accuse the babysitter?

Why why why?

Danny's advice continued to haunt him. He knew Hazel didn't have long; he saw the nurse weigh her, his stomach twisting as the numbers went in the wrong direction.

He finally stood in front of Sally's room, the morning of her release. Where would she go next? He couldn't think that far. The nurse helped her into a wheelchair, and he grabbed the handles, pushing her toward the elevator.

Her eyes blinked, full of suspicion. "What's going on? Where are you taking me? Where's Morgan?"

"Shhh," he said. "Morgan's okay. You have to meet our daughter."

✦

Hazel never made it home, never saw the inside of their house. Her ashes, sealed in a pewter urn, were displayed on the mantle, awaiting some unknown destination. The park? Their backyard? She had no memories, no history.

Charles studied Hazel's urn night after night, his eyes stinging as the guilt played again and again, like a stuck record player. Christ, if only he had noticed Sally's changing body sooner, he could've interfered. Gotten her the medical and psychiatric help she so desperately needed. Why did he threaten to take Morgan away? Why did he push Sally over the edge?

He couldn't shake the truth: *I didn't do enough to save Hazel.*

✦

Almost two weeks after Hazel died, the detective attacked with full force. Charles met him down at the station, ready to claim back his son. But then Jameson read him his legal rights, as if he was about to get arrested.

"But Sally confessed," Charles said. "I heard her. Isn't that enough?"

"Unfortunately, we can't go on your word," Jameson said.

Charles closed his eyes, his brain foggy and befuddled. "When's this going to end? I just want to go home. Morgan needs me."

"Well," Jameson said, flipping through his notepad, "we talked to your neighbors. They said they heard screams around 11:30 that Friday night. When you were at home, alone, with Morgan."

"What?" Charles's eyes sprung open. "It was the TV—I was watching TV, the show *Survivor*. Morgan was asleep."

"You originally said you were watching *Lost*."

The second detective—Rodriguez—went on to say the evidence was piling up against him: his tattered knuckles, Sally's bruise, the neighbor's report.

"But ..." Charles swallowed down his fear. "Is Sally actually blaming me?"

"We're talking to her next," Rodriguez said.

"And the babysitter, too," Jameson added.

"Alyssa didn't do it," Charles said, clenching his fists. "Go talk to Sally. She's staying with a friend from work. Robin." He pulled out his phone and scrolled to Sally's latest messages. Her pleas to come home. Her determination to prove her own innocence. He ignored most of them, sending only one reply: **I'm not even allowed home right now.**

"Here's the address," Charles said, holding out his phone. Jameson scribbled the details on his notepad. "It was Sally," he added. He felt empty, as if every remaining emotion—good and bad—had been scraped clean.

Chapter 41

Sally

The next twenty-eight days

Sally struggled to remember what happened. She made it to the road, so close to freedom, and then Charles showed up, then he vanished. A bright light. More darkness. A baby's cry—not Morgie. Then alone in a cell, no, the hospital, another room. Her brain cloudy, dulled, but different than before. Her belly aching, the bump gone, a searing, painful scar in its place.

Then Charles came back and took her to see the baby.

He had named her Hazel. *Because of her eyes.* She was ten days old.

"You can hold her," the doctor said. Or a nurse. Someone.

"Can I?" Sally squeaked. She didn't know what rights she had anymore.

"Yes," a voice said. "Of course."

They lowered the baby into her arms, bundled in a lilac blanket. Who bought her this blanket? Sally embraced her daughter, tentatively, trying not to hold *too* tightly, but afraid of dropping her. She bit her lip, sweat dripping down her back.

The baby's eyes fluttered open, and Sally gasped, her own eyes filling with searing tears. The baby, Hazel, made a little squawk, the resemblance of a scream or a cry, or maybe a coo? Sally's breasts swelled, a few drops of milk soaking through her flimsy robe, milk her baby would never drink. The doctors had said she could pump but she couldn't use any of it right now due to all her medications.

Sally lightly brushed Hazel's cheek. Just ten days ago she hadn't even known this baby existed and now, here she was. Breathing. Squinting up at Sally. She wondered who this girl would become, what this beautiful little being would do with her life. A dancer? An astronaut? An artist? A mother?

The nurse rambled off Hazel's medical complications. But Sally couldn't—wouldn't listen. Right then, she held her baby. And Charles stood nearby. She tried her best to cherish the moment.

She sang "Twinkle, Twinkle Little Star," watching Hazel's eyes scan her face—a mix of curiosity and fascination. The regrets wormed their way deeper and deeper: *Why didn't I ask for help sooner? Why did I drink so much? Why why why?*

In the end, the questions didn't matter. Hazel died four days later, before she got the chance to know Sally—the good, the bad, the love, the mistakes. Hazel died before she ever had a chance to be something.

✦

Sally's friend Robin took her in, offering a saggy couch, a threadbare blanket, and a lumpy pillow. It was better than nothing. Sally managed to squeak out the words—*The babysitter hurt my baby*—and Robin shook her head in disbelief, wiping away tears of shock.

"I can't believe everything you've been through," she commiserated, hugging Sally.

Robin was studying pre-law, so she knew the right people. She snagged a lawyer before Sally's next interview. "He'll work pro bono. Help you get your son back."

Sally nodded, trying to believe in a hopeful future. She held her breath as she followed the detective into the interrogation room. *I can still be Morgie's mother,* she told herself. She wouldn't let him go. Not after losing Hazel.

Jameson laid out the X-rays and his chubby finger stabbed the image of Morgan's broken rib, repeatedly. "Our forensics team did a deeper analysis and pinpointed the exact time of the accident to three o'clock, Friday afternoon. When you were alone with Morgan."

She blinked. "You can do that?"

"Yup." Jameson folded his arms across his chest, leaning back, a satisfied smirk on his face.

"He's bluffing," the lawyer said. "My client believes the babysitter is fully responsible for Morgan's injuries and wants to move forward with—"

"No," Sally said. The sobs came fast. "It only happened once. I only shook him once. I swear."

It was just one little shake.

What happened next cemented itself forever in her memory: The sharp click of handcuffs. Riding in the back of the cop's car—the bulletproof plastic window walling off her words, her uncontrollable sorrow. Watching in disbelief as they dabbed each finger on paper, a permanent record of her one mistake. Then standing in the stark corridor, phone in her hand, she called Charles—she had no one else.

"I'm so sorry," she said.

Charles said he'd pay the bond, but he didn't want to see her. "Not yet," he said coldly.

After she nestled the phone back onto the wall, the cop led her down the hall. At least this, her being the guilty one, meant Charles would be allowed back home. He could see Morgan. Morgan would have one parent. She tried to see the positive.

They released her and she stood in the massive parking lot, once again squinting up to the cloud-dotted sky, wondering: *What do I do next?*

Only silence followed.

Chapter 42

Charles

Three weeks later

"Sally," the judge began. "You've been charged with felony child abuse. Do you understand this?"

"Yes." Sally nodded.

"Please, tell me what happened."

Charles squirmed in his seat. The courtroom was stifling hot, the heat blasted too high against the sudden October chill outside. Jameson had notified him about the court date, after Sally's confession. Open to the public, on Halloween, of all days. In a way, it made sense, that this unbelievable nightmare would come to a peak on a day of trickery and spookiness—except there would be no treats. Charles cringed when a reporter snapped his picture on the front steps of the courthouse.

Sally took the judge through the details: Morgan screaming, her trying to appease him, to calm him. Grabbing him around the ribcage. "It wasn't me," Sally told the judge. "That person—it was like a different me."

Charles leaped to his feet and grasped the wooden railing. "Why didn't you tell me?" he roared. "Was it the pregnancy hormones? Post-partum depression? What happened?"

The judge pounded her gavel, and a bailiff came toward him, but Charles couldn't stop. "Why, Sally? Why didn't you tell me right away?"

"It was only one time," Sally said, not turning to face him.

Charles sighed into his hands, the blast of air fogging his glasses. "That doesn't make it any better."

The bailiff took him by his elbow and pulled him into the aisle.

"Morgan's brain may never be the same!" Charles shouted. "All because of what you did."

The judge's gavel resonated across the courtroom. The bailiff dragged Charles toward the exit. Before they reached the door, he saw Alyssa cowering in the back row, her face slick with tears.

✦

Afterward, Charles learned that Sally's lawyer managed to plead her charges down to a misdemeanor, getting her a twenty-four-month probation period instead of jail time. Sally had to sign a form agreeing to temporarily suspend her parental rights until she met all the requirements the court outlined in her probation agreement.

They weren't officially married so there were no complicated legal forms to fill out, no fifty-fifty splitting of the house. With one swift click, her Denny's earnings were transferred to her new account.

The judge said Sally could come home to gather her belongings, but she wasn't allowed to see Morgan until she completed the specified hours of counseling, parenting classes and community service, and then only with supervised visits. Nobody gave Charles a heads up. The doorbell rang a little over a week later, on a Saturday afternoon, and Charles opened the door to Sally, swaying on their front stoop. A pair of oversized movie-star sunglasses hid her eyes.

"Jesus, Sally," Charles said. "Come in."

She didn't say anything. Just went about her business, pulling a suitcase from the closet, throwing in clothes, scooping up crusted bottles of shampoo, then yanking down the ladder to the attic.

"I need my mom's stuff," she muttered

"I would've brought the boxes down for you. You should've called," he said. "Here, let me help."

She held up a hand, her lips pressed so hard they turned white. "I've got it," she huffed before climbing up the ladder.

His mom beckoned from down the hall. "Let me take care of this. Go into Morgan's room. Lock the door."

He followed her command. After closing the door and flicking the lock, he crouched on the floor, knees hugged to his chest while Morgan played with his toy train. A steady *choo choo choo* as it charged around the tracks. Charles strained to listen to their voices behind the door.

"I can't even hug him goodbye?" Sally's pained screech chipped at his heart like a mallet to stone.

His mother mumbled a response, her tone firm and authoritative.

"Just one hug ... I'm still his mom ... *please—*"

Another round of *choo choo choo* and a sharp command from Charles's mother. Morgan paused, his eyes darting curiously to the door. But then he clapped his hands in delight as the train looped around the rickety wooden tracks.

Charles licked the salty tears off his lips, finally standing and flinging open the door. He ran out of the house as Sally was pulling away in a U-Haul van. He chased after her until the van screeched to a halt. She unrolled the window.

"I'm sorry I didn't see what was going on," he said, leaning over and trying to catch his breath. "Why didn't you ask for help before it got that bad? Why?"

She pressed her hands together, muttering under her breath as if praying to God, her eyes still hidden by her sunglasses.

"Sally. Where are you going? Aren't you going to do the counseling and get help? To be there for Morgan?"

"I think it's better for everyone if I just leave," she said, her voice flat. The window slid up, she revved the engine, turned the corner, and faded into the distance.

He stormed into the house, barged into their room, and stared at Sally's side of the closet, empty and barren, coat hangers askew. One lone blouse abandoned on the floor. He tore at it, buttons flying, his voice a stream of guttural sounds. His mom closed the door.

✦

The months passed by in a blur, his mother nagging him to throw out the family pictures. "Start afresh. It's no use having her negative energy around." She waved a dismissive hand in the air, as if to brush away Sally's troubled aura. He picked up a frame. The newborn photoshoot, Morgan bundled between them, like a fat burrito with a wrinkly face poking out.

But whenever he started packing away their past, Morgan would grab a picture frame, toddling with outstretched arms, giggling, "Maaa ..." His face glowed with delight; that traumatic Friday afternoon seemingly forgotten. Morgan chose, Charles liked to believe, to preserve Sally's broad smile, her infectious laugh, her silky-soft skin. Morgan chose love, over everything else. Charles tried to do the same. He even found himself typing out the beginnings of a text from time to time: **I love you. I really do.** But his body would tighten, and, holding his breath, he would press backspace until the words disappeared.

Then came February 4—the two-year anniversary of their pretend wedding, the ceremony they'd thrown together for his family. Something in Charles snapped. Without thinking, he pulled out a cardboard box from the hall closet, grabbed a roll of packing tape, and started shoving in one framed picture after another. He didn't even bother with bubble wrap. He stretched tape across the top, nicking his finger on the cutter. "Ouch!"

Sucking on the wound, he stared at the box. He knew he couldn't throw everything away; Morgan was bound to ask: *Who was my mom?* He needed to have something to show him when that day came.

He hauled the heavy box into the basement. The playpen, the one under hot debate, was long gone. The gun sold to a local pawn shop, his hunting days over. Charles had even thought about moving. His mom kept pushing it—"There's plenty of room at my place. Lots of single women. Or, you know, you could always give Beth a call?" The thought made his balls shrivel, his heart ice over. Oh, the things Beth would say if she stomped back into his life. Though it was probably time to hunt her down, get that divorce. Or at least apologize for what he'd done—might as well tidy up all the messes in his life.

His mother had been coming and going since "the incident" last September. Charles quit his job at Print Solutions, coasting on meager savings, keeping his regular Uber shifts. He half-heartedly scanned online job listings but the thought of starting over made his brain seize, and he'd slam his laptop shut with a defeated sigh. Sensing his dour outlook, his mother slid a generous check across the counter: "You need time to heal."

After hiding the pictures in the basement, he busied himself with making coffee—pouring in the beans, adding water, turning on the machine. The kitchen sparkled, one benefit to having his mother around, spraying and sterilizing and polishing everything obsessively. It smelled like Lysol. The times she left to go tend to his father, he was left in a bind. Find a new babysitter or beg Alyssa to come back?

He eventually caved and called Alyssa, having vowed never to text babysitters again. "I know you hate me, but I'm sorry. So sorry. And really, Morgan loves you." He knew he couldn't take everything away from Morgan with one quick swoop.

His mother protested: "You can't trust these babysitters."

"But Mom," Charles said. "Alyssa never did anything wrong. Remember?"

"Hmmm, well," she huffed. "You can never be too careful."

They had a meeting over it, Mandy and Alyssa and himself. Mandy was fervently opposed to the idea while Alyssa insisted on helping out. They agreed she could babysit based on one stipulation: Charles needed to install some Nest security cameras. As they left, Mandy briefly touched his shoulder, her eyes cloudy with despair. "I lost a baby too. Around the same age as Hazel." He nodded, unable to voice a response. A wordless moment of shared pain and grief communicated it all.

Now Charles sipped his coffee, letting the memory of Sally and her pictures dissipate. Morgan's cry crackled over the monitor. He took a final hit of caffeine before heading down the hall.

"How's my little boy?" He held him close, rubbed his back, their chests rising and falling together—reassurance that his cracked rib had healed. Charles imagined, as he often did, how much worse the damage would've been if Sally had shaken Morgie as an infant. He rambled off his gratitude as he carefully lowered him to the floor. So careful, always careful, as if his boy were a Jenga game—one wrong move and he would crumble to pieces.

"Maaa ..."

Charles turned to where Morgan pointed. Three pictures remained on the wall, Sally's deep brown eyes peering down at them.

"That's right. That's your mama."

"Mama," Morgan said, his eyes expectant and curious, as if trying to say: *Where did she go?*

"Let's go watch TV," Charles said, ignoring the crack spreading across his heavy heart.

✦

Charles returned home from his Uber shift, lugging grocery bags up the front steps, his thoughts on Sally. They'd recently passed the one-year mark of the shaking. Was she planning on coming back? On a whim, he'd texted her a picture of Morgan with his cake about two months ago, the day after that exhausting birthday party, and it took Sally two agonizing days to reply with a simple **Thank you.** Nothing more.

He sighed and pushed the door open, only to be assaulted by one of Morgan's screaming fits. Charles's mother banged a pot with a wooden spoon, repeatedly, her forehead dripping with sweat. "Nothing will get him to stop!" she wailed. "Make him stop! He needs to stop. I can't take it!" She flung the spoon across the room. It hit the wall with a resounding thud.

"Mom!" Charles yelled, staring at the fallen spoon. "What the hell, Mom?"

Morgan's wails continued, his little fists now hammering into Charles's shins. Charles dropped the bags, scooped up his shrieking son, and bounded outside. He tried Alyssa's trick—strapping him in the stroller and racing around the block, lifting the front wheels up and down like a makeshift roller coaster, *bump bump bump* along the sidewalk. He ignored the concerned looks from neighbors and the wary glances from random joggers, his lungs aching from the exertion, breathing through the heaviness of another muggy afternoon. Miraculously, Morgan's screams slowed to giddy hiccups, his fists knocking together in baby sign language: *more, more, more.*

Charles gaped at his son's transformation as they slowed down to a more manageable speed. If only, he thought, if only Sally had known about this—a quick and easy escape from hell, a guaranteed way to placate their baby boy's misery, preserving their own sanity.

He shivered.

If only ...

Chapter 43

Simon

Almost eleven months after the incident

Simon stood barefoot in Mandy's kitchen, the new Keurig machine groaning like a sleep-deprived owl. Nibbling on stale toast, he reviewed the list Mandy had left him, his finger tapping on each item: *Pack kitchen but leave enough plates out so we can still eat, label each box so we know where to find everything ...* As if he'd never moved before.

His line-up of past relationships was nothing to brag about: headstrong women who wanted a solid someone to prop them up, to sweep up their messes, making the realities of law disappear. Love can do that, cause you to turn a blind eye and ignore the red flags waving loud and clear. He knew Mandy was different. She scurried about, haunted by her troubled past, but her eyes showed another story—a sweet vulnerability that stilled his heart. And, of course, he loved the way her petite body fit snugly in his arms, her forever-ruffled auburn hair, the way her glasses slid down her button nose. His only regret was he didn't get to her before that jerk Ian did.

He poured his coffee, then wandered throughout Mandy's quiet apartment, sizing up the workload that awaited him. They'd only known each other for roughly ten or eleven months, and apart from the rocky start with the child abuse investigation, everything had escalated into "yes, this is right." At a surprising speed. But wasn't that how it goes?

Mandy had since rebooted her career, plowing through grad school classes at night while Alyssa toured potential colleges, and now the girls were off to that elite med summer school in Boston. He smiled, hoping his presence had helped. It had, right?

He thought about how he'd chased Alyssa down after their middle-of-the-night encounter last September. Something in his gut had warned him, maybe the way her eyes flitted and twitched when he'd confronted her in the parking lot? He'd trailed behind her, keeping adequate distance—this wasn't his first time stalking someone—until she'd pulled into a playground around the corner from Whispering Wind drive. Wasn't that where Morgan lived?

He watched as Alyssa slumped in a swing, motionless, a shadow child under the moon's watchful glow. Tentatively, he approached her.

She jumped, but remained seated. "What the hell? Are you following me?"

"I knew you weren't going to Walgreens," he said, claiming the swing next to her.

"Why do you care?" She swiped tears off her cheeks.

"I don't want you to do anything stupid, you know. What with the—"

"Don't say it."

"Why'd you come here?" He surveyed the park, a massive dinosaur slide lurking behind a cluster of trees.

"I used to bring Morgan here," she said. "You know, the kid you think I beat up."

Simon sighed. "I know Jameson and Rodriguez were extra rough on you today. I'm sorry. They like to twist things around, see if you'll crack. They're dealing with pressure from higher up since things have been dragging on too long ..."

Alyssa leaned over and shoved her phone in Simon's face, an image of Morgan's chubby face filling the screen. "Like I would ever hurt this baby? I mean, I love him. I really do."

Simon nodded as Alyssa swiped from photo to photo: Morgan at this very park, Morgan sprawled across a carpeted floor, Morgan sleeping with Elmo nestled in his arms. Then: A tall man standing next to his car, duffel bag slung over shoulder.

"Hold on. Why do you have a picture of—?"

Alyssa yanked back her phone. "I—I wanted to know what you were up to before … before I knew you were a detective," she stammered. "I thought, like, you were a criminal or in the CIA or something …"

Simon chuckled. "Looks like you might need to rethink your career choice. You've got a real flair for detective work."

Alyssa shrugged in response.

"Let me tell you, there's a fine line between the good guys and the bad ones," Simon began. "Someone has it all together, they make one mistake and cover it up, then another, and before you know it, their entire life has unraveled."

"Is that what's happening to me?"

"Oh, Alyssa. Of course not." He rose to his feet. "You did everything right. You even put your own feelings aside, staying up all night to hunt down Sally, making sure she was safe. That was, well, damn courageous if you ask me. Not many people would do that."

Alyssa looked away, rubbing at the back of her head.

"C'mon, let's get you home before your mom wakes up and has another missing-child panic attack."

Simon now shook his head at the memory, feeling queasy at how close Jameson and Rodriguez got to pinning it on Alyssa. Luckily, Sally confessed and they could slam dunk the case shut—neatly and cleanly. That was always a victory in the office. No loose strings.

He drained his coffee mug, ran his fingers through his hair, then pulled out the stack of flattened U-Haul boxes. Mandy had ordered uniformly sized boxes, saying they'd make everything easier. "Baby," he'd responded, "moving is never easy." After moving more times than he cared to admit, he knew this to be one of those hard-and-fast rules of life. Like taxes. And death.

Their new house was in Durham—they could never afford the skyrocketing prices in Oak Wood. It meant a new high school for Alyssa's senior year, plus a longer commute for himself, but hey, people adjust.

Mandy's list instructed him to pack up Alyssa's closet first since she never used anything in there. It made him uncomfortable, riffling through his soon-to-be stepdaughter's belongings. (He hadn't popped the question yet, but he'd used his bonus to buy the ring and couldn't wait to see it on Mandy's delicate hand.) Anyway, Mandy had insisted he get a head start on the packing since they'd only have a few days to move before school started—and he knew better than to argue.

Alyssa's entire closet fit into four large boxes. He bent over, scribbling a quick description on each: *Coats and shoes. More coats. Dresses. Rope ladder and stuffed animals.*

He swept out the cobwebs and wiped down the closet's shelves. Something creaked underfoot and he knelt, noticing a loose floorboard. He pried it open and inside sat a small box. He glanced over his shoulder, wondering if he should investigate. Did this even belong to Alyssa?

Curiosity got the better of him. Sitting on Alyssa's bed, he examined the box's contents: an old watch, a photo of what appeared to be a kindergarten-aged Alyssa with a scruffy-looking guy—her dad? There was also a letter addressed to Jess with a postmark from Wyoming. That's odd, he thought. Beneath it all, he found a folded piece of paper. He opened it.

July 13

Dear Dad,

Thanks for your letter. Please keep sending them to Jess's address, I don't want Mom to know we're in touch (eventually I'll tell her, I promise).

And wow, that's amazing you're remarried with a baby on the way. Do you know if it's a boy or girl? I can't believe I'm going to be a big sister again!

I got so close to running away, that's how bad things got. But I didn't want to be like Sally—running from everything. I fought too hard to get to where I'm at. I really want to meet you and am saving up for a plane ticket. Do you think I could come for Christmas, maybe?

Now that I know you're actually out there—alive and real—I need to tell you something. I'm scared to even write it but I'll hide this letter until it's safe to send.

Simon paused, glancing at the door, even though he knew he was all alone. What was he doing, invading Alyssa's privacy like this? But a sliver of rage surged through him. Ian was a terrible husband—a terrible person. He abandoned them and left Mandy scrambling on her own. He didn't deserve a second chance with Alyssa. Hell no.

Hands trembling, he continued reading.

Let me start by saying that Sally confessed. Jess and I went to the open court thing and Sally told the judge it was a one-time incident. She shook Morgan! Holy shit, Sally actually broke Morgan's rib! And she kept him in the basement—waaaaayyyy before the shaking. That was abuse, right?

But here's the thing—it wasn't ALL her. That night I was babysitting, after I'd texted Charles and Sally, Morgan cried out again. It was late and I didn't turn on the lights because I didn't want him to fully wake up. I carried him to the kitchen to get more milk and I don't remember what happened but somehow the cat got under me and next thing I knew, I was falling backwards. I hit my head on the floor. And I think, maybe, my arms swung out, then yanked back in as I fell? It all happened so fast. I held Morgan tightly and made sure he didn't fall onto the ground. He didn't hit his head—that part wasn't me. But did I cause him whiplash? Or make his broken rib worse by squeezing him too hard? Dad, you've got to believe me, Morgan seemed okay. I really thought he was okay.

I'm babysitting for him again, even though Mom's not happy about it. I was legit nervous, too. But Charles needed all the help he could get. And here's the really scary part: Morgan doesn't seem okay. He's almost two and still not talking. He doesn't dance and laugh like he used to. He holds his head a lot, like he's in pain, and OMG, did I—or me and Sally—cause serious damage?

It's eating me up and I don't know what to do. I'm about to go away to this Future Doctors of America thing in Boston and I can't screw anything up. I can't have my life ruined over this.

What would you do???

Love,

Alyssa

A punch landed in Simon's stomach. He looked at the date—a little over two weeks ago. He remembered seeing Alyssa hunched over on the couch one night, frantically scribbling while she sniffed back tears. She must've been writing this letter.

He quickly folded up the letter, carefully placed it back in the box, and sealed it away under the floorboard. Stumbling out of Alyssa's room, the morning's buoyant rays attacked him, his thoughts crashing into chaos.

What have I done?

But how big of a deal was it, really? From the way Alyssa described it, she slipped and fell while holding Morgan. Would that force cause significant damage? And jeez, what were the chances that would happen on exactly the same day Sally shook him? He closed his eyes. It was true that crazy shit like this happened, like that guy who ran over a kid leaving the doctor's office, a kid who had just been fitted with a fresh cast and handed a new pair of crutches.

But the doubt—oh, that annoying doubt—started to fester. Was Sally coerced into believing she was the sole culprit? Meanwhile, Alyssa managed to carry this secret while Sally was exiled to the land of damaged, guilty mothers.

He walked toward the stack of Mandy's uniform boxes. Their future life together—ready to take flight. He wrung his hands, sweat saturating his shirt as his breaths came faster and deeper.

A decent detective would do the right thing.

Chapter 44

Sally

The same day

Four days after Morgan's second birthday, on a Monday, Sally heard her phone beep—the custom double beep for Charles. Could it really be? She finished wiping down her plate, rolled up the bread bag, and lowered herself onto her one chair, a folding chair she'd rescued from the curb.

And there he was. Morgan. His vivid blue eyes, honey-blond hair. He looked so much bigger. In front of him sat a massive dinosaur cake, the nose chopped clean, a number candle—two. How was he already two? Orange frosting smeared across his beaming face, more teeth than she'd ever seen on him. In the background stood a blurred Nancy, surrounded by dinosaur balloons, along with Alyssa. Wait, Alyssa went to his birthday party?

She shook her head, her teeth already tearing into her nails. The moment of delightful surprise crushed by the sinking truth: *I'm not there.* What she would give to go back and try again. Redo.

If only I'd put him in his crib, instead of grabbing him ...

She stared at the picture for at least an hour, maybe longer. Zooming in to Morgan's face. This was her boy. His actual birthday had come and gone without pause—she'd blocked it out, along with everything else. But now, seeing him at his party, so blissful—it sliced her heart in half. Did he miss her?

After two days, she finally worked up the courage to write Charles back: **Thank you.**

He wrote nothing in return. She obsessively checked her phone, typing out several drafts:

I'm sorry.

Tell Morgie I love him.

I miss him.

I wish ...

But the words never did justice, never seemed to adequately sum up what Sally had done, what she was feeling.

What am I feeling?

✦

The sun blazed down on Sally as she tugged on her wide-brimmed straw hat and slid on her pink sunglasses. She wore a full swimsuit, necessary to cover the scar. She lightly touched her abdomen, feeling the subtle ridge. *Hazel.* A piercing pain throttled behind her eyes.

She spent her days here, on this golden beach in Florida. It wasn't her dream, it wasn't California, but it would do. She'd picked this town, Clearwater, after her probation officer approved her request to transfer to Florida back in November, shortly after her conviction. He'd explained to Sally that this was a "low-level" probation case since she didn't have to come in for regular urine tests or anything like that—she just had to stay out of trouble. After typing *best small coastal towns in Florida,* she closed her eyes and tapped at random. Number fifteen. She climbed into the U-Haul van, toting a lineup of orange bottles, prescriptions to keep her stable, pills that made her numb—the hurt and pain slowed to a trickle, like thick syrup on a cold winter's morning.

She landed a part-time job at a small cafe—The Fisherman's Bounty—tucked away in the shade on the beach's edge, behind a scattering of postcard-perfect palm trees.

At first, the staff asked where she came from. "What's your story?"

My mom died of cancer, so I moved here to start over. Who doesn't love a tragic story that ends in a brave rebirth? It contained enough truth, apart from the omitted details: abusing one baby, causing the other to die.

✦

Shortly after arriving in Clearwater, Sally joined a local parenting class, even though she was pretty sure she couldn't be a mother again. Either way, her probation officer needed an emailed copy of the facilitator's signed form every week. The class met Sunday afternoons in a conference room at the library. She picked the faded turquoise chair next to the window.

The other moms shared their stories of struggle while munching on stale muffins and sipping tepid coffee.

"She won't listen," one mom vented, her eyebrows knitted together in frustration. "I tell her no, don't eat that crayon. But she does it anyway. I just don't know what to do."

The other moms chimed in.

"Just pack the crayons away."

"I've got a homemade recipe for crayons. One hundred percent organic, super safe to eat. I'll text it to you."

"You need to praise her when she *doesn't* eat the crayons. Positive reinforcement."

Sally stared out the window, her fingers tracing the edges of her teeth. How simple life would've been if her biggest concern had been Morgan eating crayons.

"Sally," the facilitator asked one evening. She sported a mannish crew cut and white, bushy eyebrows. Sally hadn't seen eyebrows like that since that gruff detective. "Is there anything you'd like to share tonight?"

The rain pounded on the roof, the windows gray and bleak, the palm trees limp and defeated. Sally whispered, "No."

"Are you sure? It might help get it off your chest." The facilitator flashed a smile. "This is a judgment-free space."

The put-together moms smiled and nodded in unison, like a pack of lemmings: *Yes, yes. We're here for you.*

Something snapped and without pause, she blurted, "I shook my baby. Broke his rib. Gave him a concussion."

The room inhaled sharply. Were they shocked that Sally had committed such an act, or scared shitless because they, too, sometimes possessed the same out-of-control, exasperated feelings? Or, were they stunned she'd actually admitted it? Either way, their faces screamed: *What kind of mother are you?*

The facilitator pulled her aside before she left. "That was really brave of you."

Sally shrugged, watching the rain slam against the windows, realizing she'd forgotten an umbrella. No wait, she didn't own an umbrella in this new life. "The damage's been done," she said. "I just have to live with it for the rest of my life."

The older woman's eyes deepened. "You're not alone," she said.

But I am, Sally wanted to say.

A few weeks later, Sally tried attending another parenting class at a quaint coffee shop on the other side of town. These moms sat cross-legged on the carpeted floor while their babies and toddlers crawled and bounced and dribbled trails of snacks around them. Nobody asked Sally where her children were.

One mom shared how her baby's cries rattled her to the core. "I can't believe I'm sharing this, but one time I was tempted to just throw her down the stairs."

The surrounding moms scooted closer, hands gently caressing this mother's back.

With an understanding nod, the facilitator said, "It's completely normal to have these feelings. The difference between a good mother and a bad mother is if you actually *do* hurt your baby."

Sally stopped going after that, until her probation officer reminded her the parenting classes were legally required in lieu of jail time. "The judge said you have twelve months to complete this, along with the counseling and community service hours."

So, gritting her teeth, Sally kept her head down as she listened to the other moms offering endless words of support while her guilt wormed its way deeper and deeper.

✦

For the past ten months, Sally's evening ritual, after her work shift ended, started with wading deep into the sea, until she could no longer touch the murky sand. She would then tread water, letting her breath settle, the warm waves caressing her broken soul.

Tonight's shift dragged longer than usual, a black fog drifting in by the time she made it to the shore and changed into her swimsuit. It had been forty days since Charles had sent the picture of Morgie with his cake. She checked her phone again. Nothing. Taking a heavy breath, she headed into the water, and, once deep enough, sank below the surface, focusing on the muffled sounds, a boat in the distance—probably a night tour full of drunken tourists. She drifted deeper into the reprieve, ignoring her throbbing lungs, willing herself to stay a little longer, just a few more seconds.

The end is near.

But the mere stubbornness of her lungs forced her back to the surface. She heard a distant cry and, body tensing, scanned the dark shore. Was Morgan drowning? Was he hurt? Of course not. She knew Charles would never let any harm to come to Morgan. Right now, those cries belonged to someone else's baby.

Sally sighed. *You're not Morgan's mother anymore.*

After making her way to solid ground, she walked the length of the beach, the crescent moon providing a weak outline of the worn path ahead, dozens of footprints waiting to be wiped clean by the restless ocean. She broke into a run, memories of her mom on the sidelines, cheering her on.

On the way back, she passed the exasperated mother and the wailing child, the father hovering next to them like a useless flagpole while the mom rocked, shushed, cooed, and urgently rammed a pacifier into the baby's mouth. The baby threw his head back, letting loose an ear-shrieking wail, and Sally cringed, the screams digging deep into her heart. Today, she realized, it happened today, one year ago—on September 7.

Glancing out at the endless water, she adjusted her clingy swimsuit, goosebumps piercing her skin. This vast ocean would take her, happily. Sweep her away, wash her bones into nothingness.

✦

Later that night, she dug through her purse and at the bottom, creased and almost forgotten, she found the social worker's card. Even after a year of suffering and agony, Ms. Flynn's words echoed loudly: *We never want to separate children from their mothers.*

The therapist basically said the exact same thing during Sally's mandatory counseling sessions. Sally shredded Flynn's card into tiny pieces and flung them out the window like confetti. "You're wrong! You wanted nothing more than to shame me. To take him away. To make me suffer. It was an accident. One mistake. Well, are you happy? You win!"

A motorcycle revved its engine down the road. A bird took flight, shooting her a disapproving scowl. Sally slammed the window shut. She lived in a one-room apartment above someone's garage, consisting of a single hot plate, a tattered Craigslist mattress thrown on the floor, a humming box fan blowing a thin layer of dust into the air. Her mom's boxes lined the wall, remnants of their once-happy life together.

She paced the floor, scratching at her face. She never cashed the $1,000 check from Charles's mother, slipped to her with a hushed threat: *Don't even think about coming back.* A bitter taste surfaced at the memory—the closed door to Morgan's room, Nancy's hard face. Charles bounding down the street after her. Why didn't she go back? She'd recently finished all the requirements—the parenting classes, counseling, plus fifty hours of community service time at the John Hopkins Children's Hospital in Palm Harbor. Somehow, she could do right with the cancer kids, just not her own.

The therapist said she could likely start doing supervised visits with Morgan now. But Sally couldn't bring herself to call the social worker. She didn't want to see Charles's disappointment; the way Morgan would continue loving her, despite everything she'd done.

In her bathroom, Sally scooped up the row of orange bottles and popped off each lid, pausing before shaking hundreds of pills into her hands. With a gravelly scream, she dumped the pills into the toilet and watched as the water gurgled and swirled, sucking away her numbness. She expected someone to stop her, to reprimand her, but once again, she was all alone.

Chapter 45

Sally

Almost four months later

"We're ready for you," a nurse said.

Sally clutched her gold-studded Louis Vuitton purse and smoothed her skirt before following the nurse down the hall. She knew the ritual—temperature, heart rate, blood pressure, the right answers to the essential questions: *Yes, I'm taking my prenatals. No smoking. No alcohol.* Afterward, she hopped onto the examination table.

The technician entered. "How are you feeling today, Mrs. Klein?"

She beamed. The shimmery ring on her hand was one hundred percent real—a 1.5 carat diamond, an extravagant wedding in Greece sixteen days ago, a legit husband. She'd learned her lesson and locked this one in fast.

"I'm feeling great."

"Any morning sickness?"

"Nope."

"Well, why don't you lay back and we'll take a look," he said, lubing up the wand. "Any plans for New Years?"

"Oh gosh, is it really time for a new year?"

"Yep, time sure flies." He punched some keys, adjusted the monitor.

"It sure does," Sally agreed, rubbing her stomach in a steady circle. "We'll probably take it easy, rest up and all."

"That's good." He lifted her ivory-laced blouse and maneuvered the slick wand across her almost-flat stomach. She'd dropped nearly twenty pounds in the seven weeks between ditching her meds and conceiving this baby. How, she didn't know. It was all a blur.

Watching the murky screen, she waited for the flashes of static to sharpen into focus. "Is that—?"

"That's your little one," the technician confirmed. "Measuring right on track. It's a little early to confirm the sex, but the estimated due date's July six."

A tingle traveled the length of her body, causing her toes to curl in delight. She ignored the pang of coincidence: *Morgan's birthday is also in July.*

The technician left and the OB came in next. "I see you transferred from another clinic."

"Yes," Sally said, "the other place was always overbooked. Plus, this place is closer to home."

The OB flipped through her paperwork. "You wrote here you haven't had any previous pregnancies."

"That's right."

His eyes darted to the clipboard, then to Sally. "But, uh, your scar?" He nodded toward her pink C-section scar as Sally used a tissue to wipe off the gel goop.

"I had a tummy tuck."

"Oh," he replied, followed by an awkward silence. He exhaled. "Just so you know, if you had any pregnancies or births in the past—living or not—it's crucial we know. We want to ensure that you and this baby have the safest delivery possible. If that *was* a C-section, then we need to schedule another C-section to avoid any risks—"

"It was a tummy tuck," Sally said, sitting up and flashing the smile she used to use on stage, during her past beauty pageants.

"Okay then. And what about getting your past medical records sent over?"

"Oh, about that." She paused, licking her lips. "My primary doctor's practice closed, and I haven't had any luck tracking them down. But I know my history and if there's something you need to know, I can tell you."

"Hey, these things happen. The receptionist out front can try to sort it out. Really, we just need details on your vaccines, medications, family history, and, like I said, any past pregnancies."

"Sure thing."

"Will anyone be attending your birth?"

"It'll just be me. My husband, Mr. Klein"—she took a deep, satisfied breath—"he works long hours and travels a lot. He's on a business trip right now—Japan." Truth be told, she'd never shared the complicated details of her past with him. She'd tried, in the beginning, but could never find the right words. Some things were better left unsaid.

I'm a new person now.

"That's absolutely fine," he said. "Many women birth alone."

The OB left her alone to change. But she couldn't move, something about this room whisking her back to Charles, when Morgan was growing inside of her.

Morgan had appeared again last night, floating into her dreams like he always did. He seemed older, like five or six, and they were running together on the beach, lifting beach towels above, like wings flying them to another world. And then Morgan was standing on tiptoes, pressing his face into the smudged glass, *oohing* and *aahing* at the array of ice cream flavors below. At this age, he had an adamant opinion: "Chocolate's yummy. Pineapple's yucky."

He was his own person.

A gentle knock on the door yanked Sally out of the trance.

"Everything okay, Mrs. Klein?"

"Yes, I'm fine." She studied the walls of the examination room, the familiar despair prickling her stomach.

Morgan's better off without me, she reminded herself.

With an exhale, she slid off the table and pulled on her clothes. She used the side exit to avoid the receptionist's pesky questions about her medical past.

✦

Back at home, Sally opened a stack of packages—baby bottles, diapers in a range of sizes, a solar system mobile, and a dozen pearly-white onesies. She tossed the onesies directly into the washing machine, knowing it was best to wash any residual store germs and chemicals off brand-new baby clothes. Once the dryer dinged, she sat on their periwinkle couch, methodically folding each onesie into a neat stack. The Christmas tree twinkled and shimmered in the corner while "Silent Night" gently hummed in the background. She liked to indulge in Christmas music even after the holiday passed, just like her mother used to do.

In the baby's nursery, she placed the onesies in the top drawer, then pulled out the stepstool to secure the mobile directly above the baby's crib. She gave it a good tug to make sure it would never, ever fall.

Her phone rang—an unknown ringtone. She climbed down from the stool. She didn't recognize the number. Every nerve in her body tightened.

"H-hello?"

"Sally?"

"Who is this?"

"It's Simon." A pause. "Detective Simon Wilton. With the Oak Wood police department."

Her heart screeched to a halt. "What do you want?"

"Look." He cleared his throat. "I found something about five months ago, back in July, some information regarding Alyssa and Morgan. I'm sorry I didn't reach out sooner ... I didn't know if I should, but now, after all this time, I can't let it go." His voice cracked. "You deserve to know the truth."

"What are you talking about?" A coolness crept across her skin, her stomach turning rock-hard.

"It appears something happened to Morgan under Alyssa's watch. She slipped and fell backwards, while holding him. Over a year ago, on the same day you ..." He trailed off.

"What?" Sally said, her voice barely audible.

"Based on this evidence, it's possible you weren't solely responsible for Morgan's injuries."

Several seconds of silence lapsed. A strange buzzing rang in her head as she struggled to find her breath.

"Sally, are you still there?"

She managed to nod.

Then: "We can reopen the case, if that's what you want. You don't need to carry this guilt alone."

Chapter 46

Sally

Later that night

Sally wrestled against the bed sheets, the air conditioner cranked as high as it could go to try to cool her down. It didn't help—her body burned with rage and confusion, unsure of what to do next.

Simon's words spun around her: *We can reopen the case. We can reopen the case.*

But what did that mean? What would happen next? She would need to tell her new husband, a man she hadn't been searching for but who'd appeared out of nowhere, a couple of weeks after she'd thrown out her mood-stabilizing medication and moved to Miami for a change of pace. He'd bought her one mojito after another and before she knew it, she was waking up with a crushing headache in his high-rise apartment, his body snug around hers like a missing puzzle piece. She tried to take control of her life, rushing out the door to get the morning after pill, then asking her doctor for birth control—"Give me the strongest stuff." But none of that worked. Somehow, she was destined to keep having babies.

She couldn't complain though, not really. This new man opened the door for her new life. Telling him the truth would crush him: *I left behind a son, a sweet boy who's almost two and a half.* A boy she'd hurt with her own hands.

But was it all me?

Flicking on her nightstand light, she checked her phone. She'd sent her new husband the ultrasound picture from earlier that day, the floating blob that would be her third baby, but his first. He'd responded with a string of smiley faces and high-fives, a firework, a baby bottle, and then a gif with a chubby baby doing a booty shake in a diaper.

That was *before* Simon's call. Before she choked out something to Simon about needing to call him back.

By 3:00 a.m., she'd given up on sleep. She paced their bedroom floor, gnawing at her nails—a habit she'd forced herself to give up after meeting her new man, after starting her new life.

But leaving your past behind was turning out to be harder than she thought.

She started flinging clothes into a suitcase, sneakers, a sweater, toothbrush, shampoo, conditioner. In the bathroom closet, she pulled out a storage bin labeled "feminine products." Buried under a pile of pads and tampons, she pulled out the framed picture of Morgan, the one of him clutching the little duck. It was only taken about two years ago, but now, cut free from his life, it felt like decades ago.

Is this how it feels for moms who give their babies up for adoption, she wondered. Like a part of your heart was snipped off, never to feel whole again.

She tossed the bag into the Tesla, her husband's wedding gift to her. He wasn't due back from Japan for five more days. She had time.

✦

It took her over fourteen hours to drive from Miami to Oak Wood, pulling into Whispering Wind drive a little after 6:00 p.m. She parked two houses down, across the street, wearing generic sunglasses she'd bought at a Shell station, her ponytail tucked into a black baseball cap. Nobody would suspect her. But still, her fingernails tapped against her teeth as she took quick breaths. She studied their front door and Charles's car, their old station wagon.

Time stood still. Sally's cheeks flushed, sweat gathering under her armpits, even though it was late December. New Year's Eve, in fact.

After an hour, she saw a light blue car pull up and park beside Charles's car in the driveway. Sally held her breath. Out bounded Alyssa, her hair cut short, the ends tinged yellow. As she flung her backpack over her shoulder, Sally saw a flash of silver—a nose ring. That punkish friend must have done this to her, convincing her to live it up during their senior year.

Sally pressed her fingers into her temples, the sleep deprivation and long drive making her thoughts go fuzzy, her insides coiling. Her new baby gave a little kick. Or maybe it was just nerves? Blinking back tears, she wanted to charge at Alyssa, grab her, demand why she didn't tell them what happened.

Why did you lie to all of us?

But the irony hit her—they had *both* lied. They were each trying to preserve their own self, their own future. In a flash, Sally saw Alyssa's life ahead—actually finishing a college degree, becoming whatever she wanted to be, meeting someone, having a family.

She would be a gentle mother, Sally thought. Kind, patient, calm. *Like the kind of mother I wanted to be.*

Alyssa disappeared inside the house, a house where Sally once belonged. Twenty minutes passed and then Charles emerged, smoothing back his damp hair. He was wearing a black button-up shirt and black slacks, a sparkly silver tie glistening under the remaining sunlight. A tie? He hated ties.

Sally's heart constricted. Was he going on a date? To a New Year's Eve party? To a bar to flirt with ladies? But he was terrible at flirting.

Charles sped away and Sally's phone started ringing beside her, an upbeat Salsa tune. It was him—her new husband. She swiped the call to silent, brushing tears off her cheeks. The sun began to fade, saying goodbye to yet another year. A year where Sally never got to see her little Morgie. Her body grew cold, sitting, waiting, watching.

Why am I here?

She turned on the engine and slowly maneuvered the car around, parking directly in front of the house. Maybe she could catch a glimpse of Morgan through the window? Or would Alyssa take him for a walk?

Her heart jumped to double speed at the thought. Would Morgan remember her? She'd last seen him in his hospital room, right before she slipped away and headed to the Greyhound station—over fifteen months ago. That was too long for a toddler.

She heard a light scratching at the door and froze. Adjusting her sunglasses, she slowly peeked out the window. Nothing. Nobody. But the scratching came again, followed by a sustained meow.

Cracking the door open, Moops jumped right into her lap, as if not a single second had passed. Sally closed the door, her heart exploding.

"Charles kept you after all," she said softly, stroking his fur. Moops circled around a few times before settling down, rubbing his face against her thigh, his gentle purrs filling the car.

Sally pushed up her sunglasses and rested her head against the headrest, her eyes still glued on the house. The curtains were drawn. It was nearing Morgan's bedtime. What would Alyssa do if Sally simply rang the doorbell and begged to see her son? Would she call the cops? It wasn't against her probation guidelines to travel across state lines, but she needed to arrange official supervised visits with the social worker. An impromptu visit wouldn't be good.

She'd causally asked her probation officer last week what would happen if she got pregnant with her new husband, just to be prepared. He'd reassured her she could keep it—the past crime was a separate case and wouldn't affect a new baby.

Patting her stomach, she whispered, "You're safe."

And now I know what happened, Sally thought. Alyssa slipped and fell, with Morgan in her arms. Simon said it was a backwards fall, according to Alyssa's letter, and that Morgan didn't hit his head. That fall, though—that could've been what caused his rib to break.

If Sally came forward with Simon's evidence, the charges against herself could be dropped, or at least lessened. She could be a good mother after all.

But you were still the one who shook him.

Eventually tiredness took over and Sally's eyes fluttered shut, holding Moops in her arms. Ms. Flynn stomped into her dream, all stern and tight-lipped, and Sally asked her what she needed to do to redeem herself.

Is it too late?

Flynn explained the logistics of supervised visits while Sally choked back sobs. She couldn't bring herself to share what Alyssa had done—her supposed part in Morgan's injuries. Sally's life was already ruined from that day. Alyssa, however, still had a chance.

"No, Sally," Flynn said. "*You* still have a chance. One mistake doesn't need to define who you are forever."

Next came fireworks blasting across the sky, cheers and shouts as everyone welcomed the new year. Sally was at a party, stumbling through the crowd in way-too-high heels, searching for someone. Who? Around her people embraced with fresh kisses and enthusiastic hugs while peals of laughter rippled across a gentle breeze. She saw Charles, standing near the bar, his arms open for her. He was smiling.

"Sally." His voice so calm, so solid.

Everything went blank. And then, somewhere from far away, a sweet tender voice floated in.

"Mama."

Epilogue

Morgan

Almost two years after the incident: Wednesday, July 22

Morgan touched his head. He often got a deep owie that itched inside, somewhere behind his eyes. Resting his cheek against the carpet, he closed his eyes and waited for the ouch to pass. And when it did, he picked up his dump truck and continued driving it across the living room floor with a loud *vrooom* sound.

At the end of the day, after brushing teeth and a bubbly bath with his new shark, and then Daniel Tiger jammies, he looked up at her. The three pictures on the wall. The name often got stuck or scrambled, but the *maaa* sound always came out.

"Mama," Daddy reminded him.

"Mama," Morgan repeated. He remembered the feel of warm lips on his cheek, a finger brushing away a tear. Her eyes—brown? He usually forgot color names—the colors blurring and then focusing.

Morgan chanted her name out loud, over and over, and Daddy's face drooped into an upside-down smile, like Eeyore. He looked sad. But why?

Morgan learned that other kids had mamas, or mommies, or moms. He saw them at preschool, women tall and short, fat and skinny, bending down and scooping up their babies, slobbering them with kisses. They always smelled yummy—those other mommies—like pancakes or cinnamon rolls or bubble gum ice cream. Some kids even had two mommies.

But Morgan, he only had Daddy. And Grandma. And Lissy.

But no mama.

He couldn't describe the feeling that came next—a tummy ache? A sniffly cold? *I hurt.* He wanted a mommy, too. He wanted *his* mommy to come and pick him up. To read him stories. Daddy told him she used to read him stories, but he couldn't remember any of that.

Where did she go?

Sometimes at night she'd arrive in his dream, like an angel riding a cloud. She'd laugh—*oooh, that was the sound of her laugh.* Sweet and fuzzy and giddy, like Elmo. Elmo laughed just like that.

He snuggled up to her and his fingers and toes tingled, like drinking hot cocoa with Daddy or unwrapping Christmas presents or riding his tricycle around and around and around until he became so dizzy he couldn't see straight.

And in the dream, he saw her crying. *Maaa,* he said, for he'd already forgotten her name. Again. He tried to hug her, but she faded away, like a balloon floating beyond his reach. His insides tangled up like spaghetti noodles twisted around a fork.

Morning stirred him out of the dream, and he blinked at the light peeping under his Cookie Monster curtains. He sat up. The bright orange balloon floated by the door—the number three. Daddy had told him last night that when he woke up it would be just three more sleeps. Three more sleeps until he turned three.

Three, three, three.

The door creaked open and Moopsie sneaked in. He always liked to come in for morning cuddles. It made Morgan's heart warm, feeling his vibrating purrs against his chest.

But it wasn't the same as having a mama.

His head felt yuck again—a *thub thub thub* sound inside—so he closed his eyes and stuck his thumb in his mouth, listening for the sound of his mama's voice.

She's coming to my birthday party, he told himself.

She'll be here.

Acknowledgements

This book wouldn't have been possible without an entire team of supportive people in the background, helping push me across the finish line.

I want to thank all the experts and professionals who took time to help me fine-tune the medical and legal logistics for this novel. Liz Fleming, Kaity Granda, Shelley Hoekstra, Robert Klink, Artemis Parvati, and Moriah Ruthford—you guys are amazing and played such a critical role in making this novel as realistic as possible.

I workshopped this book for almost two years with the Durham Writers Group, led by the fearless Jonathan Giles, and I want to thank everyone who listened to my monthly installments, offering detailed and insightful suggestions along the way.

A big thanks goes to Katey Schultz and her "Deep Revision" workshop, which helped empower me with the necessary revision techniques needed to refine and polish my manuscript.

I was blessed to have an extensive team of beta readers ready to dive in and offer extensive feedback on my later drafts. Ana Barton, Janet Best Dart, Liz Fleming, Jonathan Giles, Diana Neunkirchner, Victoria Olsen, Stephanie Rosenblatt, Willam W. Weddendorf, and Lori Wile—you were all so supportive, honest, and kind with your constructive feedback for this book. I'm so grateful.

A special thanks to Wanda Freeman, who offered feedback on several drafts, did a round of copyediting and proofreading before I started submitting to agents, and responded to countless panicked messages about a particular word choice, sentence, or scene. You've become a wonderful and dedicated friend—I don't know where I'd be without you!

A heartfelt thanks to John Sibley Williams who helped me create and polish my agent querying package. Some say writing these promotional materials is harder than writing the actual novel—I totally agree!

Thank you to my literary agent, Jennifer Weis, who read my manuscript in one day and said "yes!"—proving that an aspiring novelist can be plucked from the infamous slush pile. Jennifer's insightful suggestions and edits helped push this story to the next level, and I feel so lucky to have her unwavering support and belief in me as a writer (and I look forward to working together on many more books to come!).

I'm forever grateful for Jessica Bell at Vine Leaves Press (VLP), who saw my despairing post on Twitter about potentially shelving this book after a slew of "positive rejections" from other publishers. I get it, the Shaken Baby Syndrome can be a dark, controversial, taboo subject—something most people don't want to talk about and a topic that hasn't been covered in fiction before (as far as I know). And yet, Jessica was brave enough to fully embrace it. The entire editorial team at VLP has been beyond fantastic, including the supportive developmental edits with Melanie Faith, in-depth copyediting with Richard Bradburn, and the wonderful guidance and communication with publishing director, Amie McCracken. Thank you all for making my lifelong dream of becoming a published novelist finally come true.

And to my Writing in Jammies group: I love you all. Thank you for the continual support, accountability, and camaraderie as I tackled the final edits and formatting for this book—and for pushing me forward when I got stuck in obsessive-mode. Hanging out with you talented writers is the highlight of every week!

Finally, I wouldn't be where I am today without my family's dedicated support throughout my writing journey. To my parents and grandparents, who truly believed I would one day be a published author when I started writing stories at age five. To my aunts, uncles, cousins, nephews, niece, and everyone else: I'm so grateful for your support. To my husband, Cliff, who ensured I was well fed before whisking the kids off for adventures so I could have solid blocks of time to focus, while always reminding me to "Never ever give up on your dream." And to my children, who changed my life, making me realize how challenging, exciting, and rewarding motherhood can be. I love you all.

Resources

If you want to learn more about the Shaken Baby Syndrome, including how to help prevent it, warning signs to watch out for, and where to get help after a baby has been hurt, please refer to the following resources:

The National Center on Shaken Baby Syndrome (NCSBS): https://www.dontshake.org/

The Shaken Baby Alliance: https://shakenbaby.org/

Childhelp® National Abuse Hotline®: Call the free and confidential 24-hour hotline to speak to a counselor or visit https://www.childhelp.org/parent-resources/shaken-baby-syndrome/

Vine Leaves Press

9783988321374